PENDRAGON
THE MERCHANT OF DEATH

D. J. MACHALE

SIMON AND SCHUSTER

For Evander

SIMON AND SCHUSTER
First published in Great Britain in 2003 by Pocket Books,
an imprint of Simon & Schuster UK Ltd.
1st Floor, 222 Gray's Inn Road, London WC1X 8HB
A CBS COMPANY

This edition published by Simon & Schuster UK Ltd, 2008

Originally published in the USA in 2002 by Aladdin Paperbacks, an
imprint of Simon & Schuster Children's Division, New York.

Copyright © D.J. MacHale, 2002

A CIP catalogue record for this book
is available from the British Library

ISBN 978-1-84738-405-8

This book is a work of fiction. Names, characters, places
and incidents are either a product of the author's imagination or
are used fictitiously. Any resemblance to actual people living
or dead, events or locales is entirely coincidental.

10 9 8 7 6 5 4 3 2 1

Printed by CPI Cox and Wyman, Reading, Berkshire RG1 8EX

ACKNOWLEDGEMENTS

Launching a new series, whether on television or in print, is a daunting task. Writing it is the easy part. The hard part is getting it published or produced so family and friends aren't the only ones who get to read it. To that end, there are several people who should be thanked for helping get Bobby Pendragon's adventures out into the world. Many thanks go to Rob Wolken and Michael Prevett at AMG, who supported the vision in spite of the long odds. Also thanks to Richard Curtis, who guided me through the strange waters of the publishing world while always keeping his sense of humour and doing his best to keep mine. My trust and respect for the way Peter Nelson and Corinne Farley handle my scary legal matters grows with every new project. I will always be grateful to them for watching out for my best interests and not making me read all the paperwork. Lisa Clancy gets big accolades for the many creative insights that helped make this first book the best it can be and because she was the first one who had the guts to say, "Yes." Many thanks to Micol Ostow for always being cheerful and always having the answers. A very big thank you goes to my nephew Patrick McGorrill, who was the first age-appropriate test audience for the manuscript and gave me some creative ideas on how the rings should work so Bobby could send his journals to Mark. Thanks also to his mum, Carol, for wading through an early draft and helping find some of the holes. But the biggest thank you goes to my wife, Evangeline, who dutifully read each chapter as it was created and gave the encouragement and affirmation I needed to keep pushing forward in spite of all my doubts. If not for these people, the book you now hold wouldn't exist.

DENDURON

I hope you're reading this, Mark.

Heck, I hope *anybody's* reading this because the only thing that's keeping me from going totally off my nut right now is getting this all down on paper so that some day, when it's all over, it'll help prove that I'm not a total whack job. You see, two things happened yesterday that changed my life forever.

The first was that I finally kissed Courtney Chetwynde. Yes, *the* Courtney Chetwynde of the bites-her-lower-lip-when-she's-thinking, stares-right-into-your-heart-with-her-deep-grey-eyes, looks-unbelievable-in-her-volleyball-uniform, and always-smells-a-little-like-roses fame. Yeah, I kissed her. It was a long time coming and it finally happened. Woo-hoo!

The second thing was that I was launched through a wormhole called a "flume" and got jacked across the universe to a medieval planet called "Denduron" that's in the middle of a violent civil war.

But back to Courtney.

This wasn't your average "nice to see you" peck on the cheek. Oh no. This was a full-on, eyes closed, starting with tight lips but eventually morphing into a mutual open-mouth probe thing that lasted for a good thirty-second lifetime. And we were close, too. Like *real* close. I was holding her so tight I could feel her heart beating against my chest. Or maybe it was my heart. Or maybe our hearts were bouncing off each other. I have no idea. All I know is that it was pretty cool. I hope I get the chance to do it again, but right now it's not looking so good.

I guess it's kind of dumb to be fixating on the glorious Courtney Chetwynde when the real problem is that I'm afraid I'm going to die. Maybe that's why I can't get her out of my head. The memory of that kiss is the only thing that feels real to me right now. I'm afraid that if I lose that memory I'm going to lose everything, and if that happens then . . . well, I don't know what will happen then because I don't understand *anything* that's been happening to me. Maybe by writing it all down, it'll start to make some sense.

Let me try to piece together the events that led to my writing this. Up until yesterday I was living large. At least as large as any normal fourteen-year-old guy can live. School came pretty easy; I kicked ass in sports; my parents were way cool; I didn't hate my little sister, Shannon, usually. I had excellent friends, with you sitting right on top of the list, Mark. I lived in this major house where I had my own private space to play music or whatever and nobody bugged me. My dog, Marley, was the coolest golden retriever there ever was; and I had recently macked with Courtney Chetwynde. (Did I mention that?) How much more goin' on can you get?

The thing is, I also had an Uncle Press.

You remember him? He was the guy who always showed up at my birthday parties with some special surprise. He wouldn't just bring a pony, he'd bring a *truckload* of ponies for a minirodeo. He's the guy who turned my house into that laser-maze game. Was that great or what? He's the one who was throwing the pizzas at my party last year. Remember that guy? Every once in a while he'd show up, out of the blue, and do something amazing like take me flying in a private plane. Yeah, he was a pilot. Another time he gave me this computer that was so advanced, it wasn't even in stores yet. You know the calculator I have that you input numbers by talking to it? That was from Uncle Press. I gotta tell you, he was the coolio uncle everybody wished they had.

But there was always something a little mysterious about Uncle Press. He was my mum's brother, but she didn't say much about him. It was almost like she felt weird talking about him. Whenever I asked, she'd shrug and say something like, "Oh, you know him, he's his own man. How was school today?" Basically, she'd dodge the question.

I don't know what he did for a living, but he always had boatloads of money. I figured he probably had some top-level government job, like doing research for NASA or something and it was all hush-hush. So I didn't ask too many questions. He wasn't married, but sometimes he'd show up at the house with some odd character. One time he brought this lady over who never said a word. He said she was his "friend", but I got the feeling she was more like his "girlfriend". I think she was African or something because she was real dark-skinned. And beautiful. But it was strange because she'd just stare at me and smile. I wasn't scared or anything because she had soft eyes. And maybe she didn't talk because she didn't know English, but still it was kind of creepy.

I'd have to say that my Uncle Press was the coolest guy I'd ever met. That is, until yesterday.

The county semifinal basketball game was last night. You know how important I am to that team. I'm the highest scoring point guard in Stony Brook Junior High history. I'm not bragging; that's just the way it is. So for me to miss that game would have been like Kobe Bryant missing a Lakers playoff game. Okay, maybe I'm not *that* important, but it would not have been cool for me to bail on that game. Mum and Dad had already left for the gym with Shannon. I had a ton of homework and I knew I'd be fried afterwards, so I had to get it done before leaving. I had just enough time to scarf down a banana and some Pop-Tarts, feed Marley, jump on my bike, and blast over to school. At least that was the plan. I can't help but think that if I had done my homework just a little bit faster, or decided not to throw the tennis ball with Marley, or even waited till I got to school to take a leak, none of this would have happened. But it did.

I grabbed my pack, headed for the front door, threw it open and came face to face with . . . Courtney Chetwynde.

I froze. She froze. It was like somebody hit the pause button on two lives. Except there was nothing static about what was racing through my brain. The crush I had on her dated back to when we were in grade school. She was always so . . . perfect. But not in that unattainable she's too good for everybody way. She was beautiful and smart and great at sports and she laughed and told jokes. I think that was the key. The fact that she told jokes. Maybe that sounds stupid, but if you tell jokes it shows you're willing to look stupid. And if you've got the whole package going on and are still willing to let people laugh at you then, man, what *else* do you want?

Of course I wasn't the only one who felt this way about Courtney. I was one in a long line of admirers. But she was standing at *my* front door. Instantly, every synapse in my brain started firing to try and find the perfect, spontaneous thing to say. The first words out of your mouth in a time of crisis can colour someone's opinion of you forever. It either shows that you're totally in charge and ready to handle any situation with composure and wit, or that you're a blundering idiot whose mind will freeze at the first sign of pressure. This all flashed through my brain in the few nanoseconds while we were on "pause". Now it was my move. She came to the house, it was my turn to respond. So I hitched my pack up on my shoulder, leaned casually against the doorjamb, gave her a little smile and said: "Yo."

Yo??? That's not even a real word! Nobody says "Yo" unless they're impersonating Sylvester Stallone, which I was definitely *not* doing. I was all set for the smile to drop off her face in crushing disappointment as she turned and left without saying a word. Instead, she bit her lower lip (which meant she was thinking) and said:

"Hi."

That was good. "Hi" isn't much higher up on the cool scale than "Yo". I was back in the game. It was time to start playing.

"What's up?" I said.

Okay, maybe I wasn't ready to play just yet. It was easier to lob the ball back into her court. It was then that I noticed something weird. Courtney looked nervous. Not out of her mind scared or anything, but a little bit uncomfortable. My confidence soared. She was just as tense as I was. That was good.

"I know you've got to get to the game and all, I don't want to make you late," she said with a little embarrassed smile.

What game? Oh, right, the county semifinal. Somehow it had slipped my mind.

"I've got plenty of time," I lied casually. "C'mon in."

I was recovering nicely. As she walked past me to come inside I got that faint hint of rose fragrance. It took every ounce of willpower not to do a huge-old sucking inhale to try and grab every ounce of that wonderful smell. That would have been dumb and this was definitely not the time to do something dumb because Courtney was now inside my home. She was on my turf. I closed the door behind her and we were alone.

I had no idea what to do next. Courtney turned to me and I made contact with those amazing grey eyes. My knees went soft. I prayed she didn't notice.

"I wasn't sure if I should come here," she said tentatively.

"I'm glad you did," I shot back with perfect timing. I kept the ball in her court, yet still managed to make her feel at ease. I was on fire.

"I'm not really sure why I picked now to come. Maybe it was to wish you good luck in the game. But I think it's more than that."

"Really?" Perfect comeback.

"I'm not exactly sure how to say this, Bobby, but since we were kids, I've had this . . . feeling about you."

Feeling? Feeling is good, unless she feels like I'm an axe murderer or something.

"Oh?" I shot back. Noncommittal, nonaggressive, perfect.

"Man, I feel like such a geek saying this." She broke eye contact. I was losing her. I didn't want her to chicken out so the best thing I could do was throw her a bone.

"Courtney, there are a lot of words that come to mind when I think of you, but 'geek' is definitely not one of them."

She looked back to me and smiled. We were back on track.

"I'm not really sure how to say this, so I'll just say it. There's something about you, Bobby. I know you're a brain and a jock and popular and all, but it's more than that. You've got this, like, I don't know, this aura thing going on. People trust you. They like you. And it's not like you're trying to show off or anything. Maybe that's part of it. You don't act like you think you're better than everybody else. You're just this really good guy—" she paused before going on, then the bombshell — "who I've had this incredible crush on since fourth grade."

Nothing in my wildest fantasy could have prepared me for that. I was speechless. I hoped my mouth wasn't hanging open in stupefied shock.

"I'm not really sure why I'm telling you this now," she went on. "But I have this weird feeling that if I didn't, I might never get the chance again. And I wanted to tell you how I felt . . . and do this."

That's when it happened. The kiss. She stepped forward, hesitated a second to see if I'd stop her (yeah right, like there was danger of *that* happening) and we kissed. I won't rehash the details, but suffice it to say I was a happy guy. It was the most amazing thirty seconds of my life.

It was the thirty-first second when it all came crashing down.

My eyes were closed, but I could see a whole future full of Courtney and Courtney's kisses. I don't know if it's possible to kiss and smile at the same time, but if it is, I did. And then I opened my eyes, and it was over.

"Hi, Bobby."

Uncle Press was standing there! Where did *he* come from? I pulled away from Courtney so fast that she still had her eyes closed. Actually, she looked kind of goofy for a second like she was kissing air, but she recovered fast and believe me, I didn't laugh.

"Uncle Press! Hi!" I probably should have said, "Yo!" that's how stupid I felt. I'm not sure why, either. We weren't doing anything wrong. We were just kissing. Granted, it was the big-league kiss of all time, but it was still just a kiss. Once Courtney realised what was happening, she went from zero to full-tilt embarrassed. She wanted to be anywhere but there, and I wanted to be there with her. She backed towards the door.

"I . . . uh . . . I'd better go," she stammered.

"No, don't go." I didn't want to take the heat alone, but Uncle Press had other things on his mind.

"Yes. You should go." Short, blunt, simple as that. Something about the way he said it made a red flag go up in my head. This didn't sound like Uncle Press. Normally he's the kind of guy who would think catching his nephew macking was pretty funny. In fact, that's exactly what happened when he caught me making out with Nancy Kilgore on the back porch. He just laughed. I was embarrassed as hell, but he got a real charge out of it. He'd bring it up every once in a while, just to jazz me. But not in front of anybody else, which made it okay. This time was different though. This time he wasn't laughing.

"Good luck tonight. I'll be cheering," said Courtney as she took a step . . . and walked square into the door. Ouch. Uncle Press leaned over and opened it for her. She gave him a quick, embarrassed nod of thanks, then shot me a look with the slightest hint of a sly smile. Then she was gone. Uncle Press closed the door and looked at me.

"I'm sorry, Bobby, but I need your help. I want you to come with me."

Again, this didn't sound like Uncle Press. He was a loose kind of guy. My guess was he was in his fifties, but he didn't act like a geezer. He was always goofing around, never seemed to take things all that seriously. But tonight, he was dead serious. In fact, it almost seemed as if he looked a little . . . scared.

"But, I got a game. County semis. I'm already late."

"You didn't seem too concerned about that a few seconds ago," he shot back.

Good point. But I really was late, and it was a big game.

"Mum and Dad are already there with Shannon. If I don't show up – "

"They'll understand. I wouldn't ask you to do this if I didn't think it was more important than a basketball game . . . or kissing that beautiful girl who just left."

I was prepared to argue on that last point, but man, he was acting pretty intense. It was weird. Then, as if he were reading my mind he said, "Bobby, you've known me all your life. Have you ever seen me like this?"

I didn't need to answer. Something was definitely up.

"Then you know how serious this is," he said with absolute finality.

I didn't know what to do. At that very minute there was a team waiting for me to help them win a county title. Not to mention a family, friends, and an almost-girlfriend who would be expecting me to trot out on to the court. But standing in front of me was a guy who was my own flesh and blood who needed my help. Uncle Press did a lot for me as I was growing up and never asked for a single thing in return. Until now. How could I turn him down?

"You promise to explain things to my coach, Mum and Dad, and Courtney Chetwynde?"

Uncle Press actually gave a small smile, just like he used to, and said, "They'll understand."

I tried to think of any other reason why I shouldn't go with him, but came up empty. So with a sigh I said, "All right then, let's go."

Instantly Uncle Press opened the front door. I shrugged and started out.

"You won't need that bag," he said, referring to my pack. I'm not sure why, but that sounded strange, and a touch ominous.

"What's this all about, Uncle Press?"

If he had answered the question truthfully, I would have run upstairs to my room and hid under the bed. But he didn't. All he said was, "You'll find out."

He was my uncle. I trusted the guy. So I let my pack fall to the floor and headed for the door. Uncle Press didn't follow right away. I looked back and saw that he was looking around the house. Maybe I imagined this, but he seemed a little sad, as if this was the last time he was going to be here. After a few seconds he said, "You love this place, don't you? And your family?"

"Well . . . yeah. Of course," I answered. What a dumb question.

He took one more wistful look around, then turned to face me. The sad look was gone. In its place was the determined look of a guy who had business elsewhere.

"Let's go," he said.

He walked past me and headed down the front path to the street. Uncle Press always dressed the same way, in jeans, boots, and a dark brown work shirt. Over this he wore a long, tan, leather coat that reached down to his knees. It flapped in the wind as he walked. I'd seen that look many times before, but for some reason, this time it gave him the air of someone for whom time has stood still. In another time and place he could have been a dusty cowboy striding into town, or a military emissary carrying vital documents. Uncle Press was indeed a unique character.

Parked in front of my house was the sweetest looking motorcycle I ever saw. It looked like one of those multi-coloured Matchbox racers that I had played with not too long ago. But this bike was very big and very real. Uncle Press always did things in style. He grabbed the extra helmet from the seat and tossed it to me. I buckled up and he did the same. He then gunned the engine and I was surprised to hear that it wasn't very loud. I was expecting some growling, gut-churning hog sound. But this bike was almost quiet. It sounded like, well, a rocket that's about to ignite. I hopped on the seat behind him and he glanced back to me.

"Ready?" he asked.

"No," I replied honestly.

"Good. I'd be surprised if you were," he shot back. He then kicked the bike into gear, hit the accelerator, and the two of us flew down the quiet, suburban street that had been my home for fourteen years.

I hope I'll see it again some day.

◉ SECOND EARTH ◉

. . . I hope I'll see it again some day.

Mark Dimond looked up from the stack of parchment papers in his hand and took a deep breath. His heart was racing. The words on the pages before him seemed as if they were written by his best friend, Bobby Pendragon, but the story they contained was impossible. Yet there it was. He glanced at the pages again. What he saw was frantic writing. Bobby's writing in smudged black ink on some kind of old-fashioned yellow parchment. It looked real, it felt real, but so much of the story these pages contained felt about as close to reality as a fevered dream.

Mark sat safely locked in the second stall from the door of the third floor boys' bathroom at Stony Brook Junior High. It was a rarely used bathroom because it was at the far end of the building, near the art department, way off the beaten track. He'd often come here to think. Occasionally he even used the toilet for its intended purpose, but mostly he came here to get away. At his feet were a pile of carrot ends. He'd been nervously gnawing on them as he scanned the pages. Mark had read somewhere that carrots improved your vision. But after months of almost constant carrot intake, he still had to wear glasses and only had a mouthful of yellow teeth to show for his efforts.

Mark knew he wasn't a full-on nerd, but he wasn't running with the cool kids, either. His only contact with the world of "the accepted" was Bobby. They grew up together and were about as tight as two friends could be. As Bobby started to grow up and become popular, Mark kept one foot firmly planted in kid-world. He still read comics; he still kept action figures on his desk. He didn't really know popular music, and his clothes were, well, functional. But that didn't matter to Bobby. Mark made him laugh. And Mark made him think. The two would spend hours debating issues as diverse as First Amendment rights and the relative merits of Pamela Anderson before and after cosmetic surgery.

A lot of Bobby's jock friends would dump on Mark, but never in front of Bobby. They knew better. Mess with Mark and you'd be messing with Bobby, and nobody messed with Bobby. But now, somebody was indeed messing with Bobby. Mark held the proof right there in his hands. He didn't want to believe what the pages told him. Under normal circumstances he would have thought it was some goofy joke that Bobby thought up. But some things had happened that made Mark think this might not be a joke. He leaned back against the cool tile wall and his thoughts brought him back to something that had happened the night before.

Mark always slept with a night-light. He was afraid of the dark. This was his secret. Even Bobby didn't know. Though sometimes Mark thought the night-light was worse than no light at all, because a night-light made shadows. Like the dark jacket hanging on the back of a door that looked like the Grim Reaper. That nasty vision happened more than once. It didn't help that without his glasses, Mark could barely see things clearly beyond the end of his bed. Still, the occasional rude awakening was much better than sleeping in the dark.

The night before, it had happened again. Mark was lying in bed, drifting in and out of sleep. He opened one groggy eye and in his stupor he thought he saw someone standing at the foot of his bed. His mind tried to tell him it was just the shadow cast by a passing car, but his gut told him to wake up. Fast. A surge of adrenalin shot through him and his brain went on full alert. He tried to focus his nearsighted eyes on the interloper to confirm it was just his backpack. No go. He couldn't tell what it was. So he groped his bedside table, knocked over a mug full of pens and his Game Boy, but managed to grab his glasses. When he finally jammed them on to his nose, he looked to the end of his bed . . . and froze in fear.

Standing there, lit by soft moonlight streaming in through the window, was a woman. She was tall and dark-skinned. She wore a colourful wrap that draped off one shoulder, revealing an incredibly taut, muscular arm. She looked to Mark to be a beautiful African queen. Mark dug his heels in and pushed his back against the wall behind his bed in the futile hope that he'd crash through and escape out the other side.

The woman simply raised a finger to her lips and gave a soft "shhh" sound. Mark froze in absolute, paralysing fear. He looked into the woman's eyes and something strange happened. He grew calm. As he thought back on this moment, he wasn't sure if she was hypnotising him or casting some kind of spell because, oddly, his fear slipped away. The woman had soft, friendly eyes that told Mark he had nothing to be afraid of.

"Shaaa zaa shuu saaa," she said softly. Her voice sounded like warm wind through the trees. It was pleasant and soothing, but it made no sense. The woman then walked around the bed and sat next to Mark. Mark didn't jump away because, for some reason, this all felt . . . right. A leather pouch hung from a cord around her neck. She reached into it and pulled out a ring. It looked to Mark like one of those school rings you see on college kids. It was silver with a slate-coloured stone mounted in the centre. There was some sort of inscription engraved around the stone, but it was written in no language Mark had ever seen before.

"This is from Bobby," she said softly.

Bobby? Bobby Pendragon? Mark had no idea what was happening, but the last thing he expected was to hear that this strange woman who appeared in his bedroom in the middle of the night had something to do with his best friend.

"Who are you? How do you know Bobby?"

She gently picked up Mark's right hand and slipped the ring on to his finger. It fitted perfectly. Mark looked at the strange ring, then back at the woman.

"Why? What's this?" he asked.

The woman touched a gentle finger to Mark's lips to quieten him. Mark immediately felt his eyes grow heavy. A second before he had been about as wide awake as anyone can be, but now he felt weary enough to fall asleep on the spot. He felt the world slipping away. In an instant, he was out.

The next morning Mark woke up at the usual 6:15 with the alarm clock blaring. His first thought was that he hated alarm clocks. His second thought was that he had had the strangest dream. He chuckled to himself, thinking he should cut down on the raw vegetables before bedtime. He then reached over to hit the snooze button . . . and saw it.

There, on his finger was the ring the woman had given him. Mark sat up in bed quickly and stared at it with its grey stone and strange inscriptions. It was real. He could feel it. It had weight. It wasn't a dream. What was going on?

He dressed quickly and left the house without telling his parents what had happened. There was only one person who could explain this to him. Bobby Pendragon. But something had already happened with Bobby that gave him a queasy feeling. Last night was the county semifinal basketball game . . . and Bobby hadn't shown up. His parents were there, his sister was there, but not Bobby. After the first half he went over to ask the Pendragons where Bobby was, but they had already left. Very strange.

And Stony Brook lost. Badly. Everybody at the game was buzzing, wanting to know what had happened to their star. Nobody knew. When Mark got home he called Bobby's house, but there was no answer. He figured he'd see him in school the next day and get the story. Then he went to sleep and had his strange night visitor. Now Mark wanted to know a lot more from Bobby than why he hadn't shown for a basketball game.

When Mark got into the school building, the number one topic of conversation was The Game.

"Hey Dimond? Where's your superstar pal?"

"He blew it!"

"This better be good, Dimond!"

"What's the story?"

Everyone was yelling at him about Bobby. That could only mean one thing. Bobby hadn't got there yet. Of course, Mark didn't have any answers, so he shrugged and kept walking. He went to Bobby's locker, but Bobby wasn't there. Instead there were more angry kids waiting to ambush him.

"He chickened out, didn't he?"

"Couldn't take the heat!"

Mark dodged them and went to Bobby's homeroom. Bobby wasn't there, either. Where was he? Something was definitely wrong.

And then it happened. It started as a twitch at first, but quickly grew. It was the ring. It was moving. It felt like it was squeezing and releasing, squeezing and releasing.

"Dimond! Hey, Dimond! Where is he?" More kids were closing

in. This was not a good time. Mark didn't know what to do, so he grabbed the ring with his other hand and ran. He blasted through kids, bumping into more than he dodged. A couple of older guys pushed him back, nearly sending him sprawling, but Mark somehow stayed on his feet. The bell rang and everyone headed for homeroom, but Mark didn't stop until he reached his own personal Fortress of Solitude – the boys' bathroom on the third floor.

He ran to the centre of the room and held his hand out as if it didn't belong to him. The ring was still moving, squeezing and releasing like a heartbeat. Then the grey stone started to sparkle. An instant before it had been a solid grey mass; now it sprang to life like a brilliant diamond. Beams of light shot from the ring and filled the room.

Mark couldn't take it any more. He yanked off the strange ring and threw it. It hit the tiled wall and bounced to a stop in the centre of the bathroom. The beams of light continued to shoot from the stone and dance across the ceiling and the walls, making the room look as if it were alive with beautiful, dazzling stars.

Then Mark watched in awe as the circular band started to grow larger. It slowly got bigger and bigger until it was about the size of a Frisbee, and in the centre of the now impossibly large band was a black hole where the floor should have been. The ring had opened up a dark portal to . . . somewhere. From deep within this portal, Mark could hear the faint sound of musical notes. It wasn't a melody; it was a jumble of sweet sounding tones that grew louder and louder.

Mark backed away from the strange ring, not sure if he should turn and run or stay and watch the show. He was fascinated and terrified at the same time. The musical notes coming from the portal got so loud that Mark had to cover his ears. Whatever was happening, he didn't want any part of it any more. So he turned and ran for the door. He was just about to throw it open when . . .

Everything stopped. The musical notes ended so abruptly it was like somebody threw a switch to cut the power. The dazzling light show ended also. The only thing that didn't stop was Mark's pounding heart. Whatever had just happened, it was over now and Mark tried to calm down. He took his hand away from the door and looked back into the bathroom. What he saw was the ring on the floor, right where he had thrown it. It was back to its normal size and the stone had returned to its original solid grey colour.

But something else was there too. Lying on the floor next to the ring was a scroll of paper. It was yellow parchment that had been tightly rolled and tied with a thin leather strap. Whatever the event had been with the ring, the result was that it had deposited this scroll here on the bathroom floor.

Mark approached the scroll cautiously, bent down, and picked it up with a sweaty hand. It was indeed rolled paper. Nothing scary about it. Just odd. Mark tugged on the leather cord that kept it together and gently unrolled the paper. There were four sheets, all filled with writing. Mark looked at the first line of the first page, and what he read hit him like an electric charge. He couldn't breathe. He couldn't think. This strange parchment was a letter . . . to him.

It began: *I hope you're reading this, Mark.*

DENDURON

There wasn't much I could ask Uncle Press from the back of a speeding motorcycle. Between the whine of the engine, the blast of wind rushing by and the fact that both of us were wearing these high-tech helmets, conversation was impossible. So I was left with my own imagination to try and figure out where we were going and why.

One thing was clear though. We were leaving town. I lived in a quiet, peaceful, okay *dull* suburb of New York City. I'd been into the city a few times with my parents, mostly to go to events like the holiday spectacular at Radio City or the Macy's Thanksgiving Day Parade. Then there was that one time you and I, Mark, hopped the commuter train to catch that James Bond flick. Remember? Other than that, the city was pretty much a mystery to me.

On the other hand, it didn't take a New York cabbie to realise Uncle Press was steering us into a section of the city that by anybody's standards would be defined as . . . bad. This was not the New York I'd ever seen, except maybe on a TV news report about some nasty crime that had just gone down. Once we shot off the Cross Bronx Expressway we were smack in the middle of the badlands. Burned-out buildings were everywhere. Nobody walked on the streets. It all looked empty and desolate, yet I had the eerie feeling that many sets of eyes were locked on us from the dark windows of the derelict buildings as we cruised by. And of course, it was nighttime dark.

Was I scared? Well, judging by the fact that I wanted to puke and I held on to Uncle Press so hard I expected to hear one of his ribs crack, I'd say yeah, I was scared. Uncle Press guided the motorcycle towards one of those old-fashioned kiosks that marked the stairs leading down to the subway. We bounced up on to the kerb and he killed the engine. As we glided to a stop, suddenly everything became quiet. Granted, I'd been riding on the back of a motorcycle for the past half hour and after that *anything* would seem quiet. But this was *really* quiet, like a ghost town. Or a ghost city.

"This is it," he announced and jumped off the bike. I jumped off too and gratefully removed my helmet. Finally, I could hear again. Uncle Press left his helmet on the bike and headed for the subway entrance.

"Whoa, hold on, we're going to leave the bike and the helmets?" I asked with surprise. I couldn't believe it. He didn't even take the keys out of the ignition. I'm no expert on crime, but I could pretty much predict that if we left this gear here, it would be gone before we blinked.

"We don't need it any more," he said quickly and started down the subway stairs.

"Why are we taking the subway?" I asked. "Why don't we just stay on the bike?"

"Because we can't take the bike where we're going," he answered with a matter-of-fact tone. He turned and headed down a few more steps.

I didn't move. I wanted answers, and I wasn't taking

another step until I got some. Uncle Press sensed that I wasn't following him, so he stopped and looked back at me.

"What?" he asked, with a little bit of frustration.

"I just blew off the most important game of my life, my team is going to crucify me tomorrow, and you want me to follow you into the subway in the worst part of New York City? I think I deserve to know what's going on!" This had gone far enough and if I didn't get some answers, I was walking. Of course I wasn't exactly sure of where I would go if Uncle Press left me there and went on alone. I figured it was a safe risk, though. After all, he was my uncle.

Uncle Press softened. For a moment I saw the face of the guy I'd known all my life. "You're right, Bobby. I've asked you to do a lot on faith. But if we stop for me to explain everything, we may be too late."

"Too late for what?"

"There's a group of people who are in trouble. They're relying on me to help them, and I'm relying on you to help me."

I was flattered and freaked at the same time. "Really? What kind of trouble?"

"That's what would take me forever to explain. I'd rather show you."

I didn't know what to do. Even if I wanted to run away, I had no clue of how to get out of there. And here was this guy, my uncle, staring me straight in the eye and saying he needed me. There weren't a whole lot of options. I finally decided to divulge the single overriding thought in my head.

"I'm scared." There, I said it.

"I know. But please believe me, Bobby, as long as it's in my power, I won't let anything happen to you." He said this with such sincerity, it actually made me feel better . . . for about a second.

"What happens when it's *not* in your power?" I asked.

Uncle Press smiled, and said, "That won't be for a while. Are you with me?"

They say that just before you're about to meet your doom, your life flashes before your eyes. Surprisingly, that didn't happen. I didn't think of the game. I didn't think of my family. I didn't even think of Courtney Chetwynde. I just thought about me and Uncle Press. Here and now. I took that as a good sign. So I mustered all the bravura I could and said, "Hey, ho, let's go."

Uncle Press let out a laugh like I hadn't heard from him in a long time, then turned and rushed down the stairs. As I watched him disappear into the dark hole of the subway, I did my best to pretend I wasn't being an idiot by going along with him. When I got to the bottom of the stairs, I saw Uncle Press standing in front of a wall of graffiti-covered plywood that blocked the entrance. The station was closed and by the looks of the old wood, it had been closed for a long time.

"Well, that's a problem," I said glibly. "No go, right?"

Uncle Press turned to me and with the sincerity of a sage teacher imparting golden words of wisdom, he said, "There are no problems, only challenges."

"Well, if the challenge is to catch a train at a station that's closed," I countered, "then I'd say that's a problem."

But not for Uncle Press. He casually reached towards the wall with one hand, grabbed one of the boards and gave it a yank. It didn't seem as if he pulled all that hard, but instantly four huge boards pulled loose in one piece, opening up an avenue into the darkened station.

"Who said anything about catching a train?" he said with a sly smile.

He effortlessly dropped the large section of boards on the

stairs and stepped inside. I had no idea Uncle Press was that strong. I also had no idea why we were stepping into a closed subway station, at night, in the worst section of the city.

Uncle Press then poked his head back out. "Coming?"

I was half a breath away from turning, running up the stairs, and giving myself a crash course in motorcycle driving. But I didn't. Chances are the bike was already stolen anyway. I had no choice, so I followed him.

The station had been closed for a long time. The only light came from street lamps that filtered down through grates in the pavement. The soft glow cast a crisscross pattern against the walls that threw the rest of the station into darkness. It took a while for my eyes to adjust, but when they did I saw a forgotten piece of history. At one time this was probably a busy station. I could make out ornate mosaic tile work on the walls that must have been beautiful when new, but was now a mess of grimy cracks that looked like a giant, dirty spiderweb. Rubbish was everywhere, benches were overturned, and the glass around the ticket office was shattered. In a word, it was sad.

As I stood on top of the cement stairs, the derelict station began to show signs of life. It started as a faint rumble, that slowly grew louder. The station may have been closed, but the subway trains still ran. I saw the headlight first as it beamed into the opening, lighting up the track and the walls. Then the train came – fast. There was no reason to stop at this station any more so it rumbled through like a shot, on its way to somewhere else. For a brief moment I could imagine the station as it had looked in better days. But just as quickly, the image was gone, along with the train. In an instant, the place was deathly quiet again. The only sign that the train had been through was the swirling pieces of crusty paper caught in its slipstream.

I looked to Uncle Press to see if he were appreciating this forlorn piece of old New York history the same as I was. He wasn't. His eyes were sharp and focused. He quickly scanned the empty station looking for . . . something. I didn't know what. But I definitely sensed that he had just notched up into DefCon 2. He was on full alert, and it didn't do much to put me at ease.

"What?" was all I could think of asking.

He started quickly down the stairs. I was right after him. "Listen, Bobby," he said quickly, as if he didn't have much time. "If anything happens, I want you to know what to do."

"Happens? What do you mean happens?" This didn't sound good.

"Everything will be fine if you know what to do. We're not here to catch a train, we're here because this is where the gate is."

"Gate? What gate?"

"At the end of the platform are stairs that lead down to the tracks. About thirty yards down the track, along the wall, there's a door. It's got a drawing on it, like a star."

Things were going a little fast for me now. Uncle Press kept walking quickly, headed for the far end of the platform. I had to dodge around pillars and overturned rubbish bins to keep up with him.

"You with me?" he asked sharply.

"Yeah," I said. "Stairs, door, star. Why are we – "

"The door is the gate. If for some reason I'm not with you, open the door, go inside and say, 'Denduron'."

"Denda-what?"

"Den-du-ron. Say it!"

"Denduron. I got it. What is it, some kind of password?"

"It'll get us where we're going."

Okay, could this have been any *more* mysterious? Why didn't we just say "abracadabra" or something equally stupid? I was beginning to think this was all some kind of big old joke.

"Why are you telling me this?" I asked nervously. "We're going together, right?"

"That's the plan, but if anything – "

"Stop right there!"

Uh-oh. We weren't alone. We both stopped short and whipped around to see . . . a cop. Busted. For what I'm not sure. Trespassing, I guess.

"You boys want to tell me what you're doing down here?" The cop looked confident – no, cocky. He was a clean-cut guy, with a perfect khaki-coloured uniform, a big badge, and an even bigger gun. At least it was still in its holster. Even though we were busted, I was actually kind of relieved to see him. To be honest, Uncle Press was starting to freak me out. I didn't think he'd gone off the deep end or anything, but this adventure was getting stranger by the second. Maybe now that a cop was here, he'd have to explain things a little better. I looked up to Uncle Press, expecting him to answer the cop. I didn't like what I saw. Uncle Press was staring the cop down. I could sense the wheels turning in his head, calculating. But what? An escape? I hoped not. The gun on the cop's hip looked nasty. There was a long moment of silence, like a standoff, and then somebody *else* joined the party.

"Can't you leave me in peace?"

We all shot a look over to a dark corner where a pile of rubbish sat. At least it looked like a pile of rubbish, until it moved and I saw that it was a homeless dude. Correction, he had a home and we were standing in it. He was a big guy, and I had no idea how old he was because all I saw was a tangle of hair and rags. He didn't smell so good either. He pulled himself to his feet and shuffled towards us. When he spoke, it was with a kind of slurred, crazy-speak.

"Peace! That's all I want! Little peace, little quiet!" he jabbered.

Uncle Press squared off and stood firm, glancing quickly back and forth between the cop and the homeless guy. He was thinking fast, calculating.

"I think you two had better come with me," the cop said to us calmly. He wasn't rattled by the new arrival.

I looked to Uncle Press. He didn't move. The homeless guy got closer.

"Castle! This is *my* castle! I want you all to – "

"What?" asked Uncle Press. "What do you want us to do?" I couldn't believe he was trying to talk to this crazy guy. Then the platform started to rumble. Another subway train was on its way.

"I want you all to go away! Leave me alone!"

For some reason this made Uncle Press smile. Now I was totally confused. Whatever he was trying to calculate, he had his answer. He turned away from the homeless guy and faced the cop.

"You don't know this territory, do you?" he said to the cop.

Huh? What was that supposed to mean? Behind us, the light from the subway train started to leak into the station. It would be here in a few seconds.

The homeless guy started waving his arms for emphasis. "You! I'm talkin' to you! I want you out of my castle!" he yelled at the cop.

I was afraid the cop would pull his gun on the guy for his own protection. But he didn't. He just stood there, staring at Uncle Press. They looked like two gunslingers, each waiting for the other to blink. Then he gave a little smile and said, "What was your first clue?"

"The uniform. City cops in this territory wear blue, not khaki," answered Uncle Press.

This guy wasn't a cop? Then who was he? The train horn blared and the screeching of metal wheels on track grew closer.

"I'm flattered though," said Uncle Press calmly. "You came yourself."

Uncle Press knew who this guy was! The homeless guy kept getting closer to the cop, or whoever he was.

"That's it! That's it! If you don't git now I'm gonna – "

Suddenly the cop snapped a look to the homeless guy. It was a cold look that made me catch my breath. It stopped the homeless guy in his tracks. The cop stared at him with an intensity I'd never seen. The guy froze, and then began to shake like he had a fever.

The subway horn blared. The train was almost in the station.

The homeless guy looked as if he wanted to get away, but the cop's laserlike gaze had him locked in place. Then, something happened that I won't forget as long as I live, though I wish I could. The homeless guy opened his mouth and let out a horrifying, anguished cry. Then he ran. But he didn't run away, he ran for the tracks! The train entered the station in a blur, and this guy was running towards it.

"No! Stop!" I shouted. But it didn't matter. The homeless guy kept running . . . and jumped in front of the train!

I turned away at the last second, but that didn't stop me from hearing it. It was a sickening thud, and his scream was suddenly cut off. The train didn't even stop. I'll bet no one on board knew what had happened. But I did and I wanted to puke. I looked to Uncle Press, who had a pained look. He wiped it away in the next instant and looked back to the cop, who stood there with a smug little smile.

"That was beneath you, Saint Dane," said Uncle Press through clenched teeth.

Saint Dane. That was the first time I heard the name. I had the grim feeling it wouldn't be the last.

The cop, Saint Dane, gave an innocent little shrug and said, "Just wanted to give the boy a taste of what is in store for him."

I didn't like the sound of that.

And then Saint Dane began to transform. I couldn't believe what I was seeing, but it was real. His face, his clothes, everything about him changed. I watched in absolute, stupefied awe as he became a different person. His hair grew long and straight till it was over his shoulders. His body grew until he was nearly seven feet tall. His skin became ghostly pale white. His clothes changed from the khaki brown cop uniform, to an all-black suit that vaguely reminded me of the Far East. But none of that mattered as much as his eyes. His eyes grew icy blue and flashed with an evil intensity that made me understand the sheer force of will he possessed that could make someone jump to their death in front of a speeding train.

There was only one thing that didn't change. He still had a gun. And I was surprised to discover, so did Uncle Press. With an expertise that made me feel as if he had done this sort of thing many times before, Uncle Press reached into his long coat and pulled out an automatic. Saint Dane went for his gun as well. I stood frozen. Ever hear the term "deer in the head-lights"? That was me. I couldn't move. The next thing I knew I was on my butt on the floor. Uncle Press had shoved me down behind a wooden bench. We were protected from Saint Dane, but for how long?

Uncle Press looked at me, and in a voice that was way more calm than the situation warranted, said one simple word, "Run."

"But what about – "

"*Run!*" He then dived out from behind the protection of the bench and started shooting. I stayed there long enough to see Saint Dane dive behind a pillar for protection. Uncle Press was a pretty good shot because the tiles on the pillar splintered and shattered as they were slammed with his bullets. It was clear what he was doing. He was keeping Saint Dane occupied to give me time to run. But run where?

"Bobby, the door!"

Right! The door with the star and the abracadabra. Got it. I started to crawl away, when Uncle Press called to me, "Watch out for the quigs!"

Huh? What's a quig? Bang! A tile shattered right near my head. Saint Dane was now shooting back, and I was the target! That's all the encouragement I needed. I ran. Behind me the sound of the blasts from the gun battle rang through the empty station. It was deafening. I ran past a pillar and *bang*! A bullet pulverized another tile. Pieces of flying tile stung the back of my neck. That's how close it was. I got to the far end of the platform and saw the stairs leading down to the tracks, just as Uncle Press described. I stopped for a second, thinking I'd have to be crazy to crawl down on to subway tracks. But the alternative was worse. It would be easier facing a subway train than that Saint Dane guy. So I took a quick breath and climbed down the stairs.

Once I was down on the tracks, the gun battle seemed far away. I still heard the occasional crack of a gun, but I was now more concerned about what was in front of me than behind. For a moment I thought I should go back and help Uncle Press, but jumping into the middle of a blazing gun battle didn't seem like such a hot idea. I could only hope that he could handle the situation. The only thing I could do was follow his instructions.

It was dark. I had to feel my way along the greasy wall to make sure I didn't accidentally step on the tracks. I'd heard about the infamous electric "third rail" that powered the trains. If you stepped on that thing, you were bacon. So I stayed as close to the wall as I could. Uncle Press said this door was about thirty yards down from the platform. I tried to picture a football field to visualize how far thirty yards was. It didn't help. I figured I'd just keep moving until my hand hit this mysterious door. My biggest fear was that I'd miss it and then . . .

Grrrrrr.

A grumble came from behind me. What was that? Was it a train? Was it power surging through the third rail? It was neither, because I heard it again and it came from a different direction.

Grrrrrr.

It sounded like growling. But I didn't think rats growled, so it couldn't be rats. Good thing. I hated rats. I looked around slowly and in the dim light, I saw something that nearly made my heart stop. Across the tracks, looking straight at me, were a pair of eyes. They were low to the ground and caught the light in such a way that it made them flash yellow. It was some kind of animal. Could this be the "quig" Uncle Press had told me to watch out for? Or maybe it was a wild dog. Whatever it was, it was big, and it had friends, because more eyes appeared. It was a pack of animals gathering, and their growling told me they weren't friendly. Gulp. My plan was to do everything I could not to threaten them. I decided to move very slowly, very deliberately and make my way towards the door and . . .

GRRRRRRR!

Too late! The entire pack of dogs, or quigs, or whatever they were leaped from the shadows and charged me! Suddenly the third rail didn't seem all that dangerous. I turned and ran. There must have been a dozen of them. I could hear their teeth gnashing and their claws scratching on the metal rails as they bounded over one another to get to me and . . . and I didn't want to think of what would happen if they did. I remember having a fleeting thought that maybe they'd hit the third rail and vaporize, but that didn't happen. My only hope was finding that door. It was so dark I kept tripping over stones and rubbish and railroad ties and everything else down there, but I kept going. I had no choice. If I fell, I was mincemeat.

Then, like a lifeline to a drowning man, I saw it. The only light came from dirty, old bulbs strung above the tracks, but it was enough for me to see. Recessed into the cement wall was a small door with a faint star shape carved into the wood. This was it! I ran up to the door, only to discover there was no door handle. I couldn't open it!

I looked back and saw the pack of animals nearly on me. I only had a few more seconds. I leaned my weight against the door and it opened! The door opened in, not out! I fell inside and quickly scrambled back to close the door just as – *slam slam slam!* – the animals hit the door. I leaned back on the door, desperate to keep them out, but they were strong. I could hear their claws feverishly scratching at the wooden door. I couldn't keep them out for long.

Now, I'm going to stop my story here, Mark, because what happened next was far more important than those animals who were trying to get me. I know, hard to believe, but it was. Obviously the wild dogs, or the quigs or whatever they're called, didn't get me. If they had, I wouldn't be writing this.

Duh. I think what happened next was the single most important event of this whole nightmare. As scary and as strange as everything was that had happened up till then, there was no way I could have been prepared for what was waiting for me beyond that door.

While I was trying to keep the animals out, I looked at the space I'd just entered. What I saw was a long, dark tunnel. It wasn't big, maybe about six feet high. The walls were made of craggy, slate grey rock. It didn't look as if it were drilled out by a machine, either. It was crude, like somebody dug the tunnel with hand tools. I couldn't see how far the tunnel went back, because it dropped off into blackness. It could have gone on forever.

I didn't know what to do. If I tried to run down the tunnel, the instant I left the door the animals would burst in and be on me. Not a good move. I was stuck. But then I remembered what Uncle Press had told me. There was a word. He'd said to go inside and say this word. He'd said it would get us to where we were going. What was that word? Dennison? Dandelion? Dandruff? I couldn't really see how saying a hocus-pocus word could get me out of this predicament, but it was the only choice I had.

Then I remembered it. Denduron. It meant nothing to me, but if it was going to get me out of this, it would be my favourite word in the world. So I put my back to the door, planted my feet, looked into the dark tunnel, and shouted out:

"*Denduron!*"

Instantly the animals stopped beating against the door. It didn't sound like they ran away; they were just suddenly not there. I took a chance and stepped away from the door and . . . nothing happened. At least, nothing happened with the door. The tunnel was another thing altogether.

It started as a hum. It was low at first, but the frequency started to grow. I looked into the tunnel and watched in wonder as the walls started to twist and move. I was looking down the barrel of a huge, flexible, living pipeline. Then the walls started to change. They went from solid grey to clear! These craggy walls suddenly looked as if they were made of crystal, or diamonds. Light was everywhere, as if it were coming right from the walls themselves.

It was truly an amazing sight. So amazing that I didn't stop to wonder what it all meant. That's when I heard the music. It wasn't a recognisable tune or anything; it was just a bunch of soft, sweet notes that were all jumbled up. It was almost hypnotic. The mixed-up notes got louder and louder as if they were coming closer.

The thing that brought me back to myself was a strange sensation. I stood at the mouth of the tunnel and felt a tingling throughout my body. It wasn't horrible, just strange. The tingling grew stronger, and I felt an odd but unmistakable tug. I didn't realise it at first, but it soon dawned on me that I was being pulled into the tunnel! Some giant, invisible hand had got hold of me and was pulling me in! I tried to back away, but the force grew stronger. Now I started to panic. I turned and tried to find something, anything to grab on to. I fell down and dug my nails into the ground, but nothing worked. I was being sucked into this horrible tunnel, and there was nothing I could do to stop it.

This is the point. This is where my life changed. What happened next turned everything I had ever known, everything I had ever believed in, everything I had ever thought to be real, totally inside out.

I got sucked into the rabbit hole, Mark. And I was heading for Wonderland.

◉ SECOND EARTH ◉

Mark had to get out of this bathroom. The little stall was closing in on him. He tried to jump up off the seat, but a loop on his pack was caught on the flusher handle and all he managed to do was fall back and flush the stupid toilet. He pulled his pack free, jammed the parchment papers into it, then fumbled for the lock to spring himself from the stall. He was so flustered he couldn't even work the simple latch. Finally, mercifully, he slammed it back and threw the door open to see . . .

Standing there was Andy Mitchell. He was leaning casually against the wall, smoking a cigarette. "Jeez, you been in there a long time, Dimond. Everything come out all right?" Mitchell gave a stupid grin like this was a truly clever line.

Mark froze for a second, feeling as if he had been caught doing something wrong.

"I'm f-f-fine." When Mark got nervous, he had a little stutter. It wasn't a horrible thing, just something that came out under stress.

Mitchell expertly flipped his cigarette across the room and it landed in one of the urinals. Bull's-eye. Ordinarily Mark would have been grossed out by that, but his mind was on other things right now.

"It's cool," said Mitchell. "What you do in the privacy of the can is your business. What's in the pack?"

Mark clutched the pack to his chest as if it contained precious papers. Which in fact, it did. His mind raced. What was the one thing he could say that Mitchell would accept and not ask more questions? The answer was clear.

"P-Playboys."

Mitchell gave a lascivious grin. "You dog. Lemme see." He reached for the pack but Mark yanked it away and backed towards the door.

"S-Sorry. I'm late." Before Mitchell could say another word, Mark turned and ran from the room. He didn't know where he was going, but he ran anyway. The words from the pages kept running through his head. Could this story be true? This was the kind of stuff you saw in the movies or read in graphic novels. People made this stuff up for entertainment. It wasn't real.

He probably would have dismissed the whole thing as a work of fiction, except for the strange visitor he had the night before and the ring on his finger that made these pages appear on the bathroom floor. They were both real as can be. There was no logical explanation for what happened, so therefore all the normal rules of reality had to be tossed out of the window. He needed to talk to Bobby. But if this story were true, Bobby was indisposed at the moment and not available for questioning.

It was nine thirty in the morning. Mark and Bobby should have been in geometry class. Of course, Mark wasn't there because he was too busy running frantically through the empty halls of Stony Brook Junior High like a nutburger. Somehow geometry didn't seem all that important right now. But he swung by the classroom anyway, praying that he'd find Bobby sitting at his desk.

Mark approached the door warily. He took a breath and looked in to see that Bobby's desk was empty. Not good. Mark didn't know where to turn. He had to talk to somebody, but who? He wanted to share what was going on, but more importantly, he needed confirmation that he wasn't totally out of his mind. That's when the answer came to him. There was one person who could verify part of the story. Courtney Chetwynde.

The gym classes at Stony Brook were normally segregated, boys from girls. The only time the classes were coed was for gymnastics when they had to share the apparatus. The rest of the time there was a huge, collapsible wall drawn between the boys' gym and the girls' gym. However, there was one other exception to the rule.

That was Courtney Chetwynde. When it came to team sports, Courtney didn't play with the girls. She was tall and strong, and the advantage she had over most girls was unfair. So even though it went against every rule of the school system and the county and the state, Courtney was allowed to play with the guys. No one complained, either. The girls were just as happy not to have to deal with her whupping up on them all the time. And after she proved herself to the guys, which took all of thirty seconds, they welcomed her. And they didn't cut her any slack either. In fact, most of the guys feared her. When Courtney played, it was full speed all the way around.

And her game was volleyball.

Wham! Courtney leaped high over the net and spiked the ball off the head of her poor opponent. The guy was stunned silly and Courtney landed gracefully before the ball hit the ground.

"Point break," she said with a smile. Courtney never showed mercy. It was her serve now and the ball was bounced to her.

"C'mon, C. C."

"Let's go!"

"Game point!"

Courtney had a killer serve and everyone expected this to be the final nail in the coffin. But as she walked to the service line, something caught her eye. It was Mark Dimond. The little guy was waving at her frantically from outside the gym door. As soon as he got her attention, he started motioning for her to come over. Courtney raised a finger as if to say, "Wait one second," but that made Mark wave even harder. He would not be denied.

Courtney frowned and tossed the ball to one of her teammates. "You serve," she said and headed towards Mark.

"What?" the teammate yelled in shock. "It's game point!"

"I know. Don't blow it."

The guys watched her in wonder for a moment, then turned back to the game with a shrug. Though none of them would admit it, the guys from the other team breathed a little sigh of relief.

Courtney headed straight for the door and threw it open to find Mark waiting in the empty hallway.

"This had better be good," she said impatiently.

Mark waffled back and forth nervously, shifting his weight from foot to foot. Courtney watched him for a second and then said, "You have to pee?"

"N-No. I . . . I . . . it's about Bobby."

Courtney's grey eyes focused. "Where is he? Why didn't he play last night?"

Mark hesitated as if not wanting to ask the next question. But he did. "D-Did you guys make out at his house last night?"

Courtney stared at him, not exactly sure she heard what she thought she just heard. Then she blew a gasket. "That's what you got me over here for? He missed the biggest game of the year and . . . wait a minute . . . did Bobby tell you about us? I'll kill him!"

"C-Courtney . . . wait . . . it's not like that." Mark tried to stop her angry tirade, but Courtney was on a roll.

"I don't care who he is. He can't go around telling private stuff that – "

"Stop!" shouted Mark.

Courtney did, mostly because she was so surprised Mark had made such a bold move. That wasn't like him. They both looked at each other, not sure of where to go next.

Mark now had her attention and it was up to him to make the next move. When he spoke, it was slow and thoughtful. He didn't want to stutter and he didn't want to make a mistake. So he pushed his glasses back up on his nose and said, "I think something strange happened to Bobby. What went on between you two last night was a part of it. I . . . I'm sorry if it upsets you, but I've got to know. Did you two make out at his house last night?"

Courtney tried to read Mark. He was a shy guy and the fact that he'd ask a personal question like this was hugely out of character. Clearly there was more going on here than guys bragging to each other about getting to first base with a girl. She could see it in his eyes. Mark was scared.

"Yeah," she said. "We did. Where is he?"

"I . . . I don't know," he said, downcast. "I hope he's at his house. Will you come with me and talk to him?"

The two held eye contact for a long time. Courtney was trying to read Mark's thoughts, and Mark was praying that Courtney would come with him so he could share some of the burden of what he knew. Maybe she could even help him figure things out.

Courtney walked past Mark and gave him a simple, quick, "Let's go."

Courtney was now on a mission. She wanted to talk to Bobby. If she had to go to his house to find him, so be it. Mark was relieved that he now had an ally, but he had no idea how to tell Courtney what he knew, or if she'd believe him. For now though, he was happy just to have someone to talk to.

The Pendragons lived on a quiet cul-de-sac not far from school. It was lunchtime, so Courtney and Mark figured they could reach Bobby's house, get to the bottom of what was going on, and be back at school before anyone missed them. As they hurried up the street, Mark had to walk quickly to keep up with Courtney's long, purposeful strides. He wanted to tell her about the visitor he had had the night before, and the ring, and the parchment with Bobby's story, but he was afraid she'd dismiss him as a mental case. He had to choose his words carefully.

"Do you know Bobby's Uncle Press?" he asked cautiously.

"Yeah."

"Did, uh, did you see him last night?"

"Unfortunately. He's the guy who caught us making out."

Mark's heart sank. Not that it mattered if Bobby and Courtney made out, or that they were caught by Bobby's uncle. The problem was, Courtney's answer confirmed more of the story contained on the parchment papers. Mark feared that if some of the story were true, then maybe all of it was true. The thought made him sick.

They were nearly at Bobby's house now. Mark hoped that Bobby would be there to settle everything. He imagined walking up to Bobby, holding out the parchment paper, and seeing Bobby burst out laughing. Bobby would say it was all a goof and that he never expected them to think it was real. It was a prank, like Orson Welles's "War of the Worlds" radio broadcast that made everybody think the Earth was being invaded by Martians. That's what Mark was hoping for, but what they both saw in the next instant dashed that hope entirely.

Two Linden Place. That was the address. Mark had been there a thousand times. Ever since kindergarten they'd trade off playing at each other's house. Bobby's house was like his second home. Mrs Pendragon called Mark her second son. That's why nothing could prepare him for what he was about to see. Courtney and Mark walked up the path that led to the split-rail fence that surrounded Bobby's front yard, and stopped cold. They both looked at 2 Linden Place, stunned.

"Oh my god," was all Courtney could whisper.

Mark couldn't even get that much out.

Two Linden Place was gone. The two of them stood together, wide-eyed, looking at a vacant lot. There were no signs that a house had *ever* been there. Not a single piece of wood, brick, stone, or blade of grass existed in the space. The ground was nothing but dirt. Mark looked to the huge maple tree where years before Mr Pendragon had hung a tyre swing for the boys. The tree was there, but there was no swing. Even the branch that had been rope-scarred by years of swinging was clean. No marks. Nothing.

Courtney broke first. "It's the wrong address."

Mark said softly, "It's not the wrong address."

Courtney wouldn't accept it. She stormed onto the empty lot. "But I was here last night! There was a path to the house right here! And the front door was here! And Bobby and I were standing . . ." Her voice trailed off. She looked to Mark with dread. "Mark, what happened?"

Now was as good a time as any. Even though he had no idea what had happened, seeing the empty lot confirmed his worst fears. Everything he had read on the pages from Bobby was true. He had more questions than he had answers, but he did have some answers, as strange as they were. He wanted to share them with Courtney. Knowing all this by himself was too tough. So he reached for his backpack and took out the yellow parchment papers.

"I want you to read something," he said. "It's from Bobby." He held out the pages to Courtney, who looked at them, then back to Mark. Reluctantly, she took the pages from him and sat down. Right there. Right in the middle of the empty lot at Two Linden Place, not far from the spot where she and Bobby shared their first kiss.

She looked down at the pages and started to read.

DENDURON

I thought my life was over. All that was left was to wait for the pain. Would it come fast and hit me hard? Or would it start at my feet and gradually work its way up my legs, over my body, and zero in right on my head in a brilliant, searing flash of agony before everything went dark?

I was voting for fast. But it didn't come fast. In fact it didn't come at all. There was no pain. I didn't die. Instead I found myself falling through this snaking tunnel. It was like sailing down one of those water-park rides. But the water-park rides are actually more violent than this. Now that it's over, I can look back on it and actually say it was kind of fun. But that's now. At the time, I was freaking out.

Once I realised I wasn't being sucked into some giant waste disposal, I opened my eyes and looked around. It felt like I was moving fast.

Like I wrote before, the walls of the tunnel were craggy, like rocks. But they were translucent, too, as if they were crystal. The strange thing was, it wasn't a bumpy ride. I was flying along, feet first like on a playground slide, but it felt like I was floating. I couldn't feel the walls of the tunnel. There were many twists and turns, but I didn't get slammed against the walls or anything, like you do when you hit the turns on a water slide. It felt like I was floating on a magic carpet that knew exactly where it was taking me.

There were sounds, too. They were soft notes, like from a tuning fork. All different notes. Pretty notes. They were the same kind of notes I heard when the tunnel came to life, but much further apart. That's one of the reasons I could tell I was going so fast, because I was sailing past the notes. The sound would come up fast from up ahead, and then flash past me and disappear behind. It was a strange sensation.

I looked back the way I came and there was nothing but crystal tunnel for as far as I could see. I looked down between my feet and it was the same thing. Snaking tunnel. Infinity.

After a while I got used to it, sort of. There was nothing I could do to stop anyway, so I figured why fight it? Now, here's the freaky thing (as if everything up to this point wasn't freaky enough). I could look out beyond the crystal walls to see that it was dark out there. I figured that made sense, I was underground, after all. But when I looked harder, it seemed as if the blackness was broken up by thousands and thousands of stars.

I know, screwy, right? I had started in an underground subway and was going deeper underground from there, so how could I be looking at stars? But that's what it looked like. Why should this make any more sense than anything else?

I don't know how long I was flying. Three minutes? Three months? My normal sense of relativity had long since gone bye-bye. I'd given myself over to the experience and wherever it took me, and for how long, it just didn't matter.

And then I heard something different. It wasn't one of the soft notes that had been my guides on this bizarro journey.

This sounded, well, solid. It sounded craggy. It sounded like I was coming to the end of the line. I looked down between my feet and saw it. The end. The twisting, bright tunnel ended in darkness, and I was heading for it, fast. All around me the walls of the tunnel started to change. They were transforming from the translucent crystal back to the slate grey craggy rocks that I had seen at their start near the subway.

The panic returned. Was I about to hit the centre of the Earth? Wasn't there supposed to be a core of molten magma there? Was this magical flight just a prelude to a fiery death? Whatever was going to happen, it was going to happen now. So I did the one and only thing I could think of to prepare myself for the end. I closed my eyes.

But the end wasn't a fiery crash at all. I got the same tingling feeling that I had felt at the mouth of the tunnel. Then there was a shower of sound. All the sweet notes I had been hearing gathered together the way they did at the beginning of my journey. I felt as if a heavy weight were pressing against my chest. The next thing I knew, I was standing up. The musical notes faded away. I had been gently deposited somewhere by the magic carpet.

It was strange having to support my own weight after having been weightless for the journey. I was like an astronaut returning from space who needed to get used to gravity again. I opened my eyes, looked back, and saw the tunnel. It looked exactly like the mouth I had entered back at the subway. It was grey and dark and stretched out to nowhere.

I had arrived safely. But where was I? Another subway station? In China maybe? I turned around to know where the tunnel had deposited me and saw that I was at the entrance to some sort of cave. Now that I had my wits back, I realised that I was cold. The sharp sound I had heard during the last stretch of my journey was a howling wind. Wherever I was, I wasn't underground any more.

I took a few shaky steps away from the mouth of the tunnel and entered the cave. As I walked into this larger space, I noticed that the cave was marked by the same star symbol that was on the door in the subway. It was carved into the rock at about eye level. Weird.

I then saw light pouring in from an opening on the far side of the cavern. It was so bright that it made the rest of the cave seem pitch black. I was suddenly overcome by the feeling that I had been in the dark way too long. I wanted out, and that light showed me the way, so I stumbled along to reach it. When I got there, I knew that it was indeed the way out of the cave. The light also told me that it was daytime. How long had I been in that tunnel? All night? Or was it daytime in China? My eyes weren't accustomed to the light, so I had to cover them and squint. I stepped outside and immediately realised it was even colder out here. All I had on was my Stony Brook warm-up top over a T-shirt, so the wind cut through me instantly. Man, it was freezing! I took a few steps and looked down to see – snow! The ground was covered with snow! That's another reason it was so bright. The sun reflected off the snow and blinded me. I knew it wouldn't take long for my eyes to adjust, so rather than duck back into the cave to get warm, I waited till I could see. I wanted to know where I was.

After a few seconds, I gingerly took my hands away from my eyes. My pupils had finally contracted enough to let me see, and what was there waiting for me nearly knocked me off my feet.

I was standing on top of a mountain! And this was no small ski mountain like we go to in Vermont. This was like

Everest! Okay, maybe not that big, but I felt like I was on top of the world. Craggy snow fields stretched for as far as I could see. In the far distance, way down below, I could see that the snow gave way to a green, lush valley, but it was a long, steep trip between here and there.

One question kept running through my head. "Where in heck am I?" Good question, but I had no one to ask. So I turned to go back into the safety of the cave to get my act together and figure out some kind of plan. Just before I turned back I saw, scattered several yards away from the mouth of the cave, these yellowish, kind of smooth, pointed rocks about two feet high. They jutted up out of the snow like stalagmites. Or stalactites. I can never remember which is which. They stuck up and came to a sharp point. I had no idea what they could be, but the word "tombstones" kept creeping into my head. I shook that particularly morbid thought out of my brain and trudged through the snow back to the cave.

That's when I saw the strangest thing of all. The sun was just rising up over the rocks that formed the cave. But I had just been shielding my eyes against the sun that was shining from the other direction! How could that be? I looked behind me to see that there wasn't just one sun. There were three! I swear, Mark, there were three suns in opposite corners of the sky! I blinked, thinking my vision was just screwed up or something, but it didn't help. They were still there. My mind locked up. I didn't know what to think, but there was one thing I knew for sure – I wasn't in China.

I stood there on top of this mountain, all alone, trainers getting wet in the snow, staring up at three blazing suns. I'm not ashamed to admit this, I wanted my mum. I wanted to be sitting in front of the TV fighting for the remote with Shannon. I wanted to be washing the car with Dad. I wanted to be shooting hoops with you. Suddenly the things I had taken for granted in life felt very far away. I wanted to go home, but all I could do was stand there and cry. I really did. I cried.

Then the sound came again, from inside the cave – the same jumble of musical notes that had sucked me into the tunnel and dumped me here. Someone else was coming. Uncle Press! It had to be! I ran back into the cave, overjoyed that I wasn't going to be alone any more. But then another thought hit me. What if it wasn't Uncle Press? What if it was that Saint Dane guy? The last time I had the pleasure of hanging with that dude, he was shooting at us. And I've got to tell you, getting shot at isn't like what you see in the movies, or with Nintendo. It's real and it's terrifying. I could still feel the sting on the back of my neck where I got hit by the shattered pieces of tile.

I didn't know what to do, so I stopped in the middle of the big cave and waited. Whoever it was would be coming out of the tunnel. Would it be Uncle Press or Saint Dane? Or maybe those freakin' dogs that wanted to eat me. Wouldn't that be just perfect? Who was it going to be? Friend or foe?

"Bobby?"

It was Uncle Press! He walked out of the tunnel with his long leather coat flapping against his legs. I could have hugged him. In fact, I did. I ran over to him like a little kid. If this were a movie, I'd have been running in slow motion. I threw my arms around him with the feeling of pure joy and gratitude that I wasn't alone any more, and that my favourite guy in the world wasn't shot dead by that Saint Dane guy. He was safe.

This feeling lasted for about, oh, three seconds. Now that my fear of impending doom was gone, reality came flooding back. And there was only one person responsible for my being here. Uncle Press. Someone I trusted. Someone

I loved. Someone who yanked me from home and nearly got me killed about eight times over.

I pushed away from him with a shove that was hard enough to knock him off his feet, because that's what I wanted to do. I wanted him to feel how angry I was. But as I saw before, Uncle Press was strong. It was like trying to push over a wall. All I managed to do was knock myself off balance and fall on my butt.

"What the hell is going on!" I shouted as I scrambled back to my feet, trying not to look like an idiot.

"Bobby, I know you're confused about — "

"Confused? Confused doesn't begin to cover it!" I stormed over to the mouth of the tunnel and screamed, "Denduron. *Denduron!*" I'd say *anything* to get out of there. But nothing happened.

"This is Denduron. We're already here," he said as if that were supposed to make sense.

"Okay then," I looked into the tunnel and screamed, "Earth! New York! The subway! There's no place like home!" I ran into the tunnel, hoping the magical notes would pick me up and fly me home. But nothing happened. I came back out and got right in Uncle Press's face.

"I don't care what this is about," I said with as much authority as I could generate. "I don't even care where we are. I care about going home and going home now! Take . . . me . . . home!"

Uncle Press just looked at me. He had to know how angry and scared I was, so I think he was trying to choose his next words carefully. Unfortunately no matter how carefully he chose his next words, there was no good way of saying what he then told me.

"Bobby, you can't go home. You belong here right now."

Boom. Just like that. I backed away from him, stunned. I

didn't know what to do. I didn't know what to think. I wanted to cry. I wanted to hit him. I wanted to reason with him. I wanted to wake up and find this was all just a horrible nightmare.

Uncle Press didn't say anything. He just watched me and waited for me to get my act together. But with all the confusing information that had been so rudely inputted into my poor little skull, all I could squeak out was a single, simple question. "Why?"

"I told you. There are people here on Denduron who need our help," he said slowly, as if to a little kid, which made me even more angry.

"But I don't know these people!" I shouted. "I don't care about them. I care about me. I care about getting me home. What is it about that you don't understand?"

"I understand perfectly. But that can't happen," he said firmly.

"Why? What's so important about these people? And where is here anyway? Where is this . . . Denduron?"

"That's hard to explain."

"Try," I said. I was getting fed up with all the mystery.

Uncle Press sat down on a rock. I took that as a sign that he was ready to start helping me understand things.

"We are far from Earth, but this isn't a different planet in the sense you're thinking. It's a territory. Like Earth is a territory."

"Territory, planet, what's the difference? It's just words."

"No, it's not. If we had a spaceship and blasted off from here and went to the place where Earth is, it wouldn't be there. At least not the way you know it. When you travel through the flumes – "

"Flumes?" I repeated.

"That's how you got here. Through a flume. When you

travel to the territories through flumes, you're not just going from place to place, you're moving through space and time. I know that's hard to comprehend, but you'll get it."

I was not so sure I wanted to get it. Maybe it was better to stay ignorant. I looked at Uncle Press and for the first time it hit me that this guy wasn't the person I thought he was. I always knew he was a mysterious character, but now he was way more ozone-esque than I could ever have imagined.

"Who are you?" I asked. "Really, you're not a normal guy."

Uncle Press smiled and looked down. Somehow I had the feeling that this wasn't going to be an easy answer either.

"I'm your uncle, Bobby. But I'm also a 'Traveller'. Just like you are."

Another new word. "Traveller." I didn't want to be a "Traveller". I wanted to be Bobby Pendragon, point guard on the Stony Brook basketball team. But that life seemed pretty far away right now.

"So if we're not on Earth, why is it like Earth? I mean, I can breathe and there's snow and normal gravity and all."

He answered, "All the territories are pretty much like Earth, but not exactly."

"You mean, like the three suns here?"

"Good example."

"And those weird yellow stone things sticking up out of the snow?"

Suddenly Uncle Press got tense. "Where? Outside? How many are there?"

"Uhh, I don't know. Ten. Twelve."

Uncle Press shot to his feet and started pulling off his coat.

"We gotta go!" He dumped his coat on the ground and hurried to the far side of the cave where there was a pile of dried branches. He started pulling at them.

"What's the matter?" I said, confused and more than a little worried.

He turned to me and raised a finger to his lips to "shush" me. He continued pulling branches off the pile and spoke quietly, as if not wanting to be heard.

"Quigs," he said.

Uh-oh. Quigs. Not a new word. I hated that word.

"Those aren't quigs. Quigs are like dogs, right?" I asked hopefully.

"Depends on the territory," he whispered. "On Second Earth they're like dogs. Not here."

"So what are . . . quigs?" I asked, but I wasn't really sure I wanted to know.

"They're wild animals that are special to each territory," he explained. "Saint Dane uses them to keep the Travellers away from the flumes."

There was that name again. Saint Dane. Somehow I knew he'd factor back into this equation. But how was it possible for a guy to "use" a wild animal to do anything? Before I got the chance to ask, Uncle Press pulled off the last branches to reveal a jumble of fur and leather. Animal pelts. He then started taking off his shirt.

"We can't wear Second Earth clothes in this territory. Put these on," he said as he lifted up a nasty looking piece of skin.

"You gotta be kidding!" was all I could say.

"Don't argue with me Bobby. These will keep you warm."

"But — "

"No buts. Hurry!" He said this in a stage whisper. He really was afraid of the quigs. I figured I should be too, so I started taking off my clothes.

"Even my underwear?" I asked, horrified at what the answer would be.

"They don't wear boxers on Denduron," he said, which is exactly what I didn't want to hear. This was going to be uncomfortable. I followed Uncle Press's instructions and dressed in the leather and fur. There were even leather boots that were kind of soft, which was good because they didn't wear gold-toe sweat socks on Denduron either. As we took more of the clothing off the pile, something else was slowly revealed. I picked up one last furry pelt, and saw a two-man sled! It looked sort of like the sled you see in Alaska for sled dogs, but there was nothing modern about this thing. The runners were slats of wood, the sides were made of branches, the seats were woven out of some kind of cane, and the steering mechanism up front was fashioned out of huge antlers. Fred Flintstone would have been proud. But there was something else about this sled that made me nervous.

Lashed to either side were long, deadly-looking spears. The shafts were carved from smooth tree branches. The tips were made of hammered-out metal and looked surgical sharp. The tails had some sort of feathers attached for stability. As crude and low-tech as the whole rig was, these bad boys looked pretty lethal. They hung on either side of the sled like prehistoric sidewinder missiles, ready for launching.

"What about your gun?" I asked hopefully. "Can't we use that on the quigs?"

"There are no guns in this territory," he answered, then stopped working for a moment and looked me dead in the eye. "We can only use what the territory offers. That's important. Remember that. Okay?"

"Yeah, sure, whatever."

He then shoved something into my hand. It was a small, carved object that hung from a leather cord. It looked like . . .

"It's a whistle," he said, reading my thoughts. "Keep it handy."

I wanted to ask why, but at this point it didn't really matter. I just hoped Uncle Press was as good with a spear as he was with a gun, because a little whistle sure as heck wasn't going to protect us if things got hairy. I followed orders and put it around my neck.

"You ready?" he asked.

"No," was my usual reply. Though honestly, I was. I felt a little like a caveman, but the strange clothes fitted me fine. Where they were too big, I tied them tight with leather straps the way Uncle Press showed me. I was actually pretty comfortable. The only bad thing was I really wished I could have kept my underwear. There was going to be some major league rash action going on here and they probably didn't have talcum powder on Denduron either.

Uncle Press started dragging the sled towards the light and the entrance of the cave. I helped him pull.

"When we get the sled in the snow, hop on and sit in the back," he instructed. "I'll get us going and steer from the front. If we're lucky we'll be gone before the quigs wake up."

"What if we're not lucky?" was the obvious next question.

"We can't outrun them. Our only hope is to get one of them."

"Get? Define 'get'."

He didn't. We were at the mouth of the cave. Uncle Press looked at me.

"I'm sorry for this, Bobby, I really am. All I can say is that sometime soon you'll understand why it had to be this way."

He said this with such conviction that I actually believed him. The thing was, I was afraid to believe him. Because if what he had been saying was true, I'd have no choice but to face whatever trouble lay ahead. And based on what had happened so far, it wasn't going to be fun.

"I hope you know how to drive this thing," I said.

"Hold on tight," was his answer. Yeah right, like I planned on waving my hands in the air like on a roller coaster. Give me a break.

We pulled the sled out of the cave and on to the snow. It took a few seconds for my eyes to adjust to the light again, but when I did, the first thing I saw were the ominous looking yellow pointed rocks sticking up out of the snow. In spite of Uncle Press's fear, I didn't see how these things could be dangerous. Uncle Press motioned silently for me to get in. He then went to the back and started pushing. For a clunky prehistoric bobsled, it moved pretty smoothly. In front of us was the field of yellow stones. I counted twelve of them, spread out over several yards. We glided closer to them with almost no sound. I looked to Uncle Press. He winked at me and put a finger to his lips as a reminder to be quiet. After a few more yards, we were right in the middle of them. Uncle Press manoeuvred the sled carefully so as not to disturb anything. That's when we started to pick up speed. The slope was growing steeper. I looked ahead and suddenly I wasn't worried about the quigs any more. We were about to set sail down a steep, craggy, boulder-strewn, snow-covered mountain on a rickety piece of wood that was held together by leather straps. Compared to that, how horrible could some two-foot-tall animals be?

I was about to find out.

We were nearly out of the field of yellow stones, when right in front of us the snow started to shake. There was only one stone left, but one was enough. Suddenly, right in front of us, the snow cracked and the yellow, pointed stone started to rise up. But it wasn't a pointed stone at all. This was a spike made of bone that stuck out of the back of the most hideous beast I had ever seen. The quig rose up out of the snow until its entire body was free. It looked like a huge, dirty-grey grizzly bear. But its head was giant, with fangs like a wild boar. Upper and lower. Spiky sharp. Its paws were oversized too, with claws the size of piano keys. Sharp piano keys. And its eyes looked like the eyes of the dogs in the subway. They were yellow, and angry, and focused on us.

Uncle Press manoeuvred the sled around the quig and ran while he pushed, trying to get more speed.

"Get the spear!" he shouted.

I couldn't take my eyes off the beast. It reared up on its hind legs and let out a horrifying bellow that I thought would wake the dead. Or at least wake the other quigs. And that's exactly what happened. Behind us, the snow around the other yellow spikes started to boil. The rest of the quigs were waking up.

"Bobby, move!"

Uncle Press jumped on to the sled and I snapped to my senses. I dived forward to grab one of the spears. We were moving faster now, bouncing over the snow. It was tough to keep my balance. I stayed low and leaned over the side to try and untie one of the two spears.

"Hurry please," came from the back. He was calm, but insistent. I turned to look and saw that there were now a dozen quigs behind us, shaking off the snow.

I shouldn't have looked. The trouble was I had almost finished untying the spear and just as I looked back, the sled hit a bump. Before I realised what was happening, the spear worked itself loose and fell off! I tried to grab it, but it was too late. It clattered to the snow, just out of my reach. Gone.

"The other one! Now!" shouted Uncle Press.

I dived across the sled to get the other spear. I grabbed it and held it tight with one hand while fumbling to untie it with the other. There was no way I was going to let this one get away. Finally I worked off the strap and the spear was loose.

"Got it!" I shouted. I fell back, holding it up for Uncle Press to grab. Once he had it, I got to my knees and looked behind us. To my horror, I saw that the quigs were now charging. It was like a stampede of snarling, vicious bears that had us in their sights. I had no idea what one little spear could do against this deadly onslaught.

"Steer!" shouted Uncle Press. "Keep it steady."

I scrambled to the front of the sled and grabbed hold of the antlers. The sled responded perfectly. Whoever built this thing knew what they were doing. Still, Uncle Press was right. We weren't going fast enough to lose the quigs. They were getting closer.

The first quig was far ahead of the others, and it was getting dangerously close. I kept glancing back over my shoulder to see what was happening. Uncle Press was amazing. He stood on the sled, backwards, with spear in hand. I was getting used to seeing Uncle Press pull off stunts like this. Nothing surprised me any more. Like Captain Ahab hunting Moby Dick, Uncle Press waited for the quig.

"Come on. Come on. Little closer," he growled, taunting it.

The quig obliged. It was nearly on us. It charged forward with a bloodlust, ready to snap its jaws shut on Uncle Press.

"The whistle!" Uncle Press shouted back. "Blow it! Now!"

The whistle? What was a whistle going to do? But I wasn't about to argue. While keeping one hand on the steering antlers, I fumbled for the carved whistle around my neck. The beast was almost on Uncle Press. I finally managed to grab hold of the whistle, pulled the leather cord over my head, put it to my lips, and blew.

It didn't sound like anything. The thing must have been

designed like one of those silent dog whistles where the sound was so high pitched that only dogs could hear it. Well, only dogs and quigs, and quigs didn't like it. The beast suddenly opened its hideous mouth and let out another bellow that made the hair on the back of my neck stand out. It was a roar of pain, as if the high-pitched sound from the whistle was piercing its head.

That's when Uncle Press struck. He hurled the spear like an Olympic javelin thrower. The deadly missile flew straight at the quig and stabbed into its open mouth! The beast let out a choked howl as the spear plunged into the back of its throat. It stopped short, kicking up a spray of snow as it fell to its side. Blood spewed from its open mouth like a gruesome fountain.

It was disgusting. But not as disgusting as what happened next. The other quigs caught up with the first one, and rather than come after us, they all stopped and pounced on their fallen brother. It was a frenzy feed, like you see with sharks when there's blood in the water. I can still hear the sound they made as they tore into it, ripping it apart. The sound of flesh being torn away from cracking bones is not one I care to hear again. It was still alive, too. Its pained screams were horrifying. Thankfully, they didn't last long.

I took one last look back and wished I hadn't. At that moment one of the quigs looked up at us, and I saw that its mouth and fangs were smeared with the blood of its living meal. Now I knew what Uncle Press meant by "getting" one of the quigs.

"Look out!" he shouted.

I quickly looked ahead and saw we were seconds away from slamming into a boulder the size of a car. I turned the antlers, hard. The sled turned, but the back fishtailed into a skid that slammed us into the boulder. We kept moving, though the shock was so strong it threw Uncle Press to the floor of the sled. It nearly knocked me off too, but I grabbed the antlers in a death grip. It would take a heck of a lot more than a little bumping around to pry me loose. The only problem was, when I grabbed the antlers, I dropped the quig whistle. If the quigs came after us again, we'd be in deep trouble. We had no spears and no whistle. Why hadn't I left the strap around my neck?

Now we were going fast. The slope turned double-diamond steep. I could see that we were about to reach the tree line. Up to this point we only had to manoeuvre across snow and avoid some boulders. Now we were heading into a forest.

"I've got it!" shouted Uncle Press. He had made his way to the front of the sled and I was only too happy to let him take charge.

"I don't suppose we've got brakes?" I shouted.

"I wish," came the shouted answer. Bad answer. This wasn't a nicely groomed ski slope. Oh, no. We were heading full-tilt boogie into the trees. The only thing that was going to stop us now was something solid. I didn't want to find anything solid. That would hurt.

"Right! Lean right!" shouted Uncle Press. I did and he skirted us around a tree. "Stay with me! Watch where we're going! Left!" he shouted.

It was like riding on the back of his motorcycle. We both had to lean into the turns to help make them. But the motorcycle had brakes and we didn't have to drive it through a minefield of trees. This was terrifying. We were rocketing down on a rickety bobsled through a slalom course of rock-solid pine trees.

We flew past trunks with inches to spare. Left, right, right again. We were going too fast for Uncle Press to tell me which way to lean. I had to look ahead and anticipate what turns he was going to make. Branches slashed at our faces. We were so close to some trees I could hear them as we sailed past. The further down we dropped the more dense the forest became.

"There's a clearing ahead!" he shouted. "When we hit it, I'm going to turn sharp right. Hopefully we won't flip."

Yeah, hopefully. And hopefully we wouldn't launch ourselves into a rolling tumble that would land us into a tree! Not that I had a better idea.

"When I make the turn, lean hard right!" he yelled. "We're almost there."

I looked ahead and saw it. Through the trees there was a field of white. That must be the clearing. But we still had a lot of trees between here and there, and we were still moving fast. Left, left, right. A few more turns and we'd hit the clearing.

"We're gonna make it!" I shouted.

We didn't. Our left runner hit a snow-covered root that kicked us up on our right side, but we kept going. Now we were on one runner and out of control. There were only a few trees between us and the safety of the clearing when we crashed. The sled hit a tree and spun us around. The force of the collision was huge. I mean, it rocked me. But I stayed with the sled. Uncle Press wasn't so lucky. He was ejected.

And I kept going. The sled fell down off the right runner and now ran flat again, but I was lying in the back, miles from the controls. I was nearly at the clearing and for an instant I thought I'd make it. But then the sled hit a rise and suddenly I was airborne! If there was any time to abandon ship it was now, so I bailed. The sled went one way and I went the other. For a moment I was airborne, and then I beefed. Hard. The snow wasn't as deep any more, so instead of a nice cushy snow landing, I hit hard ground. It knocked the wind out of me and slammed my head against the ground.

The world became a spinning mass of white. I couldn't think. I couldn't breathe. But I wasn't moving any more and that was good.

I'm not sure how long I lay there because I was drifting in and out of consciousness. Then I remember hearing something odd. It was far off at first, but it was coming close very fast. I feared that the quigs had finished their lunch and caught up with us for dessert, but this didn't sound like them. This sounded like horses. Galloping horses. More than one.

And then I heard Uncle Press calling to me. "Bobby! Bobby, if you can hear me, don't move. Stay where you are! The Milago will find you. They'll help you."

What did he mean? What were the Milago? I had to see what was happening. I rolled over on my side, which really hurt by the way. I must have smashed a couple of ribs in the fall. I didn't stand up though. I'm not sure I could have, even if I wanted to. My head hurt and I was really dizzy, but I clawed at the snow and crawled towards Uncle Press's voice. There was a little rise of snow, probably the one that launched me into space, and I painfully crawled towards it on my belly. When I got to it, I cautiously peeked over the top.

I was relieved to see Uncle Press standing on the edge of the clearing, not far from me. He was okay. Come to think of it, he looked a lot better than I felt right then.

To the far right of the clearing, closing fast on him, were the horses I heard. And there were riders on the horses, four of them. They looked to me like ancient knights. They wore black armour made of heavy leather. They had black leather helmets with faceplates as well. Even their horses had similar leather protection. They all looked the same, as if the armour were some kind of uniform. I also saw that they had swords. They looked to me like something out of the Knights of the Round Table.

Uncle Press gave them a friendly wave as they circled him.

"Hello!" he called out in a friendly voice. "How are you this fine day?"

We weren't in America. We weren't even on Earth. Why did Uncle Press think these guys spoke English?

"Buto! Buto aga forden," shouted one of the knights brusquely. I was right. They didn't speak English.

"No!" answered Uncle Press. "I am hunting rabbits. For my family."

"Soba board few!" barked another knight. This was weird. They were speaking some bizarro language and Uncle Press was speaking English, yet they both seemed to understand each other. I, on the other hand, understood nothing. What else is new?

The first knight pointed a finger at Uncle Press and started shouting, "Buto! Buto aga forden ca dar!" This looked bad. Whatever "Buto" meant, I didn't think it was a compliment. Uncle Press raised his arms innocently and shrugged, as if he didn't know what they were talking about.

"No!" he said with a smile. "Why would I spy on Kagan? I'm a miner who only cares about feeding his family."

Spy? Miner? Kagan? My head started to throb.

And then things turned sour. The first knight pulled a nasty-looking bullwhip off his saddle and slashed it at Uncle Press! Whap! It wrapped around his arm. Uncle Press let out a yelp of pain and the knight yanked on the whip, pulling him to his knees.

I tried to get up and run to him, but the pain in my side shot through my body and I lost my breath again. My head started to spin. I was seconds from losing consciousness. But I kept my eyes riveted on Uncle Press. Two of the other knights took ropes from their saddles and lassoed him like a steer in a rodeo. Then they kicked their horses and took off across the field, dragging Uncle Press along on his back!

That's the last thing I saw – these laughing, black knights on their horses dragging my uncle across the snow. As they disappeared into the woods, I lost it. My head was spinning out of control. I was going down. The last thing I remember thinking was that what seemed like only a few hours before, I had been standing in my kitchen throwing the tennis ball for Marley to fetch. And I hoped somebody remembered to take her out for her nighttime walk.

Then everything turned white, and I was gone.

END OF JOURNAL #1

◉ SECOND EARTH ◉

Mark Dimond paced nervously as Courtney Chetwynde sat on her backpack in the empty lot at Two Linden Place, reading the parchment pages. He wanted her to read faster. He wanted her to look up and tell him that everything was okay. He wanted her to find a clue somewhere in the pages that proved none of this could be real. But most of all, he wanted to turn around and see that Bobby's house was back where it should be.

Courtney took her time reading the pages and when she finally finished she looked up at Mark with a curious expression.

"Where did you get this?" she asked with no emotion.

Mark dug into his pocket and pulled out the strange ring with the grey stone. After what happened in the boys' bathroom, there was no chance he was going to put the cursed piece of jewellery back on his finger.

"It came from this thing," he said while holding the ring out gingerly. "It was like, alive. There were flashing lights and it got big and opened up this hole and there was a sound and suddenly the pages were just . . . there."

Courtney looked at the ring, looked back at the parchment papers. Mark could tell the wheels were turning in her head as she tried to make sense of everything he had just thrown at her. Finally, she stood up and tossed the parchment pages over her shoulder like yesterday's news.

"Gimme a break," she said with a sneer.

"Hey!" squealed Mark as he frantically ran after the pages. There was a slight wind that scattered them across the empty lot so he had to scramble before they blew away.

"What do you guys think I am?" Courtney barked. "Some kind of idiot?"

"N-no! It's n-not like – " Mark's stutter was back.

"You tell Bobby Pendragon that I'm not dumb enough to go for such a stupid joke."

"B-but – "

"What happens next? Am I supposed to get all worried and tell everybody that Bobby missed the game last night because he got flumed into another dimension and had to battle cannibal beasts and unless he rescues his uncle from some dark knights on horseback he might miss the next game too?"

"W-well, yeah."

"Oh yeah, that's perfect," shouted Courtney. "Then Bobby jumps out and yells, 'Surprise!' and I have to move to another state because no one will ever let me forget that I was dumb enough to fall for the most ridiculous practical joke in the history of practical jokes. I don't think so!"

With that, she snatched up her pack and started to walk away.

"Courtney, stop!" shouted Mark.

Courtney wheeled back to Mark, throwing him a look of total disdain. When you get a look like that from Courtney Chetwynde, it's really hard not to quickly dig a hole and bury yourself in it. It took every bit of strength for Mark to go on. When he spoke, it was sincere and without a trace of a stutter.

"It's hard for me to believe it too," he began. "But this isn't a joke. I don't know if everything in those pages is true, but I've seen some things that I can't explain. I swear I have. And it's enough to make me believe something totally bizarre happened to Bobby."

Courtney didn't move. Was she starting to believe him? Or was she just waiting for him to finish so she could tell him, again, what an idiot she thought he was?

Mark took the chance and continued, "I know it's a lot to swallow. But if this is all just some big old practical joke, then where's Bobby's house?"

Courtney looked past Mark to the empty lot. Mark wondered what she was thinking. Was she remembering how she had come to this spot last night, gone inside a house that was no longer here and kissed Bobby Pendragon?

"I'm scared, Courtney," added Mark. "I want to know what happened, but I don't think I can figure it out by myself."

Courtney stared at Mark for a moment more, as if trying to read his mind. She then walked past him to stand in the centre of the empty lot. She did a slow 360 around to take everything in. But there was nothing to take in. There wasn't a shred of evidence to show that a family of four, with a dog, had lived there not twelve hours before. Courtney was the kind of person who was always on top of things. It didn't matter if it was a game of volleyball, or an argument with her parents, Courtney always knew how to handle difficult situations and turn them to her advantage. But this was different. She couldn't control this situation because she didn't know the rules. Yet.

"All right," she said thoughtfully. "We can't go crazy trying to figure out everything at once. It's just too . . . too much." She was half talking to Mark and half thinking out loud. "I don't know anything about quigs or Travellers or plumes – "

"Flumes," he corrected her.

"Whatever," she snapped back. "That's all fantasy to me. But this house . . . this house being gone is about as real as it gets. If we can find out what happened to the house, maybe that'll point us towards Bobby."

Mark smiled for the first time in forever. He had an ally, and it was somebody he knew could make things happen.

"Where do we start?" he asked.

Courtney started to walk towards the street with her long, bold strides. She was now on a mission. "We've got to find his parents. No way they disappeared too."

"Excellent!" shouted Mark. They were moving forward.

Courtney suddenly stopped, whirled around, and went nose to nose with Mark.

"And I swear, Dimond," she said while jabbing him in the chest with a strong finger. "If you're pulling my chain about all this, I'll slam you so hard you'll have to reach up to tie your shoes."

"So noted," gulped Mark.

Courtney continued on towards the street. Mark followed while stuffing the parchment papers into his pack. As he was about to step on to the pavement, he took one last look back at the empty space where his best friend's house used to be. He could understand where Courtney's disbelief was coming from. The story contained in the parchment papers was tough to believe, even though some of it had proved to be true. At least the part about Courtney, that is. That was the easy part. The rest was just plain incredible. And there was a mystery too. Nowhere in the pages did Bobby say anything about his house disappearing. If everything had played out the way the pages said, when he and his Uncle Press took off on the motorcycle, the house was still here. Something happened to it after they were gone, which meant Bobby didn't know that his house was history. Oddly enough, this gave Mark some hope. Courtney was right. If they could figure out what happened to the house, then maybe they could make some sense out of what happened to Bobby.

There was another thought that nagged at the back of Mark's mind, and it was one he didn't feel comfortable sharing with Courtney. At least not yet. It had to do with the ring, and the fact that Bobby sent the pages to him. The question that Mark kept asking himself was: "Why?" If all that Bobby wrote about were true, and he was on a most incredible adventure, then why would he take the time to write down everything that happened and send it to him? Sure, they were best friends, and Bobby wrote that he hoped the pages would someday prove that he wasn't making everything up. But that didn't seem to be enough to justify doing it. Mark felt that somehow there was an important reason that he should know about what was happening to Bobby.

For now, he was happy just to be on the road to making sense of what had happened to his best friend. The logical place to start would be to find Bobby's parents, and ask them what happened to the house. So with that positive thought in mind, Mark turned his back on the empty lot and ran to catch up with Courtney. They were both sure that their questions would soon be answered, they would find Bobby, and life would return to normal in time for school the next day.

They couldn't have been more wrong.

Their investigation first took them to Mark's house. They figured it would be easier to track down Bobby's parents over the phone than by racing around town on their bikes, or by taking the bus. Mark lived on a cul-de-sac about a half a mile from Bobby's house. Rather, half a mile from where Bobby's house used to be. Of course, when he left for school that morning Mark hadn't anticipated that the fabulous Courtney Chetwynde would be paying a visit to his bedroom that afternoon. The odds of that happening were roughly the same as . . . well . . . his best friend being launched across the universe.

"Wait here," commanded Mark as he ran into his bedroom and closed the door in Courtney's face. Courtney rolled her eyes, but respected his privacy.

Mark took one look at his room and wanted to faint. He wasn't sure which was the most embarrassing: the dirty underwear and socks that were scattered everywhere; the cartoon superhero posters that he hadn't got around to taking down; the *Sports Illustrated* bikini posters that he had just got around to putting up; or the rancid smell that seemed to permeate the whole squalid mess. Mark went into overdrive. He threw open a window, scooped up an armload of the offending Fruit Of The Looms and jammed as many as he could fit behind the pillow of his unmade bed.

Then the door opened and Courtney charged in.

"Look, I've got two older brothers. It's not possible to gross me out – " She took a look at the room and stopped dead in her tracks. Mark stood frozen holding a bunch of dirty grey socks that in an earlier life had actually been white. Courtney sniffed the air and had to try hard not to gag. "I was wrong. I am totally grossed out," she managed to say. "Did something die in here?"

"S-sorry," he said in complete embarrassment. "It n-needs a little air."

"It needs fumigation. Open another window before I pass out," gagged Courtney.

Mark tossed his bunch of socks out of one window and quickly threw open another. Courtney surveyed the room, stopping in front of two posters on the wall. One was a colourful Hentai-animation superhero cartoon, the other was a gorgeous girl lying on a tropical beach in a leopard-print thong.

Courtney said, "Looks like you've got kind of a conflicted puberty versus playschool thing going on."

Mark stood in front of the posters, blocking them. "Can we f-focus on the important problem, please?" he said curtly.

Courtney got the message. Now wasn't the time to be giving Mark grief. She sat down at his desk as he quickly cleared off the F-117 model plane he had been building in order to give her room to work.

"Phone book," she said. All business.

Mark went to his cupboard in search of one. Courtney found a scratch pad of paper and opened a desk drawer to look for a pen. Big mistake.

"Well, I solved one mystery," she announced.

"What?" asked Mark hopefully.

Courtney reached into his drawer and pulled out a revolting-looking block of yellow ooze.

"I know why your room smells like a shoe," she said, holding out a rotten piece of mouldy cheese as if it were diseased. It probably was. Mark instantly grabbed it.

"Hey, I've been looking for that," he exclaimed.

Courtney rolled her eyes and grabbed the phone book Mark had found. The plan was to call Bobby's parents at work. Mr Pendragon was a writer for the local newspaper and Mrs Pendragon was the assistant librarian in town. Courtney found both numbers and called both places. Unfortunately she got the same disturbing information each time. Neither of Bobby's parents had shown up for work that day and neither had called in to say why. That was bad. She then called Glenville School where Bobby's sister, Shannon, was in the third grade. Again, she got the same answer. Shannon hadn't come to school that day. After hearing this last bit of information, Courtney slowly put the phone back down in the cradle and looked to Mark.

"They're *all* missing," she said soberly.

Mark quickly grabbed the phone and dialled a number.

"Who are you calling?" asked Courtney.

"I'm dialling Bobby's number." He did, and what he got was a recorded message from the operator that said: "The number you have reached is not in service." Mark slammed the phone down.

"That's impossible!" he shouted. "I just called him yesterday! A whole family can't just vanish!"

On a hunch, Courtney took the phone book and flipped through it. She got to the "P" section and searched for "Pendragon". She checked, double-checked, triple-checked and then announced: "It's not here. Their name isn't here."

Mark grabbed at the book and looked for himself. Courtney was right; there was no listing for "Pendragon".

"Is their number unlisted?" asked Courtney.

"No," answered Mark quickly. This seemed to upset him more than anything else. "And I'll tell you something else. Bobby and I looked up his number in this very book about a year ago. I was goofing around and next to 'Pendragon' I wrote 'Sucks'. I know, lame joke, but I did it. And now it's n-not there. It's n-not erased, it's n-not cut out, it's just . . . not there, like it was never there!"

This had got out of hand. A whole family was missing. There was only one thing to do. They had to report it to the police. This wasn't the kind of thing they wanted to do over the phone, so the two of them headed right for the Stony Brook Police Station.

Stony Brook was a little town in Connecticut that wasn't exactly a centre for criminal activity. There was an occasional robbery, or fight, but most of the time the Stony Brook Police Department kept itself busy by making sure people obeyed the traffic laws and cleaned up after their dogs.

When Courtney and Mark walked into the police station, they weren't exactly sure what they were going to say. They decided that they would stick to the obvious facts, which were that Bobby and his family were nowhere to be found and that their house was gone. Telling them about the ring and the parchment and the wild story that supposedly came from Bobby would be a bit much to throw at them at first. They spoke to a policeman by the name of Sergeant D'Angelo sitting behind the large front desk. Courtney did the talking. Mark was too nervous. She explained how Bobby hadn't shown up for the game last night and didn't come to school today. She told him how they had gone to the Pendragon's house to find that it wasn't there any more, and none of the other family members were where they should have been. Sergeant D'Angelo listened to everything they had to say and took notes on a form. Courtney had the strange feeling that the policeman didn't believe a word they were saying, but he had to go through the motions because it was his job. After he finished the form, he walked away from the front desk and went to his computer. He clicked away on the keyboard, read the screen, and occasionally glanced back to Mark and Courtney. Was he scowling? Finally, he stood up and came back to the desk to face them.

"Look kids," he said with a frown. "I don't know what you're trying to pull here, but you're wasting my time and taxpayers' money."

Mark and Courtney were stunned.

"What are you talking about?" asked Courtney. "Didn't you listen? A family is missing. Isn't that the kind of thing the Stony Brook Police should be worried about?"

This didn't impress Sergeant D'Angelo. "Pendragon, right?" he said. "Two Linden Place?"

"That's r-right," answered Mark.

"I just went through the town register," said the sergeant with force. "There is no family by that name living in Stony Brook. There is no house on Two Linden Place. There has never been a house on Two Linden Place. So the only possible explanation is that you're either pulling some kind of joke, or you're talking about a family of ghosts and no, the Stony Brook Police are not interested in tracking down a family of ghosts!"

With that, he tore up the form he was filling out and tossed it in the wastebasket. Courtney was livid. She was all set to leap over that desk, grab the smug cop and force him to go to their school where everybody knew Bobby. She might have done it too, except for one thing.

The ring in Mark's pocket started to twitch.

Mark's heart instantly leaped into his throat.

Courtney leaned closer to the desk, looked up at the cop and said angrily: "I don't care what your computer says. I know the Pendragons! Bobby is my – "

Mark grabbed Courtney by the hand and pulled her back with such force it actually made her stop talking.

"We gotta go," was all Mark could say. In his pocket, the ring was starting to shake harder.

"No way! I'm not going until – "

"Courtney! Let's go!" He shot her a look that was so intense she got the message. She didn't know what was going on, but she knew Mark was serious.

Mark backed towards the door, pulling Courtney with him. But Courtney wanted the last word with D'Angelo.

"I'm coming back!" she shouted. "And you better hope those people are okay or it's going to be on your head!"

Mark pulled her out of the door, leaving Sergeant D'Angelo alone. The policeman sniffed, shook his head, and went back to reading the newspaper.

Outside the station, Mark pulled Courtney into an alley to get away from the main street. Though Courtney was bigger and stronger than Mark, he would not be denied.

"What is your problem?" she shouted.

Mark dug into his pocket and pulled out the ring.

"This," he said while holding it out in front of him.

The grey stone had already turned crystalline and rays of

light once again shot from its centre. Courtney watched in wonder as Mark placed the ring on the pavement and took a few steps back. The ring twitched, flipped over, and started to grow.

"Oh . . . my . . . god," Courtney breathed, dumbfounded.

Within the growing circle was a black portal where the road should have been. From this portal came the musical notes that Mark had heard in the boys' room at school. The sparkling lights flashed against the walls of the buildings and even though it was daytime, they shone so brightly that Courtney and Mark had to shield their eyes. The musical notes grew louder, the stone gave off one last blinding flash, and that was it. The lights ended, and the music stopped.

"Is that it?" asked Courtney.

Mark walked cautiously over to the ring. It sat on the road, right where he had left it. It was once again back to normal size and the stone had returned to its original grey colour. But something else was there too. Lying next to the ring was another scroll of parchment paper tied with a leather cord. Mark reached down, picked it up gingerly, and turned to Courtney.

"Mail's in," was all he could say.

DENDURON

Uncle Press is going to die tomorrow.

So much has happened since I wrote to you last, Mark. It's been strange, scary, confusing and sometimes even sort of — dare I say it — fun. But the bottom line is, Uncle Press is going to die tomorrow.

Right now I'm sitting in a small cavern that must be two hundred feet underground. I'm writing this by the light of a candle because there's no electricity. I'm looking around and all I see are rocks. Tons and tons of black rocks that look as if they might collapse on my head at any second. I'd better stop thinking about it because I'm freaking myself out. The cavern isn't going to collapse. I'm safe here, at least for now. The guy who is in trouble is Uncle Press.

I'm telling you this because I need your help. I'm going to ask you to do something for me that is pretty dangerous. Under normal circumstances I'd never ask you to do something like this, but it's the only thing I can think of that might help me save Uncle Press. I'd understand if you didn't want to do it, but before you decide I want to tell you all that's happened since the last time I wrote to you. Once you know everything, then you can decide.

I ended my last letter right after Uncle Press was dragged off by Kagan's knights, and I blacked out. Have you ever blacked out, or fainted? It's not like falling asleep at all. When you fall asleep, you never know the exact moment it happens. You just kind of lie there, waiting, and the next thing you know, bang, it's morning. But when you pass out, you can feel yourself slipping away. It's not a good feeling. Waking up afterwards isn't much better. There's a moment where you're not really sure where you are and what's going on, then suddenly everything rushes into focus and you're snapped back to reality. It's a pretty rude experience.

Of course, in this case, even after I snapped back to reality I still didn't know where I was and what was going on. The first thing I saw was a face. A girl's face. For a second I thought it was Courtney. But once my brain started to click I realised this girl didn't look anything like Courtney. She was totally beautiful. (Whoa, that sounded bad. Not that Courtney isn't totally beautiful, but this girl was, well, different.) I'd say she was my age, maybe a little older. She had dark skin and eyes that were so brown they looked black. Her hair was dark too. It was tied in a long, tight braid that reached halfway down her back. She wore the same kind of weird leather skins that Uncle Press had made me put on, but on her they looked pretty good because she had an amazing body. She had to be an athlete or something. Seriously, this girl was cut like an Olympic sprinter. No fat, all muscle, totally awesome. And she was tall. Maybe a few inches taller than me. If I saw her at home I'd guess she was of African descent. But this wasn't home.

I lay flat on my back as she looked down at me with absolutely no expression. I couldn't tell if she was glad I was alive, or getting ready to finish the job the quigs started and kill me once and for all. We stayed that way for a few seconds, with neither of us moving. Finally I swallowed to make sure my voice would work and croaked out, "Where am I?" No points for originality but hey, I wanted to know.

The girl didn't answer. She stood up and walked to a table that had a couple of wooden bowls. She picked one up and held it out for me, but I didn't take it. Who knows what she was trying to give me? It could have been poison. It could have been blood. It could have been some vile-tasting liquid that they consider a delicacy here, but would make me puke.

"It is water," she said flatly.

Oh.

I took it. I was thirsty. The girl then walked over to the door and stood with her arms folded. I took a drink and looked around to get my bearings. I was inside what looked like some kind of hut. It wasn't big, maybe the size of my living room at home. There was only one room with six walls. Is that a hexagon? The walls were built of stones that were held together by dried mud. There were a few holes which passed for windows and one big opening for a door. The ceiling rose to a centre point and was made of interwoven tree branches. The floor was dirt, but it was so hard it might as well have been concrete. I was lying on a low bench-thingy that was made out of lashed-together logs. The top was woven out of straw or something. It was comfortable enough, but I wouldn't want to spend a whole night there. There was a bunch more of these beds lined up in the hut, which made me think this might be some kind of hospital. It made sense. After what I'd been through, I belonged in a hospital.

It was like I had stepped into a time machine and been sent back a few thousand years to an age when people built their world out of anything they could get their hands on . . . and didn't care much for personal hygiene. Oh, yes, did I mention the place smelled like a locker room for goats? It made me wonder if the mortar holding together the stone walls was really mud, or something disgusting that would make me retch if I knew what it was.

I looked over at this amazing girl. She stood there, staring back. Was she a friend? An enemy? A guard who was standing watch until one of those knight guys came in to drag me off like they did Uncle Press? A million thoughts ran through my head, but one thought stood out above all others.

I had to pee.

The last time I took a leak was before Courtney showed up at my house. When was that? A million years ago? Judging by how my bladder felt, it was at least that long. So rather than lie there and wet my leather pants, I started to get up.

"Hey," I said. "I've got to — "

As soon as I moved, the girl flew into attack mode. She instantly crouched down and whipped out a wooden pole that must have been strapped to her back. It was about five feet long and well-worn from use. She held the weapon steady with both hands, and I saw that each end was stained shiny black from hitting things I didn't even want to imagine. Scarier still were her eyes. They were dead-set focused on her target, which happened to be me.

I froze. No way I was going to stand up or she would have whacked me so fast my head would hit the ground before my feet did. I didn't want to move at all for fear of setting her off. We both stayed that way, waiting for the other one to make the next move. One thing I knew for sure, it wasn't going to be me. And if she took a step towards me, I'd be off that bench and out of the window headfirst.

Then a voice called from outside, "Buzz obsess woos saga!" At least that's what it sounded like; I'm not exactly sure of the spelling. Someone stepped in through the door. It was a woman dressed in the same crusty leather clothes that apparently were fashionable in this neighbourhood. She actually looked like an older version of the girl who was about to brain me. But as powerful as this woman looked, there was something about her that made me feel as if she could possibly be my saviour. I think it was her eyes. They were kind eyes. No anger there at all. When she looked at me, I knew it was going to be okay. She looked familiar, though I can't imagine where I could have met her before. She gave the younger girl a stern look and the girl reluctantly responded by putting her weapon away. Whew. Disaster averted.

The woman then turned to me and said, "Forgive my daughter. She often takes herself too seriously."

New info. This was a mother-daughter team. I guess I shouldn't have been surprised. They looked alike. I wondered what Dad looked like. He must have been a linebacker. I still didn't feel comfortable moving. This woman seemed cool, but after what I'd been through I wasn't taking any chances. She walked up to me, knelt down by the bench and gave me a kind smile.

"My name is Osa," she said softly. "My daughter's name is Loor."

"I . . . I'm Bobby and I'm not from here," was all I could think of saying.

With a smile, Osa said, "Neither are we. And we know exactly who you are, Pendragon. We've been waiting for you."

Whoa! She knew who I was! A million thoughts flashed through my brain, but one in particular jumped out. If they knew who I was, then why was amazon girl over there ready to beat my brains out? I figured I'd better not ask. I didn't want to tick Loor off. She might decide to yank out her stick and start wailing on me anyway.

"How do you know me?" I asked.

"From Press, of course," she answered. "He has been telling us about you for quite some time."

That's right! Now I remember where I'd seen her before. Uncle Press had brought her to our house. We had met before! I remember thinking how beautiful she was, and how odd it was that she didn't speak. The mystery was over: She was a friend of Uncle Press's. But that realisation was quickly replaced with another. Man, I'd almost forgotten. Uncle Press was in trouble. At least I think he was in trouble. Those knight boys who lassoed him and pulled him off didn't exactly look like his pals. A rush of adrenalin shot through my body and I sat up fast.

"He's in trouble!" I shouted. Bad move. Not the shouting part, the sitting up fast part. My body was one big black-and-blue mark from our bobsled crash in the forest. A wave of pain hit me like, like, well, like that stick would have hit me if Loor were taking batting practice on me. I don't know why I didn't realise it before, but I was really hurt. It felt like every one of my ribs was cracked. The pain was so intense it took my breath away. My legs went weak and I had to lie back down or I would have passed out again. Osa quickly grabbed my shoulders and gently lowered me back on the bench.

"It is all right," she said in a soothing voice. "The pain will not last."

How could she know that? Unless maybe she thought I was about to die. Nothing short of death was going to stop this burning pain any time soon. But what happened next was nothing short of amazing. I lay there taking short quick breaths because deep breaths made the pain even worse. Osa then reached out and gently put her hand on my chest. She looked into my eyes and I swear, Mark, it was like I melted. The tension totally flew out of me.

"Relax," she said softly. "Breathe slowly."

I did. Soon my heart stopped pounding and I could take a deep breath. But most amazing of all, the pain went away. I swear. A second before I was hurting so bad I couldn't even cry. Now it was gone. Completely.

Osa took her hand away and glanced over to Loor for a reaction. Loor turned away. She wasn't impressed. But I sure was. It was some kind of miracle.

"How did you do that?" I asked while sitting up and feeling my ribs.

"Do what?" was Osa's innocent reply.

"Are you kidding?" I shouted. "My ribs! I was like, dying. You touched me and poof, I'm off injured reserve."

Osa stood up and said, "Perhaps you were not hurt as badly as you thought."

"Yeah right," I shot back. "I know what pain is, especially when it's mine."

That's when Loor decided to join the party.

"We are wasting time," she said in a peeved voice. "Press is being held by Kagan."

I didn't care much for Loor's style, but she was right.

"Who is this Kagan dude?" I asked.

"There are many things you must learn," said Osa. "Press was to begin teaching you, but until he returns the task will be mine. Come."

She walked over to the hole in the wall that was a door and stood next to her daughter. They both looked at me, which I took as my cue to follow. I stood up, ready to feel the pain in my ribs shoot back. It didn't. Amazing. I then looked at Loor to see if she would spring into attack mode again. She didn't. So far so good.

"Shouldn't we find Uncle Press?" I asked.

"We will," responded Osa. "But first you must learn about Denduron."

Denduron. Right. That's where I was. There wasn't much I liked about Denduron so far, and I couldn't imagine finding out anything else that would make me like it any more. But I didn't have a whole lot of options, so I followed the others towards the door. I took two steps and then stopped, remembering something very, very important.

"Uhhh, where do I go to, uh, you know, I've got to – "

"Relieve yourself in there," Loor said coldly, pointing to a far corner of the room where there was a wooden screen separating a small space from the rest of the hut.

"Great, thanks," I replied and hurried towards it. When I looked behind the screen I learned two things. One was that these people didn't have indoor plumbing. The toilet was nothing more than a hole in the ground surrounded by a circle of stones. Not exactly comfy. The second thing was that the mystery of why this place smelled so bad was solved. I guess these people hadn't figured out that an outhouse should definitely be "out" of the house. Man, it smelled like a sick elephant had been using this thing. But what the heck, it wasn't my house and I had to go bad. So I held my breath against the stink and then took about five minutes to figure out how to undo the leather clothes. I guess these people hadn't yet discovered zips, either. It was during this that I realised the furs I had been wearing were gone. I guess somebody took them while I was unconscious. That was fine by me because if I'd had to get through another layer, I would have wet myself for sure.

After I finished, I hurried across the stone hut to catch up. I didn't know what I was expecting to find outside, so I guess no matter what I saw it would have been a surprise. But when I stepped outside, I had to stop and catch my breath because I had just stepped into another world, and it was like nothing I had ever seen before. The hut I had just come from was in the middle of a village of stone huts. They all looked the same, more or less, with stone walls and roofs made of woven branches and straw. There were no decorations of any kind to distinguish one from the next. Some had smoke curling up from stone chimneys, which meant there were fires burning inside for cooking and for heat. The roads and pathways that snaked between the huts were dirt, well-worn and narrow. And why not? It's not like they had to worry about cars or anything. All the huts were built around a big grassy area kind of like a town square, with a large, round platform about ten feet across at its centre. The base of the platform was made of stones like the huts, and it was topped by a surface made of lashed-together logs. The setup reminded me of those towns that have a gazebo in the centre of a park for concerts and stuff. But the stage was empty now. No shows today.

The village was busy with people doing whatever people do in a village like this. They were hurrying here and there, some carrying baskets of food, others moving a herd of goats. They all wore the same kind of leather clothes I was wearing, so even though I felt out of place, I probably didn't look it. The people who looked out of place were Osa and Loor. As I described them to you, they were both tall, dark-skinned, and athletic looking. There were no other people of colour in this village. Just the opposite. The people of Denduron were the palest people I had ever seen in my life. It was like they never saw a day of sun in their lives. That was strange because even though it happened to be overcast just then, I had seen three suns in the sky from on top of the mountain. Could it be that the suns here didn't give you a tan? Or was it mostly always overcast, like Seattle or something? Whatever the reason, it was pretty obvious that Osa and Loor were not from Denduron, just as they had said.

The village had been cut out of a forest. Looking one way, beyond the huts, was vast farmland. I could see many people working out there, tending to crops. Looking off in the opposite direction I saw the mountain where Uncle Press and I had made our idiot bobsled run to escape the quigs. Any other direction showed nothing but forest. Not that I'm an expert anthropologist or anything, but this first brief look at the village made me think of books and movies I'd seen about Europe back in medieval days. The only thing missing was some huge castle that loomed over the village.

Osa and Loor let me stand there for a few minutes so I could take in the surroundings. I was about to join them, when suddenly I was grabbed from behind and spun around.

"Ogga ta vaan burr sa!"

It was a little guy with long scraggly hair, an eye patch over one eye, and a smile that showed more spaces than teeth. On each of his fingers was a different ring that looked to be braided out of rope. Ten fingers, ten rings. The guy was grubby, but he sure liked jewellery. I had no idea what he wanted until he shoved a furry-looking thing at me. I jumped back, but then realised it was some kind of woolly shirt, like a jumper.

"Ogga ta vaan," he said again with a smile as he shoved the piece of clothing at me. I figured he was harmless and that he wanted me to take the thing. Hey, what the heck? Maybe it was a local "welcome" custom. It was kind of chilly and this leather shirt thing I was wearing wasn't keeping me all that warm. So I smiled back at him and reached for it. But just as I was about to take it, the little guy pulled it back, held out his hand, and rubbed his fingers together. Yes, he was giving me the international sign, no, I guess it was more the intergalactic sign for "you want it, you pay for it". This weird little guy was trying to strike a deal for the jumper.

"Figgis, leave him be!" said Osa as she stepped between us.

"Mab abba kan forbay," said the little guy innocently. At least I think it was innocently. His language made no sense to me.

Osa looked at Figgis and said, "He has only just arrived. Go sell your wares somewhere else."

The guy was a salesman. He seemed to deflate in disappointment and started to walk away, but then he turned back and gave me a sly, toothless smile. From out of his grungy shirt he held up a shiny red apple, trying to tempt me. It looked good.

"Go!" commanded Osa.

Figgis snarled at her and ran away.

"Figgis would sell you his breath if he could," she explained. "They say he wears that patch because he sold his eye to a blind man."

Nice. That's a fairly disgusting image.

"Osa," I asked. "Are you from Earth?"

Osa laughed and looked to Loor to share the joke that I didn't get. Loor didn't laugh back. Big surprise.

"Why do you think that?" she asked.

"You know English," I said.

"You are wrong, Pendragon," she said. "I do not understand a word of English. Come." She left me there and continued walking with Loor.

Huh? I could be mistaken, but I thought sure we were

speaking English. I should know. Aside from a little classroom Spanish, it's the only language I know. This was getting frustrating. Every time I thought I was starting to get a handle on things, something would come along and pull the rug out from under me. I figured I'd better get used to it.

Osa and Loor were already way ahead of me, so I had to run to catch up. I had to jog to keep pace with their long strides while making sure to keep Osa between me and Loor. I liked the mum, but I didn't trust the daughter. I kept catching her throwing me these "you aren't worthy to breathe air that could go to someone more deserving" looks. She was giving off a major cold vibe. I figured it would be best to stay out of her way.

"I don't understand," I said to Osa. "How can you say you don't know English if you're speaking it?"

"I am not speaking English," she answered. "You are speaking English. I am speaking the language from Zadaa, which is our home territory."

"Sounds like English to me," I said.

"Of course it does. That is because you are a Traveller."

This was getting more confusing by the second.

"So, you're saying that Travellers understand all languages?" Logical question, right?

"No," came the illogical reply. "Travellers hear all languages as their own. And when they speak, others will understand them no matter what their native language."

Cool. If this were true, maybe I'd have a shot at getting better than my usual lousy C in Spanish class. Still, something didn't fit.

"Okay, so how come when that Figgis guy spoke it sounded like blah, blah, blah to me?"

Suddenly Loor jumped in front of me. I had to put on the brakes or walk into her. That would have hurt.

"Because maybe you are not a Traveller!" she said with a challenging snarl.

Ahhh! Suddenly it all came clear. Loor didn't think I was who I was. That's why she was acting all strange and aggressive. Of course, I wasn't even sure myself who I was supposed to be, so there wasn't anything I could say to convince her that I was me. Or I was who I was. Or . . . you get the idea.

Again Osa came to my rescue saying, "The reason you did not understand Figgis is that you have not yet learned to hear. You understand us because we are Travellers, but Figgis is not. You must learn to hear, without trying to listen."

Say what? Hear without listening? That sounded like fortune cookie logic.

"How can he be a Traveller? He is just a boy!" Loor said to her mother vehemently. "He is soft and frightened. He will do more harm than good."

Wow. How's that for an ego pounding? Ouch. Unfortunately though, she was right. I *was* soft and frightened. Maybe I wasn't a Traveller after all. Frankly, it wouldn't kill me to find out I wasn't, no matter how much it would have helped my Spanish grades. I was beginning to think that maybe this was all some big mistake and they would send me home.

Osa looked at me with those dark, knowing eyes, but spoke to Loor saying, "No, Pendragon is a Traveller. But he has much to learn." Then she looked at her daughter and said, "And you seem to forget that you are but a child yourself."

Loor stormed off in a huff. I got the feeling she didn't like being told she was wrong. Osa turned to me and said, "You will find that she is not always so angry."

"Hey, no big deal," I shot back. "Just so long as she isn't angry at me!"

Osa smiled and walked on. I followed, and she began to tell me about Denduron.

"The people who live in this village are a tribe called the Milago," she began. "As you can see they live a simple life. They grow all their own food and live peacefully with the other tribes of Denduron."

Milago. Uncle Press had used that word just before those knights showed up. He said they'd find me, so I guess they are the good guys.

"What about those knight-looking guys who attacked Uncle Press?" I asked. "Are they Milago too?"

"No," answered Osa. "That is what I want to show you."

We continued walking out of the village and along a path in the woods for about a quarter of a mile. (I judge all distances by the track at Stony Brook High. It's a quarter of a mile around, and it felt like we walked about the distance of that track.) We broke out of the woods into a clearing and I was yet again hit with an amazing sight. Remember how I said the only thing missing from this medieval village was a big old castle looming over it? Well, as it turns out there was a big old castle, it just wasn't doing any looming.

Here's what I saw: When we emerged from the path through the trees, we came upon a huge, open field of grass. We walked across this rolling field until we came to a cliff on the far side. Down below the cliff was water. Yes, we were at the edge of an ocean as vast and as blue as the Atlantic. The sea was to my right, and I turned to look down the coast — an uneven, craggy shoreline with big, rocky cliffs. I saw that the cliff we were on was actually one side of an inlet. Looking down over the edge, I saw wave after wave of seawater crashing on the rocks below. Far below. We were so high above the water I started getting sweaty palms. I'm not good with heights. I looked up and straight ahead to the cliff on the far side of the inlet to see that the land on top was covered with more lush sea grass that waved in the ocean breeze. Then what I saw *below* that grass took my breath away.

Built right into the face of the cliff was a monster fortress. It looked as if it were literally carved out of the rock that made up the bluff. I could see several levels of stone balconies where knights like the ones who attacked Uncle Press were keeping guard. They marched back and forth with lethal-looking spears over their shoulders. I'm not exactly sure what they were guarding against. Marauding fish, I suppose.

I counted five levels of balconies, so this fortress was big. Osa must have read my mind because she said, "You are only seeing the outside wall of the palace. It is built far into the cliff. It is a village in itself."

From what I saw so far, these people didn't have any heavy-duty construction equipment, so this place was chiselled out of the rock by hand. It must have taken centuries to dig such a huge building out of hard rock using simple tools.

"There have always been two tribes here," she continued. "The Milago work the land, the Bedoowan are the soldiers and rulers. At one time many of the tribes of Denduron were at war. The Bedoowan protected the Milago from marauders, and in return the Milago provided food. Each tribe relied upon the other, while they remained very much apart. It lasted that way for centuries, with both tribes living in relative harmony. But the Bedoowan were powerful and power can lead to arrogance. It was forbidden for a Milago to marry a Bedoowan, or even to become friends. As so often happens in situations like this, the Bedoowan began to look upon the Milago as their slaves."

"But still, they protect the Milago, right?" I asked.

"There have not been invaders here for many years. The need for protection no longer exists," said Osa.

"So the Milago guys still do all the work and the Bedoowan guys do . . . what?"

"That is a good question. The Bedoowan are ruled by a royal family, with the role of monarch passed down to the eldest child. There was a time, not too long ago, that the Bedoowan monarch wanted to break down the barriers between the two tribes and allow them to become one. But he died and left the monarchy to his firstborn. There are some who believe that the father was murdered by those who did not want the Bedoowan to give up their superior position."

"And let me guess: The new monarch likes having slaves and wants to keep the two tribes apart," I said.

"Yes," she said. "The Milago are afraid to even say the name . . . Kagan."

There was that name again. I was beginning to get the picture, and I didn't like it.

"The knights who attacked Uncle Press thought he was spying on Kagan," I said. "But Uncle Press pretended that he was a miner. Are there mines here?"

"Yes," she said with a sad breath. "That is the worst part of the story."

Oh great, it gets worse. Just what I wanted to hear. But before Osa could continue, I heard the sound of a far-off drum. It was a steady, booming sound that came from the direction of the Milago village.

Loor ran up to us and said breathlessly, "It is the Transfer. Hurry." She took off, running back the way we came.

Osa looked at me and said with concern, "Stay close to me. Do not let them see you." With that she took off after Loor.

As I told you, these two were athletes. But I didn't care

how fast they were, I was going to keep up with them. I caught up and kept right on Osa's tail as we beat feet along the path back to the Milago village. Good thing it was only about a half mile away, or I would have bonked for sure.

As we approached the village, I saw that everyone was gathering towards the central area with the stage in the middle. I guessed there was going to be a show after all. People came in from the fields, emptied from their huts, and generally left whatever they were doing to crowd around the platform.

I was all set to join the crowd when Osa grabbed my hand and pulled me in another direction. The three of us climbed on top of one of the stone huts and positioned ourselves on the roof so we could get a good view of the show.

"They must not see us," cautioned Osa. "We are not a part of this."

Whatever. No biggie. We had the best view in the house anyway. So I settled in and wondered what the performance was going to be. Maybe some Milago musicians, or some school play thing.

I looked out on the meeting ground, and saw the Milago villagers gathered in a wide circle around the central platform, which wasn't empty any more. On top of it was some kind of contraption that looked like a seesaw. On one end was a seat, on the other was a big, wide-mouthed basket. Standing on the platform next to the gizmo was one of Kagan's knights, beating on a drum. I hoped the purpose of this guy was to signal for everyone to gather, because if this was the whole show, I wasn't impressed. The deep booming sound echoed across the village. His rhythm was pretty lousy too. Standing next to the platform were six more knights. They stood to attention, each holding a nasty-looking spear in front of them. The Milago villagers gave these guys a wide berth. I would have too. They didn't look friendly.

It started to dawn on me that none of these people looked as if they were getting ready for a good time. There wasn't an excited air of anticipation that comes before a fun event. No one spoke, or laughed or joked. Except for the booming drum, it was deathly quiet. These people all had a look of dread on their faces.

Osa then tapped me on the shoulder and pointed to the far side of the clearing. I looked to see a group of four Milago villagers walking slowly towards the assembly. They were all men who were covered with dirt from head to toe. Not that any of these Milago people were all that clean to begin with, but these guys were pretty gnarly. The black dirt really stood out boldly against their pasty-white skin. The four men were carrying a large basket filled with craggy rocks of all sizes. Some were as large as bowling balls, others were much smaller. But the thing that really stood out about them was that they were blue. And I mean bright blue, like dazzling sapphires. I had never seen anything so stunning.

"The stones are called 'glaze'," whispered Osa. "There are mines throughout this area. The Milago mine for glaze day and night."

"I guess it's valuable," I said, stating the obvious.

"Very," she answered. "Glaze is the foremost reason why Kagan wants to keep control over the Milago. Glaze has made the Bedoowan wealthy. They trade with merchants from all of Denduron. So long as the Milago mine for glaze, Kagan remains a powerful monarch."

So Kagan and the Bedoowan weren't only lazy bullies, they were greedy bullies who forced the Milago to do their dirty work. Nice guys. I wanted to ask more questions, but suddenly the drummer stopped pounding and an ominous silence fell over the village. The four miners brought the basket of glaze to the platform and carefully placed it down. The whole thing was starting to take on the air of a ceremony. The Transfer is what Loor called it.

That's when I heard the sound of a galloping horse. Someone was coming straight down the path where we had walked out to the ocean, and he was coming fast. The weird thing was, nobody turned to look. Nobody but me, that is.

As the horse came charging out of the forest, I saw that riding it was a guy who looked like he knew what he was doing. He was a big guy, with long dark hair, wearing some kind of leather armour similar to what the knights had on, but his armour didn't look like it had seen many battles. It was clean and unscarred, unlike the knights' armour, which looked pretty beaten up. As he galloped up to the circle of villagers, they parted to give him access to the platform. Good thing too, because he didn't slow down. I think if the people hadn't moved, he would have ploughed over them. Already I didn't like this guy.

"Is that Kagan?" I whispered.

Osa and Loor exchanged secret looks, like there was something going on that they didn't want to tell me about. I caught the look and I didn't like it.

"His name is Mallos," answered Osa. "He is Kagan's chief advisor."

Mallos, Kagan, Osa, Loor, Figgis . . . was I the only guy around here who had a first and a last name? This Mallos guy rode his horse right up to the platform and stopped. My guess was the show was about to begin. He sat there on his horse and surveyed the assembled crowd like he owned them. None of the Milago returned his look. They all stood with their heads down, avoiding his gaze. It didn't take a genius to figure out that they were afraid of him. Mallos then turned in his saddle and looked right up to where we were hiding on the roof.

"Stay down!" ordered Loor with a strong whisper.

We all ducked down further, trying to press ourselves into the roof to make ourselves smaller. But I could still see Mallos. As his horse kicked at the dirt, he sat there stock still, looking towards us. It was like he knew we were there. But that was impossible. There was no way he could have seen us.

That's when it happened. As I looked back at him, I was hit with a realisation so shocking that it made me gasp in surprise. I think the thing that tipped it were his eyes. As far away as he was, I knew those cold blue eyes. How could I forget?

Osa and Loor both sensed my surprise and looked at me questioningly.

"Saint Dane," I said softly.

"You know him?" whispered Loor with total shock.

"Yeah, he tried to kill me back on Earth just before I got flumed here," I said. I couldn't believe those words had just come out of my mouth. There was a lot going on in that one little sentence. It would have sounded like fantasy about twenty-four hours ago, but right now it made all too much sense. Osa and Loor exchanged concerned looks again.

Then Loor whispered to me, "He followed you to Second Earth?" She said this as if it were an amazing thing to have happened. I shrugged and nodded a silent "yes". It was the first time she looked at me with something other than total disdain. Up until now, she acted as if I were less important than the dirt on her boots. But now her look was one of, well, curiosity. Maybe the fact that I survived an encounter with Saint Dane proved that I wasn't so soft after all. Of course I wasn't about to tell her that all I did was run for my life. I wasn't an idiot.

Looking down at Saint Dane, or Mallos, or whatever he called himself, I got hit with a strong wave of "I want to go home". But that wasn't going to happen any time soon. I was stuck here looking at a guy who had tried to kill me. Could he see me? Was he going to kick that horse into gear and come charging towards the hut? We'd be trapped up here on the roof. All I could do was hold my breath.

It felt like a lifetime, but Saint Dane finally turned away. I could breathe again. With a wave of his hand he said sharply, "Begin!"

Whoa. He spoke English. Did that mean he knew English, or that he too was a Traveller and that's why I could understand him? That question would have to wait, for the main event finally began. One of the miners who had carried in the basket of glaze stepped forward. He was a big guy and something about the way he carried himself told me he was in charge. Whatever was about to happen, this guy didn't seem too happy about it. Every move he made was stiff and forced, as if the pressure of doing what he had to do was physically painful.

"That is Rellin," whispered Osa. "He is the chief miner."

Guess I nailed that one. Of course, he was another one-name guy.

Rellin stepped up on to the platform and turned to the crowd. He then held out his hand and gestured to someone. The crowd parted and a man stepped forward to join him on the platform. He was a tall skinny guy, which I point out only because of what happened next. The skinny guy walked over to the seesaw thing and sat down on the end with the seat. Since there was no weight on the other side, he tipped his end down to the floor of the platform. Rellin gestured to the other miners and the three guys lugged the basket of glaze up onto the platform, placing it near the opposite end of the seesaw. What were they going to do? Measure the guy's weight in glaze?

"They make a Transfer every day," explained Osa. "Mallos chooses one of the Milago, and that determines how much glaze they must mine for Kagan the next day."

I was right. Measuring the guy's weight in glaze was exactly what they were going to do. The big seesaw was a scale. The miners reached into the basket of glaze and were about to pick up the first few stones to begin the process when Saint Dane barked, "No!"

The miners stopped. Everyone held their breath, waiting for Saint Dane's next move. Saint Dane surveyed the crowd, then pointed.

"Him," he said with no emotion.

There was a general rumbling of discontent within the crowd. Two of the knights pushed roughly past a few of the villagers and grabbed the man Saint Dane had pointed to. He was a much bigger man than the first guy. The rules had just changed, and Rellin didn't like it.

"Mallos ca!" he shouted. He was ticked and started yelling angrily at Saint Dane. I won't write the words as I heard them because, as you know, his language made no sense to me. I'll just tell you the translation that Osa gave me.

"Mallos has chosen a different subject for the Transfer and Rellin is telling him that it is not fair," Osa explained, though I'd pretty much figured that out on my own. "He is pleading with Mallos to use the choice he made yesterday."

I could see why. This new guy was much heavier than the original guy. If they had mined enough of the glaze to balance with the first guy, there was no way they'd have enough to balance with the second guy. Rellin begged Saint Dane for fairness. Saint Dane didn't flinch. He looked at Rellin like he was a bug. Then one of the knights stepped up to Rellin and slapped him on the side of the face with his spear. Rellin spun around and I could see the fiery anger in his eyes. He was already bleeding from the smack on his cheek. I could tell he was a breath away from leaping at the knight's throat. But he didn't. That was smart because the other knights were standing right there, ready with their weapons. He would have been hammered.

"Look at me, Rellin," commanded Saint Dane.

Rellin looked up at his enemy on the horse.

"Being a loyal subject, you should want to do more for Kagan than is expected of you," Saint Dane said with an arrogance that even made *my* blood boil. "Are you telling me that you are doing the least amount of work that is necessary?"

Rellin answered with a seething yet controlled tirade that Osa translated for me.

"He is arguing that mining glaze is difficult and dangerous. Every ounce they pull from the mines comes at a huge cost. He says they mine as much as they possibly can."

Saint Dane snickered and said, "We will see."

He then gestured to the knights. One of them jumped up onto the platform, grabbed the skinny guy who was sitting on the end of the seesaw and pushed him off the platform. Then the other two knights dragged the heavyset guy up on to the platform and jammed him down into the seat. This guy was scared. He looked to Rellin with pleading eyes, but there was nothing Rellin could do.

"Now," said Saint Dane. "You may begin."

The miners looked to Rellin, who gave them a slight nod. They had no choice, so they went to work taking the glaze from their basket and putting the stones on the opposite end of the seesaw.

"What happens if they don't make the weight?" I asked Osa.

"Let us hope you do not have to find out," came her ominous answer.

The miners quickly placed the glaze stones on the scale, starting with the larger ones and working their way down to marble-sized ones. The villagers' eyes were all focused on the scale. My guess is that no one was breathing. I know I wasn't. When the miners were about halfway through, the seesaw began to move. Ever so slowly, the heavy man on the opposite end of the scale began to rise. As soon as he felt himself move, a look of relief came over his face. Maybe there would be enough glaze stones to balance him after all. With renewed hope the miners continued to pile the stones on the scale. Slowly the scale moved and the heavyset man rose into the air.

I could feel the mood of the crowd beginning to turn. They were going to do it. They had mined more than enough glaze that day, just as Saint Dane had demanded. With the last few small stones, the scale rose until it was perfectly level. It took every last one they had, but they made it. If this had been a World Series game, the crowd would have erupted into a cheer. But this was no game. Even though I could sense their joy and relief, no one made a peep. I saw them secretly exchanging little smiles of joy. There were even a few quick, secret hugs. It was a good moment. Even Rellin looked relieved, though he tried not to show it. Throwing victory back in Saint Dane's face would not have been a smart thing to do.

Saint Dane didn't react. I couldn't tell if he was happy they had mined so much extra glaze, or ticked that the Milago had met his unfair challenge. He swung his leg over and jumped down from his horse. He climbed up on to the platform and looked at the level scale with a slight smile. Suddenly the mood of the crowd grew tense again. What was Saint Dane doing? He looked to the heavyset man who was swaying on the end of the scale. The man looked down, afraid to make eye contact. Saint Dane then walked to the end of the scale where the glaze stones were piled into the basket.

"Well done, Rellin," he said. "You have mined quite a large amount of – " He suddenly stopped talking, and leaned in closer to the basket of glaze stones. Throughout the crowd people started holding one another's hands for strength.

Saint Dane gazed into the basket of stones and said, "Rellin! I am surprised at you. There is a stone in here that is not pure glaze!"

Uh-oh. Rellin made a move to run to the basket, but two of the knights held him back. Rellin yelled something at Saint Dane, but it didn't matter what he said. Saint Dane reached into the basket, grabbed the largest glaze stone, and picked it up. Instantly, the scale tipped and the heavyset man slammed down on to the platform, hard. Saint Dane carried the stone over to Rellin and held it up to his face.

"You know that Kagan only accepts stones of pure glaze," he said through smug, clenched teeth.

Not that I'm a geology expert or anything, but that stone looked just like every other stone in the batch. Saint Dane was changing the rules again.

"You know what must happen now," he said with mock sadness.

Apparently the heavyset men knew it too. He scrambled to his feet and jumped down off the platform. He wanted out of there, fast. But the knights grabbed him and held him tight.

"What's happening?" I asked Osa.

Osa didn't answer. She kept staring at the scene with sad

eyes. I figured I was going to find the answer soon anyway and turned back to watch the last act of this drama.

One of the other knights quickly grabbed a heavy chain that was attached to one end of the wooden platform. He pulled on it and half of the platform top lifted up like a trapdoor. Underneath there looked like . . . nothing. The platform was built over a huge hole.

"It is the first mine shaft that was dug here in the Milago village," Osa said without taking her sad eyes off the scene. "It is a pit that reaches down farther than the eye can see. I am afraid there are many lonely bones resting on the bottom."

My mind was racing. I couldn't believe what I was seeing. They were going to toss this guy down the mine shaft!

"Why don't the Milago do something?" I said. "There are hundreds of them! Why don't they stop it?"

The knights dragged the heavyset man closer to the open pit.

"Bagga! Bagga va por da pey!" he cried. It was horrible.

No one in the crowd moved. No one tried to help the poor guy. Even Rellin. It was like they knew it was futile. I noticed that next to me, Loor reached to her back and grabbed hold of her wooden weapon. But Osa put her hand over her daughter's.

"You know it is not the time," she said softly.

Loor didn't release her weapon at first. I could feel her tension. One push, and she would be down there, swinging away. But today was not that day. She kept her eyes on the scene and released her grip on the weapon.

The knights dragged the screaming heavy man up to Saint Dane, who looked at the poor guy without a trace of sympathy and said, "If you weren't such a glutton, you may have lived to see another day." Saint Dane then nodded at the knights, and they dragged the poor, screaming man towards the open pit.

"Ca . . . ca!" he pleaded. "Maga con dada pey! Maga con dada! Moy fol wife, and two children! Please! I must take care of them! They will be alone!"

The scene was so horrifying that it wasn't until later that it hit me . . . I could understand him. It sure sounded like English, but it didn't make sense that he suddenly would have switched languages. Osa said that the Travellers had the ability to understand all languages, and since I was suddenly able to understand this man, maybe I was a Traveller after all.

But I didn't think about that until later. Right now I was witnessing the most gut-wrenching moment I could imagine. The two knights dragged the heavy man closer to the open pit. Suddenly a woman jumped out of the crowd and tried to pull him away from his executioners. She was in tears and begging for mercy. She must have been the man's wife, but her brave effort didn't help. She was quickly grabbed by another knight and thrown to the ground. She lay there in the grass, sobbing.

The knights finally got the man to the edge of the pit and were about to push him in, when the man suddenly stopped wailing. Up until this point he had been crying and begging for his life. But now he stopped fighting and stood up straight. I swear, there was a look on his face that was almost calm. The knights didn't know how to react. They weren't used to someone being calm during the worst moment of their life.

The heavy man turned and faced Saint Dane, and in a distinct, strong voice he said, "My only regret is that I will not live long enough to see Kagan suffer the way we have all suffered."

Saint Dane chuckled and said, "None of you will live that long, for that day will never come." He then gave a quick, almost imperceptible nod and the two knights pushed the doomed man backwards into the pit. His wife screamed, but the guy didn't let out a sound. One second he was there, the next he was just . . . gone. Hopefully his death would be quick and he'd now be in a better place than this horrible village.

The knight holding the chain let it go and the wooden platform fell down with a boom. Saint Dane walked up to Rellin, who looked him right in the eye. Saint Dane then pointed to the man's sobbing wife.

"We will use her for tomorrow's Transfer," he said with pleasure. "She seems quite light. It should make for an easy day. Please thank me for being so considerate."

Rellin looked at Saint Dane and for a second I thought he was going to spit in his face. But he didn't. Instead, he gritted his teeth and said, "Thank you."

"You're welcome," Saint Dane said with a smile. With that he strode to his horse, jumped into the saddle and was just about to ride off when he once again looked back towards us. Actually, it was more like he was looking right at me. I could feel it. He knew I was there. Was all of this a show for me? Saint Dane laughed, kicked his horse and rode off through the stunned crowd back towards the Bedoowan palace.

The knights pushed a few of the miners towards the basket of glaze with their spears. The valuable stones had to be delivered to Kagan and it was clear that they weren't the ones who were going to carry them. That was a job for their slaves. The miners picked up the basket from the seesaw and started the long walk towards the palace. The rest of the villagers slowly started to disperse. Not a word was spoken. A few people went up to console the poor woman who had just lost her husband, but most simply headed back towards their homes. They had been through this horror before, and they probably would go through it again.

But I hadn't. I was frantic. I had just witnessed a man murdered in cold blood. It was even more horrible than the poor homeless guy who Saint Dane hypnotised into running into the subway train back in New York. That was awful, but it didn't seem real. This was very, very real and I didn't understand it. My emotions were all over the place. And yes, I'm not ashamed to admit it, I was crying. They were tears of anger, and fear, and sadness for a man I didn't even know. And for his family. I didn't care that I was crying in front of Loor or anybody else. I was out of control.

"Why didn't they do something?" I shouted at Osa. "They could have ganged up on the knights. They could have pulled the guy away. Why didn't they stop it?"

Osa was as calm as I was upset. She said, "If they had done anything, Kagan would have sent an army to punish them. They had no choice."

I looked to Loor and was surprised to see that she too looked upset. She may not have been ranting the way I was, but her icy calm was cracked. I even thought I could see a tear in her eye. Maybe there was a heart beneath that tough exterior after all.

Still, I didn't buy what Osa was saying. "So what? They should have done something," I cried. "If they don't do something, it'll never stop."

Osa put a hand on my shoulder, and I could feel myself starting to calm down. But what she said next was the last thing I wanted to hear.

"They are going to do something, Pendragon. They are going to take destiny into their own hands and rise up against Kagan. That is why we are here. We are going to help them. *You* are going to help them."

These words hit me like a bolt from the blue. Uncle Press

had told me there were people who needed our help, but I had no idea he was talking about an entire village of people who were at the mercy of a vicious army that didn't think twice about killing people in cold blood. This was crazy. I felt bad for these people, but there was nothing I could do to help them. I didn't care how tough this Loor person was, those knights were killers. And there were only three of us . . . four if you counted Uncle Press. What good could we do against an army? No, this was crazy. I made up my mind right there that the first chance I got, I'd get away from these nutburgers and get back to that flume thing. If it brought me here, then there had to be a way for it to get me back home. Yes, that was the answer. I was going to get myself out of here and kiss this place good-bye – with or without Uncle Press.

◉ SECOND EARTH ◉

"Hey, you kids!"

Mark and Courtney looked up from their reading to see Sergeant D'Angelo calling to them from the front of the building. The two had been sitting there the whole time, reading the pages from Bobby.

"Run!" yelled Mark. He started to get up, but Courtney grabbed him by the seat of the pants and pulled him back down.

"Why?" she asked him calmly. "We're not doing anything wrong."

Mark had to think about that for a second. She was right, all they were doing was sitting in the alley, reading. Nothing illegal about that. So then why was this policeman yelling at them? Courtney looked to the cop, but didn't budge.

"What do you want?" she yelled.

"I want to talk to you," came the reply.

"Then you come to us," Courtney yelled.

Ouch. Mark winced. Courtney was being pretty disrespectful. Okay, so maybe the guy dissed them before, but he was still a cop. Mark was sure he was going to arrest them.

D'Angelo took a few steps towards them with his hands on his hips, and said in a downright civil tone, "I want to talk to you about the Pendragons."

"Why?" asked Courtney, oozing scepticism.

"Because I believe you," answered D'Angelo.

Mark and Courtney shot each other a look. Victory! He must have found Mr and Mrs Pendragon. They both jumped up to go to the cop. Mark made sure that Bobby's half-read journal was tucked securely in his pack, and the two followed D'Angelo back into the station house.

Once inside the sergeant led them past the lobby and continued on through the back offices. Mark thought this was kind of cool. He had never been behind the scenes at a real police station. The experience wasn't exactly what he had expected. On TV, police stations had a lot of activity. There were always cops leading handcuffed perps towards interrogation rooms, and detectives taking statements and SWAT teams hurrying to some mission and generally a ton of cop-type hubbub. But not here in Stony Brook. Here a guy was making a phone call to Domino's for pizza, and another guy looked bored while playing FreeCell on an old computer. Not exactly a beehive of electrifying police activity. Very disappointing.

"I've got to be honest," said D'Angelo as he led them through the station. "I thought you two were pulling a number on me until I spoke with Captain Hirsch."

"What did he say?" Mark asked.

"Ask him yourself," said the sergeant as he opened a door and motioned for Mark and Courtney to enter. The two walked into a conference room with a large metal table surrounded by eight chairs. It was a plain room with a huge mirror that covered most of one wall. Sitting at the head of the table was a pleasant-looking man wearing a suit. When the kids entered he stood up and smiled, but both kids sensed that he was troubled. Good. He should be. There were troubling things going down.

"Hi, guys. I'm Captain Hirsch," the man said. "Thanks for coming back."

Courtney went right up to the mirror and stuck her nose to the glass while cupping her eyes to block out the light.

"This a two-way mirror?" she asked. "Who's back there? You interrogating us?"

Hirsch looked to D'Angelo and the two chuckled. "Yes, it's a two-way mirror," said Hirsch. "But nobody's back there and we're not interrogating you."

Courtney kept trying to look through the mirror. She didn't believe him.

"Why don't you two sit down and relax," said the sergeant.

Mark and Courtney took seats next to each other at the table. D'Angelo stood by the door. Hirsch sat down and looked at the kids. The kids looked back at Hirsch. Hirsch nervously pulled at his eyebrow. It seemed as if he didn't know where to begin, so Courtney being Courtney, decided to kick things off herself.

"So how come you suddenly believe us about the Pendragons?" she asked Hirsch.

"Mr and Mrs Pendragon are good friends of mine," he said. "My son Jimmy plays basketball with Bobby."

"Jimmy Hirsch!" shouted Mark. "I know him. Strong forward."

Captain Hirsch nodded. This was good. Now they had an adult on their side. And he was a cop. A captain, no less. Now things were going to start happening.

"When was the last time you saw Bobby?" he asked them.

Mark knew the answer, but it was up to Courtney to give it.

"Last night at his house," she answered. "About an hour before the game."

"Did he say anything that would make you think he was going away?" came the next question.

Courtney and Mark looked at each other. They knew exactly where Bobby had gone. If the story on the parchment were true, then they knew how Uncle Press had taken him on the back of his motorcycle and left for a place on the far side of the universe called Denduron. But neither of them were sure if the outlandish story was really true, and they didn't want to sound totally insane. Besides, the pages didn't explain what had happened to the Pendragons' house. Mark and Courtney had decided before going to the police that they'd stick to the facts that could be proved. And it was pretty easy to prove that the house was gone. So without discussing it again, they both decided to stick with the original plan.

"I was talking to Bobby at his house," answered Courtney. "His uncle Press came in and I left. That's the last I saw him."

Captain Hirsch looked down at a piece of paper where he had written some notes.

"Right. Uncle Press," he said out loud, though it seemed like he was thinking it more than saying it. Hirsch looked like he wanted to say something, but wasn't sure if it was a good idea or not. He looked to Sergeant D'Angelo for guidance.

"I think you should tell them, Captain," said the sergeant.

"T-Tell us what?" asked Mark.

Obviously these policemen had some disturbing information. Captain Hirsch stood up and paced nervously.

"After you spoke with Sergeant D'Angelo, he told me about your visit," began Hirsch. "Frankly, he didn't believe you because he couldn't find any information on the Pendragons."

"But you know them," interjected Courtney.

"Yes, I know them," said Hirsch. "I've been to their house many times."

"And the house is gone!" added Mark.

Hirsch didn't continue right away. He looked at the two kids, then to Sergeant D'Angelo. Finally he said, "Yeah. The house is gone. This may be a small police department in a small town, but we have access to pretty much any piece of information that's part of the public record," he said. "After you came in here, we did a computer search for the Pendragons . . . and found nothing."

"What do you mean 'nothing'?" asked Courtney. "No police record?"

"No, I mean absolutely nothing," said Hirsch. A hint of frustration was creeping into his voice. "No birth certificates, no driving licences, no social security numbers, no bank accounts, no deeds, no electric bills, no school records, no credit cards, no nothing! The Pendragons didn't just disappear – it's like they never even existed!"

Hirsch paced faster. He was getting upset because what he was saying didn't make sense, yet it was true.

Finally Mark said, "B-But they do exist, don't they? I mean, we know them."

"I know!" snapped Hirsch. "I've had dinner at their house. I've driven Bobby to Boy Scouts. Here's another one for you: We scanned back copies of the newspaper where Mr Pendragon works and couldn't find a single article he had written. But I remember reading them. I've discussed some of those articles with him."

This was getting stranger by the second. Disappearing is one thing. But having someone's whole history vanish seemed downright impossible.

"W-What about Uncle Press?" asked Mark nervously.

"Again, nothing," answered Hirsch. "There is nothing we can find to prove that any of these people ever existed. . . ."

"Except in our memories," added Courtney.

That was a chilling thought. If what the captain said were true, the only thing left of Bobby and his family were the memories they all held . . . and the parchment papers in Mark's bag. Captain Hirsch sat back down at the table and looked to the kids with pleading eyes. This had turned his orderly policeman's mind inside out.

"Kids," he said with a touch of desperation. "Help me out here. If there is anything you can add, anything that might help us figure out what happened to the Pendragons, please tell us."

Mark and Courtney had plenty to add. It was all sitting in Mark's backpack on the table in front of them. All they had to do was slide it over to Captain Hirsch. He would read the pages and take over. That's what adults did. They took over and fixed things. It wasn't Courtney's call — the letters were to Mark. If they were going to tell the police about the pages, it would have to be Mark's decision.

Courtney saw that he was staring at the pack. She knew exactly what was going through his mind. He was debating whether or not to give over the pages. He then looked to her and they made eye contact. Courtney wished that she had some way of helping him make the decision, but she honestly didn't know the right thing to do. So she gave him a slight, helpless shrug that said, "You're on your own."

"Well?" asked Hirsch. "Can you guys think of anything else?"

Mark took a deep breath, turned to Hirsch and said, "No. We're just as confused as you are."

Decision made. Courtney picked up on Mark's lead and added, "Yeah. We're pretty freaked out."

Hirsch took a deep, tired sigh and stood up saying, "Okay, we're going to start an investigation. Tell your parents, tell your friends, tell anybody who'll listen. If they hear anything about the Pendragons, have them call me. Okay?"

Courtney and Mark nodded. Hirsch then gave each of them a business card with his phone number on it. Mark grabbed his pack and they headed out.

Once they were out of the building, they walked silently for a long while. The police station was right near Stony Brook Avenue, which was the main business street in town. Most of the shops and restaurants were there. Since there was no mall in Stony Brook, the "Ave" as they called it was where everybody hung out. But Courtney and Mark weren't interested in any of the temptations that the Ave held that day. They walked by the CD Silo without even a glance into the window; they weren't tempted by the smell of the best french fries in the world coming from Garden Poultry Deli; they had no interest in ice cream from The Scoop; and they didn't even think of going to the library. The front steps of the library was where everyone stopped first on a trip to the Ave because you were sure to find someone you knew there.

But not today. Not for Courtney and Mark. Somehow these familiar haunts didn't seem so familiar any more. Everything looked the same, but the last few hours had opened their eyes to the possibility that the world didn't work exactly the way they thought it did. Between Bobby's adventure and the strange disappearance of the Pendragons, everything they'd ever believed was thrown into question. With thoughts like this running through their heads, somehow grabbing a box of fries at Garden Poultry Deli didn't seem all that appetising. So the two walked past the usual places where their friends hung out and went into a small, quiet pocket park that was sandwiched between two buildings. They sat down on a park bench and stared at the ground.

Finally Mark looked to Courtney and asked softly, "Should I have told them about Bobby's letter?"

"I don't know," was Courtney's reply. "I don't know what to think any more."

Mark tried to put his feelings into words. "I have a feeling," he began, "that there's an important reason Bobby is sending me his story."

"Why? We haven't even read what he wants yet," said Courtney.

"Yeah, I know. But I think it's more than that. I've got a feeling that something big is going on and Bobby's only one part of it. There's some serious stuff going on here. I mean like, cosmic stuff. Am I being weird?"

"Weird?" chuckled Courtney. "How could anything sound weird now?"

"Exactly! The idea of Travellers who understand languages, and territories, and flumes that send you across space and time . . . that stuff changes everything we know about how things work."

This made Courtney fall silent. Mark was right. Up until now she was only thinking about Bobby and the Pendragons. But the implications of what they were reading were totally huge. Too huge to comprehend.

Mark continued, "As we were sitting with the police, I thought about what might happen if I gave them Bobby's story. I came up with two possibilities. One was that they'd announce it to the world, there'd be a huge furore and we'd be smack in the centre of it. Remember, I might still get more pages. I don't think Bobby would want that kind of uproar, especially if he wants me to help him. If he did, he would have started right off by telling me to take his story to the newspapers."

"What's the other possibility?" asked Courtney.

"The exact opposite might happen. The stuff Bobby wrote about might be so disturbing to the world that they'd bury the whole thing and pretend it never happened . . . kind of like the aliens from Roswell, or the Kennedy assassination. People don't like to hear that their nice, orderly world isn't what they thought it was. I wouldn't blame them; I'm not so thrilled about it myself."

"There's a third possibility," added Courtney. "People may think we're responsible. Everyone always wants easy answers and the easiest answer is that we made the whole thing up. It would be easier for people to think it's all a hoax than to believe there are people who jump through wormholes and travel through the universe."

It was hard to believe that only a few hours ago their biggest concern was that Bobby Pendragon had missed a basketball game.

Courtney looked to Mark and asked, "What do you think we should do?"

Before he could answer, someone reached in from behind, grabbed his backpack and yanked it out of his hands! Courtney and Mark looked up in surprise.

"What'cha got, Dimond? More magazines?" It was Andy Mitchell, the kid who'd caught Mark in the boys' room reading Bobby's first journal. He fumbled with the clasps on Mark's pack, trying to open it.

Mark jumped to his feet, shouting, "M-Mitchell. G-give it back!"

Mark lunged at him, but Mitchell danced away.

"Aw, c'mon," laughed Mitchell. "Don't you want to share?"

He held the pack out towards Mark. Mark swiped at it, but Mitchell pulled it away and laughed.

"How bad you want it back?" Mitchell taunted. "Bad enough to swim with the rats for it?" He backed towards a storm drain in the kerb. It was plenty big enough for the pack to fit through.

"Don't!" Mark shouted desperately.

Mitchell dangled the pack over the drain. "What'll you give me for it?"

"What do you want?" asked Mark nervously.

Mitchell thought for a moment, then spotted something on Mark's hand. "I'll trade the pack . . . for that big old ring"

Mark couldn't give up the ring, no way. But he didn't want to lose the pages, either. He hadn't read what Bobby wanted him to do yet.

"Think fast, Dimond," snickered Mitchell as he dangled the pack over the storm drain. "The pack or the ring . . . pack or the ring."

Mark didn't know what to do. Suddenly, a steely-strong hand clamped down on Mitchell's wrist. He looked up and came face to face with Courtney. She had been calmly watching the scene from the bench. She might not have known how to deal with the mysterious disappearance of Bobby and the Pendragons, or the fact that the world had just turned upside down, but the one thing she knew how to handle was a bully like Andy Mitchell. She squeezed his wrist and stuck her nose in his face.

"Drop that in the sewer," she said through clenched teeth, "and you're going in after it . . . headfirst."

They stood that way for a long moment. Finally, after what seemed like a lifetime, Mitchell smiled.

"Jeez. I was just kidding around," he said.

Courtney reached over with her other hand and grabbed the pack. Once she had it, she let Mitchell go. He pulled away quickly, while rubbing his wrist to get the circulation flowing again.

"It was just a goof," he said, trying to save face. "Where'd you get that butt-ugly ring anyway?"

Mark and Courtney stared at the guy until he felt so uncomfortable that the only thing he could do was leave.

"Jeez, lighten up," he said as he turned and jogged away. Courtney tossed the pack to Mark.

"Thanks," said Mark with a bit of embarrassment. Now that the crisis was over, he knew he hadn't handled it well.

"I hate that weenie," she said.

"We've got to go somewhere and finish reading this," Mark said seriously. "I'm nervous about having these out in public. Let's go back to my house."

"Uh-uh," Courtney said uncomfortably. "No offence, but your room is like . . . rank."

Mark looked down, embarrassed.

"Hey, don't sweat it," she said with a smile. "All guys' rooms are rank. It's just the way it is. Let's go to my house."

It was a short walk to Courtney's house, and neither of them said much along the way. Both had their minds on the pages. There were a lot of questions to be answered, but one stood out above all others: What was the dangerous favour that Bobby wanted Mark to do for him? Courtney was dying to know. So was Mark, but he wasn't all that sure he liked the idea of having to do something dangerous, no matter how important it was. Up until now, Mark's idea of doing something dangerous was to ring somebody's doorbell on Mischief Night and run away. Given what Bobby was going through, the stakes here were a wee bit higher than that.

They arrived at Courtney's house, which was very much like Mark's. They both lived in a quiet, suburban neighbourhood. But rather than go to Courtney's room, Courtney took Mark down to the basement where her father had a workshop. Mark had a fleeting moment of disappointment that he wouldn't get to see the inner sanctum of the glorious Courtney Chetwynde, but there were larger problems to deal with.

The two sat down on an old, dusty couch and Mark opened

his pack. He laid the precious pages out on a coffee table in front of them. The two hesitated a moment. As much as they were dying with curiosity about what happened next to Bobby, they were also a little bit frightened about what the pages contained and what new and disturbing wonders they would reveal. They each took a breath.

Then Courtney looked to Mark and said, "You ready?"

"Yeah."

They looked down at the pages and picked up where they had left off.

I was going to get myself out of here and kiss this place good-bye – with or without Uncle Press.

DENDURON

My plan was to climb back to the top of the mountain, get past those cannibal quig beasts, find the gate that leads to the flume, and get the hell out of here. Simple, right? Yeah, sure. I'm not even sure I could *find* that stupid cave again, let alone survive the climb through the snow and the quigs. Still, my mind was made up. It was better than staying here.

But it wasn't going to happen today. The suns were going down and it was getting dark. Yeah, that's right. Suns. Plural. Remember I told you there were three suns? Well, they all set at the same time, but in opposite parts of the sky. North, south and east . . . or whatever they use for directions around here. I figured I had to spend the night and sneak away once it got light. Besides, I was hungry. I hadn't eaten anything since I had a banana and some raspberry Pop-Tarts before the basketball game I never made it to.

Loor brought me to a hut that was like the one I woke up in, only smaller. In one corner was a pile of furry animal skins.

Loor pointed to them and gave me a simple command. "Sit."

I did. It was smelly, but comfortable. There was a small stone fireplace where Loor quickly and expertly made a fire that gave us light and took the chill off. Osa arrived soon after with a cloth sack that I quickly found out was full of food. Yes! We all sat around the fire and shared loaves of crunchy bread; some weird fruit that looked like an orange but you ate like an apple; and some soft nutlike things that tasted like liquorice. Maybe it was because I was so hungry, but this odd meal was delicious. I would have preferred some fries from Garden Poultry Deli on the Ave, but this did just fine. While we ate, Osa gave me some strange instructions.

"Is there someone back on Second Earth whom you trust above all others?" she asked.

It didn't take me long to come up with the answer. I told her it was you, Mark. Sure my family's cool, and of course I trust them, but a friend is someone who gives you trust because they want to, not because they have to.

Osa handed me a stack of blank parchment paper that was all yellowed and crunchy. She also gave me a crude pen that looked like it was carved from a tree branch, along with a small bowl of black ink.

"It is important that you write down all that is happening to you," explained Osa. "Every chance you get, write your thoughts, your feelings, and describe the things that you see. Think of it as a journal."

"Why?" was my obvious question.

"Because you will send them to your friend for safekeeping," she answered. "I will not lie to you, Pendragon. This is a dangerous journey. If anything should happen to you, this journal will be the only record of what you have done."

Yikes, that sounded grim. It was like she was asking me to write out my last will and testament. Part of me wanted to refuse because doing what she asked made me feel like I was going along with the programme. And I definitely was not. On the other hand, what she said made sense. If anything happened to me, nobody would know the real story. I didn't like that. If I was going to go down, I wanted everybody to know why.

"How are we going to get it to Mark?" I asked.

"Write first," she said. "When you are ready, I will show you."

That was interesting. If she could get these pages to you, that meant she knew how to use the flume in the other direction. Maybe this would be my chance to find a way home. So with that in mind, I took the pen and went to work. I set myself up next to the fire, using a piece of wood on my lap as a desk. It took a while to get the knack of using the pen because it wasn't exactly a Bic Rollerball. I had to dip the pointy end in the ink and scratch the words out on the paper. It was a pain, but after a while I got to where I could write a whole sentence without having to re-dip.

Across from me, Loor was doing the same thing. It felt like we were doing homework together. As she scratched out her thoughts on the same kind of parchment paper, I couldn't help but wonder what she was writing about me. I knew she thought I was a toady boy, but maybe having survived a brush with Saint Dane gave me a little more credibility. On the other hand, who cares? Tomorrow, I was out of here.

That's how I spent the rest of the night. I wrote for a while and when my eyes got heavy I sacked out on the animal skins. I'd sleep for a little bit, then wake up and write some more. Loor did the same thing. Osa was in and out of the hut. She'd come in to put some wood on the fire, then leave again. I wondered if she was getting any sleep at all. I got as far as writing about Uncle Press being captured by Kagan's knights, and then I crashed for good. The next thing I knew, Osa was gently shaking me to wake up.

"It is morning, Pendragon," she said softly.

I was sleeping deeply and had to force my eyes open. There was light in the hut, but I could tell it was early because there were no shadows and the birds were singing. I looked around to see that the fire had gone out and Loor was gone.

"Give me your journal," she commanded.

I sat up and gathered the pages I had written. She took them, rolled them up, and tied them with a leather cord. She then walked to the centre of the hut, sat down cross-legged and placed something on the floor. It was a big old clunky silver ring with a grey stone mounted in the centre. From where I was sitting I could see there was some kind of inscription engraved around the stone, but I had no idea what it meant. Osa looked to make sure I was watching, then reached down to the ring, touched her finger to the stone and said, "Second Earth."

What I saw next sent a bolt of adrenalin through me so quickly that I was shocked out of any last remnant of sleep. The grey stone in the ring started to glow. It acted like the flume had when it brought me here. The flume was made of grey rock, just like the ring. When I said, "Denduron," the grey rock of the flume had started to glow, just like the ring. Bright light shot from the facets of the stone and washed the walls of the hut, just like the lights in the flume. And like the flume, I started to hear the strange musical notes.

Then the ring started to twitch . . . and grow! The band actually stretched out and got bigger until it was about the size of a Frisbee. But inside the circle, where the floor should have been, was a hole. It was like this ring opened up a miniflume to . . . where? Osa took the rolled-up parchment pages and dropped them into the ring. The pages disappeared as if they had been dropped into a hole in the floor. Then the ring snapped back to normal size and everything ended. No lights, no sound, no hole. Just the ring. Osa picked it up and put it into a leather pouch that hung from around her neck.

"Your friend Mark has your journal," she said and got up to leave. That was it. No explanation, no nothing.

I jumped to my feet to head her off. "Whoa! You can't pull that hocus-pocus number and not tell me what happened!" I demanded.

"I told you what happened," she said calmly. "I sent your journal to Mark Dimond."

She tried to continue out of the hut, but I got in front of her.

"But how? Is that like a portable flume?" Obviously my mind was in overdrive.

"There are many things to know about being a Traveller, Pendragon," she said patiently. "Once you are more comfortable, this ring will be yours and you will be able to send your journals to Mark Dimond yourself. Until then, be satisfied to know that the power contained in the ring is similar to the power found in the flumes."

I wasn't going to give up that easily. "But how can it find Mark?"

Osa took a deep breath like she was getting tired of my questions. Too bad. She knew how this stuff worked. I didn't.

"I gave another ring to Mark Dimond," she said.

"What? You saw Mark? No wait, you went to Earth? When? How? Did you tell him I'm here? Did you see my parents? Did you – "

Osa put a hand to my mouth to shut me up. She was gentle, but firm.

"I went to Second Earth and gave Mark Dimond the ring," she explained. "That is all. I saw no one else. No more questions."

She took her hand away and started out of the hut.

"Just one more," I called after her.

Osa turned back to me, waiting to hear.

"Does this ring thing work both ways? I mean, if we can send things to Mark, can he send things to us?"

Osa smiled. It was the kind of smile I'd see from my mother when I thought I was being clever about trying to keep something from her. That smile said "I know exactly what you're thinking, smart guy. You can't fool me."

"The rings can transport small objects, but they only work for Travellers," was her answer. "Mark Dimond would not be able to send you anything. Now if you wish to bathe yourself, there is a river that runs a few hundred feet south of the village."

She left and my mind went into hyperdrive. This ring business had just opened up a whole new world of possibilities. Maybe I didn't need to get all the way to the top of the mountain after all. Maybe the ring could grow big enough for me to jump into it. And if I'm a Traveller, then the ring will work for me! Yes! For the first time in a long while, I felt as if I had a shot at taking control of my life again. When the time was right, I'd get the ring from Osa and punch my ticket out of here. That was the new plan and it felt good. Heck, anything would be better than climbing that mountain and getting past the quigs. So with a new sense of hope, I left the hut to start the day.

The suns were just creeping up over the horizon and I saw it was going to be a clear day. The first thing I wanted to do was find that river and wash. Not that I'm a clean freak or anything, but the animal skins I was wearing weren't exactly cottony fresh. I'm not sure which smelled worse: me or my clothes. A quick splash of water would be a good thing, so I picked my way through the Milago village in search of the stream.

The village was just waking up. Smoke drifted up from chimneys in all the huts. A few women scurried along carrying firewood. In the distance I saw farmers already working out in the fields. I also saw a pretty depressing sight. A group of men trudged into the village on a path that led from the woods. I figured they were miners since they were covered with dirt, like the miners who had brought glaze to the Transfer ceremony the day before. Could these guys have been working all night? I then saw another group of miners pass them going in the other direction. I realised this was some sort of change in shift. The day crew was taking over from the night crew.

As bleak as this scene was, it wasn't the depressing part. The thing that really hit me was that nobody talked. Nobody. They didn't even make eye contact with one another. They just went about their business, doing their work or their chores or whatever it is they probably do every single day, but with absolutely no human interaction. I guess it didn't surprise me. After what I had seen the day before, I realised that these people were prisoners. Kagan's army had stolen everything they could from them, including their souls. There was no joy in this place. No hope. They probably didn't want to make friends with anyone because they never knew who might be Kagan's next victim. So they kept to themselves, living in their own personal, tortured world.

It feels kind of weird to admit it, but as I stood there watching these people going about their dreary lives, I started to cry. Normally I'm not a crying kind of guy. Yeah, a couple of times I got weepy during a movie when somebody's dog died or something. But this was different. This was real. I stood in the centre of this village and it was like I could feel a huge weight of sadness press down on me. The thing is, no matter how bad somebody's life gets, it can always get better. Things pass and life goes on. Like for me. As bad as things were for me right then, I had a shot at getting home. There was hope. But for these people, there was no escape. Their future was just as bleak as their present. This was their life, and the hopelessness of it brought tears to my eyes. For that one brief instant, I could feel their pain.

But you know something? It didn't last long. If anything, it made me want to get out of there even more. Yeah, I felt bad for them, but it wasn't my problem. This struggle had been going on for a long time and nothing I could do was going to change it. I had to worry about myself right now, so I wiped away the tears, put my head down, and started to look for the path that led to the river. I had only walked a few feet when somebody grabbed my shoulder and whirled me around.

"Crabble nectar?" It was Figgis, the strange little guy who tried to sell me the sweater before. He was holding up a leather pouch that looked full of liquid. "Very delicious. Very rare. Only four quills."

I assumed quills were like Denduron money.

"Thanks, no," I said and walked on. But Figgis jumped in front of me. This time he held out a thing that looked like a crude bumbag that was woven from dried straw.

"Twenty quills!" he announced while tying it around his waist to demonstrate.

Even if I wanted to buy it, I didn't have any quills, so this was a waste of time. I tried to push past him but he blocked my way again.

"Ten quills, since you are new!" he offered.

He could tell that I wasn't interested, but he was desperate to make a sale so he quickly yanked off one of the ten rings that he wore on his fingers.

"Two quills!" he shouted.

"I'm sorry, dude, I don't have any quills," I said.

This guy seemed to be all about cash, so I figured that telling him I didn't have any would make him back off. It didn't. He grabbed my arm and pulled me towards him so fast that I didn't have a chance to stop him. He leaned in close and whispered something in my ear like he was giving me some information of dire importance.

"Tak is the way. It is the only way. Rellin knows this." I could feel his hot breath on my ear. He smelled like a goat. I wanted to retch. "Remember tak. Remember me." He then let go and scampered off and disappeared into the activity of the village.

That was weird. What was tak? He spoke about it with such passion that it made me think it must be something pretty special. It was like he was tempting me with it. Maybe it was illegal and he had to be careful about selling it.

It also felt kind of weird that I understood what he was saying. The day before his words made no sense. Now I heard them as if he were speaking English. But according to Osa, he wasn't speaking English. He was speaking the Denduron language, but I heard it as English. Still, there were some words that didn't translate into English like "quill" and "tak" and "crabble". I guess those are things that are special to Denduron, and therefore don't have an English translation. Whatever it was he was selling, I didn't want any. So I continued on towards the river.

A path snaked out of the village in the opposite direction from the ocean. Since I hadn't been there yet, I figured it must be the way to the river. After walking about a hundred yards through the forest, I began to hear the sound of rushing water. A few yards further along, I hit it. The path ended at the bank of a river that looked to be about twenty yards across. I knelt down on the bank and dipped my hand in. Yeow! It was like sticking my hands into a bucket of ice. I'm sure it was fed by snowmelt from the mountain, and rivers fed by snowmelt are frigid. But I was feeling all crusty from sleeping in animal skins and breathing smoke from the fire, so cold or not, I had to get wet. I took a deep breath and splashed water on my face. Wow. It was like a thousand needles stinging me, but it actually felt pretty good. I took a big gulp and swished out my mouth. I wished I had my toothbrush, but this would have to do.

That's when I heard the *crack* of a broken branch. Somebody was nearby! I heard someone humming a sweet tune. It was coming from just a few yards away. I think under normal circumstances I would have turned and left, but something compelled me to investigate. Remember how I described the people of this village? There was no joy here. There was only the sad business of survival. So hearing a pleasant tune being hummed felt out of left field. It made me want to see who it was. As strange as this seems, knowing that one of the Milago would actually want to hum a song made me feel that there might be some hope left in these people after all.

I remember going on a hike with my dad once through a forest that had been recently destroyed by fire. We were surrounded by nothing but the burned and black remains of what had once been a wonderful, green thicket. It was sad, until I saw that growing out from beneath a fallen log was a single, green fern leaf. As horrible as the devastation was, this one leaf was proof that one day the forest would return to normal. Hearing this tune coming through the woods made me think of that single fern leaf and I wanted to see who was singing it. So I quietly sneaked through the brush towards the sound. When I pushed back the final branch between me and the singer, I saw that it wasn't one of the Milago after all.

It was Loor. She was kneeling on a rock with her back to me, washing out some clothes. I was disappointed at first, but this posed another interesting puzzle. As I told you, Loor is a hard case. I don't know much about the territory where she and Osa came from, but it didn't take a genius to figure out that these two were warriors. Osa had a calm way about her. She reminded me of one of those Black Belt guys who are so confident in their fighting abilities that they are actually gentle people. Of course, if you messed with them, they'd kick your ass. Loor, on the other hand, didn't have that calm thing going on. She seemed ready for a good ass kicking all the time. Maybe it was because she was young and hadn't got that wisdom comes with age thing. It didn't matter though, all I knew was that she scared the hell out of me. But seeing her on this rock, with her hair undone and humming a sweet tune seemed completely against character. Maybe there was a soft side to her that she kept hidden somewhere below all that macho stuff. Way below. She was facing away from me and had no idea I was there. Her long hair fell across her shoulders. It was deep black, and beautiful.

Now before you go thinking I was some kind of perv watching her from the bushes, you gotta realise that I was stuck. If I made a sound, she'd turn and see me watching her and probably pick up her stick and start playing Bobby the piñata boy. I wouldn't blame her. My only hope was that she'd finish washing up and walk back along the river towards the path without ever knowing I was there. So I stood rock still, doing my best to look like a tree.

After what felt like a lifetime, Loor stood up and started to braid her hair . . . and that's when I heard it. Another crack of a branch told me that somebody was walking up behind me. My heart pounded. I thought for sure that Loor would hear this, turn around, and catch me standing there like a doofus. I also thought that whoever was behind me was about to see me doing a peeping Tom number on Loor. But I was afraid to leave because Loor would surely catch me. None of these scenarios was very good.

What I didn't realise was that there was another scenario that was worse than all the above.

"I've been looking for you, Pendragon," came a deep voice that made Loor turn quickly in surprise. I turned too, and what I saw made my knees buckle. Standing behind me was one of Kagan's knights! He towered over me holding a spear in one hand and a rope in the other.

The guy had me. In that instant I felt sure that Saint Dane, or Mallos, or whatever he called himself had sent this guy to bring me in, the same way they got Uncle Press. And I knew one other thing – I wasn't going to go easily. So before the knight could make a move, I made my own move. I turned and ran for the river.

Loor didn't have time to react and I made another snap decision. She was coming with me. As she scrambled to her feet, I launched myself into a full-on, horizontal, flying tackle. I hit her and we both went sailing off the rock into the river.

Cold? You don't know cold until you jump into a river swollen from melted snow. The only reason it wasn't frozen solid was because it was moving so fast. But the truth was, I didn't care. If this river could get us away from that knight, it didn't matter to me if it froze the blood in my veins. I could always get warm later.

We hit the river in a tumble of arms and legs. The water was flowing so fast that it swept us downriver and away from the knight. There was no way he could catch up with us. I looked back and saw him standing on the shore looking stupid. He wasn't even going to try and catch up.

My attention went from getting away from the knight to surviving the river. You know when you first jump into the ocean you get a jolt of cold, but then your body quickly adapts and you get used to it? Well, not here. The river water was too cold for that. It felt like my body was actually freezing stiff. But I had to fight it, because we were in rapid whitewater, and that meant there were rocks. I heard once that if you're caught in rapids like this, the best thing to do is point your feet downriver and go with it until you hit a calm patch where you can swim to the side. That was the plan, but Loor was making it tricky. She held on to me so tightly that I was having trouble moving my arms to manoeuvre. I had to get away from her or we'd both drown.

"Feet first!" I yelled. "Float on your back!" I tried to push away, but Loor wouldn't back off. Then she said the three words I never expected to hear from this macho warrior girl. They were the three worst words you could hear in this situation, but she said them just the same.

"I cannot swim."

Oh, great. No wonder she was clinging to me. This was bad. The river was swirling us around and every time we hit a drop, both our heads went under. Each time we came up sputtering, and I didn't know how long our luck would hold out. I had to take control somehow or we were going to drown, or bash our heads into a rock and then drown. I thought maybe we could make a train with both of us on our backs. She'd go feet first and I'd cradle her from underneath while using my arms to guide us like a rudder.

"Feet downriver!" I shouted. "Face up, lie on me!"

She didn't move. She couldn't. It wasn't that she didn't want to, it was because she was paralysed with fear. I can't imagine what it's like not being able to swim, but it must be terrifying. And with her strength, there was no way I could pry myself loose. We hit another drop and both went under again. No sooner did we come up for air than we both slammed into a rock. I barely felt it because Loor took most of the hit with her back. It must have been crushing, because it made her loosen her grip on me. Instantly I grabbed her and flipped her on to her back.

"Grab my legs," I commanded. She did. I was on my back too, with Loor between my legs. My arms were now free to steer and keep us afloat. My train idea was working. Now if we could only ride this out until the rapids stopped.

"Use your legs to keep us off the rocks," I said. Loor was scared, but she had enough of a grip to start thinking again. While I paddled frantically, she kicked us away from a few sharp rocks. We then hit another drop and went under again. I could feel Loor starting to squirm away from me, but I held her tight with my legs. In a few seconds, we were above water again.

Then I was hit with a terrifying thought. What if these rapids led to a waterfall? There was no way we could survive that. I had to force the idea out of my head, because there was nothing I could do about it now.

We hit a few more drops, bounced off another rock or two, and then mercifully, the river grew calm. We made it through the rapids and there was no waterfall waiting. But we weren't safe yet because Loor still couldn't swim. My junior lifeguard training took over at this point and I began to tow her to the side. She was so tired and beaten that she didn't have enough strength left to fight me, so it wasn't all that tough to bring her along. Soon we were dragging ourselves out of the freezing water and crawling up on to the bank. We lay down on the gravel, totally exhausted, totally beaten up, but alive. Luckily the three suns were now higher in the sky and they were starting to give off some warmth.

After I caught my breath, I sat up on my elbows and looked at Loor. She lay flat on her back, still breathing hard. I have to admit, now that we were safe, I was feeling pretty good about myself. Not only did I save the big, bad warrior girl from one of Kagan's knights, I also saved her life a dozen times over on the river. I couldn't wait for her to admit that I wasn't the lame wad she thought I was. But of course I wasn't going to fish for a compliment. That wouldn't have been cool. It had to come from her. So I waited. And waited. And waited some more. But she didn't say a word. What was up with that? I was getting kind of ticked off. Not that I was expecting a full-on "Oh, Pendragon, you're my hero!" but a simple "Thank you" would have been nice. Still there was nothing. Finally I decided to break the ice.

"You okay?" I asked.

"No thanks to you," came the reply.

"What?" I shouted and sat up straight. "I saved you from drowning!"

"But if we had not been in the river, I would not have needed help," she said as if she were totally ticked off at me.

"But if we weren't in the river, we would have been attacked by Kagan's knight!" I shot back.

Loor finally sat up and looked at me. She didn't say anything at first, but her hard look made me feel like some sort of lower life-form.

"You were hiding in the bushes, watching me," she said. Gulp. *Busted.* "If you had come out to speak with me," she went on, "I would have told you that I was waiting for that knight."

Huh? I couldn't get my mind around this. "You were waiting for one of Kagan's knights?" I asked, dumbfounded. "Why?"

"Because he is the Traveller from Denduron and he was coming to give me information about Press. You nearly killed us both to escape from the most important friend we have here on this territory. What am I supposed to say to you, Pendragon? Thank you?"

DENDURON

I had reached a new low. The more I learned about this world the less I understood. Worse, when I finally tried to take action, I screwed up. Loor and I nearly died on that river and it was my fault. I wanted to go home. I wanted to be in my bed. I wanted to feel Marley's nose nudging me and smell her fishy dog breath. Instead I was lying cold and bruised on the bank of a river on the other side of the universe.

"Loor! Are you all right?" I heard the voice first, then saw the guy crashing through the woods. It was the knight who scared me into our whitewater adventure. As he appeared from out of the brush I could see that he wasn't much older than me. He was tall, and the leather armour made him look even bigger. He wasn't very agile though. The other knights I saw were trained, dangerous dudes, kind of like ancient marines. This guy had the gear and the look, but he acted more like a big puppy who was all floppy arms and legs. He wasn't exactly the fighting machine one would expect. He stumbled out of the woods, tripped over a root, nearly did a face plant in the dirt, then looked at us with wide, frightened eyes.

"We are fine," assured Loor.

"This was my fault," whined the knight. "I am so sorry."

Loor felt herself for broken bones. "Pendragon," she said, "this is Alder."

"Alder what?" I asked, though I think I already knew the answer.

"Just Alder," answered the knight.

Yup, another one-name guy. When does a society progress far enough to start using two names? Whatever.

"I cannot tell you how happy we are that you have arrived, Pendragon," said Alder enthusiastically. "Now we can begin."

Uh-oh. What did he mean by "begin"? I was getting sick of being one step behind everybody else.

"Begin what?" I asked.

Alder looked at Loor like he was surprised I didn't know what he was talking about. He should get used to it. I looked at Loor too. Obviously they hadn't told me everything. Loor gazed across the river. I could tell she was debating whether or not to answer. Her jaw was clenching. She looked back to me, stared me down for a second, and then let it out.

"You have seen how the Bedoowan tribe treats the Milago," she began. "There is more you have not seen. There is torture and starvation and disease. The Bedoowan treat the Milago worse than dogs. They do not have enough food or medicine. Half of the babies born do not live past the first few months. The glaze mines claim lives every day. If this horrible treatment is not stopped, the Milago will die out. The time has come to stop it."

I didn't like where this was going. Sure, these people had it pretty rough, and things needed to change. But what I didn't get was what my part was supposed to be in all this. I wasn't so sure I wanted to know, either.

Alder said, "The Milago are a gentle people. They are not

warriors. It has taken years of hardship to convince them to take action. If it were not for Press, they may never have been ready."

"What's Uncle Press got to do with it?" I asked.

"Press has been their inspiration," said Alder with reverence. "He has given the Milago the strength to fight back."

Things were happening fast. This was the first time I heard the word "fight", and I didn't like it. "What about you?" I asked Alder. "You're not a Milago. You're a Bedoowan. How come you're so concerned about them?"

Loor stared me right in the eye. "He is a Traveller, Pendragon," she said forcefully. "Just like I am, and Press, and my mother. That is what Travellers do. They provide help where it is needed. Are you ready for that responsibility?"

"Well . . . no," I said honestly.

"I did not think so," spat Loor with disgust.

Alder gazed at me with a look of confusion, and maybe a little desperation. "But Press has spoken of you for some time now," he insisted. "He told us that if anything happened to him, you would take his place."

"Whoa, whoa!" I said, backing away from him. "Uncle Press didn't fill me in on any of this! All he said was that there were some people in trouble who needed our help. I figured all we had to do was give somebody a ride somewhere, or maybe help move some furniture. I didn't know he was talking about leading some freakin' revolution!"

Loor spun to me with fire in her eyes. "That is the word exactly," she said with passion. "Revolution. The Milago have been preparing to revolt against the Bedoowan. Press has made them believe they can succeed. Without him, they will not have the strength to fight and they will all die. I do not know why, but he has made the Milago believe that you are able to lead them as he would. That is why you are here, Pendragon. That is what you must do."

I felt like I was in the river again, being swept along with no control. My heart was beating about as fast as it had in the river too. I'm not a revolutionary, Mark. The closest I ever came to being in a fight was the time you and I wrestled over who was gonna bat first in Wiffle ball. That doesn't exactly qualify me to lead a revolution.

"Look," I said, trying hard not to let my voice crack. "I feel bad for these people and all, but I'm not up to this. You say I'm a Traveller? Fine, whatever. But up until two days ago I had no idea any of this even existed! How can I suddenly lead a revolution?"

"But you must," said Alder seriously. "The Milago believe that you will take over for Press."

"Then go get Uncle Press!" I shouted. Alder then looked down at the ground. Obviously something was wrong.

"Where is Press now?" she demanded.

Alder kept his eyes on the ground and said, "He is being held in the Bedoowan fortress. Kagan has sentenced him to death. He will be executed tomorrow at the equinox."

Oh, man! Uncle Press was going to die! Could things get any worse? Loor spun away from Alder and picked up a rock. With a roar of anger, she reached back and threw it across the river. It was like she was channelling her anger and frustration into this one, mighty throw. She stormed towards me like an enraged bull. I took a few steps back, expecting her to take a swing at me. But she didn't. Instead she stuck her nose in my face and seethed. "I do not understand why Press believes in you. You are a coward, you are weak, and you do not care for anyone but yourself. But you are a Traveller, and you will begin to act like one. It is time you saw the truth," and with that she gave me a shove backwards. I had to pinwheel my arms to keep from falling over.

Alder said meekly, "You know I cannot go with you."

"I know," answered Loor. "Meet us after dark."

She gave me another shove and walked off. I didn't know what else to do, so I followed her. We didn't say much on our walk back to the Milago village and it gave me a chance to digest all that I had just learned. I guess that Travellers are some kind of cosmic do-gooders. That's very noble and all, but I didn't volunteer for this particular honour. Just the opposite. I didn't want any part of it. Everyone kept telling me that I was a Traveller and that I had a responsibility, but who the heck made me a Traveller? I don't remember signing up. Maybe it's like the army where you get drafted. But if I were the guy in charge of drafting Travellers, I sure as heck wouldn't pick somebody like me! They should have picked a Navy SEAL or a SWAT guy or better still, one of those WWF muscle heads. They shouldn't have picked a fourteen-year-old gym rat. Even if I wanted to help the Milago, the second I opened my mouth they'd know I was a fraud. No, the best thing I could do was stick to Plan A, and that was to get to the flume and get out of here, ASAP.

There was one thing that bothered me though. Uncle Press was in trouble. No, worse. He was going to die the next day. But what could I do? If I went after him, Kagan's knights would cut me to ribbons and we'd both be dead. I was in a horrible situation.

When Loor and I got back to the village we were greeted by Osa, who looked at us with concern. My guess is she could tell that things were going badly. Before Osa could ask what had happened, Loor said, "He must see the mines."

Osa didn't ask why, she just looked at her daughter and gave a weary sigh.

"Come with me, Pendragon," said Osa and started to walk off.

"What if I don't want to see the mines?" I asked, because I didn't.

Osa looked at me with these intense, piercing eyes. She wasn't scolding me. She wasn't trying to intimidate me either. This is hard to describe, but the look she gave me was one of absolute certainty. The look said: "You will come and see the mines because that is what you must do." Maybe it was a kind of hypnotisedm, but the instant she looked at me, I knew I had no choice. So I followed her. Weird, huh?

Loor didn't come with us and Osa didn't invite her. It was just the two of us and that was fine by me. As we walked through the Milago village, I started to notice something I hadn't seen before. Whenever we passed one of the Milago, they would give me a quick glance. We'd make eye contact and then they'd quickly look to the ground and continue on their way. It was weird. It was like they were watching me, but afraid to acknowledge that I was there. Up until now, I thought they didn't even know I existed. Nobody talked to anyone else and they certainly didn't talk to me. That is, of course, except for Figgis. He was the only Milago who spoke to me. Everybody else kept to themselves. Yet here they were, checking me out. I was betting these villagers were looking at me and thinking: "How can this be the guy who's going to lead our revolution? He's a wussy kid!" And they were right.

I followed Osa back to the path that led to the ocean. We walked a few yards into the woods and I saw that there was another, smaller path that led off to the right. This is the path we took and it led us to a clearing where there was a large foundation made of stone. It looked much like the stage in the centre of the village where the Transfer ceremony took place, but there was no wooden platform covering it. There was a huge wooden frame built over the foundation with a large pulley attached. A thick rope looped over the pulley and dropped down into the hole. Two burly men were hauling on the rope, bringing up something from below. The setup kind of reminded me of one of those old-fashioned wishing wells where the bucket would be dropped down on a rope and then hoisted out with water. But in this case, they weren't hoisting up water, they were hoisting up glaze. The two men brought the large basket to the surface, grabbed it, and emptied it on to the ground. A few craggy glaze stones tumbled out. The two looked at each other and sighed. Apparently this wasn't a very good haul. I remembered that they had to bring out enough glaze to balance with the wife of the man who was killed the day before. They added the new stones to a larger pile next to the foundation. There wasn't much there. If they didn't bring up more glaze, the poor woman would join her husband at the bottom of the pit. A cold chill went up my spine.

Osa walked to the foundation, sat down, and swung her legs over the side. "Be careful," she commanded. And with that, she lowered herself over the side. Where was she going? Did she jump? I walked up to the edge, looked down, and saw that there was a ladder attached to the side. Osa was climbing down into what looked like a bottomless pit. In no time she disappeared into the gloom. I looked over at the two miners. Sure enough, they were looking at me. But the second we made eye contact, they looked away and went back to work. I'm not sure what was creepier: knowing that everyone was checking me out, or climbing down a rickety ladder into the dark unknown.

"Now, Pendragon!" echoed Osa's voice from below.

I reached over the side and tugged on the ladder to make sure it was sturdy. I swung my legs over, grabbed the ladder and started down. It was a good thing the pit was dark, because if I could have seen all the way to the bottom, I'm not sure I would have had the guts to climb down. The ladder itself was crudely made from saplings lashed together, but it was strong. After climbing down several feet, I found that the foot of the ladder rested on a stone ledge. But this wasn't the bottom. The top of another ladder was leaning on the ledge next to this one and since Osa wasn't there, I figured I had to climb down it as well. In all, there were fifteen ladders. Unbelievable. This pit was deep. Every third ledge had a tunnel that led horizontally away from the pit. I figured that these were abandoned sections of the mine. Probably when the glaze ran out on each level, they would tunnel deeper and deeper and deeper.

Finally I reached the bottom, where Osa stood waiting for me. There was light down here too. Small candles were everywhere. It wasn't exactly bright, but once my eyes adjusted, I could see just fine. There was one tunnel leading away from the pit, and that's where Osa went. I followed her obediently. The tunnel was carved out of the rock; I could stand up straight, but Osa had to crouch down a bit. It was a good thing I wasn't claustrophobic.

"The main shaft was built generations ago," she explained. "But when they discovered a rich vein of glaze at this level, the miners decided to do things differently."

"What did they do?" I asked.

Osa didn't have to answer. After a few more yards the tunnel emptied out into a humongous cavern. The ceiling must have been thirty feet high. It was spectacular. Leading off from the cavern were many other tunnels. It was like we were at the centre of a wagon wheel and the tunnels, like spokes, led out from the centre in all directions. Down each tunnel was a set of miniature tracks. I had seen pictures of gold mines before and I figured these tracks were for the ore cars.

"Once it was discovered that this was the level to find glaze, the tunneling started to spread out in all directions," she explained. "There are miles and miles of tunnels. It is so complex that miners have lost their way and wandered for days."

I had to admit it was pretty impressive, especially because these guys did all of the work by hand. We stood to the side of the cavern and watched the activity. There were no powerful mining machines here, just the strong backs of Milago miners. Some were pushing carts full of dirt, others emptied the carts in the centre of the cavern and sifted it for bits of glaze. I also heard the distant sound of pickaxes ringing against stone as the miners laboured to stretch the tunnels in their search for more glaze.

"The miners work day and night," Osa explained. "It is the only way they can possibly meet Kagan's unreasonable demands."

She reached down and picked up one of the miners' tools. It was a metal pickaxe with a wooden handle. "These tools are forbidden on the surface because they are made of metal," she told me. "The penalty for using a metal tool on the surface is death."

Now that she mentioned it, I didn't remember seeing anything made of metal on the surface. All the tools that were used above were made from wood or from stone. It was like the Bedoowan were trying to keep the Milago back in the stone age, except for when it came to getting their precious glaze, of course.

I began to notice that there was an odd smell to the mine.

It wasn't a horrible smell, in fact it was kind of sweet. "What is that smell?" I asked.

Osa didn't answer, but motioned for me to follow her. We walked across the large cavern, stepping across the railroad tracks. As we approached the far side I began to make out something that made me shudder. I hadn't seen it before because the light was so dim, but now that we were here I could see things plainly. To be honest, I wished I still couldn't see, but I did. Lying on the floor of the cavern were dozens of miners. They looked horrible. Some moaned in pain, others just sat there with blank looks.

"They look sick," I said.

"They are," came the sad reply. "The smell is a gas that is released when the glaze is separated from the rock. It is a poison that slowly destroys your ability to breathe."

"We're breathing toxic fumes?" I asked, ready to bolt back to the ladders.

"Do not worry," she said calmly. "You must breathe it for years for it to be of concern."

I looked at the sick miners and said, "These guys have been breathing it for years?"

Osa nodded sadly. "It is a painful death."

"Why don't they go up into the fresh air?" I asked with horror.

"They have no strength left," was the grim answer. "These poor souls are in the final stages of the disease. They will die here."

I took a few steps back from the sick miners. I'm ashamed to admit it, but I was afraid I might catch this nasty disease from them. Suddenly the huge cavern didn't seem so huge any more. The walls felt like they were closing in and I wanted out of there in a bad way. Maybe I had a touch of claustrophobia after all.

"Why did you have to show me this?" I demanded to know.

"Because it is very important that you understand how desperate the situation is for the Milago," Osa said.

I wanted to scream. Osa was setting me up. She was showing me how bad these guys had it so I'd feel sorry for them and agree to lead their revolution. But why? Osa didn't seem like a fool. She could see that I wasn't the kind of guy who could lead a revolution. Her daughter figured it out pretty quick. Why wasn't Osa with the programme? I didn't want to argue here in front of these poor miners, so I headed for the tunnel that led to the ladders.

"Where are you going?" she asked.

"Home!" was my simple reply. I hurried across the cavern, hopping over the railroad tracks and dodging the ore cars. Then just as I was about to enter the tunnel that led to the ladders, somebody ran in front of me. It was Figgis. But this time he didn't stop to try and sell me something. He was in a hurry and I'm not even sure he knew it was me who he cut off. I watched the little guy run down the tunnel towards the ladders and was about to follow him when I felt the ground start to shudder. Uh-oh, was this an earthquake? Or a cave-in? A second later there was a huge explosion! I spun to look where the sound came from and saw black smoke billowing out from one of the tunnels. Many of the miners were looking at the smoking tunnel with confusion.

Now, I'm no expert, but these guys have been doing this mining thing for a long time. Surely they had been through an explosion like this before. You'd think that they would have instantly kicked into emergency gear and either evacuated the mine or started damage control. There could be miners trapped in there who needed to be rescued. But that's not what happened. The miners just looked to each other with a mixture of fear and confusion. It was like they didn't know what to do.

Finally Osa called out, "Are there men in there?"

One of the miners shouted out, "Rellin!" This seemed to wake the others up. They quickly came to their senses and headed for the smoking tunnel to rescue their leader. One of the miners tied a rope around his waist, boldly fought the smoke and entered the tunnel. Another few miners held the other end of the rope. I guess the idea was that if he passed out, they could drag him back to safety. Brave guy.

The ground didn't shake again. Whatever damage the explosion caused was only in that one tunnel. I didn't feel I was in any danger and I wanted to stay and see if Rellin was okay.

"How often do they have explosions like that?" I asked. Osa kept staring at the smoking tunnel and then said something I never expected to hear.

"What is an explosion?" she asked.

Huh? How could she not know what an explosion was? This woman knew everything there was to know. It couldn't have been a language thing because Travellers understood all languages.

"You know," I continued. "Explosion. That big bang. From dynamite or something."

Osa looked at me with confusion and said, "I have never seen anything like that happen here, nor in my home territory. You are saying that loud noise caused the damage? Like lightning?"

This was deeply weird. Though maybe it explained why the miners reacted the way they did. They probably had no idea what happened either. But then what had caused the explosion? Maybe they tapped into some underground gas pocket.

Before we could talk more about it, the miners holding

the rope began to frantically pull on their end. Other miners gathered to watch with concern. They stared into the smoky tunnel, waiting to see what came out. After a few seconds, the miner on the other end emerged from the smoke and in his arms . . . was Rellin. The chief miner was full of black soot and there were traces of blood around his forehead, but he was okay. Dazed, but okay. He was helped to sit down and brought a leather skin full of water to drink. Rellin took a long drink, swished it in his mouth, and spit.

Then an odd thing happened. Rellin looked up at the other miners, gazing at each one in turn, and began to laugh. The other miners didn't know what to make of this. Maybe the total relief from his brush with death came out in nervous laughter. Or maybe he was crazy. I sure didn't know and from the confused looks of the miners, they didn't know either. I have to admit, it was kind of creepy. I think Osa felt the same way because she put a hand on my shoulder and said, "We should go to the surface."

She didn't have to tell me twice. I was down that tunnel and up those ladders in an instant. As I climbed, I looked up at the circle of blue sky that grew larger and larger the higher I got. It was the light at the end of a long, dark tunnel and I couldn't get to it fast enough. When I poked my head out into the fresh air, I took a deep breath and promised myself that I would never go down in that hell hole again. One of the miners who hoisted up the basket of glaze was leaning against the wooden frame of the pulley system, watching me. The other miner was gone.

Then I sensed something strange. For some reason the miner didn't turn away after we made eye contact. He kept on staring at me.

Osa poked up out of the hole, jumped on to the

ground, and said, "Tell me more about this thing you call . . . explosion."

Before I could answer, Osa's attention was caught by something behind me. I turned to look and saw the miner who had been staring at me. Osa walked past me with her eyes fixed on the man. He just stood there, still looking at me with a dumb expression on his face. Osa walked right up to him, stared at him for a moment more, then quickly spun back towards me and shouted, "Pendragon, run!"

"Huh?"

Before Osa could say another word, the miner toppled over and fell at her feet. My eyes fixed on the wooden arrow that was sticking out of his back. Yeah, the guy was dead. That wasn't a dumb look on his face, it was a dead look. I had never seen a dead man before. I couldn't move. Osa ran to me, grabbed my hand, and started to drag me towards the forest. We had only gone a few steps when four of Kagan's knights leaped out in front of us. Now I knew what had happened to the miner.

"We've come for the boy," they announced. There was no mistaking it this time. Unlike the knight named Alder who I mistook for an enemy back by the river, these guys were not on our side. They carried clublike weapons and, judging from the poor dead miner with the arrow sticking out of his back, they wouldn't hesitate to use them for whatever mayhem they thought fit.

Osa didn't move, but I could feel her tense up. She let go of my hand and slowly turned sideways. I knew what this meant. It was exactly what we were taught to do in karate class. Turning sideways made you a smaller target. Yeah, there was going to be a fight and I was in the middle of it. Osa wasn't about to make the first move. She was too smart for that. If something was going to happen, it would be the knights who would start it.

One raised his club and took a step towards us. I froze. Osa bent her knees, ready to defend herself. The knight let out a bellow, began to charge and . . . whack! He suddenly went down in a heap as if he had been shot. The other knights were just as surprised as I was, but I saw the reason for it before they did.

Standing behind them was Loor, holding her wooden stave. Nice shot. She had another weapon and quickly tossed it to her mother. Osa caught it and crouched into attack mode. Now they were both armed and the odds became a little better. But still, these knights were professional fighters. I wasn't so sure how these warrior women would do against them.

Things happened fast. Before the knights could recover from the surprise of seeing their buddy do a face plant, Loor grabbed the club from the hand of the knight she had just whacked and in one quick movement she threw it to me. I caught it just as Loor took up position next to her mother. It was now three-on-three. Well, two-and-a-half-on-three because the chances of me using that club to attack one of those hairy knights were about the same as me sprouting wings and flying out of there.

"Fight, Pendragon," commanded Loor.

At that instant the three knights charged. Osa and Loor ran to meet them. I stood frozen. My prediction about Osa and Loor being warriors turned out to be a hundred per cent correct. These two were awesome. They swung their long wooden weapons like martial arts experts. If I weren't so terrified, I probably would have enjoyed the show. They spun and twirled the long staves so quickly they were nothing more than blurs. The knights, on the other hand, fought awkwardly. They would swing their clubs, but the women would either bat the attack away with a deft flip of their stave, or dodge out of the way and answer the attack with a ringing smack to the body. If this were a toe-to-toe slugfest, I would have bet on the knights. But Osa and Loor never stood still long enough for the knights to get a solid shot at them. It was like watching lumbering bears being attacked by vicious bees. And the bees were winning.

The only problem was that the knights were armoured. It was going to take more than a few defensive blows to stop these guys. But I was certain that Osa and Loor were going to take care of them, so I began to relax.

Bad move. That's when one of the knights charged me. He had his club held high and screamed like he was getting up the energy to take my head off. I didn't know what to do. I should have held out the club to protect myself. I should have ducked and then attacked. I should have thrown the club at him to slow him up. But I didn't do any of those things. All I did was take a few steps back in fear, trip, and fall down on my butt. I was dead meat. The knight was almost on me. I could see the rage in his eyes. This was going to hurt. A few more steps and he would be within swinging range.

But then, Osa threw her wooden stave at the guy like a javelin and it hit him right in the knees. His legs buckled and he fell to the ground, hard. Loor was on him instantly. She gave him a ringing whack with her stave, and the knight crumpled unconscious. Two down.

Loor looked at me and I could see the fire of battle in her eyes. "Fight, you coward!" she commanded.

Osa ran up and shouted, "No! Take him. Hide him!"

Loor wanted to stay and fight beside her mother, but Osa was in charge.

"He must not be taken. Go!" commanded Osa.

There wasn't time for argument because the other two knights were back on the attack. Reluctantly Loor grabbed me by the arm and yanked me to my feet. I have to tell you, Mark, I never felt so helpless and embarrassed in my life. I was a complete wuss. You always wonder how you might react in times of danger. You always have these visions that you'll rise to the occasion and be the hero and save the day. Well, let me tell you, that fantasy couldn't be any further from the truth than what was happening to me. I'm ashamed to admit it, but I was like a frightened baby.

As Loor pulled me away towards the forest, I glanced back to see what was happening with Osa. What I saw was incredible. She was even better on her own. This amazing warrior woman fought both knights at the same time. She spun, thrust, parried, and rarely missed the mark. It seemed almost easy.

Loor and I dived out of the clearing into the woods, then turned back and hid to watch the end game. I knew that Loor wanted to be in there fighting beside her mother. It was killing her to be here, baby-sitting me.

"Your mother is amazing," I whispered to Loor.

Loor didn't comment, but I knew she felt the same way. A few moments later, it was all over. The knights had been losing steam and after a few more ringing blows, they both collapsed to the ground either unconscious, or too exhausted to move. Osa remained in a crouch and swept the air with a quick 360 to be sure the fight was over. She then straightened up, spun her wooden stave like a ninja master and slipped it into its leather strap that ran across her back. The battle had been won.

"You don't deserve this, Pendragon," Loor spat at me.

She was right. I didn't. These two women had risked their lives for me, and there was no way I was capable of living up to what they expected of me in return. But as bad as I felt, the real horror of the situation hadn't yet hit. Loor and I stood up and started back into the clearing. Osa saw us. She took a few steps towards us, then suddenly stopped. Loor saw this and quickly put her hand out to stop me as well. Something was wrong. Were the knights waking up? I looked at Osa, who slowly returned to her fighting stance. She was back on full alert and started to reach for her wooden stave. I looked around the clearing, but there was no movement at all. The knights lay unconscious where they had fallen. Why was everyone so tense?

A second later I had my answer – a moment that will forever haunt me. I first heard a rustling and thought someone was coming through the bushes. I soon learned it wasn't in the bushes. It was coming from above. It was in the trees. I looked up and saw to my horror that perched up in the trees were four more knights. These knights weren't armed with clubs. They had bows and arrows. I had forgotten that the miner was killed with an arrow. These knights had been there the whole time, watching the spectacle. And now they were about to make their move.

Osa stood in the middle of the clearing, unprotected. Loor was about to run to her, but Osa yelled out, "Hide him!"

This made Loor stop. It must have taken every bit of will-power to go against her instincts and obey her mother, but that's what she did. She backed off, grabbed my hand, and that's when it started.

The knights let loose with their arrows, all aimed at Osa. The brave woman wore no armour. There was nothing to protect her from this deadly rain. All four arrows hit their mark, and Osa crumpled to her knees. Loor let out a pained little sound and started to run for her, but I grabbed her. By now the knights had already reloaded, and if Loor had run to her mother, she would have met the same deadly fate. We stood there for a second, looking into the doomed woman's kind eyes. Maybe I was imagining things, but as I write this now I could swear that she gave us a little smile.

The knights unleashed another volley of arrows. But these weren't meant for Osa. These were aimed at us. Luckily we were protected by trees and they all ended up missing us or slamming into branches. But it was enough to throw Loor back into action. She grabbed my hand and off we ran into the forest, leaving behind her mortally wounded mother.

Loor knew the forest well. Keeping up with her was like running with a deer. She leaped over fallen trees, skirted boulders, and blasted through a thicket. We weren't going in a straight line either, and I realised that this journey was all about shaking the knights who might be trailing us. I was getting tired and had a nasty stitch in my side, but there was no way I would complain. Not after what these women had done for me.

We eventually made our way around to the far side of the village, where Loor brought me to a stone hut. I wasn't exactly thrilled with her choice of hiding places. All it would take for a knight to find us was a quick search of the village. But I soon found out that Loor had other things in mind. She quickly dived on the pile of animal skins that was lying along one wall and pulled them aside. Beneath was the same hard-packed earth that all the hut floors were made of. Loor took her wooden stave and started to scratch at the dirt. With a couple of quick digs, she unearthed a wooden ring. She threw her stave down, grabbed the ring and pulled. It was a trapdoor!

"This leads to the mines," she said in explanation.

Oh, great. I had promised myself never to return to those mines. It was a promise that lasted a good twenty minutes.

"The Bedoowan are afraid of the gas," she said. "They never go into the mines." She threw open the trapdoor to reveal another crude ladder leading down. Here we go again. She motioned for me to go first. Loor followed quickly and closed the door behind her. We climbed down only one ladder. It led to a small tunnel that we had to crouch down in to walk along. I could tell that it was angled downward.

"There are many of these small tunnels," she said. "They bring air to the miners."

So basically we were walking along a ventilation shaft. Made sense. But since this was only for ventilation, there were no candles to show us the way. It was like walking through ink. I kept one hand out in front of me in case a wall decided to jump out. But I wasn't going fast enough for Loor. She barged ahead and took the lead. She moved much faster and it was easier to follow her than it was to follow nothing. I just hoped she knew where she was going.

This ventilation tunnel led to a much wider tunnel with some ore car tracks. I figured this must have been one of the early mining tunnels that was dug before the Milago built the big cavern. We followed this tunnel for several minutes until it emptied out into a familiar space. It was the mine shaft where Osa and I first climbed down. When was that? It felt like a century ago, but it was more like an hour. We came out on one of the rock ledges and I saw that we were only three levels down from the surface. The familiar circle of blue light beckoned from above.

Loor stood out on the ledge and looked up. She was obviously debating with herself about something and it didn't take long for me to find out what it was.

"Go to the bottom," she commanded. "I will meet you there. Go!" She stared at me until I started to climb down the ladder. As soon as I started down, she began to climb up. Just as I figured. She wanted to go to her mother. I hung on the ladder and watched her climb to the surface. I know I should have kept going down as I was told, but I couldn't. Osa had put her life on the line for me, and I had to find out how she was. So after wrestling with the decision for a few seconds, I started to climb up.

When I reached the last ladder before the surface, I heard something coming from outside. I didn't know what it was at first, and when I finally recognised it, it made my heart sink. It was Loor. She was humming the same sweet song that I'd heard her humming by the river. I pulled myself up out of the mine shaft and what I saw then, broke my heart.

Loor was sitting on the ground next to the stone foundation. She cradled Osa's head in her lap and stroked her hair while slowly rocking back and forth as if lulling a baby to sleep. I didn't know if Osa was dead or alive. Lying next to her were the four arrows that had hit her. Loor had pulled them out. I stayed where I was because I didn't want to intrude. Loor was a proud girl and I was sure she wouldn't want me to see her cry.

I glanced around the clearing and saw that the knights were gone. The archers in the trees probably dragged off their unconscious buddies. The body of the Milago miner was still there though. He lay on his back, staring up sightlessly into the sky.

That's when I saw Osa's hand move. She reached out weakly and took her daughter's hand. She was alive! I quickly ran over to see if I could be of any help. Loor didn't acknowledge that I was there, except that she stopped humming her song. But Osa knew I was there, and she looked up at me with tired eyes.

"Do not be sad," she said with a weak voice. "Either of you. This is the way it was meant to be."

I had trouble holding back my tears. Osa wasn't going to make it.

"I . . . I'm sorry, Osa," was all I could get out.

Osa then took her hand away from Loor and reached for the leather pouch around her neck. It was the pouch where she had put the silver ring.

"Take this, Pendragon," she said. "Use it as you see fit."

I took the pouch and pulled out the ring. Osa nodded encouragement, so I put it on the ring finger of my right hand. Oddly enough, it fitted perfectly.

"You are both at the beginning of a long journey," said Osa as she grew weaker. "Pendragon, I know you do not feel you are up to the challenge. You are wrong."

I nodded, but I didn't believe her.

Osa continued, "Halla is in your hands. Remember that. Let it be your guide. Together you two will – " Osa caught her breath, gave a little shudder and closed her eyes. They would never open again.

This was a painful moment. Of course, I felt sympathy for Loor. The girl had just lost her mother. But I, too, felt loss. In the short time I had known Osa, I had developed an affection for her. She was the one voice of reason in the storm of confusion that I had been swept into. I trusted her. I felt safe with her. And my trust had proved to be well placed, for she had sacrificed her own life to save mine. That's a debt that can never be repaid.

I wanted to comfort Loor but I didn't know how. I struggled to find the right words, but Loor spoke first. "Go down into the mine, Pendragon," she said. "I will meet you there."

I wasn't about to argue. I just nodded and stepped away. Before I climbed down on to the ladder I said, "I'm sorry, Loor."

Loor didn't acknowledge me. She just sat there, still cradling her mother. As I climbed down the ladder, I could hear that she was once again humming the tune from the river. I had to fight back my tears.

I climbed all the way down to the bottom of the mine and found my way into the giant cavern. Once there I saw that it was business as usual. There was no day here and no night. All signs of the excitement from the explosion were gone. I didn't know what to do, so I found a quiet corner and sat down to try and think. To say that my mind was a jumble of conflicting thoughts was an understatement. I spun the silver ring on my finger. This strange piece of jewellery might actually be my ticket home. But as much as I wanted to use it, the idea of bolting out of here made me feel incredibly guilty. For some reason that I still didn't understand, everyone was expecting me to help these poor people fight for their freedom. Stranger still, an amazing person had just given her life so that I could live to carry out that mission.

I wished I knew what to do. If there was something these people needed that I could deliver on, I'd gladly do it. But lead a revolution? That's insane! I sat there for a while and even got a little bit of sleep. Finally Loor arrived carrying a basket.

"Come with me," she ordered. So I got up and followed her. She led me down one of the mine tunnels that didn't look as if it were active. A few feet along we came to an opening to a small room that had been cut from the rock. It was set up like one of the huts with animal fur bedding, a table, and candles for light.

"This is where we come when Kagan is looking for us," she explained. "You will be safe here." She then handed me the basket and I saw that it was full of bread and fruit. I needed to eat, but I didn't have much of an appetite.

I took a chance and asked, "Where's Osa?"

"She was taken to the village," said Loor with no emotion. "Tomorrow I will take her to Zadaa."

Zadaa. That was the territory where Loor and Osa came from. So that meant Loor knew how to use the flumes to get around. And if she was going to bring her mother's body back home, I couldn't imagine she planned to climb back to the top of that mountain to get there. There must have been another way to use the flumes.

There was some serious tension in this little stone room just then. Loor was angry, but I wasn't sure how much of that anger was aimed at me. I was upset and sad and to be honest, a little scared of her. She had a nasty temper and if she decided to take it out on me, there'd be nothing left of poor Bobby Pendragon except a stain on the wall. I decided not to push Loor by talking. So I sat down on the animal fur and tried to act invisible.

Loor was like a caged cat, pacing back and forth. What I feared was that her anger would build to a point where she'd explode and take me apart. In a strange way, that was exactly what happened. But it happened in a way that I never expected. She didn't hit me. She didn't insult me. She didn't even scream at me. All of those things would have been understandable. But what she did hurt much more.

"I am taking you home tomorrow," she said flatly. "You do not belong here."

Whoa. That was the *last* thing I expected to hear.

"But . . . what about the revolution?" I asked lamely.

"You think you cannot help these people because you are not a warrior," she said. "But the Milago do not need a warrior. They need someone they can trust. You are not that person."

This took me by surprise. Obviously I was not a fighter like Loor, and I was not exactly the brave, hero type. But trustworthy? Come on! I could be trusted. I was a good guy. Where did she get off calling me untrustworthy?

"Why do you say that?" I asked.

She looked me right in the eye and said, "How can someone be trusted who only thinks of himself? From the moment you arrived, you have plotted to get away. It did not matter how much the Milago need help. It was always about getting home."

I was feeling a little defensive at this point. I thought she was being unfair and said, "Okay, maybe you're right. But I was kind of thrown into this mess without a whole bunch of warning. It's a lot to ask someone to turn their life upside down in a day!"

"I know, Pendragon," she said. "The same thing happened to me. But there is a difference between you and me and it has nothing to do with fighting."

"And what's that?"

That's when she let me have it.

"You saw how my mother died," she said, trying to hold back emotion. "I would have done anything to save her. But you . . . I do not understand how you can only think of yourself when your uncle is about to die."

Those words hit me hard. She was right. Uncle Press was in trouble. I knew it ever since that sled had landed us in the snow bank. Yet I was planning on leaving without even trying to help him. I had been so worried about saving myself that I didn't think for a second that Uncle Press needed me. Loor was right and I was ashamed.

"That is why you are of no use here, Pendragon," she said with finality. "The Milago need someone to have faith in. You are not that person." She turned and headed for the door, but just before she left she said, "After you get some sleep, I will bring you home. You can go back to the life you miss so dearly and forget that any of this ever happened. I suppose in time you will also forget about Press." And she left.

I had just learned something about myself and I didn't like it. Could I really be that selfish? Everything Loor said was dead on. Sure I cared about Uncle Press, but I convinced myself that there was nothing I could do to help him. But was that true? Or was it just an easy way to get out of trying? Did I even let my mind think of the possibility of trying to rescue him? I spent the next few hours questioning myself. Memories of the past few days played over and over in my head. I was haunted by the vision of the guy who was coldly thrown to his death because the Milago hadn't mined enough glaze. I continued to see the horror of Osa fighting for her life and ultimately losing to a shower of arrows. I remembered the look on Loor's face when she wanted to help her mother, but chose instead to protect me.

But most of all, I remembered Uncle Press. I thought back to my first memories of him. He was always there for me. It was sad testament that my last memory of him was going to be the sight of him dragged off by Kagan's knights. That wasn't right. That was not the way it should end. And that's why I need your help, Mark.

After I finish writing this journal, I'm going to put down some instructions on a separate piece of parchment. That way you can keep it with you. I think you should keep my journal separate and in a safe place. Osa was right. It's important that I write down everything that's going on. If I never get back, these words are the only record of what happened to me. Treat them like gold, buddy.

I don't know if it's fair of me to ask you to do this. I'm beginning to think that I don't deserve it. If you can't help, I'll understand. No harm, no foul. I'm still going to do what I have to do anyway. I'm not even sure if the help I'm asking for will do any good. I'm winging it here. The real wild card is Loor. She may not give me a chance, and without her help the odds are going to be really against me. But you know, it doesn't matter. One way or another, with or without her, I've made up my mind.

Tomorrow I'm going after Uncle Press.

END OF JOURNAL #2

◐ SECOND EARTH ◑

Courtney finished Bobby's second amazing journal and placed it down on the table. Mark had finished a few minutes earlier and was already looking over the additional piece of parchment paper that Bobby had included with his latest missive. It took a while for her to say anything. The story contained on the pages from Bobby was getting more fantastic with each new paragraph, and she had to let it sink in. Finally she looked at Mark and asked, "What does he want you to do?"

Mark stood up and paced Courtney's dad's workshop as his mind tried to work its way around the task at hand. On the additional piece of parchment, Bobby had outlined a job for Mark to do that was fairly simple, yet still dangerous.

"It's a list," explained Mark. "He wants me to put together a bunch of stuff and get it to him."

Courtney grabbed the paper and looked over the list. "Get it to him?" she exclaimed. "How?"

Mark grabbed the list back and shook it at her. "Th-That's the hard part," he declared nervously. "He wrote out instructions. First I'm supposed to try and use the ring the way Osa did. But if that doesn't work, which it shouldn't because I'm not a Traveller, then he wants me to find the gate to the flume in the subway station."

"You mean the abandoned subway in the Bronx with the killer dogs?" asked Courtney in disbelief. "That's like . . . suicide."

"Y-Yeah, tell me about it," Mark exclaimed.

Courtney and Mark fell silent. It was a dangerous favour that Bobby was asking.

Finally Courtney asked, "But you're gonna do it, right?"

"Of course!" Mark answered quickly, as if he were insulted that she even had to ask. "You think I'd blow off my best friend? Gimme a break."

"Then I'm going with you," said Courtney without a hint of doubt.

"N-No way," said Mark quickly.

"Yeah way!" Courtney shot back. "You need somebody to cover your butt."

"Who'll cover *your* butt?"

"I can cover my own butt," said Courtney with her usual cockiness.

It was hard to argue with that. Courtney *could* cover her own butt. But Mark doubted that she'd ever had to do it in a place like the badlands of the South Bronx against a pack of vicious quig-dogs and a demon killer by the name of Saint Dane. No, he was pretty sure Courtney hadn't encountered that particular challenge before. But then again, he didn't want to do this alone. The idea terrified him. He thought over the dilemma for a good five seconds and then asked, "You sure you want to help?"

"Absolutely," she said as she grabbed Bobby's list back. She looked it over and then announced. "I get why he wants some of this stuff . . . a torch, a watch . . . but what's he going to do with a CD player?"

"You're asking me like I should know?" Mark said sarcastically. "None of this makes any sense to me."

Courtney scanned the list again and then said, "Uh-oh, he wants some stuff from his house."

"Yeah, I saw that," said Mark. "But I can substitute other things."

This raised another tough issue. Courtney threw a sober stare at Mark and said, "If we can get things to Bobby, that means we can tell him his family disappeared."

Mark had to think about this. Courtney's instincts were right. Bobby had to know what was going on, even though they didn't really know themselves. The only thing they knew for certain was that the Pendragons had vanished.

"Bobby should know," said Mark cautiously while still working out his thoughts. "But not yet. There's nothing he can do about it now."

"But it's his family," countered Courtney.

"I know," said Mark. "But so is Uncle Press. I don't know what Bobby's got planned, but he has a shot at saving his uncle. I'm not sure there's anything he could do here to help find his family."

Courtney realised that Mark was right. Bobby needed to do what he had to do on Denduron. There would be plenty of time after that to find his family. Besides, the police were already working on the case. What more could Bobby do?

"We'll tell him after he's back for good," said Mark with finality.

"And what if he doesn't come back for good?" asked Courtney. "Mark, I think we should tell our parents what's going on."

"N-No! We can't!" shouted Mark.

"Why? Maybe they can help!" said Courtney hopefully. "It would be much safer if we *all* went to the subway with the stuff! Right?"

Mark really wanted to agree. He wanted to dump this all on an adult who had more authority than he had. But he felt certain he knew what would happen if they did. He chose his words carefully and said, "Courtney, I'd love to tell our parents and get their help and go to this subway station with Captain Hirsch and armed cops from the Stony Brook Police. But you know what would happen if we told them? They'd stop us. They'd probably lock us up. Then they'd all sit around and try to logically figure out what's going on and by the time they came to any decisions it could be too late for Bobby . . . and for Press."

Courtney let Mark's words sink in. The guy was kind of a dweeb, but he was a smart dweeb. If they told their parents it would be all over. They had to do this on their own. Mark quickly gathered up the parchment papers and started rolling them up.

"We can get this stuff together in a couple of hours," he said. "The trick will be to sneak out without our parents knowing – "

"Whoa, whoa," interrupted Courtney. "You're not thinking of doing this tonight, are you?"

"Well, why not?" said Mark innocently.

Courtney spoke to Mark slowly and deliberately, as if he were a child. She wanted him to understand exactly what she was saying. "This is important," she said. "But by the time we get this stuff together it'll be dark and something tells me that going where we have to go isn't too safe after dark."

This made Mark think. They were heading into a rough part of town and rough parts of town got rougher after dark. They definitely had a better chance of pulling this off in the daylight. It was more important to get it done than to get it done fast.

"You're right," said Mark. "I'm not thinking straight."

"Yeah, you are," said Courtney. "You're just excited. Let's split the list, get the stuff, and then meet back here tomorrow morning."

That made sense. Tomorrow would be the day. Courtney

searched for a piece of paper and a pen so she could write them each their own list. She picked up the piece of parchment paper with Bobby's instructions and looked at the yellowed paper with the blotchy writing for a long time. Mark could see that something else was on her mind. He waited for her to pull her thoughts together. Finally Courtney turned to Mark and asked, "What was she like?"

"What was who like?" asked Mark.

"Osa. She gave you the ring, right? What was she like?"

It was true. Mark had almost forgotten. He had actually met one of the characters from Bobby's adventure. She was in his bedroom. Mark put the rolled parchment pages down and allowed his thoughts to drift back to the night before.

"She was like a dream," he said softly. "But the thing I remember most is that when she looked at me, I felt . . . safe." Mark looked down to the ring on his finger and continued, "And now she's dead. I guess she wasn't able to make things safe after all."

The two took a moment to grieve silently for a woman they only knew through the pages of Bobby's journal. Then Courtney picked up her pen and began to write. There was work to be done. They went over Bobby's list and picked the items they felt they could each find most easily. Courtney made out the two lists, then with the plan of meeting back at her house at seven A.M. the next day, they split up and went to work.

Mark went home and brought Bobby's parchment papers with him. Bobby had asked him to treat them like gold and that's what he planned to do. Mark had a hiding place that no one in his family knew about. His attic was full of old furniture. Tucked way in the back was an ancient rolltop desk that hadn't been moved since before Mark was born. The drawers of the desk were locked and his parents never tried to open them because they didn't have the key. But Mark did. He had found it hidden on a lip under the desk when he was eight years old. He never told his parents because they didn't really care, but for him it was the perfect place to hide his most treasured possessions. His special stash included mint condition *Mad* magazines; baseball cards for rookie Yankees Derek Jeter, Bernie Williams, and Mariano Rivera; some Star Wars action figures that were still in their original packaging; a report card from the seventh grade that had two Ds . . . just to remind him how easy it is to screw up; and an assortment of other small items that had special value to him alone.

Every so often Mark would go up in the attic to look over these treasures. It always made him feel good, like visiting old friends. He especially liked to check out the toys. He was too old to be playing with them, but they always brought him back to a fun time in his life, if only for a moment. It was a pleasure that no one had to know about.

When he opened the drawer this time, he wasn't hit with the familiar warm wave of nostalgia. As he looked down at all his good junk, he had the strange feeling that it belonged to someone else. And in a way, it did. It belonged to the old Mark, the innocent Mark of yesterday, whose biggest concerns were about finishing homework on time and battling the acne that was running wild on his nose. But that was yesterday. Today he had to deal with issues that not only affected life and death on the far side of the universe, but raised serious questions about the reality of life in his own backyard. It wasn't until Mark opened that drawer that he realised how much he had changed in the past few hours. He wanted to pick up the Chewbacca figure and let out a Chewie roar. He wanted to flip open a *Mad* magazine and laugh at "Spy vs. Spy". He wanted to walk the dog with the whistling yo-yo he had kept since his day at the state fair when he was six. Instead he found a cardboard box, pulled out the drawer and dumped everything into it. He closed the box and shoved it under the desk alongside all the other dusty, long-forgotten boxes full of long-forgotten stuff. It was like putting aside his old life to make room for the new one.

This desk drawer was still going to be the place for Mark's most valued possessions, but they were no longer the trinkets that held warm memories of childhood. This would now be the place to hold Bobby's story. He carefully placed the rolled scrolls in the wooden drawer. They fitted perfectly, front to back. Mark made a mental note that there would be room for many more scrolls. He usually kept the desk key in his bedroom desk, but that didn't feel secure enough any more. His mother had given him a silver chain that she used to wear when she was his age. It had a peace symbol on it and Mark had it hanging from his bedroom mirror. Mark took the chain down and replaced the pendant with the key. The chain then went around his neck, never to be away from him again. He now felt reasonably secure that Bobby's pages were safe. Or at least as safe as he knew how to keep them.

At seven A.M. sharp Courtney's doorbell rang. When she opened the door, Mark was standing there wearing a large backpack from L.L. Bean.

"Did you sleep?" he asked.

"No," she answered. "Did you get any more pages?"

"No," he answered. "Let's get this party started."

They went down to Courtney's dad's workshop, where Courtney had laid out all of the items from her half of the list.

"Where are your parents?" Mark asked her.

"They left for work."

"You know we have to skip school to do this," Mark said.

"Do you care?" asked Courtney.

Mark didn't have to answer. The two stood there looking at the items, not sure of what to do next. Courtney broke the tension.

"Try the ring thing," she said.

Mark scanned the items and picked out the torch. It was roughly the same size as the rolled parchment pages and as good a candidate as any. He then took off the ring and put it on the floor. He knelt down, put his finger on the grey stone and looked at Courtney.

"Go for it," she encouraged.

"Denduron," whispered Mark. Nothing happened. "Denduron," he said again, this time a bit louder. Still no reaction from the ring.

"Let me try," said Courtney and knelt down. She touched the ring and shouted, "Denduron!"

They both looked at the ring, but it lay motionless on the ground.

"I g-guess we're going to the subway," Mark said soberly.

Courtney jumped up and started to pack the gear into Mark's backpack. She moved fast, as if she were afraid she might chicken out if she stopped to think too much about what lay ahead.

"I got a train timetable," she said efficiently. "We can take the commuter train to 125th Street, then catch a subway from there." When she finished packing, she closed up the buckles on the pack and looked at Mark. It was time to go.

"Courtney," said Mark sheepishly. "I'm scared."

The two let that admission hang in the air for a moment, then Courtney straightened up and said, "You know something? I'm not. We're gonna do this."

It may have been a bold bluff, but seeing Courtney being her usual confident self gave Mark hope. Maybe they could do this. So he hoisted the pack on to his back and the two started for the train station.

Stony Brook Station was at the bottom of the Ave. It was

early so the platform was still packed with business commuters in suits who were on their way to work in New York City. Courtney and Mark had to keep one eye out for any parents who might know them and question why they weren't in school. They saw one guy who Mark knew from Boy Scouts, but they saw him in time to make sure they boarded a different car when the train pulled into the station. They didn't need to be so cautious. All the commuters had their heads buried in their newspapers and didn't look at anyone else on the platform.

The train ride into New York was a quiet one. The commuters who weren't reading were asleep. It would have been hard for Courtney and Mark to discuss their mission for they definitely would have been overheard. Mark looked at the commuters reading their morning papers and had to laugh to himself. They were all reading articles about the stock market, or about sports, or about a speech the president had given at some parade. But whatever news they were reading about couldn't compare to the very real story that he and Courtney were living out right in front of their noses. Mark could imagine the headline: LOCAL BOY FLUMED ACROSS THE UNIVERSE TO LEAD REVOLUTION. Now *that's* a news story.

All Courtney wanted to do was take these few minutes to relax. She knew that once they stepped off this train their adventure would begin and she wanted to be calm enough to handle whatever came their way. So she laid back in her seat, closed her eyes and tried to keep her heart from beating as fast as it was.

In no time they arrived at their stop, 125th Street in Manhattan. The train would continue on from there to Grand Central Station, where most of the commuters were heading. But 125th Street was much closer to the Bronx, so with a silent nod Courtney and Mark got off the train.

They had always heard their parents say that this was a bad section of town. They weren't entirely sure what was meant by bad, but they were nervous just the same. One thing was certain. This wasn't suburban Connecticut. They were in New York City with all the traffic, noise, and people congestion that New York is famous for. Courtney had a map of the New York City subways and had carefully plotted out a route to get close to Bobby's abandoned subway station. It was a short walk from the 125th Street commuter trains to the nearest subway stop and they made it with no problem. They descended into the underground station, bought their tokens, and hit the trains.

The subway trip to the Bronx was uneventful. The neighbourhoods of New York that they travelled through were filled with people from all different nationalities and ethnic backgrounds and none of them were monsters. They were all just people going to work or going to school and generally living their lives. Under other circumstances, Courtney and Mark might have enjoyed this. But these weren't other circumstances. They were on a mission.

After changing trains twice, they arrived at the subway stop that was nearest to the abandoned one that Bobby had described. They climbed back up into the sunlight to see a Bronx neighbourhood that was just as busy and diverse as the one where they had first gone underground.

According to their map, Bobby's subway stop was three blocks east from where they were. As they walked those few blocks, neither of them said it but each secretly wished that the subway station where Bobby and Uncle Press had gone, wouldn't be there. They each held a slim hope that none of this was true and that Bobby was making the whole thing up. Those hopes totally disappeared when they reached the corner of a busy intersection and looked across to the far side.

"Th-That's it, isn't it?" asked Mark nervously.

Courtney didn't have to answer. The station was exactly what Bobby had described. It was a small kiosk covered with cracked green paint. Mark gave a nervous look to Courtney, but Courtney kept her eyes on the building. She didn't want Mark to see that she was starting to get nervous. Instead, she stepped off the kerb and headed for the building. Mark had no choice but to follow. When they got to the kiosk, they looked down to see a cement stairway that was covered in rubbish and debris. This was definitely an abandoned station. After a quick glance around to make sure nobody was watching, they ran down the steps. They hit a landing, turned, and were faced with the boarded-up entrance that Bobby had described.

Courtney reached out, grabbed hold of one board, and pulled it aside as easily as Uncle Press had done. She had just opened up a dark doorway into the underground. Before they had the chance to change their minds, Courtney ducked in and disappeared. Mark took a scared breath and was right after her. He had to squeeze through with the pack, but he made it and closed the board up behind him. Everything was playing out exactly as it had for Bobby. But Courtney and Mark were now hoping that this is where the similarity would end. Neither of them wanted to run into Saint Dane or the quigs. They walked down the last few steps into the abandoned station and stood shoulder to shoulder, with every sense on full alert.

"I feel like I've already been here," Mark said in awe. Indeed, everything was just as Bobby had described. It was a lonely station that hadn't seen passengers in years. Then they heard the distant rumble of an oncoming subway train. In a few seconds the train blasted into the station and thundered through without slowing down. This seemed to kick them back into gear.

"C'mon," said Courtney, and headed for the far end of the platform.

"Wait," said Mark and quickly took off the pack. He opened it up and dug deep down inside.

"What are you doing?" asked Courtney.

As he dug through the pack Mark said, "I brought a little insurance." He found what he was looking for and pulled out a package wrapped in brown paper.

"Was that on the list?" asked Courtney curiously.

"No, it's a little something I added." He unwrapped the paper to reveal two huge, succulent steaks. He held them up proudly. "A bribe, just in case we run into some hungry quigs."

Courtney had to smile. "I don't care what anybody says, you're good." She then grabbed the steaks and walked off. Mark smiled proudly at the compliment, but then the smile dropped when he realised it wasn't exactly the greatest compliment in the world. He picked up the pack and hurried after her.

They reached the end of the platform and saw the small set of stairs leading down to the dark tracks.

"This looks hairy," declared Mark. "What if the gate door isn't there?"

"Everything he described so far has been true," said Courtney. "I've got to believe this will be too."

Just then they heard another train approaching. They took a few steps back from the edge of the platform and a few seconds later, the train flashed through, moving fast. The idea of being down on those tracks when a train came through was a frightening one.

"Gulp," said Mark.

"Don't think, move!" shouted Courtney. She ran to the edge of the platform and disappeared down on to the tracks. It was kind of like jumping into cold ocean water. The longer you thought about it, the more reasons you'd come up with to wait. It was better just to do it and that's what she did.

Mark was right behind her. He ran across the platform and hurried down the stairs to find Courtney below, pressing her back against the wall.

"I can't believe I did that," she said, panting hard.

"Yeah, me neither, but don't stop now," he added.

With Courtney in the lead, the two made their way cautiously along the tunnel. It was dark and they didn't want to risk wandering out on to the tracks so Courtney kept one hand on the grimy, greasy wall.

"How far did he say the door was?" asked Courtney.

"I don't remember," was Mark's answer. "Just keep – " That's when he heard it.

"What was that?" he asked.

"What was what?"

"I heard something, like a growl." Mark grabbed one of the steaks back from Courtney and held it out. "Gooood doggy! Goooood doggy!"

Then Courtney heard it too. It was faint, but unmistakable.

"That's not a growl," she said. "That's a train! Another train is coming!"

A blast from the train's horn told them she was right. Another train was coming and the two were caught. They didn't know which way to run.

"I'm going back!" shouted Mark and turned to run back for the platform. But Courtney grabbed him by the pack and held him tight.

"No!" she commanded. "We can't be far!"

She turned and continued to make her way along the wall as Mark pushed her from behind. It was getting hard to see because the train had just rounded a curve ahead and its headlight was shining right in their eyes. And it was coming fast.

"Hurry!" pleaded Mark.

Courtney desperately felt at the wall, then tripped over a switch and fell to her knees. Mark quickly pulled her to her feet and pushed her forward. The train was now getting dangerously close. The racket from the wheels on the track was deafening. There wasn't much space between the wall of the tunnel and the track.

"We're not going to make it!" Courtney shouted. "Press against the wall!"

Mark pulled off his pack and flattened his back against the wall. The train was only a few yards away. The two held hands tightly. Mark closed his eyes. Courtney pressed against the wall and slid her hand out in one last desperate attempt to find the door. She leaned forward a few more inches . . . and her hand found something.

"I got it!" she shouted.

The train was right there. Its horn blasted. Courtney held on tight to Mark's hand and dived for what she hoped was the gate. She pushed against the dark recess and it gave way. Courtney and Mark tumbled inside just as the train flashed by. In seconds it was gone and all was as quiet as it had been only a few moments before. Courtney and Mark lay on the ground, totally out of breath. It took a minute for them to get their heads back together, and when they did they both looked up and saw it at the same time.

"Whoa," was all Mark could say in awe.

It was the rocky grey tunnel. With their eyes fixed on the craggy portal, they both stood up. Courtney then hurried back to the wooden door they had just come through and poked her head outside.

"It's here," she announced. "The star, just like Bobby said."

She came back inside to join Mark, who kept staring into the tunnel.

"This is it," he said with growing excitement. "It's all true. Everything Bobby wrote is true."

This was as far as Bobby's instructions took them. In his letter, he wrote for them to come to the gate and wait. But wait for what? They stood there for a few minutes, not exactly sure of what to do next. Finally Courtney looked at Mark with a mischievous smile and said, "I'm going to try it."

She took a step towards the mouth of the grey tunnel, but Mark pulled her back.

"Don't!" he yelled nervously.

"Why not? If Bobby can do it, I can do it," was her typical Courtney-esque response. She shook Mark off and stepped into the mouth of the flume. Mark backed away and watched nervously as Courtney faced the depths of the endless, dark tunnel. She stood up straight, gave a quick glance to Mark, then turned back towards the darkness and said, "Denduron!"

Nothing happened. Zero. They could hear the word echo back from the tunnel, but besides that, nothing.

"It's gotta be the same as the ring," said Mark. "If you're not a Traveller, you don't have the power."

Courtney backed out of the tunnel with a look of definite disappointment. She was psyched to take the magic carpet ride of light that Bobby had described, but it was not meant to be. "So why is it that Bobby has the power?" she asked, a little bit peeved. "What makes him so special that – "

"Shhh!" Mark held his hand up to quieten Courtney.

"What?" asked Courtney.

"Do you hear that?"

Courtney listened and then said, "It must be another train coming."

"No," said Mark as he strained to listen harder. "It's not a train. It sounds like . . . like . . . music."

Courtney listened harder, and soon she heard it too. It *was* music. Far off music. But it wasn't a tune. It was more like a jumble of sweet, high notes.

"I've heard that before," exclaimed Mark. "When the ring opens up." He glanced down at the ring on his finger, but the grey stone wasn't glowing. No, this music wasn't coming from the ring. Courtney looked into the tunnel, and what she saw made her jaw drop open in surprise.

"Uh, Mark," she said numbly. "You looking at this?"

Mark was also looking down the tunnel and what he saw made his jaw fall open as well, for there was something coming towards them. It was a pin spot of light, like the headlight on the front of a far-off train. As it drew closer, the light grew larger and the sweet music grew louder.

"D-Do we want to run?" asked Mark with a shaky voice.

"Yeah," answered Courtney. "But we can't."

As the light came nearer, they saw that the grey walls of the tunnel were beginning to change. It was like they were disappearing. The grey, craggy rock walls were transforming into clear crystal, just as the grey stone of the ring had done. Beyond the clear walls was a vast star field. The light grew so bright that Mark and Courtney had to shield their eyes. The music grew louder as well. Without thinking, the two backed away until they hit the far wall. They were trapped. It was too late to find the door and get out of there. All they could do was cover their eyes, crouch down, and hope that it would soon end.

With one final burst of light, the room fell dark and the music stopped. All was quiet and calm. Slowly Mark and Courtney lowered their arms from their faces to see what had happened. What they saw seemed more impossible than anything they had seen so far. Yet there he was, plain as can be.

It was Bobby. He stood at the mouth of the tunnel looking a little dazed. He glanced around to get his bearings, then saw Mark and Courtney cowering against the far wall. Nobody knew what to say. They all just stared at each other for a good long time. Finally Bobby let out a simple, calm, "Yo."

That broke the ice. Mark and Courtney jumped up, ran to him and all three threw themselves into a tight group hug. They didn't need to say anything. This one unplanned action said it all. It was a release from all the fear, uncertainty, and sadness that had been building up in them since the adventure began. They stayed this way for some time, until Bobby finally said, "Okay, I'm choking here."

Reluctantly they all let go and took a step back from each other. They waited a second and then all three ran at each other again for another hug. This time they all started to laugh.

"You guys are the best," said Bobby, but then something dawned on him and he pulled away from the group. He looked right at Courtney and said, "Wait, what are you doing here?"

"I showed her the journals," admitted Mark. "I'm sorry. I couldn't deal on my own."

Bobby had to think about this. He thought that he was writing to Mark and Mark alone. But it was a big responsibility that he threw at his friend and Bobby realised that maybe sharing it was a good idea. If there was anybody who could help him deal, it was Courtney. So he smiled reassuringly at his friend and said, "It's cool, Mark. I'm glad you did. Does anybody else know?"

Courtney answered, "No, just us."

"That's good," said Bobby. "At first I was thinking everybody should know, but now I'm not so sure. This is all pretty heavy."

"That's what we thought," said Mark.

Bobby added, "There's going to be a time when everybody should know, but not yet, okay?"

Courtney and Mark nodded. There were all on the same page.

"Are my parents freaking out?" Bobby asked.

There it was. The question they didn't want to answer. Mark

and Courtney gave each other a quick glance. They had already decided it wouldn't be a good idea to tell Bobby that his family had disappeared. He had enough to worry about as it was. But they didn't want to lie to him. Mark didn't know what to say, so Courtney jumped in, saying, "Everybody's really worried about you."

It wasn't a lie; people were definitely worried about him. It just wasn't the whole truth. But it was the right thing to say because Bobby then said, "I hate to keep them in the dark, but I think they'd be more worried if they knew what was really going down. So don't tell 'em anything, okay?"

Both Courtney and Mark nodded quickly. Whew. They just dodged a bullet. Bobby then spotted the L.L. Bean pack that Mark and Courtney brought.

"Did you get everything?" he asked as he quickly poked through the contents.

"Every bit," answered Mark.

"Any trouble getting here?" Bobby asked.

Courtney answered, "No sweat."

Bobby looked back to his friends as if he were seeing them for the first time. What he saw were two people who came through for him in a big way when they really didn't have to. "I don't know how to thank you guys," he said sincerely. "I don't deserve friends like you."

Courtney and Mark answered with smiles.

"Bobby," said Mark sheepishly. "Is it true? I mean, what you've been writing about?"

"Yeah," was Bobby's answer. "Weird, huh?"

Courtney and Mark started to ask more questions but Bobby cut them off by saying, "Guys, I don't know any more about what's going on than what I wrote. I don't know why I'm a Traveller. I don't know where Denduron is. I don't know *when*

Denduron is. I've got a million questions and no answers. And I'm scared as hell."

Yes, there were many questions but none of them had any answers. Finally Courtney took a step towards Bobby. She hesitated, as if what she was about to say would be difficult. She finally gathered the strength and said, "Don't go back. That's not your world back there. It's not your life. You belong here. All you have to do is walk out of that door with us. Nobody would know. Please, Bobby, stay here."

Bobby looked at Mark. Mark nodded to him as if agreeing with Courtney. "You're home now, Bobby," he said. "Stay here."

Bobby hadn't thought about the possibility. It would be so easy. All he had to do was walk away. He was home now. He was safe. It was so tempting. He didn't answer at first because this was the most important decision he ever had to make in his life. He looked around him, looked down into the dark tunnel, and then to the L.L. Bean pack full of stuff his friends had brought him. He had made up his mind.

"There are a ton of things I don't know," he said soberly. "But there's one thing I do know for certain. Uncle Press is going to die unless I do something."

The others dropped their heads. Bobby was right. If he stayed, Uncle Press was doomed.

"But there's more," Bobby added. "I'm not the guy to help those people fight their revolution. I don't know why they think I am, but I'm not. The guy to help them is Uncle Press. If he dies, they don't stand a chance. I gotta go back and get Uncle Press for the sake of the Milago, too."

Bobby picked up the pack and swung it on to his back.

"What're you gonna do with that stuff?" asked Mark.

"I'm not exactly sure," answered Bobby, "but I better think of something fast." He tightened up the straps on the pack and took a step back towards the flume. "I'm no big hero," he then said.

"I'm going to try to save Uncle Press and then get out of there. I'd just as soon not stick around for the real fireworks."

"We'll be waiting for you," said Mark.

Everyone looked at each other, not entirely sure of what to say. It was time for Bobby to go.

"There's nothing I can say to thank you guys for doing this and for hanging on to my journals," Bobby said.

"Just keep 'em coming, dude," said Mark with a smile.

Bobby smiled and then the three once again joined in a group hug.

"I'll write as soon as I can," said Bobby and pulled away. Everyone was holding back tears. Bobby had turned to the flume when Courtney asked, "Is Loor really as gorgeous as all that?"

Bobby winced. Busted. "You weren't supposed to see that," he said sheepishly. "She's not my type."

"No?" said Courtney with a sly smile. "I think she and I have something in common. We can both kick your ass."

Bobby laughed at that. Of course she was right.

"Get home safe," she added.

"Soon as I can," was his reply. Mark gave him a wave and Bobby turned back to the flume. He stepped in, took a breath, and said, "Denduron!"

Instantly, the flume reactivated. The walls started to shimmer, the musical notes grew loud, and bright light blasted out from somewhere far inside.

Bobby turned back to them and gave a quick wave. "Later!" he said.

Then, in a flash, Bobby was gone. The light and the music trailed away inside the tunnel, transporting Bobby to his far-off destination. Soon all was quiet once again. The two stood there, staring into the dark, empty tunnel. There was nothing left to do now except to start the long journey home.

"Uh-oh," Mark said.

"What?" asked Courtney nervously.

Mark held out his hand and they both saw that the grey stone in the ring was starting to glow. Mark quickly took it off and placed it down on the ground. They each took a step back and watched as the ring grew larger and light blasted out of the stone. The familiar musical notes were heard again as the light built in intensity. There was a flash, and just as quickly as it started, it was over. The ring lay still on the ground. Next to it was another rolled-up parchment.

"How could he have written so fast?" asked Courtney.

Mark picked up the pages and started to unfurl them.

"Something tells me that time here and time there aren't relative," said Mark.

"Huh? English please," demanded Courtney.

"I think Denduron might not only be in another place," explained Mark. "It might be in another time. It could be thousands of years ago, or a million years from now. The flumes not only travel through space, I'll bet they travel through time as well."

Courtney didn't quite get this, but then again she didn't get much of anything that was happening. Mark unfurled the pages, gave them a quick glance, then looked up at Courtney with a smile.

"I was right. It's from Bobby."

DENDURON

I messed up big time, guys.

I tried to take charge and do the right thing, but I'm afraid I only made things worse. It's been a wild ride since I saw you two in the subway, but the bottom line is that as I write this journal, we are on the verge of a catastrophe that could rip Denduron apart. It's not all my fault, but I'm afraid I pushed it closer to the edge. First I gotta backtrack to what happened since I wrote last. I finished my last journal before I saw you two, so I should tell you what happened before the trip I took to Second Earth where you gave me the backpack. As much as I was over-the-moon psyched to see you guys, I wish I had never made that trip, because that trip is one of the reasons we're on the edge of disaster.

When Osa was killed, something snapped in my head and I was able to think clearly. It wasn't anything dramatic like I suddenly realised I had to fulfil my destiny as a Traveller and lead the Milago to victory or anything like that. No way; gimme a break. It was about Uncle Press. I was ashamed of myself for not trying to help him. My only defence is that I had a whole lot of wild stuff thrown at me all at once and I was having a tough time keeping my head on straight. But when Osa died, it was like a wake-up call. And my loss wasn't even on the same scale as the loss was for Loor. Osa was her mother. I imagined what it would be like to lose my own mum. I take that back. I couldn't imagine what it would be like to lose my mum. The thought was just too horrible.

Osa didn't deserve to die. All she was trying to do was help some people find a better way of life. So was Uncle Press. He was trying to help the Milago and because of it, he was going to be put to death. Was that fair? I didn't think so, and I realised that somebody had to step up and say so. Unfortunately I also realised that the only person who could do something was me. I say "unfortunately" not because I didn't want to help him, but because I knew I wasn't exactly the best candidate to stage a Schwarzenegger-style commando assault on the Bedoowan palace and fight my way out with Uncle Press in tow. That particular fantasy was going to stay a fantasy. Still, I had to do something. And if I was going to have any chance at all, I needed help. That meant Loor. There was nothing I could say to Loor that would make her feel any better about what had happened to her mother. Man, she must have hated me. But she was the only person I could go to for help, so I had to take a shot.

I wandered out into the main cavern of the mine to look for her. I found her sitting cross-legged on the far side of the cavern, alone, carving a small piece of wood. It looked like she was sculpting a small face that was half sun and half moon. She was really concentrating on the work and I didn't want to disturb her, so I waited until she said something first. For several minutes she ignored me and continued to carve. Finally I think she figured out that I wasn't going to leave so she said, "This is a szshaszha. On my territory it symbolises the end of one life and the beginning of another. I will give it to my mother for it is said to bring luck in the next life."

"That's pretty cool," I said.

"It is an old fairy tale that has no meaning," she spat back sharply. "But my mother believed in these things and I will respect that."

I guess I said the wrong thing again. I was ready to chicken out and leave her alone. I had to force myself to stay and go through with this.

"I'm not going home tomorrow," I said trying to sound stronger than I felt. "I'm going after Uncle Press."

This made Loor stop her work and look up at me. I did my best to hold eye contact without blinking. I wanted her to know how serious I was. But then she burst out laughing. Obviously the idea of my going up against the Bedoowan knights was pretty funny to her.

She stopped laughing and said sarcastically, "Why, Pendragon? So you can watch him die the way you watched my mother die?"

Ouch. That was cold.

"No, I'm going to rescue him," I said trying to make it sound like I could make it happen.

"Go to sleep," she said dismissively. "I am tired of looking at you."

She was starting to tick me off. Yeah, she had been through a lot, but she didn't have to treat me like a turd. I stood my ground and said, "You told me I didn't care about my uncle. You're wrong. I care enough to go in that fortress and get him out."

She scoffed and said, "The Bedoowan knights would shred you before you got close to your uncle."

"You're probably right," I said. "That's why you're going to help me."

Loor shot me a surprised look. Uh-oh, maybe I was coming on too strong. She slowly stood up to her full height and looked down at me. It was all I could do to keep myself from backing off because if I did, I'd be lost.

"Why should I help rescue your uncle when my mother died trying to protect you?" she said with a seething intensity I'd never seen before.

"That's exactly why you should help me," I said, trying to keep my voice strong. "We both know that I'm not the person to lead the Milago against the Bedoowan. But Uncle Press is. I want to rescue him because he's my uncle. And if you care about the Milago as much as you say you do, then you should want to rescue him because these people need him."

Loor didn't move right away. I thought I saw something in her eyes. Was it a moment of doubt? She backed away from me and picked up her wooden weapon from the floor of the cavern.

"There is a meeting," she said coldly. "I will allow you to come."

A meeting. Cool. I didn't know what it was about, but at least she had thawed enough to include me. That was a start. She stepped forward and pointed the end of her weapon at me threateningly. "I will not protect you, Pendragon," she said. "If you come with me, you are on your own."

With that sweet little promise delivered, she walked off. I wasn't sure what to do until she turned back over her shoulder and barked, "Come. Now!"

I wasn't sure where we were going, either, but I was willing to follow her and find out. She led me back up the ladders to the surface. Night had fallen and the stars made it bright enough to see clearly. Loor glanced around quickly, probably looking for any knights that might still be hanging around looking for us. Good idea. I looked around too, but all was quiet. I followed her back into the Milago village and straight to the hut where I first woke up. When we ducked inside, I saw that I was right about this being a hospital, sort of. Two of the wooden benches now had occupants. But these two weren't here to get well. It was Osa, and the miner who was killed at the mine shaft. This is where they were keeping the bodies until doing whatever they were going to do with them. I supposed I should have been creeped out, but I wasn't.

There were two other people there as well, only these two were alive and well. It was Alder, the knight who Loor said was the Traveller from Denduron, and Rellin, the chief miner. They were sitting cross-legged in front of a fire that was burning in the hearth. Loor walked right over and sat down as well. I figured this was the meeting Loor had invited me to, so I sat down across from Loor.

Rellin started the meeting by saying, "I am sorry about your mother, Loor. She was a good person. I speak for all the Milago when I say how grateful we are to you and your people for coming here to help us. It saddens me that it had to end this way."

Loor was quick to respond and said, "I thank you for your sympathy, but my mother's death does not end things. We will still lead the Milago to their freedom."

Rellin looked nervous. Suddenly there was tension in the air. I felt it and Loor felt it. I'm not sure what Alder felt because I didn't know him well enough.

"No," Rellin said with finality. "It is over. There will be no fighting." With that declaration he got up to leave. But Loor jumped up and stopped him. Rellin's comment had taken her by surprise.

"How can you say that, Rellin?" she asked. "If the Milago do not break free of the Bedoowan, you will all die!"

"And if we fight them we will die much sooner," said Rellin. "My people are not warriors. You know that, Alder." He looked to Alder, who dropped his head. Rellin then looked back to Loor and said, "And you know that too, Loor. We would have no chance in a fight with the Bedoowan knights. We would be slaughtered."

Loor didn't give up. "Remember what Press said? You may not be warriors, but you are strong. He said the Bedoowan do not have the character to resist if the Milago stand up for themselves. He said – "

"Press is gone!" shouted Rellin. "And now Osa is gone as well. Who is left to lead us in this mad quest? You? Him?" He said this while pointing at me. "You are children. Your motives are noble, but it is time to end these foolish dreams."

With that he turned and stormed out of the hut. The meeting was over. I could tell that Loor wanted to go after him, but she didn't. She may have been a warrior, but she didn't have the words to change his mind.

"He is wrong," said Alder softly. "The Bedoowan are not as strong as Rellin thinks."

Loor walked slowly towards the body of her mother. She looked down at the fallen woman, then touched her arm as if trying to gain strength from her. She took the wooden szshaszha she had been carving and placed it in her mother's lifeless hand. Man, this was tearing my heart out. I can only imagine how Loor felt.

"He is lying," she said with finality.

Alder looked up quickly. This surprised him as much as it had me.

"Say what?" was all I could come back with.

"Rellin has wanted to fight the Bedoowan all of his life," she explained. "His anger and hatred are far greater than his fear. I do not believe that he has changed his way of thinking so quickly."

Alder stood up. He looked as confused as I felt.

"Then why did he say there would be no fight?" he asked.

Loor kept her eyes on her mother and answered, "I do not know, but something has changed. Something he has not told us about. Maybe he does not trust us because we are so young."

I thought back to the other two times I had seen Rellin. The first was at the Transfer ceremony. Though I was far away, I felt his hatred for the Bedoowan. The other time was in the mines after the explosion. After he was rescued, he had that strange laugh that felt so out of place. Loor was right. Something odd was happening.

"He trusted your mother, didn't he?" I asked.

"Of course," came her quick reply.

"Then he would have told her if things had changed and she would have told you, right?" I asked.

"Are you saying that I am wrong?" she asked.

"No," I answered quickly. "I'm saying that if you're right, then something strange is going on and the fact that he didn't tell your mother about it makes me kind of nervous."

We all let this hang in the air for a while. Finally Alder said, "So what do we do?"

I knew the answer to that. So did Loor, but I wanted to say it first.

"We rescue Uncle Press," I announced. "We've got to get him back here."

I shot a look at Loor. She didn't have to say a word. I knew what she was thinking. Rescuing Uncle Press was exactly what we needed to do and she had decided to help me. She then looked to Alder and said, "This will be a difficult fight, Alder. You will have to reveal to them that you are a Traveller."

Alder stood up proudly and said, "I knew this day would come. I am ready."

"Whoa, whoa!" I said while stepping between them. "Who said anything about a fight?"

Loor scoffed and said, "If you think we can get into the Bedoowan fortress, find Press, release him, and get out without a fight, you are not only a coward, you are a fool!"

Loor's macho act was starting to get old, but I didn't want to make her angry by telling her so. I had to stand up to her or she'd walk all over me.

"Yeah?" I said trying to match her bravura. "The goal here is to get Uncle Press out, and if you think the three of us have any chance of doing that by fighting Kagan's knights, then maybe *you're* the fool!"

Loor didn't have a comeback. Alder put the icing on the cake for me by saying, "He is right, Loor. If we charge in fighting, we will be killed before we find Press."

This bothered Loor. It was obvious that her first reaction to problem solving was to come out swinging. But she wasn't an idiot, and she was beginning to realise that her way might not have been the best way in this case.

"Then what do we do?" she asked. "Ask Kagan politely to release Press? Maybe if we said *please* it would happen."

Whoa, the muscle head was capable of sarcasm. Maybe she had more going on than I gave her credit for.

"The only chance we have is to sneak in there without

them knowing," I said. "The longer we can stay invisible, the better chance we have of getting Uncle Press out."

Alder was getting excited. He said, "Yes! I know a way to get in. And I know every corridor of that fortress. There are passageways and tunnels that are rarely used."

Loor didn't like being told she was wrong, especially by someone she didn't respect, which was me. But I think she was smart enough to know that my way made more sense.

She said, "And do you have a plan for what to do after Alder gets us into the palace?"

The fact is, I did. Sort of. It wasn't really a plan as much as it was a bunch of ideas. Unfortunately all my ideas needed things that didn't exist here on Denduron. I needed a bunch of stuff from back home.

"If I got a message to my friends back home," I asked, "is there a way for them to send me something from there?"

Loor stepped away from me. She knew the answer, but I think she was reluctant to tell me. I was still pretty new to this whole Traveller thing. Maybe she wasn't sure she could trust me with all the secrets yet.

But Alder didn't have the same concerns. "Of course there is," he said innocently. "You can flume back to your territory and get whatever you want."

I was beginning to like this guy. Could it be as simple as that? All I had to do was go back to the flume and I could get home? Cool. But there was still the tricky issue of having to climb back to the top of that mountain to get to the gate. There's no way I could do that in time to get home, then get back here to rescue Uncle Press before he was executed. Besides, I'd probably get eaten by those quigs anyway.

"That's no good," I said. "Is there another way?"

"You do not need to go to the mountain," said Loor. "There is another gate in the mines that is not guarded by quigs."

Oh, yeah! This was getting better by the second. And maybe best of all, by Loor giving me that piece of information, she was allowing herself to trust me. Maybe we could work together after all. Now that I was certain I could get home, my mind started to calculate all of the things I could get that would help us sneak into the fortress. The thing that was so cool is that the people of Denduron knew nothing about life at home. They would be blown away by something as simple as a torch. Man, talk about power! I wasn't exactly sure how it was going to work, but I was beginning to think that we might really have a chance of getting Uncle Press out of there.

Loor took me back down to the mine. It was an uneasy truce that we had going. We both knew we needed each other, but neither of us was too happy about it. The first thing I did was go back to the small cell-like room where Loor made me wait before, and finish my journal. I also wrote out the list of items and the instructions that I sent to you. Once they were ready, I rolled them up and did exactly what Osa had done when she sent you my first journal. I took off the ring, put it on the ground, touched the grey stone, and said, "Earth!"

But nothing happened. I tried again. Nothing. I was suddenly hit with a terrible thought. Osa told me that the power only worked for Travellers. What if I wasn't really a Traveller? I was doing exactly what she did, but the ring didn't work. Maybe I wasn't a Traveller after all!

Loor had been watching from the doorway. Before my panic got any worse she said, "You are not from Earth. You are from Second Earth."

Oh. Right. That's what Osa said. Second Earth. Did that mean there was a First Earth? I made a mental note to ask that question later. There were more important duties at hand. I touched the stone and said, "Second Earth!" Sure enough, that was the ticket. The stone began to glow, the ring grew, the musical notes played, and I dropped the journal with my list into its centre. It disappeared and all returned to normal. Cool. But then I was hit with another thought.

"Loor," I asked. "How will I know when to flume back to Earth . . . uh . . . Second Earth? It could take a long time for my friends to get the stuff together."

Loor gave me the straightest answer I'd had since my arrival. And she seemed unsure of herself, like it didn't make sense to her, either.

"I do not fully understand how," she began. "But when Travellers fly through the flumes, they will always arrive when they need to arrive."

It was then that I realised that Loor didn't know much more about being a Traveller than I did. Sure, she put on this tough front, but I think she was still trying to get her mind around the concept.

"My mother began to explain it to me," she added. "She said the flumes travel through time as well as through space. But why a Traveller always arrives at the time they need to arrive was not made clear to me."

"So you're telling me that when I flume to Earth – "

"Second Earth," she corrected.

"Yeah, whatever. When I flume to Second Earth I'll arrive at the same time that my friends arrive at the other end?"

"Yes."

"Does that work both ways? Forward and back?" I asked.

"What do you mean?"

"I mean, if I left right now, would my friends be waiting for me already? Even though I just sent the list a minute ago?"

"I think so," she answered.

"Then let's go!"

Loor led me back into the large cavern and then into a tunnel on the far side. This was an ancient tunnel, more so than the others. There were some loose rocks scattered over the ore-car tracks, which told me there hadn't been any miners through here in a long time. The walls also looked to be a bit rougher than the others, as if they hadn't quite perfected their digging techniques when this tunnel was gouged out of the earth.

We had walked for quite a while when I asked, "How do you know we're going the right way?"

Loor answered by raising up her hand. She was wearing a ring that was identical to mine. I couldn't believe I hadn't noticed it before. I guess when you're in the Traveller Club, everybody gets the special ring. But the thing was, the grey stone was letting off a very slight glow.

"My mother showed me this gate a few days ago," she explained. "She also showed me how to tell if a gate is nearby. The stone will tell you."

Sure enough, I looked at my own ring and saw that the grey stone was starting to glow. Then as we rounded one more bend, I saw it. Embedded in the rock was a wooden door.

Several yards farther down the tunnel was another opening. There was a pile of stones in front of that, as if it had just recently been dug out. Beyond this opening was an old ore car on the tracks. The thing probably hadn't been moved in decades.

"How do you know it's this tunnel and not that one?" I asked.

Loor pointed to the wooden door. There was a star symbol

carved in it, just like the door in the subway back in the Bronx. We walked inside and I saw the familiar tunnel that led to nowhere and everywhere. I took a few steps towards it and then turned back to Loor.

"What do I do?" I asked.

"I think you know," she answered.

Yeah, I did. I walked a few steps farther into the mouth of the tunnel when Loor called to me, "Pendragon?" I turned back and she said, "Your uncle is a good man. I want to rescue him too."

I thought that was pretty cool. I nodded to her, then turned to face the darkness and said, "Second Earth!"

You know what happened next.

DENDURON

I didn't want to leave you guys. When I took the flume back to that subway station, my thoughts were all about Uncle Press and the mission ahead. But once I got there and saw you both, I remembered how much I missed my real life. The small time I had spent on Denduron put my head in an entirely different place, but when I saw you two I suddenly felt like I had never left home. There was a moment where the idea of stepping into that flume and jumping back to Denduron was impossible. You were right, Courtney; it would have been easy. All I had to do was walk away.

But then I remembered Uncle Press and I knew what I had to do. I had to come back. Maybe it would have been better if I had stayed with you because I've made things worse than they were. Good intentions aren't always enough. You have to be smart and sometimes I think that I'm not that smart. I'll tell you what happened and you be the judge.

When I took the flume back to Denduron, I was greeted by Loor. The first thing she said was, "I was not sure if you would return."

I got all indignant and said, "Hey, give me a little credit, would you?" Of course she was absolutely right. I almost stayed on Second Earth, but I didn't want her to know that. I wanted her to think that I was confident in our mission.

She said, "We are both tired. We must get some sleep before we begin."

"Do we have enough time?" I asked. I knew that Uncle Press was to be executed at "the equinox", whatever that was. It could have been in ten minutes for all I knew.

"The equinox is at midday tomorrow," she explained. "When the three suns are one in the sky. We have enough time for a short rest."

Now I understood. The equinox was noon. Loor and I walked back to the small room in the mine. She didn't ask me about what was in the backpack and I wasn't about to start explaining. That would come later. But there was one item I wanted, so I took it out. It was my digital watch. I had no idea what time it was, but if we were going to sleep, I didn't want to end up sacking out for ten hours and waking up too late. I set the alarm to go off in two hours. That's just a long nap, and my tank was empty. Still, a few hours of sleep was better than nothing.

Loor watched me curiously as I set the watch alarm. She even jumped back with surprise when it beeped. I assumed they didn't have watches where she came from. It made me feel like I had one up on her for a change. But more important, her surprise at the beep meant my guess was right. To the people of Denduron, the simple things I could pull out of this pack would seem like huge magic. Throwing someone off balance, even for a short time, might mean the difference between success and failure. Or between life and death.

When I dug the watch out of my pack, I also found the extra surprise you put in there, Mark. You are the best. You know how much I love Mars Bars and the one you stuck in that pack was the most delicious treat in the history of treats. Thanks. I even offered a piece to Loor. I thought that was pretty nice of me, since I didn't have much hope of finding another Mars Bars around these parts. She took the bite-sized piece, popped it cautiously into her mouth and instantly spit it out. What a waste! I guess they don't have chocolate bars on her territory either.

"Next time you wish to feed me poison, warn me first," she demanded.

"What are you talking about? Where I come from this is a major treat," I said, still laughing.

"Then you come from a strange place, Pendragon," she said while taking a swig of water to wash the taste out of her mouth. It was like I had given her a brussel sprout or something.

This was the first time Loor and I weren't totally tense around each other. We were like two normal people doing normal things. Believe me, it wasn't like we were suddenly buds or anything, but it gave me the courage to ask her a question.

"What else did your mother tell you about being a Traveller?" I asked. I figured the more information I had, the better chance I had of getting out of here alive.

Loor didn't answer and busied herself arranging the animal pelts on her side of the cell floor. I knew she heard me, so I didn't ask again. I had just about given up on her when she said, "You may not like what I have to say."

Oh, great. More good news.

"If it's important," I said, "I should hear it whether I like it or not."

Loor sat down on the pelts and leaned her back against the wall. In spite of what I had just said, I wasn't so sure I wanted to hear this. But I had to.

"I have only known for a short time that I am a Traveller,"

she began. "I do not know much more than you do. But there is something my mother told me that is important. Maybe more important than saving Press and helping the Milago."

This sounded big. She had my full attention.

"I know you want to know why we are Travellers, but I do not know. That is the truth. My mother said that I would understand someday, but for now it was not important. What she did tell me though, is that we must understand our mission."

"Mission? You mean there's more to this than helping the Milago?" I asked.

"Yes," she said. "My mother explained that there are many territories, and they are all about to reach an important time. A 'turning point' she called it. It is a time when the outcome will either send the territory towards peace and prosperity, or plunge its people into chaos and destruction."

"So the battle between the Milago and the Bedoowan is some kind of turning point for all of Denduron?" I asked.

"That is what my mother said," she continued. "If the Milago break free of the Bedoowan, then Denduron will continue to exist in peace. But if the Bedoowan triumph it could be a disaster that will destroy the entire territory."

That was huge. This struggle wasn't just about helping these poor miners, it was about saving the whole territory.

"How did she know all this?" I asked. "That's like predicting the future!"

Loor shrugged and said, "It is part of being a Traveller. Someday we will understand this. But for now we must know that the Travellers' mission is to go to the territories that are about to reach their turning point and do all we can to help guide events in the right direction. That is why my mother was here; that is why Press is here. That is why you and I are here."

This was all a little cosmic for me. I thought I was finally getting my mind around how things worked, but I was only scratching the surface.

"Then who is Saint Dane?" I asked.

"Saint Dane is a Traveller like us," she said. "But he has been working against us. He wants the territories to turn the wrong way and create pandemonium."

"But . . . why?"

"When we find that answer, we will know all there is to know," she said. "Right now, I do not have those answers. Now go to sleep."

Yeah, right. Sleep. She just revealed that we have the future of Denduron in our hands, not to mention other territories that might be headed for trouble, and I was supposed to nod off to dreamland? And to make things just a little bit more interesting, there was a killer out there trying to stop us. I saw what this Saint Dane dude was capable of. Sweet dreams, Bobby boy! I was on the verge of a major brain haemorrhage and had to try and calm down. I told myself that none of this had anything to do with me. I had one goal and one goal only: to rescue Uncle Press. After that, I was out of here. If Uncle Press wanted to stay and try to change the course of history, that was his choice. But for me, I was catching the next flume home.

This gave me a little comfort and I tried to get some sleep. But before I put my head down I asked, "Is that it? Is there anything else you're not telling me?"

Loor didn't even open her eyes. She was nearly asleep. But she managed to say, "That is all I know, Pendragon. Is that not enough?"

Oh, yeah. That was plenty. It was time for lights out. I thought I would have trouble knocking off, but the truth was I was so exhausted, I didn't even remember my head hitting the fur. That was great, except that it felt like I had just closed my eyes when my watch alarm went off. Two hours felt more like two seconds. Man, did I go out hard! I had one of those weird waking-up moments and didn't know where I was. It seemed like I was in my bed at home and my first thought was, "I gotta walk Marley." But in no time, the reality of my situation came hurtling back. I sat up and tried to clear my head.

Loor wasn't there. After a stretch and a yawn, I went to my pack to do an inventory and saw that the clips were undone. Somebody had been going through my pack! I quickly threw it open and did a quick scan. It looked like everything was still there, though it was definitely rummaged through. I was pissed. I clipped the pack shut and went looking for Loor.

I walked back into the now familiar main cavern of the mine. It was business as usual out there. These poor guys never stopped. I briefly wondered what had happened with the latest Transfer ceremony and if they had mined enough glaze to balance with the woman Mallos had chosen. I hoped so, but there was nothing I could do about that. I needed to find Loor and get the rescue show on the road.

I scanned the cavern and something caught my eye. Walking out of a tunnel to my left was Rellin. He walked along quickly while speaking with another one of the miners. The weird thing was, these guys actually looked happy. Rellin slapped the guy on the back like they had just shared some joke and the guy took off running somewhere. Now, these guys had nothing to be happy about. The last time I spoke with Rellin he had pretty much condemned his entire tribe to a slow death by refusing to stand up against Kagan. Why was he happy all of a sudden? When he got farther away, I went to take a look down the tunnel they had just come from.

I entered to find that it was another abandoned avenue. The ore-car railroad tracks were old and rotten. This must have been one of the first tunnels they dug off the main cavern. I wondered how long ago that was. Years? Decades? Centuries? I also wondered why Rellin and the other miner were down here. I found my answer a few yards in. As with many of the other tunnels, there was a chamber dug out of the rock off to the side. But unlike the cell where I had just slept, this one had a wooden door to it. I took a quick look around to see if I was being watched, then opened the door and went inside.

It was a room about twice the size of the one I had just slept in, and this one was packed full of equipment. At first I thought this was where they kept their mining tools, but on closer inspection I saw the truth. This wasn't digging equipment, this was an armoury loaded with weapons! There were hundreds of spears like the ones Uncle Press had lashed to the side of the sled we rode from the top of the mountain. I was surprised to see their sharp metal tips gleaming in the light. The Milago weren't allowed to use metal tools except in the mines, but I was sure they weren't allowed to make weapons, either.

One side of the room was full of these spears. Below them were stacks and stacks of arrows. There must have been thousands. Across from them were the bows for the arrows. Probably a hundred in all. This looked to be a pretty formidable arsenal. Then I saw something that didn't quite make sense. There were large baskets placed along the back wall. I recognised them as the baskets they used to bring the glaze to the surface. These baskets were full, but not with glaze. I walked over to them and picked up one of the items inside. It was a small, sturdy stick about six inches long.

Attached to one end were two thin, leather straps about eighteen inches long. At the other end of the strap, a leather pouch the size of a baseball card was attached. I looked at the strange contraption trying to figure out what it could be. And then I got it. It was a catapult! An old-fashioned catapult! These guys didn't have rubber, so it wasn't the kind that you could stretch back and snap to propel stones. With this thing you had to hold the wooden stick and kind of fling the stone. There must have been a couple of hundred of these babies in the baskets.

As I stood there holding the catapult, I was struck with a sad thought. Rellin was right. The Milago were not prepared to do battle with Kagan's knights. These slingshots were pitiful. Sure, we all knew the story about David slaying Goliath, but that was just a story. How did these guys think they could stand a chance against trained, killer knights in armour by using these toys? The spears looked a little more dangerous. The arrows did too, but did the Milago even know how to use them? Suddenly Rellin's concern seemed very real to me. If they tried to fight the Bedoowan, they'd be slaughtered.

I was just about to drop the catapult back in its basket, when somebody reached out and grabbed it from my hand!

I turned in surprise to see Figgis. He danced away from me, swinging the catapult over his head.

"Changed your mind, have you?" he chirped. "Ready to make a trade?"

"I don't want anything from you," I said as strongly as I could.

"No? I have many things you may need," he said with a toothless smile. "How about this?"

He took something from his waist pouch and held it up to me. It was a red Swiss Army knife.

"That's mine!" I shouted and grabbed it away from him. "You went through my pack! What else did you take?" The mystery of why my pack was worked over had been solved. Figgis didn't put up a fight for it. He just cackled out a wheezy laugh.

"I know what you really need," he said slyly. "I know, I know."

"What do I need?" I asked, losing patience.

"You need tak," he announced. "I am the one, the only one who can get it for you."

Tak. There was that word again.

"What is tak?" I asked.

Figgis laughed again and reached into his waist pouch.

"Tak is the answer," he said reverently. "Tak is the hope."

Whatever tak was, it couldn't be very big because it fitted in his pouch. He was just about to pull it out . . . when Rellin walked in.

"Figgis!" he shouted.

Figgis instantly pulled his hand out of the pouch, empty. He looked incredibly guilty.

"You should not have brought him here, old man," Rellin chastised.

Figgis cowered and ran out of the room like a guilty puppy. Whatever tak was, it was clear he did not want Rellin to know that he was trying to sell me some.

"I am sorry you saw this room," he said, sounding tired. "I do not want you to think we still have hope of fighting the Bedoowan. These weapons will soon be destroyed."

Something wasn't right. Rellin wasn't telling me the whole truth. I figured since he wasn't being totally up front with me, then I should be careful about what I said to him. So I didn't mention the tak thing that Figgis was trying to sell me.

"I guess you gotta do what you gotta do," was all I could think of saying.

I didn't like being there, especially since there was something going on that I wasn't clear on. The best thing for me to do then was leave. So I walked past Rellin and out of the door. He didn't say another word to me.

Once away from there, my thoughts went back to the problem at hand, which was Uncle Press. So I ran back to the cell where my gear was. When I stepped inside that room, I saw that Loor and Alder were there and they were going through my stuff! They had it spread out all over the floor. Wasn't there any such thing as privacy around here?

"Hey!" I shouted.

Alder jumped back, embarrassed. But Loor kept right on rummaging.

"I am looking for the weapons you brought back," she said without a hint of apology. "I see no weapons here." She said this while shaking one of the yellow walkie-talkies you sent.

I grabbed it from her and said, "I didn't get any weapons. I wouldn't even know how to use a weapon."

"Then this is all useless," she spat out.

"That's what you think," I said and handed her back the walkie-talkie. I then found the other walkie-talkie and stepped to the far side of the room. I put it up to my mouth, hit the send button and said, "Boo!"

Both Loor and Alder jumped in surprise. Loor threw the walkie-talkie away like it was hot. Alder caught it and then he threw it too. Man, how excellent was that? It was the exact reaction I was hoping for.

"What is this magic?" asked Alder with wide eyes.

"It isn't magic," I said. "You gotta understand, my territory is way more advanced than here. Things like this are pretty common where I come from. It's not magic, it's science."

I picked up the small CD boom box you sent and hit Play. Instantly the first track started to play. It was a head-banger rock song with thrashing guitars that sent Loor and Alder into a panic. They covered their ears and ran to the far side of the room like frightened rabbits. It was awesome. I didn't want to prolong their agony so I turned the music off quickly. The two sat there staring at me with wide, frightened eyes.

"Still think we need weapons?" I asked with a sly smile.

Then I saw something that totally blew me away. Loor looked to me and, believe it or not, she smiled.

"I like this science," she said.

"Me too," added Alder.

So far so good. Their reactions gave me hope that my ideas might work. The trick was to use this stuff the right way and the time to do that was coming fast. I took a quick inventory and saw that you were able to get everything except for the torch. You guys are amazing. I was a little surprised to see that none of the stuff was mine though. I didn't mean for you to go out and get new stuff, or to send your own, Mark. But after I thought about it, I realised that it would have been hard for you to go to my house and get my stuff. My parents would have asked questions and that would have been tricky. So as soon as I can, I'll repay you for everything.

I gave one of the walkie-talkies to Loor and showed her how to use it. If we got split up, these would be crucial. The rest of the equipment I put back in the pack. Alder then added something that was a little surprising. He gave us each clothes that the Bedoowan wear inside the palace. They were simple trousers and jackets with long sleeves. The trousers had pockets and were tied with a drawstring. The jackets closed with buttonlike pieces of wood. They were light, almost pastel colours of green and blue. But the thing that really jumped out at me was that they were soft. The material was some kind of cotton and they were really comfortable. Even the leather shoes were comfortable. If I didn't know better, I'd guess that the Bedoowan did their shopping at The Gap. It really struck me how the Milago lived their lives wearing rough, smelly caveman skins while the Bedoowan wore these coolio, comfortable clothes that were like pyjamas.

Loor didn't want to wear them. She wanted Alder to get us armour from the knights. But Alder explained that the knights were not allowed to wear their armour in the palace. If we were seen inside wearing armour, the Bedoowan would instantly take notice and we'd be lost. Wearing the clothes he gave us was our best chance of blending in. Loor didn't like it, but she couldn't argue with the logic, so we quickly dressed in the Bedoowan outfits.

Alder also had something else of value – a map of the palace. It was crude and drawn roughly on some parchment paper, but it was good enough. It didn't show everything, but it had the key areas we needed to worry about: the cell area where Uncle Press was being held and the guard quarters where the knights stayed. Everything seemed in place except for one small detail. Maybe the most important detail of all.

"This is all good," I said. "But how are we going to get in?"

"There is a way," Alder said. "The Bedoowan do not know of it and very few of the Milago are aware. My brother showed it to me the day before he died."

Now there was some new information. Alder had a brother who died. I wanted to know what that was all about, but now was not the time for chitchat.

"Then let's go," I said.

I put on the pack and followed the others out of the cell. Rather than turn for the main mine shaft to climb to the surface, Alder led us to one of the ore cars.

"No sense in all of us walking," said Alder. "Jump in."

Wherever we were going, it was underground. Loor and I climbed into the ore car and Alder started to push. We headed down the track of yet another tunnel off the main cavern. As we passed some miners, they barely took notice of us. These poor guys were like the living dead.

Alder was a pretty strong guy and he pushed us along with ease. Luckily the tunnel was flat, so maybe it wasn't all that hard anyway. We travelled for a long time and went pretty deep into the mine. After a while it got totally dark, but it wasn't like we had to make a turn or anything, so Alder kept on pushing. As the tunnel started to grow brighter, I looked ahead and saw a small spot of light way in the distance. Before I could ask what it was, Alder said, "The tunnel leads to the sea. The end is not far from here. You cannot enter from the outside because the opening is high in the bluffs. It is to bring fresh air into the mines."

Fresh air, yeah, right. Not fresh enough to get rid of the poisonous gas that was killing all the miners. I then noticed something else weird. Throughout all the tunnels, the walls looked the same. They were made of solid, craggy rock that had been chiselled out by hand. But here it was different. Along one side of the tunnel were round, stone columns. They were wide too, maybe three feet in diameter, and looked to me like big ancient columns from Greek ruins.

"The miners uncovered these by accident many years ago," Alder said. "They are the foundation of the Bedoowan palace."

Whoa! That meant we were directly under the fortress!

"The Bedoowan do not know that the Milago have tunnelled under their palace," Alder added. "If they did, they would have closed this tunnel off and killed some miners in punishment."

There must have been about twenty of these pillars and they were roughly ten yards apart. I saw off to the side, between two of the stone pillars, another tunnel. Actually it was more like a small recess, because just inside it was a ladder. Obviously this ladder led up into the palace. Gulp.

"No one knows why this secret entrance was created," said Alder as we climbed out of the ore car. "It is older than any of the miners who are alive today."

I stood at the bottom of the ladder and looked up. I then looked back at the others. It was show time.

"Let's make sure we're all on the same page," I said. "Our plan is to get to the cell where they're keeping Uncle Press as quietly as possible. If this becomes a fight, we'll lose." I said this while looking straight at Loor. She looked away from me. I knew she agreed, but it was killing her.

"Alder," I said. "Can you get us to the cell area?"

"Yes, I think so," was his answer.

"You think or you know?" I didn't want anything left to chance.

"I know," came his more confident reply.

"Good," I said.

"But it is not going to be as easy to get back unnoticed," he added.

"And that is when we fight," said Loor.

"Yeah, whatever," I said, and turned for the ladder. Jeez, she had a one-track mind. It wasn't until I got halfway up the ladder that I realised I didn't want to be the first one up. What was I thinking? I had no idea what might be waiting for me on top. But it was too late now; we weren't about to change places while dangling in the air. So I continued to climb and ended up on a dark shelf of stone. The ceiling was also stone and it was so low that I couldn't stand up straight. The others quickly joined me.

"Now what?" I asked.

Alder knew exactly where to go. He walked a few feet along the stone ledge and then raised his hands. I looked to see that above him was a wooden door. A trapdoor! Alder pushed it up easily, then hoisted himself through it. Loor was next. She easily pulled herself up. It wasn't as easy for me. Not only was I shorter, but I had the pack on. I stood below the open trapdoor looking up and said, "Uh, excuse me? Little help, please?"

Loor and Alder both reached down, grabbed my out-stretched hands and hoisted me up as easily as if I were a child. We were now in another dark room.

"This leads to a storage room off the kitchen," Alder whispered. I figured that since he was whispering, we were getting close to where we might come across some Bedoowan.

Alder led us across the small room and then felt along one of the walls. I wasn't sure what he was looking for until he found it. There was a small notch carved into the stone. Alder stuck his fingers in and pulled. Suddenly, the wall opened up as if it were a door! We quickly went through and Alder closed the secret door behind us. When I looked back, I saw that once it was closed, you could barely see the seam where the door was. The wall was smooth, as if it were made out of plaster. That seemed weird. Everything I had seen so far on Denduron was crude and rough. This wall seemed almost modern.

I looked around to see that we were in a storage room. There were baskets of food and rough, burlap bags full of stuff. There were also stacks and stacks of earthen pots. I was hit with a bunch of new smells. For the last several hours I had been smelling that nasty, sweet smell in the mines. But now I got the definite aroma of cooking food. I had no idea what it was, but it was making my mouth water. All I could think of was how my house smelled at Thanksgiving. My stomach rumbled. So did Loor's, I'm glad to say.

On the far wall was a wooden door. Alder crept quietly to it and gently eased it open. Instantly, the sounds of banging pots and sizzling food filled the room, like a busy restaurant kitchen. Again my stomach rumbled. I wanted to get out of here as soon as possible because this was torture. Alder waved for us to come and look. Loor and I joined him at the door and peered out. What I saw gave me a total shock.

This was a busy kitchen. Several cooks scurried around carrying large, succulent roast turkeys cooked to a golden brown. Other cooks were peeling vegetables and cutting potatoes on large wooden tables. Others were stirring pots of fragrant soups that bubbled on fiery stoves. But that wasn't the shocking thing. What surprised me was how modern this kitchen was. Believe me, by our standards it was still pretty ancient looking, but not compared to what I'd seen so far on Denduron. The pots were crudely shaped and hammered out of black metal; the ovens were made of stone with fires burning inside. The chefs slid the turkeys and other roasts in and out of these ovens with long paddles. Their other utensils didn't exactly look as if they came from the mall. They were crudely made and very simple but still, this setup was light years ahead of anything the Milago had.

I saw a device that looked like a dumbwaiter. The chefs placed platters of sumptuous, steaming food into a hole in the wall, then pulled on a rope that raised the small elevator and its cargo up into the palace. They even had running water! I saw iron sinks with hand pumps that produced clean, fresh water. Unbelievable. The Bedoowan had running water while the Milago had disgusting sewerholes in their crude huts!

It was then that I noticed the kitchen workers. As they went busily about their chores, they had a different look than anyone else I had seen on Denduron. Their features were all very small and delicate, like perfect dolls. Everything about them was small. Their hands, their feet, and even their height. Their eyes were different too. They slanted down, which gave them kind of an Asian feel. They all wore outfits like we had on, but theirs were white. But the thing that jumped out the most about them was their skin. It, too, was pure white. I don't mean pale-skinned like the Milago, I mean white. Believe it or not, it wasn't creepy. In some strange way, they were beautiful people. They just happened to look like porcelain dolls.

Alder must have been reading my mind because he whispered, "The workers in the palace are not Bedoowan. They are brought from a place across the ocean called 'Nova'."

"Why don't they use the Milago to do their work?" I asked. "They make them do everything else."

"Because they do not want the Milago to see how well they live," answered Alder with a trace of venom. "They are afraid it would cause unrest."

That was an understatement. If I were a Milago and saw this I'd be downright pissed. Heck, I was getting pissed anyway. And hungry. Those turkeys smelled good.

"Look," said Loor as she pointed across the kitchen.

Standing in the doorway was a guy who was definitely not from Nova. He was so big that he filled the opening. He wore the same kind of clothes we had on and stood with his hands on his hips, surveying the kitchen. Around his waist was a leather belt from which dangled a nasty-looking club. I could feel Alder tense up.

"It is a Bedoowan knight," he whispered. "I do not like this. The knights never come to the kitchens. He must be looking for something."

"You think they know we're here?" I asked nervously.

"I do not know," answered Alder. "But if he catches us, we are finished before we even begin."

The knight stepped into the kitchen and slowly walked around to survey things. The Novans paid no attention to him and he didn't acknowledge them either. His eyes slowly scanned the room, taking everything in. We were trapped. In a few moments he would certainly enter this cupboard and find us.

Alder said nervously, "We should go back to the mines. We can wait until he's gone and then return."

"There isn't time," snapped Loor. "When he enters the door, we will overpower him and throw him into the mine."

That wasn't a good idea either. We weren't about to kill the guy; at least I wasn't about to. And he'd be sure to wake up and sound some kind of alarm. And who knew what the Novans would do if a knight entered their pantry and never came out? No, beating up the guy wasn't the answer. I quickly pulled off my pack and dug into one of the side pouches, looking for a better solution.

"What are you doing?" demanded Loor.

"I've got an idea," I answered. "If it doesn't work, we'll do it your way."

I found what I was looking for and quickly moved back to the door. The knight was only a few yards away. There wasn't much time. He looked into a large pot of soup and reached in to take a taste, the slob. That's when I took my shot.

The thing I pulled out was the laser pointer you sent. I clicked it on and aimed the red beam at the pot of soup. From where we were it was easy to see the red laser dot against the black pot. I could only hope that the knight saw it too. He pulled his hand out of the pot and started to suck on his finger to taste the soup, but still he didn't see the laser. Alder and Loor watched the scene over my shoulder. Of course, they had no idea what this laser thing was, but now wasn't the time to ask.

I jiggled the beam a little so that the red dot danced on the pot. The knight stood there sucking on his tasty finger. He was just about to reach back into the pot for a double dip . . . when he saw it. He looked at the jumping dot curiously, without even taking his finger out of his mouth. The idiot. Then I slowly moved the dot off of the pot and let it travel across the stove. The knight, with his finger still in his mouth, followed it. This was like the game I play with Marley and a torch. I'd shine the beam on the floor and Marley would jump at it. The poor dog never got the idea that the spot of light wasn't something she could get her paws on. But that didn't stop her from trying.

That's exactly what happened with the knight. I slowly moved the red laser dot over loaves of bread, past bubbling pots, across wooden tables, down along the floor and back up on the wall. The curious knight never took his eye off of it. He followed the magical red light like, well, like a dog following a torch beam. What he didn't realise, is that I was moving him farther and farther away from us.

Once his back was to us, I silently motioned to the others to get moving. They slowly but silently opened the pantry door and crept out into the kitchen. I was right on their tails, while still concentrating on holding the beam steady to keep the dumbfounded knight entertained. We quickly moved across the kitchen to the exit. The Novans didn't even give us a second look. I was the last one out. My body was already out of the door, but I leaned back in, directing the beam. Then, I turned the laser off and couldn't resist waiting one last second to see the befuddled knight's reaction. It was perfect. He stood still for a moment, then started looking around frantically. Sheesh, even Marley wasn't stupid enough to do that. I wanted to laugh out loud, but I couldn't stay to enjoy the show. We had to get moving, so I followed the other two into the palace.

We had made it. We were in. The next step was to make our way to the cell where Uncle Press was being kept. Alder was already checking the map. All Loor and I could do was follow him and try to blend in. As it turned out, it wasn't all that difficult. The palace was busy with Bedoowan people who all more or less looked and dressed like us. Yes, Loor's skin was a bit darker than most, but not so much that she stood out. If no one recognised us for who we really were, we might just make it. As we made our way through the corridors, what I saw was not only surprising, it made an anger grow inside me that I never thought possible.

The fortress was nothing like I expected. From the outside it looked like an ancient stone castle like they had in medieval times. I had seen pictures of those castles that still stood in England and the interiors were just as crudely simple as the exteriors. Here I expected to see corridors of stone and tiny cell-like rooms. I expected the floors to be of dirt and the light to come from windows or torches. You know, your basic Robin Hood–style castle. But this is not at all what we found inside the Bedoowan fortress.

The kitchen had been my first hint that all was not going to be what I thought. I'm telling you, Mark and Courtney, this place was beautiful! The walls were smooth and painted with light colours. Near the ceilings were elaborate decorative paintings done right on the walls. Some corridors had paintings of vines and flowers that stretched the whole length of the wall. Other corridors had paintings of people who were probably famous Bedoowans from the past. The ceilings were decorated with colourful chips of glass that were sculpted into beautiful patterns. The floors were all tiled with intricate marble work. And the place was totally clean. Every so often we'd pass one of the Novan servants on his hands and knees scrubbing the floors, or dusting the statues that stood on tables like this was some kind of museum.

Loor and I exchanged glances. We were both thinking the same thing. How could these people live in such elegance at the expense of the Milago people? I saw that Loor's jaw was clenching. She was angry too.

We heard music coming from a room we were about to pass. As we went by I glanced in to see a small concert going on. Three musicians sat on chairs playing oddball instruments like I had never seen before. They were string instruments, but they were shaped like human forms. It was really bizarro. The music they played was sweet and soothing. Several Bedoowans lounged around listening on big, cushy pillows. Pillows! These people had pillows! And to top it all off, they had Novan servants scrambling around serving them fruit from large platters.

The more of the Bedoowan people I saw, the more I realised that they were a pretty soft bunch . . . except for the knights, of course. All the others had this kind of baby fat thing going on. The men, the women, even the kids . . . all looked as if they needed to hit the gym. I guess that's what happens when you have nothing to do except lie around, eat stuff, and listen to lame music.

And here is the wildest thing. In every corridor along the walls there were thin glass tubes about the diameter of a nickel. These tubes stretched the whole length of every corridor, and they gave off light! Light! They didn't have electricity here, but they'd figured out some way to make artificial light! The bottom line is that these guys were incredibly advanced. By our standards they were still back in the dark ages, but compared to the Milago they were the Jetsons!

I was amazed at first, but my amazement was replaced by anger. The Milago were dying and living in squalor so that these people could get fat and live in such luxury. It was just flat wrong. The more I saw of how these people lived, the more determined I grew to get Uncle Press out of there so he could help the Milago even things out a little.

All the while I was taking in the rich surroundings, Alder had been leading us through the maze of corridors. The kitchen was on the lowest level of the palace. We had climbed one set of wide, circular stairs to the next level. According to the map, this was the level where the prisoners were kept. Finally we came to an area that was a little less fancy than the rest of the fortress. The walls didn't have paintings on them and the floors and ceilings were bare. I guessed this was where they kept their prisoners, though it was still a lot nicer than where the Milago lived. At a turn in the corridor Alder motioned for us to stop. He took a cautious peek around the corner, then turned back to us.

"There is good news and bad news," he said. "The cell where Press is being held is being guarded. That means he is still there."

"Okay," I said. "What's the bad news?"

"The bad news is that there are six knights keeping guard."

Uh-oh. I took a peek around the corner to see for myself.

Alder was right. There were six guards there. And these weren't fat and sassy Bedoowans, either. These were solid-looking knights. Each was dressed the same as we were and had the same club-weapons hanging from their belts as the knight in the kitchen. This was bad. There was no way we were getting past those guys. I sneaked back to the other two, looked right at Loor and said, "Don't even think about taking those guys on."

"We must do something," countered Loor. "Or this was all for nothing."

Alder added, "And the equinox is fast approaching."

"We gotta get the knights away from the door," I said. "You know how this place works, Alder. What can we do that would make them leave their post?"

Alder thought and then said, "It would take some sort of emergency. Something they had to respond to quickly."

"Keep going," I said. "Think."

Alder looked around. He had no clue. But then his eye caught something near the ceiling. He stared at it for a moment, and smiled. Loor and I both looked up to where his gaze was fixed. What we saw was something that looked like a pipe. It was about six inches in diameter and ran along the wall right by the ceiling.

"What's that?" I asked.

"You have something in your bag," said Alder. "It has a handle, with a jagged metal blade."

I knew exactly what he meant. I dug into my pack and pulled out the hacksaw. This one was even better than the one I asked you for, Mark. All I wanted was the small saw from my dad's workshop. But you gave me this coolio thing that folded in half to fit in the pack. Alder opened it up, locked the saw blade and felt the sharpness of the teeth.

"This is for cutting?" he asked.

"Yeah," I answered. "What are you thinking?"

Alder looked back up at the pipe in the ceiling and said, "That carries water throughout the fortress," he answered. He then looked at us with a devilish smile. It took me a second, but I figured out what his plan was and smiled back.

"You can cut through that thing?" I asked.

"Like soft fruit," was his confident answer.

Loor still didn't get it. "Why would you do that?" she asked angrily. She was ticked that we were a few steps ahead of her.

Alder answered, "I will go a few corridors over and cut out a section of the water carrier."

"It'll make a mess," I said, enjoying the thought.

"Yes, it will," he said, enjoying the idea as much as I was. "And of course the missing piece will not be found anywhere."

"That's perfect, dude. Go!" I said. Alder took off running in the opposite direction, away from the prison corridor. Loor and I hid ourselves in a small room around the corner, waiting for the excitement to begin.

"I did not think we would get this far," she said.

"Neither did I," I replied.

We waited a few minutes, but nothing happened. I was getting nervous. Loor seemed calm. She had her game face on. Maybe she was used to this prebattle moment, but my stomach was a knot of tension. I couldn't take it any more and jumped up.

"I gotta see how he's doing," I said.

"Pendragon, no!" she hissed and tried to grab me. But there was no way I could wait there any longer. I moved quickly in the direction that Alder had gone, peeking down the corridors at each junction, expecting to see him. Finally I rounded a corner and there he was. Alder was standing on a table, sawing away at the pipe. He had already sawed all the way through once and water was leaking down on him. There was a pool of water growing on the floor. But the best was yet to come. With a few final pulls on the saw, he sliced through a second time and pulled down a chunk of pipe about two feet long. The second he pulled it down, water starting gushing out like a berserk fire hydrant. Alder got doused and was nearly knocked over by the force. I sure hoped this was fresh water and not sewage. That would have been nasty. Effective, but nasty. Alder got his bearings, caught sight of me and held up the hunk of pipe triumphantly.

Then suddenly, "*Ahhhhhh!*" A Bedoowan woman had rounded the corner on the far end and saw the waterworks. The alarm had been officially sounded. Alder tucked the pipe away like a football and ran in the opposite direction from me. I was now in the wrong spot and started back to Loor. I had to force myself to walk. I didn't want anyone thinking that I was running away from the scene of the crime . . . which is exactly what I was doing. It was a good thing too, because no sooner did I slow down, than I saw the team of knights that had been guarding Uncle Press come running towards me. Or should I say, towards the screaming woman. They ran past me as if I wasn't even there. I really wanted to stay and watch the madness as they tried to stop the water. But that's not why I was here. It was time to spring Uncle Press.

When I got back to Loor, she was up and peering around the corridor towards the cell. She sensed I was near and turned to face me.

"There is only one guard left," she said. "It is my turn." She reached behind her back and from underneath her jacket she pulled a smaller version of her wooden stick weapon. I had no idea she had it. Sneaky. She was all set to charge, but I stopped her.

"No," I said as strongly as possible. "They don't know we're here yet. The longer we can be secret, the better chance we have of getting out."

"There is no other way, Pendragon," she said seething. She wanted to fight.

I took a quick glance around the corridor to see the guard standing there. Further down, the corridor ended at a balcony. My guess was that this balcony overlooked the ocean.

I had an idea.

"Can you get to that balcony without him knowing?" I asked.

Loor took a quick look, turned to see that there was a parallel corridor behind us, and said, "Yes."

"Then go. I'll send him to you."

Loor wanted to ask how, but I pushed her to go before she had the chance. I figured if the laser pointer trick worked once, it would work again. So I waited a few minutes to make sure Loor was in position, then took the pointer out of my pocket. When I clicked it on, the beam didn't work! I clicked it a few more times, I banged it, I took out the battery to clean it, but nothing worked. It was dead and so was I. I didn't know how much longer the other knights would be occupied with the water geyser, and Loor was waiting for me to do something.

I dug back in my pack, looking for an answer . . . and I found it. It was the radio-controlled stunt cycle. If the batteries failed on this baby, then we were out of luck. I wasn't as good with the stunt cycle as with my four-wheel humvee, but I understand why you guys couldn't go to my house to get it. It was going to be the stunt cycle or nothing. I still remember the day you got this for your birthday, Mark. We both picked up on the radio controls pretty quick and had that cycle taking air off ramps in no time. The plastic helmet on the driver still had the scars from all the times he landed on his head. But I wasn't planning any tricks with him today. All I wanted him to do was drive straight and smooth. If I could pull that off, then we might have a chance.

So I took the little motorcycle out of my pack, reached around the corner of the corridor, and put him on the floor. My plan was to send it slowly past the guard, but I didn't want him to see me standing there with the radio controls. I had to do this blind. I took a breath, then pushed the forward stick. The motorcycle hummed to life with that familiar whine. I wasn't sure how fast it was going, but I couldn't take the chance of looking too soon. If I sent it off course, I was dead. If I sent it too slowly, the guard might just bend over and pick it up. So I forced myself to count to ten, then I peeked an eye around the corner.

I saw exactly what I wanted to see. The guard was standing at the door, dumbfounded, staring at the little man on the motorcycle. I can't imagine what was going through his mind. I couldn't tell if he was curious or scared. Probably a little bit of both. I had the motorcycle moving on a perfectly straight line, headed for the far end of the corridor. So far so good. But just as the cycle was about to roll past him, the guard took a step forward and reached down to pick it up.

I quickly hit the throttle and the cycle shot ahead, just barely out of his grasp. Maybe I was better at this than I thought. This seemed to get the guard's curiosity up even further, and he walked after the cycle. Perfect. This was like playing a fish on a line. I teased him by slowing up. When he would bend down to pick it up, I shot it forward. The whole time he kept moving closer and closer to the balcony on the far end of the corridor where Loor was lying in wait.

With one final push on the throttle, I accelerated the motorcycle forward and it shot out on to the balcony. The guard walked out behind it. He looked down, then hesitated because he expected it to move again. But it didn't. He stared at it for a second, then suddenly bent over and snatched it up with one quick move. But his victory was short-lived because he never stood up again. Loor jumped out and whacked him with her ministick. With two quick moves she slammed the guy, pivoted, and sent him sailing over the rail into the ocean. Mission accomplished and we hadn't given ourselves away.

I quickly reached into my pocket and pulled out my walkie-talkie. "Get Alder," I commanded into the yellow walkie. Loor definitely heard me, because she took off running along the balcony and out of sight. I put my walkie-talkie away and looked to the cell door. There was nothing left between me and Uncle Press but that door. So I quickly grabbed my pack and ran for it.

It was too much to expect that the door would be unlocked, and it wasn't. There was an old-fashioned keyhole, but of course I had no key. So I dug into my pack to look for something that might help me open the door. All I could come up with was the Swiss Army knife that I had nabbed back from Figgis. I opened up the awl blade and stuck it into the keyhole, figuring I might be able to turn the lock somehow. But it didn't work. I jammed the awl up and down desperately. If I couldn't open the lock then maybe I could break it. I think that's exactly what happened, because with one final twist, the latch moved and the door opened. I was in! Or should I say, Uncle Press was out.

"Uncle Press!" I shouted as I ran in. "It's me! We've got to get – "

The small cell was empty. Uncle Press wasn't there! I didn't understand why it would be guarded if there was no one to guard. The answer came quickly.

"Ahhhhh!" Somebody jumped me from behind. He leaped up on my back, wrapped his legs around my waist, and tried to wrestle me to the ground.

"Let me outta here, ya filthy Bedoowan pig!" he shouted. The guy wasn't very heavy, or very strong for that matter. All I had to do was spin once and he went flying off. He landed on the hard floor with a loud thud that must have knocked the wind out of him. I looked down and saw that this definitely wasn't Uncle Press. It was a grimy little guy dressed in Milago skins. His hair and beard were incredibly long, which meant he'd been here for a long time.

"Where's my uncle?" I shouted.

The strange little man looked up at me with confusion in his eyes. "You . . . you are not Bedoowan?" he asked.

"No! I'm here to get my uncle. Where is he?"

The guy took a while to answer. I guess he wasn't used to this much excitement. Join the club, neither was I.

"You must be . . . Pendragon," he said.

"Yes! And I'm looking for my uncle. Do you know where he is?"

"They took him," answered the Milago prisoner. "Early, before the suns came up. He is to be executed today."

Yeah, I knew that. This guy wasn't helping much. I didn't know where to turn. Uncle Press could be anywhere. My mind raced but I didn't come up with a single answer. I was in total brain lock when my walkie-talkie came to life.

"Pendragon," came Alder's voice. "I found Press. He is not in his cell."

I grabbed my walkie and said to him, "Yeah, I know. Where is he?"

"I am with him now," he came back. "I will direct you to us. Hurry."

We were back in the game. I glanced at the Milago prisoner and said, "Now's your chance. Get out!" Then I turned and ran out of the cell. I quickly ran back towards the mayhem that Alder had caused. The water was still gushing out of the pipes and the corridor was totally flooded. Knights and Novans worked together trying to stop the flow, but they were doing a lousy job. Good. It kept them busy.

Alder then came through the walkie-talkie saying, "Go back to the stairs and climb two more levels."

Got it. I did what I was told. But when I entered the stairwell I saw something down below that nearly made my heart stop. Coming up fast from the lower level were a dozen knights. And these guys were in full battle gear, carrying spears. I think some kind of alarm must have finally sounded. They knew we were here.

One of them looked up and saw me. "There he is!" shouted the knight.

Yep, they knew we were here. The knights began to run. There was no way I could outrace these guys, so I played my final card. I pulled the CD boom box out of the pack, held it in front of me, cranked the volume and hit "Play." Instantly the thrashing rock guitar blasted out of the speakers.

It was like I had thrown a bomb at these guys. They froze in their tracks with a look of total shock on each and every face. They had never heard anything like this before and probably never would again. They turned and fled back down the stairs in total panic. Under other circumstances I would have thought this was pretty funny. Right now it just felt like victory. I left the boom box on the stairs, figuring this would be as good as putting up a gate to keep them down there.

"Pendragon, hurry!" came Alder's voice through the walkie.

As I started to run back up the stairs, I grabbed my walkie and called to him, "I'm almost on the fourth level."

"Turn left at the top and go to the end of the corridor," he instructed. "We're hiding in the last room to the left, before the balcony."

I tucked the walkie away and ran to where he told me. My mind was working ahead to the next few moves. We had to find Loor and get out. But we couldn't get back out through the kitchen because I had the knights trapped down there. There had to be another way out. Hopefully Alder had one, because I sure didn't.

I got to the top of the stairs, made the turn and ran down the corridor. I realised briefly that this corridor was more ornate than any we had seen so far. There were huge sculptures and giant paintings on the walls. It would have been pretty cool, if I weren't so scared out of my mind. But I had reached my destination. The last room on the left was where Alder and Uncle Press were waiting for me. Hopefully Loor was there too. I ran into the room and skidded to a sudden stop.

It took all of a half second for me to realise that this had gone terribly wrong. I turned to run back out, but two Bedoowan knights jumped in front of me, blocking the door. I was trapped. Slowly I turned back to see Alder standing there holding the walkie-talkie. A knight had a spear to his throat. Alder looked as if he were about to cry.

"I . . . I am sorry, Pendragon," he cried. "They were going to kill her."

Two other knights were holding Loor. One had her arms, the other held a knife to her throat.

"You should have let them," she spat out in defiance. There were a few other people in the room too. Seeing them is why I knew all was lost. One of them was Saint Dane. Or Mallos, as he calls himself here. He stood with his arms folded and a smug smile on his face. But it was the final person in the room who gave me the biggest surprise of all. This person was seated on a large, ornate throne that was decorated with cut pieces of glaze. I didn't need to be told who it was. This was the heir to the throne of the Bedoowan. This was the monarch who had their father killed so they could begin their tyrannical rule over the Milago. This was the person who ordered the deaths of Milago as easily as ordering more glaze. This was Kagan's throne room, and seated on the throne was Kagan.

The thing that surprised me though, is that Kagan was a woman.

"Hello, Pendragon," said Saint Dane. "Lovely day for an execution, don't you think?"

The one person missing from the room was Uncle Press.

DENDURON

"This is the Milago boy I have heard so much about?" said Kagan with a sneer. "His odour offends me."

Gee, thanks, lady. Nice to meet you, too. I have to describe to you guys what Kagan looked like because she was a real piece of work. First off, she was fat. Not just baby fat chubby, we're talking gordo. I'll bet she kept that kitchen downstairs pretty busy. She wore a flowing yellow toga dress that didn't do much to hide her rolls of chub. Luckily the dress went to the floor and had long sleeves because I didn't think her arms and legs would be a pretty sight. The dress didn't hide her feet, though. She wore these sandals that her toes poked out of like stuffed sausages. Not a pleasant picture. She also had a double chin of fat that hung down over the neck of her dress. Ick.

I have no idea how old she was. She could have been eighteen or thirty or any age in between. The fat stretched her skin so much that it gave her a smooth, baby look. Of course, she wasn't a baby; she was a monstrous, evil queen with fat toes. Everything about her was big. Her hands, her feet, her head, even her eyes. Oddly enough, with all of the size she had going on, her mouth was tiny. Such a little hole didn't belong on this immense, doughy face. She had long hair too. But it wasn't shiny and combed; it hung down over her shoulders and looked like it hadn't been washed in a few months. Nice, huh? She was like some kind of bizarro cartoon sumo wrestler woman.

She had multiple drapes of silver necklaces, bracelets that travelled halfway up her arms, and rings on every finger. She also had a tiara perched on top of her head that looked kind of stupid because it was too small. On any normal head it would look fine, but her big, old, round, greasy-haired dome made it look like a doll crown on a giant. Of course, all of the silver jewellery was adorned with glaze. The precious blue stones were cut in every shape and size imaginable. It must have taken the Milago miners a week to dig up this much glaze. Her throne was decorated with glaze as well. There were baseball-sized stones mounted all over the golden chair.

As I took all of this in, I kept thinking about the Transfer ceremony where that miner died because they hadn't brought up enough glaze. I can honestly say that I have never hated anyone in my life. But this lady was in line to be the first.

"Show me the toy," she commanded. Her voice was high and squeaky, like fingernails on a blackboard.

The knight who was holding Alder grabbed his walkie-talkie and handed it to Kagan with a subservient bow. She took it and inspected it from all angles.

"What sort of magic is this?" she asked.

I couldn't resist. I took my walkie, hit the send button and said, "Put it down!"

Bad move. Kagan let out a yelp and dropped the walkie like it was alive. It hit the floor with a clatter and a knight immediately crushed it with his boot like an annoying bug. I stood there holding the second walkie (which was now totally useless) wishing I hadn't pulled that stunt. Kagan hoisted herself up out of her throne and waddled towards me, her jewellery jangling as she walked. She stared down at me with those big, round black eyes, raised a meaty hand, then hauled off and slapped me across the face.

Yeow. That stung. But I wouldn't give her the benefit of letting her know how much, so I clenched my teeth and forced back my tears. I looked to Kagan and oddly enough, it seemed as if she were holding back tears too. She looked at her hand, then looked at me with genuine surprise and exclaimed, "You hurt my hand!"

Say what? Whose fault was that? I guess it was mine, because instantly two knights ran up to me and jammed the points of their spears in my neck.

"Whoa, whoa!" I yelled. "Sorry. It won't happen again!" What I wanted to say was: "Gee, sorry I hit your hand with my face, chubby." But I figured it wouldn't be a good idea to be a wise ass. Especially when I had two spears at my throat.

"Let him go," commanded Mallos/Saint Dane.

The knights pulled their spears away, but stayed on either side of me. Kagan fell back into her throne, sobbing like a pouting baby. Mallos comforted her by saying, "Shall I call the surgeon, Your Majesty?"

Surgeon? You gotta be kidding me.

"No," sniffled Kagan. "I will be brave."

Give me a break. This lady was a piece of work all right.

"He will be punished." Mallos added, "Along with his uncle."

This was bad. We came to rescue Uncle Press, and now it looked as if I was going to join him in whatever horrible fate they had planned. Some rescue, huh? Mallos then left Kagan and walked to me.

"Press will be so happy to see you," he said to me with an oily smile.

"Where is he?" I asked, trying to sound like I wasn't totally petrified.

Mallos answered me with a laugh. He turned to Kagan saying, "This boy is a spy like his uncle, like this girl" – he walked to Alder and stared him square in the eye – "and like this traitor Bedoowan." Mallos leaned close to Alder until their noses nearly touched. Alder was scared, but tried not to flinch. Mallos said, "I always knew you were a traitor, but I needed you to deliver Pendragon."

Alder dropped his head in shame and embarrassment.

Loor struggled in anger to pull away from the two knights who were holding her, but as strong as she was, these huge knights held her tight. To stop her from struggling, one of the knights gave a quick jab with the knife he was holding to her throat. My stomach turned when I saw a trickle of blood flowing down her neck. But Loor wouldn't flinch. She wouldn't let the guy know he had hurt her. I wasn't surprised.

Mallos then walked to the throne saying, "They are all conspiring to incite the Milago into a revolt against us, your majesty. And for that they should be put to death."

Things were falling apart, fast. "What do you mean 'us'?" I shouted at Mallos. Then to Kagan I said, "He's not a Bedoowan! Ask him where he comes from!"

Kagan looked at Mallos. Was there a hint of doubt in her mind? If I could expose Mallos as being a Traveller from a different territory, maybe Kagan wouldn't buy everything he had to say. It was a long shot, but the only thing I could think of.

"It's true and I can prove it. Who thought of the trick to

get me here? It must have been Mallos. Nobody else knows how those walkie-talkies work, right? A Bedoowan wouldn't know how to use that magic."

Kagan looked at the crushed walkie on the floor, then to Mallos. I was getting through to her.

"Mallos isn't a Bedoowan," I said with authority. "You can't trust him!"

She sniffed back her tears, looked at Mallos, smiled, and said, "Of course, Mallos is not a Bedoowan. He came to us many years ago from the far side of the ocean and has been my most trusted advisor ever since. Why do you tell me things I already know?"

Oh well, so much for my brilliant plan. She already knew. Kagan reached to the table next to her throne and grabbed a piece of purple fruit. It must have been past her feeding time, which was probably every five minutes. She took a big sloppy bite and a river of purple juice ran down her chin and landed on her ample chest. I wanted to puke. When she spoke, it was with a mouth full of fruit goo. Did I mention I wanted to puke?

"Why are you trying to get the Milago to make war with us?" she asked in her squeaky, annoying voice. It was weird; she sounded all innocent, like a three-year-old asking why the sky is blue. Was it possible that she didn't know how bad the Milago had it? Was Mallos really the guy who was calling the shots and using this creepy, child-woman like a puppet? I figured I'd better answer carefully.

"Because they have horrible lives," I said. "They live in dirty, mud huts and they don't have enough food. If they don't mine enough glaze, they are murdered. But the worst thing is, they're dying. The air in the mines is poisoning them. They want to fight because they are desperate for better lives."

That about summed it up. I didn't want to accuse the Bedoowan of taking advantage of them, that might get her mad. But I wanted to paint a picture of how bad the Milago had it. If Her Royal Chubness didn't know these things before, maybe now she would think twice about what her people were doing and have a little sympathy.

She took another juicy bite from her purple fruit and stared at me. What was she thinking? Alder and Loor watched her, waiting for her reaction. Mallos looked bored. Kagan then tossed the juicy wet fruit stone on the floor. Instantly a Novan servant appeared from behind the throne, cleaned up the stone, then disappeared again. No wonder this woman was so fat. She didn't have to lift a finger to do anything.

Kagan then said innocently, "That is how it always has been. The Milago dig for glaze so that the Bedoowan can trade it for lovely things. It has been this way forever."

Wow. Could she really be so clueless? She didn't think there was anything wrong with the Milago suffering and dying for them. I glanced to Loor and she had the same look of dumbfounded surprise on her face that I'm sure I had. Alder just kept looking down at the floor. I think he already knew where Kagan's head was. I wasn't sure of what to do next, but I had to say something.

"And what do the Bedoowan do for the Milago in return for their hard work?" I asked.

Kagan cocked her head in surprise, as if I were asking something she had never thought of before. It reminded me of the way Marley turns her head and her ears go up when she hears a strange sound. Before answering, Kagan reached for another piece of purple fruit and started gnawing on it. She made these little grunting, slurping sounds that turned my stomach. What a pig. The whole while she gazed off into the distance, as if she were giving some serious thought to the question I had asked. I couldn't wait to hear the answer because from what I saw, the Bedoowan do nothing for the Milago except abuse them. Alder and Loor waited for the answer as well. Even Mallos looked at the queen in anticipation.

Kagan took another messy bite of her fruit, swallowed, then looked right at me and said, "Your questions make my head hurt." She then looked at Mallos and said, "Kill them."

Whoa, bad response. Instantly the knights grabbed me and started dragging me and Loor and Alder towards the door.

Loor put up the best fight. She screamed back at Kagan, "It does not matter what happens to us! The Milago will not be slaves forever!"

That was very bold and all, but I was kind of thinking it *did* matter what happened to us. The knights dragged us out into the corridor and towards the stairs when I heard Mallos calling from behind.

"Wait," he shouted. "I wish to speak with that one!"

That meant me. The knights stopped dragging me along and Mallos approached us. He looked at me for a long while, as if sizing me up.

"Remember what happens here today, Pendragon," he said seriously. "This is how it will be. There is no hope for you. Halla will fall, and you will fall with it."

He then looked at the knights and ordered, "Take them to the box." As the knights dragged me away, Mallos called, "Remember, Pendragon!"

What was he talking about? I expected him to say something like: "The Milago are doomed!" or "You will all die a horrible death!" or some other nastiness. But instead, what he said made no sense. What is Halla? Osa had said something about Halla before she died, but I had no idea what she was talking about. More important, if I was about to die, then why did he tell me to remember what was going to happen? The way things were going, I wasn't going to live long enough to have time to forget. Believe it or not, as scared as I was, Mallos's words gave me hope. They reminded me that this was actually a larger battle than it seemed. It wasn't just about the Milago and the Bedoowan. It was about the future of the whole territory of Denduron. If Mallos threatened that he would always defeat me, then he must expect there to be more battles. And maybe that meant he wasn't planning to kill us after all. At least that's what I hoped.

The knights dragged the three of us to the circular stairway. I expected them to bring us down to the prison area, but instead we went up. We climbed one more flight of stairs and were then hurried down a wide corridor to a wooden door with a heavy lock. One of the knights pulled out a big old key, opened the door and shoved us inside. Behind us, the door slammed with a booming crash and we found ourselves in the dark. I think we were all too stunned and scared to look around. Not that there was anything to see.

"Is this it?" asked Loor, sounding bold as ever. "Is this where we will die?"

"No," said Alder. "This is not where we will die." Alder seemed pretty calm about the whole thing. It was strange. Alder was a pretty nervous guy in general, but now he acted all casual in the face of certain death. I guess of the three of us, I was the only one who was actually scared. Not fair.

"How come you're so calm?" I asked.

I didn't like his answer. He said, "Because this is the holding area. Nothing will happen to us here. When they are ready, they will bring us to the horror."

I guess that meant Alder wasn't being casual, he was in

a state of shock. He knew this was the calm before the storm. Something was coming and the thought of it was so horrible that it frightened him far beyond the point of showing nervousness.

"What will they do to us?" asked Loor.

She didn't have to wait for an answer. A door creaked open on the far side of the room and bathed the place in bright sunshine. Once the sun came in I saw this was a cell, with shackles on the walls and leg irons on the floor. Two knights in full battle gear stood at the open door. One of them motioned for us to come outside. We knew we had no choice, so we walked towards the sunlight. Loor took the lead, but before she went she turned to us and said, "I will not die without taking some of those Bedoowan animals with me." She then turned and left, with Alder and I close behind.

When we stepped into the sunshine, I was blinded and had to shade my eyes. Before they adjusted, I got a strange feeling. I think maybe it was the sound, but I had the feeling we weren't alone. Once my eyes adjusted I realised that not only weren't we alone, we were standing in a huge stadium along with thousands of other people. This was the Bedoowan version of a sports arena. It was open air. Above our heads was blue sky – we were on the top level of the Bedoowan palace. Two days before when I had looked across the inlet to the bluff above the palace, I thought it was just barren land. But now I realised that from where I was I couldn't look down into this arena that was dug below the surface.

The stadium was square. It reminded me of one of those arenas where they play tennis matches. My guess was that the place could seat a few thousand people. And it was packed. Each side of the arena held a different tribe. One side was all Bedoowan. They sat on cushioned seats with pillows for their backs. The next section was taken up by the Novan servants who sat on long bleachers. It was odd seeing so many of these pure white doll people in their white uniforms. The next section was full of Milago. It was obvious they were Milago because of their filthy leather clothes and the fact that they weren't even allowed to sit. They had to stand on stone tiers. My guess was they entered the arena from above, since they weren't allowed to walk through the palace. The fourth side was nearly empty. Halfway up the stands there was a box with a throne. Obviously this was where Kagan sat.

There were high walls with spikes built between the sections so there was no way the tribes could mingle. But even if the Milago wanted to get a little rowdy, they couldn't because there were armed knights ringing the top of the stadium. They stood as sentries, lining the entire top tier with their spears at the ready.

We stood in a section right next to the playing field below Kagan's box. There were no seats here, only a low barrier between us and the field. At least, I thought it was a playing field, but I wasn't exactly sure what game they played here. The flat area was about the size of a baseball diamond. The surface was grass, but there weren't any lines or markings that would show the boundaries for a game. It was just a plain, grass field.

I looked up at the various tribes in the stands and saw that each group acted very differently. The Bedoowan were chatting and seemed relaxed. Some smiled, others laughed. There were kids, too. It had the feel of a baseball stadium before a game. The Novans sat quietly looking down at the field. Most had their hands crossed in their laps politely and didn't move a muscle. Their faces were blank. I couldn't tell if they were happy to be here or not. The Milago were much easier to read.

They were restless. They kept glancing up at the guards that surrounded the stadium. It was obvious that they weren't here by choice, and it wasn't for entertainment.

Unfortunately I was afraid that Loor and Alder and I were the main attraction. I leaned over to Alder and asked, "What kind of game do they play here?"

Alder's eyes were riveted on the playing field. "This is no game, Pendragon," he said softly.

Before I could ask any more, I heard chimes. They were three simple notes that sounded like they came from a loud, but pleasant xylophone. All eyes turned to the empty viewing box above the playing field. I looked up too and saw two knights walk out into the box, followed by Mallos, who was followed by Kagan. She didn't wave to the crowd or anything the way you would expect a queen to acknowledge her subjects. She just lumbered to her throne and plopped herself down like a bored, spoiled little kid. She was eating again too. Big surprise. It looked like she was gnawing on a turkey leg. The entire stadium was now quiet except for the slurping and grunting sounds as Kagan finished off her latest snack. I really would have been grossed out, except for the fact that I knew whatever was going to happen, was going to happen soon. My heart started racing. I'm not sure what would have been worse – knowing our fate or not. The fear of the unknown was terrifying. Either way though, the show was about to begin.

Kagan looked up to Mallos and said impatiently, "Well?"

Mallos took a few steps forward and motioned down to the playing field. Instantly I saw a small door open on the opposite side of the field. A few seconds later somebody was pushed out from inside and tumbled down on to the grass. Obviously this guy didn't want to be here. In a few seconds I realised who it was – the scrawny Milago prisoner who was in

Uncle Press's cell. I guess he didn't get away when he had the chance. The poor guy looked scared. He pulled himself to his feet and looked around the stadium while shielding his eyes from the suns.

As if on cue, the Bedoowan spectators let out a loud, football-like cheer. This startled the guy and he stumbled away from them to the centre of the field. At the same time, the Novans applauded politely. There was no yelling or whistling from them, just polite applause that ended as quickly as it began. The Milago didn't do anything but watch in silence. The guy backed to the centre of the field because it was the one place where he could be the farthest away from everybody. He stood in the centre, alone, his eyes darting around the stands with confusion and fear. He seemed to be looking for help. Then, his eyes finally fell on me. That's where he stopped. It was creepy. I didn't know what to do. Was I the only familiar face in the crowd? Did he want me to wave or something? I looked back at him, feeling helpless.

Then something strange happened. He was a bent over, old guy who had a rounded back that I assumed came from working in the mines his whole life. But as he stood staring at me, the fear left his face. He stood up straight, pushed his shoulders back, then touched his heart and held out his hand towards me. He even gave me a small smile. I know this sounds bizarro, but I felt that somehow by seeing me, he got some kind of strength. Believe me, I have no idea why it happened. It's not like I did anything or could help him, but after he saw me, it was like he transformed. Whatever was about to happen, he was now ready, and I played some small part in that.

We didn't have to wait long to find out what was in store

for the guy. On the right side of the arena from where we were sitting was a door that was larger than the one the Milago just came through. Two knights ran across the grass field towards it. There was a big brass latch that was so heavy it took two of these big knights to release it. Once the latch was undone, they threw the door open and ran for the stands. The scene reminded me of movies I'd seen of bullfights. I looked into the dark recesses beyond this large open door and expected to see a bull come charging through.

As it turns out, I wasn't that far off. I heard movement and snarls beyond that door. All eyes were riveted on the opening, including Loor's and Alder's. Even the Bedoowan stopped their socializing for a moment to look with anticipation.

A quig beast leaped through the doorway and crouched down on all fours. The Bedoowan section let out a cheer. The Novans applauded again and the Milago cringed. Some hid their eyes, others stood straight as if the least they could do for their fellow tribesman was to honour him by having the courage to watch.

The quig scanned the arena with yellow hunter's eyes, ready to spring as soon as it found quarry. It curled its black lips back from its teeth to reveal sharp rows of deadly fangs. Even from where I was I could see drool dripping down its chin in anticipation of the hunt. My mind quickly flashed back to the quig that Uncle Press nailed with the spear and of how the other ravenous quigs devoured one of their own, ripping its flesh from the bone while it was still alive.

I glanced up at Kagan, who stared intently at the quig with a smile on her face. Without taking her eyes off the animal, she took a huge bite out of her turkey leg. At once the idea of a bullfight left me. This wasn't like a bullfight at all. This was like one of those Roman Coliseum spectacles where they threw the Christians to the lions. The Bedoowan wanted to see blood. Their wish was about to come true.

The Milago prisoner had remained still ever since the quig had entered the arena. And why not? There was nothing for him to do. He was too frail to fight and had no place to run. Mallos made a gesture to one of the knights near the arena floor and the knight threw something to the Milago. It was one of those stick weapons like Loor used. But there was no way the Milago miner could use this puny weapon to defend himself. I think it was given to him in hopes of having the battle last more than a few seconds. That's the best the guy could hope for. He picked up the weapon, but just from the way he held it I knew that he had no clue how to use it. He might as well have had a pillow to fight off the quig.

The coiled quig sniffed the air. It had caught scent of the Milago. Its body tensed, zeroing in on its prey.

I looked up to Kagan and saw that she had put her turkey leg down and was leaning over the rail in anticipation. Mallos stood behind her with his hands clasped behind his back. He turned and looked right at me. I looked away. I didn't want to see this guy any more.

Then the quig attacked. It crouched back on its legs like a cat and sprang at the poor Milago miner. The Milago turned and ran. It was heartbreaking and horrifying. He ran to the side of the arena, but there was no safety there. So he started to run around the circle with the wooden weapon dragging behind him.

Loor couldn't take it. She made a move to jump out and rescue the doomed miner, but the instant she took a step, Alder stopped her. It was a good thing, too. She wouldn't have much more of a chance against this beast than the scraggly miner.

The Milago in the stands watched silently. I could see the agony on their faces. The Novans watched silently as well. I couldn't tell how they felt about what was going on. Then I looked to the Bedoowan. The horrible thing was, these people were laughing. The sight of a Milago miner running for his life was a big joke!

The quig kept its distance from the Milago miner, almost playing with him like a cat plays with a mouse before killing it. After a few moments, the Milago miner realised it was futile to run around the ring, so he stopped and turned back to face the beast. He raised the wooden stick, but there wasn't a person watching these events who thought it would help him beat back the vicious animal. Time seemed to stand still. The Milago stood with the stick weapon at the ready. The quig crouched a few feet away, swaying its massive head. Everyone in the stadium held their breath.

And then the quig jumped. The Milago miner held up his stick to defend himself. The last thing I saw was that the quig swept it out of the way with a mighty swing of his clawed paw. The stick flew across the arena and when it landed, I was horrified to see that the Milago miner's hand was still clutching it.

I looked up towards Kagan and the other Bedoowan. What I saw there was almost as horrible as the carnage that was taking place in the arena. Kagan sat forward on her chair and clapped her hands with glee like a little girl watching clown tricks. The other Bedoowan were laughing uproariously as if this were some kind of slapstick comedy. And through it all, I could hear the sounds of the quig tearing at the flesh of the Milago miner. The doomed man gave one quick yelp and then he was silent. Luckily he died quickly. All that was left was the feeding. It turned my stomach and made me hate the

Bedoowan even more for their total lack of compassion for another living being.

Mallos looked at me and smiled. This may have been the most horrible moment of all, because I felt in that second that he had staged this whole spectacle for my benefit. The idea that I may have been responsible for this, in any way, made my stomach hurt.

The show was over quickly. I knew it was done because the Bedoowan applauded as if the quig had just staged a fine performance. The Novans applauded politely as well, though with much less enthusiasm than the Bedoowan. The Milago just watched in horror. A few of them were crying.

Then a few more chimes sounded. Instantly six knights rushed into the ring with ropes. Three of them held spears on the quig, while the others lassoed its neck and began to drag it back towards the large door. Now that it had fed, it was much more calm than before. It actually went without a fight. I saw the blood dripping from its jaws as it was led back to the door leading to the quig pens. I looked back to the spot where it had attacked the Milago miner. All that was left of the poor man was a wet, red spot on the grass. A Bedoowan knight filled a wooden bucket with water from a tap near the quig pen, then quickly rushed over to the spot of the kill and poured it on the blood. The water and blood sank into the grass as if they had never been there.

Then two more chimes sounded and a terrifying thought came to me. We were next. We had been shown what our fate would be and now it was our turn. I looked around, expecting the knights to prod us into the arena. But they didn't. I looked up to Mallos to see what he was doing. He looked back at me and pointed to the sky. I looked up and realised what would happen next.

In the sky the three suns were about to converge on each other. It was the equinox. Then I heard another door open inside the arena. It was the same door where the doomed Milago miner tumbled out before. But there were no more Milago to be executed today. What I saw at that door made my heart sink. A man stepped out into the sunlight standing up straight, with his head held high. I think I actually gasped when I saw him.

It was Uncle Press. It was the equinox, and he was the next to die.

DENDURON

Uncle Press walked defiantly to the centre of the killing ring. It was only a few days since I had seen him last, but with all that had happened it felt like it had been months. It was strange to see him dressed in the leather skins of the Milago. I was used to seeing him wearing jeans and his long coat that would flap in the wind as he rode his motorcycle. But things had changed. Though he was still Uncle Press, he also looked like any other Milago miner with his three-day-old beard and messed-up hair. But unlike the other Milago, Uncle Press had an air of confidence. The Bedoowan stopped talking and laughing. There was now tension in their section of the stands, as if this newest gladiator was going to prove to be more of a match than the last.

I looked to the Milago spectators and saw that they were watching his arrival in pretty much the same way. But rather than the look of fear they had for the poor Milago prisoner who had just been devoured, they now seemed to have hope that maybe, just maybe, the visiting team might have a shot here. Only the Novans reacted the exact same way as before. They gave Uncle Press some polite, emotionless applause.

Even though Uncle Press looked all sorts of confident, it was going to take more than confidence to beat a charging, hungry quig. Still, something about the way Uncle Press carried himself gave you the feeling that if any man could beat a quig, it would be this one. He stood in the centre of the field and looked up at all the spectators. He did a 360 turn, and stopped when he laid eyes on the Bedoowan section. I could see that he was shaking his head and knew what he was thinking. It disturbed him to think that these people were gathered to watch blood sport.

In the royal box Kagan didn't sense any of this tension. She was being her normal, oblivious self as she sat on her throne, gnawing her turkey leg. Mallos leaned down and whispered something in her ear. Kagan answered with a shrug that told me she didn't care one way or the other about what Mallos had asked her. Mallos bowed to Her Royal Chubness, then stepped to the front of the box and surveyed the people in the stadium. He raised his hands and all eyes immediately went to him. Even Uncle Press looked up to see what this evil puppet master had to say.

"People of Denduron," he bellowed. "The man you see before you has been accused of the high crime of treason. He is guilty of plotting to destroy the peaceful balance of our society and of inciting the Milago into overthrowing the great reign of our beloved Queen Kagan." When he said this, he looked to Kagan. Kagan acknowledged his look with a loud, deep belch. What a class act.

Mallos didn't react and continued, "For this crime he has been sentenced to death at the equinox, when the light is the strongest so we can all bear witness to his punishment. Let this execution serve as a reminder that the natural order must never be disrupted. To try and change the normal course of events is a crime against humanity, and punishment will be harsh and swift. Long live Denduron. Long live Queen Kagan. Death to those who oppose the throne."

Mallos then made a motion to the field and two knights ran across the grass to open the door to let in another quig. It was clear what this was all about. Mallos was using Uncle Press as an example to scare the Milago out of their rebellion. The Milago trusted Uncle Press. In seconds another quig would leap out of that dark door and attack. It would mean the end of the rebellion and the death of my uncle. And the way things were going, Alder, Loor, and I would be the next victims in the ring.

As scared as I was, I realised that there was an even bigger picture unfolding here. Uncle Press had brought us here to try and bring peace to the Bedoowan and the Milago. It was a tribal feud that Mallos (or Saint Dane) was doing a fine job of fuelling. By eliminating Uncle Press, and us, there would be nothing to stop the Bedoowan from destroying the Milago. The territory of Denduron would fall into chaos, and Mallos's evil mission would be complete.

That is, unless I did something to stop it. I knew exactly what I had to do. I was scared out of my mind, but still, I knew what had to be done. Before I had the chance to chicken out, I jumped over the barrier that separated our box from the field and ran towards my uncle.

"Pendragon!" shouted Loor with surprise. I think she was totally shocked that I was the first one to take action for a change. I hadn't told her what my plan was. There wasn't time. But she must have figured I had something in mind, so she and Alder quickly followed after me. I know what you're thinking, Mark, and you're wrong. I hadn't gone delusional. I hadn't suddenly I got all hero macho and figured I could whup up on a quig. It wasn't like that at all. But I had an idea and if I was right, it might give us all a chance of getting out of there alive.

I ran up to Uncle Press and stood beside him. I expected him to see me and be totally surprised and shout something like: "Bobby, no! Go back! Save yourself!" But he didn't. Instead he looked down at me as if he were expecting me to show up all along and calmly said, "I forgot to tell you, that Courtney Chetwynde is pretty cute."

I've got to hand it to the guy, he was cool. Maybe a little crazy, but cool.

Loor and Alder quickly joined us. Loor had scooped up the wooden weapon that the Milago prisoner had used and was ready to wield it. I was glad to see that she had separated it from the guy's severed hand first.

Then suddenly a cheer went up from the Bedoowan crowd. I knew what that meant. I looked to the animal entrance and saw a huge quig lumber out of the darkness. This one was even bigger than the first. The spines on its back grazed the top of the doorway as it came through. It seemed slower, too, but that may be just because it hadn't got its blood boiling.

Yet.

Loor jumped between us and the quig and shouted, "I will go for its eyes."

I guess she felt that fighting was the only chance we had. Big surprise. So she squared off against the beast, prepared for it to charge. She must have realised that fighting this thing would be suicide. But fighting was what she knew, so she was ready.

Uncle Press seemed oblivious to the impending danger. He turned to me and said, "I'll bet it's been an interesting few days."

Was he kidding? Here we were about to be attacked by a vicious beast with three-inch fangs and an appetite for human flesh and he was making small talk! Maybe he didn't think we stood a chance against the monster and decided to spend his last few moments in peace.

I had one last trick left from the stuff you two sent me and it was time to use it. I have to admit, this was the one item I didn't think you could come up with. I knew there wouldn't be a problem getting the laser pointer or the Swiss Army knife or the wristwatch or any of the other stuff, but I knew this last item would be tricky to find. I was thrilled when I saw it in the pack. To be honest, I hoped I wouldn't have to use it, but here I was and it was in my pocket and it was the only chance we had. Thank you, guys.

The quig spotted us. Or maybe it had smelled us. It didn't matter which because either way, it was starting to circle for the attack. Its ghastly yellow eyes were trained on us, looking for the right moment to spring. We crowded together, trying to look bigger than we were. I glanced up at the stands and saw that every eye in the stadium was on us. They were ready for the show. Only this time they were expecting a killing frenzy because there were four tasty morsels being served to the quig, not just one.

Loor said, "When it attacks, get behind me."

"No," I said with as much authority as I could gather.

Loor gave me a quick glance of surprise, then focused back on the quig. "Do not be foolish, Pendragon," she said. "I am the one with a weapon."

Before I could tell anyone what I had planned, the quig reared up on its back legs, bellowed, then galloped towards us. Loor started to run to meet the beast, but I grabbed her belt with one hand and held her back.

"Pendragon!" she yelled at me.

I didn't let go. I held her tight and with my other hand I pulled out my last trick . . . the silent dog whistle. I put it to my lips, and blew for all I was worth. Instantly the quig skidded to a stop and cried out in pain, just as the quig had done on the mountain when Uncle Press and I were speeding away on the sled. But this modern dog whistle must have produced a sharper sound than the hollow wooden whistle I used on the mountain because the reaction from this quig was much more dramatic. This quig crashed to its knees and screamed so loud I thought its head was going to explode. But I wasn't about to cut it any slack. As soon as I emptied my lungs, I took another breath and blew harder than the first time.

The quig screamed in pain. I glanced around the stadium and saw every single person staring back in openmouthed shock. Every person except for Mallos, that is. Mallos simply cocked his head to one side as if this latest development were nothing more than a minor, interesting surprise.

"What is happening?" shouted Alder.

Loor stood stunned as well. Only Uncle Press wasn't surprised. Finally he kicked into gear.

"The quig pens, go!" he commanded. Then as an aside to me he said, "Cutting it a little close, aren't you?"

He knew I had the whistle all along! How could he have known that? Maybe he didn't know I had dropped the one he gave me in the mountains. Either way, he was calm because he knew I would use the whistle to stop the quigs. I gotta say it again, the guy is cool. And I'm glad he was back in action now because my plan didn't go beyond blowing the whistle to stop the quig. I had no clue of what to do next, but Uncle Press did. That was good. His plan had us escaping through the only avenue open to us . . . the holding pen where the quigs were kept. That was bad. But he was right, there was no other way, so we all ran for the door.

The crowd watched in stupefied awe. It was Kagan who made the first move. She jumped off her throne, ran forward still clutching her turkey leg and squealed out, "Stop them!"

One of the Milago spectators yelled out an impassioned, "Run!" The other Milago spectators took his lead and started to cheer for us too. It was like they had all suddenly snapped into delirious football fan mode as they cheered for us like we were running a hundred-yard kickoff return. It was the most life I had seen from these people since I got here. Maybe seeing us escape from that ring was the first time their side had a chance of winning. For those few moments it was like every one of those Milago were down on that field with us, running for freedom.

But what lay ahead was every bit as deadly and dangerous as what we were escaping from. As we ran I continued to blow the whistle and the quig kept writhing in agony. Suddenly I felt a hand on my shoulder and I was jerked to a stop. It was Uncle Press. It was a good thing he stopped me because if I had taken one more step I would have walked right into the path of a spear that was thrown from the top of the stadium by one of the knights. The spear screamed down and stuck into the ground like a javelin in the exact spot where I was heading. I had been so focused on the quig that I forgot there were Bedoowan guards swarming the place. I looked up and saw them all running down the stadium steps towards us. Worse, several had unleashed their spears and the dark, deadly shafts were raining down on us from above.

"Keep your head up, keep moving," commanded Uncle Press.

Uncle Press had the presence of mind to grab the spear

that had barely missed me. Loor took one as well. I didn't grab one. That little metal whistle was every bit as powerful a weapon as those spears and I wasn't about to lose this one the way I lost the whistle on that sled. I'd leave the sharp stuff to those who knew how to use it.

With the Milago miners cheering deliriously and the spears stabbing the ground around us, we made it across the field and into the dark tunnel. Just before ducking in I glanced up at the royal box and at Mallos. I didn't like what I saw. I expected him to be leaning out of the box, shouting commands at the knights to stop us. After all, this was his big demonstration to the Milago and it was falling apart before his eyes. But that's not what I saw. Instead I saw Mallos standing next to the throne with his arms folded, looking calm. I could swear that he had a smug smile on his face. Maybe I was reading too much into it, but it was almost like he wasn't surprised by what was happening. No, it was like he was enjoying it! Could he have anticipated this? Were things playing out the way he wanted them to? I remembered his words to me back in the palace. Though he was sending us to certain death, he spoke as if this wouldn't be the last battle between us. Of course, the question was, if this wasn't the last battle, what was?

I couldn't think about it too long, for we were in the process of jumping into the fire outside of the frying pan and I needed to keep my head on straight. I was the last one into the tunnel and away from the falling spears. But before I got too far along I heard a command barked from behind, "Stop!"

I looked back and saw two Bedoowan knights standing in the large open doorway. They each had their spears drawn back, ready to throw, and I was way too close for them to miss. The others had already disappeared into the gloom of the quig pen ahead of me, so it was just me and the knights.

It looked as if after all I'd been through, it was going to end with one of these knights skewering me with his harpoon.

As I stood there staring back at the knights who were about to kill me, I froze . . . and stopped blowing the dog whistle. It was still in my lips, but there wasn't any blowing going on. I was too scared. That's what happens when you are seconds away from death.

The knights cocked their arms ready to throw their spears. All I could do was hold my breath and brace against the impact. My only thought was: "Oh man, I hope this doesn't hurt too bad."

That's when my saviour arrived. With a screeching howl the quig from the ring came back into play. It charged the knights from behind and slammed them both to the ground with a giant paw on each. When I stopped blowing the whistle, the quig had got its act back together . . . and now it wanted revenge. I actually felt bad for the two knights because they were seconds away from a bloody death. The quig let out an angry bellow that shook the ground. Though the two knights had been about to kill me, I couldn't stand seeing anyone die the way they were about to. So I took a breath to blow the whistle and stop the quig. Before I could blow, Uncle Press grabbed my hand.

"Save them and they'll kill you," he said soberly.

He was right. If the knights got away, they wouldn't be grateful, they'd try to kill me again. Then they'd go after the others. No, this was war, and the knights were going to be the next victims. I nodded to Uncle Press and he let me go. He walked further into the dark pen and I turned to follow. I don't think I will ever forget the sounds I heard behind me as I ran. I won't even describe them to you because it was too horrifying. I will say this: Their deaths weren't as quick as the Milago prisoner's. That's because the quig had to work its way through the knights' armour first.

For a moment I felt a surge of guilt. Not about the two knights who were being devoured, but for the poor Milago miner who had died in the ring earlier. I had been so stunned by the quickly unfolding events that I hadn't thought to use my whistle. Could I have saved him? I don't know for sure. I'll never know. My only solace came from the fact that if I had tipped my hand back then, we wouldn't have got together with Uncle Press, who was now helping us make our escape. Maybe all things happen for a reason.

But our escape was not yet complete. We now faced a different danger. We were in the bowels of the quig pen. I could only hope that there was another door somewhere that would lead us out. There had to be another way out. The trick was to stay alive long enough to find it. Sunlight sneaked in through the cracks in the rock walls, sending bright slices of light throughout the place. Because these light beams were so bright, they created deep shadows everywhere. That's what I feared. The shadows. There could be quigs lurking there, ready to spring.

The quig pen was nothing more than a big cave that had been dug out of the rock. The cavernous space was broken up by low walls made of stone that acted as corrals for the quigs. I figured that out because a few of the pens had heavy metal chains attached to the walls that I was sure were used to restrain a quig. In each of the large pens there was some kind of haylike material spread out, I guessed to soak up whatever the beasts decided to deposit. It wasn't doing a very good job, though. The place smelled vile. Remember how I described the smell that came from the latrine hole in the Milago hut? Well, multiply that by about a thousand and you'll have the smell of the quig pen. It was a combination of quig waste, rotten meat, and death.

Uncle Press turned back to me and said, "Keep that whistle handy."

Yeah, right, like he needed to remind me of that. If I held that metal whistle any tighter it would have snapped in two. Uncle Press walked on cautiously, with his spear at the ready. I walked close behind him, though I didn't like being last. I kept glancing back over my shoulder to make sure nothing snuck up from behind. After walking for a few moments, I heard something that made me stop short. It was a growl and it was coming from the pen to my right. I snapped a look and saw a quig lying there on its side. It must have been the quig that just ate the Milago prisoner, because it was looking all sleepy and relaxed. This monster had no interest in us. It was grooming itself by licking its giant paw. The blood it licked off was the final clue that it was indeed the quig who had just feasted. Gross. I continued walking while keeping my eyes on the bloated quig . . . and tripped over something. When I looked to see what it was, I swear I almost barfed. It was a leg bone. A human leg bone. I knew it was human because the skeleton foot was still attached. I scanned more of the floor and saw that there were tons of bones scattered about. It became disgustingly clear that feeding time for the quigs meant the death of more Milago.

We continued to walk along and I saw that there were many quig corrals, but no more quigs. I guess they didn't keep many down here at one time. That was fine by me. Maybe the two quigs I saw today were the only quigs down here. But looking around this dark labyrinth I saw many tunnels that led off to places unknown. There could very well be a quig down any one of them who would catch a whiff of us and come running. I wasn't about to relax until we were out of there.

Then Uncle Press stopped and held out a hand to still me. He had heard something. I listened and heard it too. Something was coming towards us. Fast. I put the whistle to my lips, ready to blow my lungs out, but Uncle Press stopped me. He wanted to make sure what it was first. Good thing too, because as it turned out it wasn't a quig. It was Alder. If I had blown the whistle, I might have woken up a napping quig.

Alder ran up to us out of breath and said, "Loor has found the way out. This way!" He then turned and ran back the way he came.

Excellent. We were one step closer to getting out of there. Uncle Press nodded to me and took off running after Alder. I followed close behind. We ran through the dark tunnels as quietly as possible so as not to sound the dinner bell. After a few turns I began to see light up ahead. We were headed towards a section of the quig pen that was brighter than where we'd been. We made one last turn around a rock outcropping and I saw why.

There was a large, round hole in the rock ceiling. I saw blue sky above. I even heard the sound of crashing waves. We were right on the edge of the bluffs. The hole was big, maybe about the size of your above-ground pool, Mark. It was just about the right size for a quig to fit through. I now saw how the Bedoowan managed the quig pen. All they had to do was shove a quig into the hole from above and it would fall into this cavern and be trapped. The only way out was through the door to the stadium. I guess once a quig was down here, it never left because the hole was too high for an animal to crawl back out. Of course, that also meant it was too high for *us* to climb out of too. Our freedom was a mere thirty feet away, but it was thirty feet straight up and out of our reach. I had no clue how we could possibly make it.

But Loor did. When Alder and Uncle Press and I arrived at the hole, she was busily tying a long vine to the end of her stolen Bedoowan spear.

"There is a rope up there," she explained quickly. "I will get it down for us to climb out."

I looked up and saw that sure enough there was a thick rope that looped down below the hole. My guess is that this was an emergency escape route for any unlucky Bedoowan who happened to stumble down here. One of his buddies could drop the rope from above for him to climb out.

"Make it fast," said Uncle Press. "We gotta get out before the knights catch up."

He was right. Even if we got out of here, that didn't mean the Bedoowan knights wouldn't be waiting for us on top. They may have been barbaric, but they weren't idiots. If this were the only way out, they would be heading for this hole for sure. The faster we got out, the better chance we had of getting away. Suddenly I was less concerned about the quigs than about what we might find above.

Loor expertly tied the long vine to the spear and stood up. She tested its weight since it was now imbalanced because of the vine. Then she looked up at her target. To be honest, I had no doubt that she would nail this on the first shot. That's how good she was. With a grunt of air, she javelin tossed the spear up at the dangling rope. It flew towards the ceiling with the long vine trailing behind like a contrail. The spear made a perfect arc through the loop of the hanging rope and careened back towards the ground. Loor had just threaded a needle thirty feet in the air. The trailing vine draped over the loop of rope with both ends now touching the ground. Alder quickly grabbed the vine and gave it a yank, pulling down the rope. Our escape route was set. Loor had done it. I told you, she was good.

Now as I looked up at that rope, all that came to mind was the dreaded rope climb in gym class. I hated that. Some guys could climb that rope like monkeys. I wasn't one of them. Sure I could get up, but it wasn't quick. And right now, speed was a good thing. But what choice did I have? None. All I could do was hope that adrenalin would help me climb this thing.

Loor started up first. I wasn't surprised to see that she climbed it like one of the aforementioned monkey boys. I don't think she even used her legs. She muscled up the rope as if gravity weren't an issue. She got to the top in seconds and climbed up through the hole. She scanned the outside and leaned back down to say, "We are alone. Hurry."

That was good. The knights hadn't figured out what we were doing yet. Maybe they *were* idiots after all. Loor then threw something down to us. I had to duck out of the way or it would have hit me. When I looked back, I smiled with relief. It was a rope ladder. I guess not all the Bedoowan were as strong as Loor. Some of the weenies had to take the easy way up, like me. I had no problem with that.

Uncle Press grabbed the bottom of the ladder and held it taut.

"Alder, go," he commanded.

Without hesitation our Bedoowan friend began his climb. He was kind of a big, clumsy guy so he wasn't as quick on the rope as Loor. Still, he was on his way up and that was good. As he climbed, Uncle Press looked to me and for the first time he smiled.

"That was a brave thing you did, Bobby," he said. "Jumping in the ring like that."

I was feeling pretty good about myself. Granted, I was pretty sure the whistle would work, but still it was a scary thing to do. Maybe I even impressed Loor. But even though I was feeling all proud, I had to act the way all good heroes act at a time like this.

"No big deal," I said with as much humility as I could muster. "You would have done the same thing."

I looked up and saw that Alder was struggling, but he was almost at the top. I took the few seconds left before it was my turn to ask something that was bugging me.

"You weren't surprised to see me," I said to Uncle Press. "How come?"

"I know you, Bobby," was his answer. "Maybe better than you know yourself. I knew you'd come after me. And since you had the whistle, I knew you'd use it."

I don't think Uncle Press realised how close I was to *not* coming. I thought back to where my head was when I first arrived on Denduron and I was ashamed to remember how rescuing Uncle Press was pretty low on my list of concerns. But you know, the bottom line is that I made the right decision. So maybe it's okay to think like a weenie sometimes, so long as you don't act like one. There's a grand philosophy in there somewhere. I'll leave it up to you guys to figure out what it is.

"You were right," I said. "Except for one thing."

"What's that?" Uncle Press asked.

"This isn't the whistle you gave me. I lost that when we hit that boulder."

Uncle Press gave me a quizzical look. It was the first time I saw doubt in his face since we started this adventure.

"I don't get it," he said. "Did you make another one?"

I held up the silver whistle and said, "No, this is from home."

Uncle Press quickly let go of the rope ladder, then swiped the whistle out of my hand.

"How did you get this?" he demanded. "Did you bring it with you?"

Uh-oh. Something told me I had done a bad thing.

"N-No," I said nervously. "I wrote to my friends and told them I needed one. Then I took the flume back to the subway and – "

Uncle Press did something stunning. He took the whistle, whirled, and threw it up and out of the hole in the ceiling!

"Throw it in the ocean!" he shouted to Loor above. "Now!"

Loor obeyed without question. She picked up the whistle and threw it. Uncle Press then spun back to me and stared me down with a look of intensity that made my knees buckle.

"I told you," he seethed. "We can only use what the territory has to offer! That's why I didn't bring the gun with me."

My mind was spinning. That's exactly what he had warned me about, but frankly, I forgot.

"Did you get anything else from home?" he asked.

Uh-oh again. Not only had I got some other things, I left them scattered all over the Bedoowan palace. I wasn't sure why this was such a bad thing, but from the look on Uncle Press's face, I had made a grave mistake. Before I fessed up we heard a noise. It came from deep down in one of the tunnels that stretched out behind us. Uncle Press and I both whirled towards the sound. We listened a moment . . . then heard it again. Yup, it was a growl. Turned out there were more than two quigs in the cavern after all and from the sound of things, our new company had just woken up.

"Climb," commanded Uncle Press.

He didn't have to tell me twice. I grabbed the rope ladder and started up. I tried to go fast, but climbing a rope ladder is not like climbing a regular ladder. A regular ladder is solid. A rope ladder is soft and swings. As soon as you put your foot on one rung, it bends down under your weight. If you're not completely balanced the ladder will twist. And if you aren't careful where you put your foot, it can easily slip off and that would be disaster. So I tried to climb fast, but the faster I climbed, the tougher it got.

Alder called down from above, "Hurry, Pendragon."

Yeah, thanks for the tip. My foot nearly slipped off a rung and I had to hang on for my life. The movement caused the ladder to swing and I had all that I could do to get my balance back. Uncle Press wasn't holding the ladder at the bottom either, which made it more tricky. I looked down and saw that he was staring off into the depths of the cavern. He must have sensed that I was watching him because without looking up he shouted, "Climb!"

Another bellow came from deep within the cavern. Only this was louder and closer. The quig had definitely picked up the scent and was on its way.

"Come on!" I shouted down to Uncle Press.

"No!" yelled Loor. "It is not strong enough for two."

"There it is!" said Alder, pointing into the cavern.

As I kept climbing I glanced back. A quig appeared from out of the shadows, stalking closer. It was hunched down like a hunting cat, with its belly grazing the ground. Any moment now it would pounce. All Uncle Press had to defend himself was the Bedoowan spear. Why had he thrown away the whistle? If I still had it, he would be safe. Now he was back in the same position he was in at the stadium, only this time I couldn't help him. I was near the top and stole a quick look down to see that Uncle Press was sliding a heavy, flat rock towards the bottom of the ladder. What was he doing? I climbed up two more rungs and was high enough now to reach up for Alder and Loor. They each grabbed one of my hands and hoisted me up.

"I'm up!" I shouted down to Uncle Press. I quickly scrambled around and the three of us looked back down into the cavern. The quig was only a few yards from Uncle Press and stalking closer. Its horrible yellow eyes were focused on him. If Uncle Press started to climb, the quig would pounce and easily pick him off. His only choice was to fight, and fighting a quig could only end in death. Not for the quig, but for Uncle Press. History was repeating itself. Someone I cared for was about to die so that I would live.

The quig stopped advancing as if it sensed that Uncle Press was more dangerous than the average Milago miner. It crouched, facing Uncle Press, who stood holding his spear at the ready.

I was surprised to see that the first one to make a move was Uncle Press. But he did a curious thing. He relaxed. He lowered the spear and held it down at his side. Why was he doing that? It was like he was giving himself up. He stepped over the heavy rock that he had pushed under the ladder and held his hands out in surrender. To the quig it must have looked as if Uncle Press were opening himself up to be eaten without a fight. The quig didn't move. It must have been just as confused as I was. But its hesitation didn't last long. It was suppertime. The quig coiled, wagged its butt, and with a snarl it launched itself at Uncle Press.

Uncle Press barely moved. As soon as the quig had committed itself, he jammed the tail of the spear against the rock that was now behind him. At the same time he dropped to one knee and angled the spear up towards the flying quig. The quig realised too late that Uncle Press had set a trap and that it was now sailing towards a six-foot spike! Yes!

The quig landed on the spear. It impaled him through the chest and came out of his back. The weapon didn't move because it was anchored by the heavy rock. Uncle Press let go of it and did a dive roll to the side just before the wounded quig fell to the ground. But the battle wasn't over. The quig was injured, but the spear didn't seem to have pierced anything major. The angry animal squirmed and screamed and writhed on the ground like a fish out of water, but it was still very much alive . . . and dangerous. Uncle Press had to get out of there fast.

He leaped for the rope ladder. The quig saw this and swiped at him, but his claws bit into the air below his feet. Uncle Press was much better at climbing than I was. He flew up the ladder as if it were rock steady. Yet the quig wasn't done. Judging from its pained bellows it was in horrible agony, but it still wanted a piece of Uncle Press. It squirmed over to the rope ladder and with a sweep of its mighty paw, grabbed on to it and began to pull. The quig must have been eight hundred pounds. There was no way this flimsy rope ladder could withstand that kind of pressure. I looked next to me to see that the top of the rope ladder was tied to a tree. The point where it was tied was dangerously frayed as if it had been rotting in the rain.

"Look!" I shouted.

Loor and Alder looked to see how the rope ladder was going to break right on top. Loor didn't stop to think. She jumped over me and grabbed on to the rope. This was crazy. The rope ladder was going to break and if Loor were hanging on when it went, she'd go down with it. Alder realised this and ran to Loor. He sat behind her, grabbed her waist and dug his heels in. Maybe the strength of two would be enough. Or maybe the strength of three. I had to help. It was crazy, but it was the only thing to do. I dived behind

Alder and grabbed him around the waist. That's when I heard the *snap!* The rope ladder broke from the tree. Loor held on tight and became the only link that kept it from falling into the pit. I could see the muscles in her arms bulge as she fought desperately to hang on. Alder held on to her and I held on to Alder but we all started to slide towards the edge of the hole. We dug our heels in, desperately trying to stop. I felt the tension in both of their bodies as we strained against the weight of the ladder, of Uncle Press, and of the quig that was pulling from below.

It felt like we were hanging on for hours, but it was probably only a few seconds. Where was Uncle Press? Did the quig get him? Were we hanging on just so that the quig could pull its bad self out from the hole and eat us? It didn't really matter, because we weren't going to be able to hang on much longer.

Then, finally, just as we were about to go over the edge, I looked up and saw the welcome sight of Uncle Press's head poke up from below. He crawled to the surface, rolled away from the rope and shouted to Loor, "Let it go!"

She did. The rope whiplashed away and we all fell back. A second later I heard the heavy sound of the quig hitting the ground below. It let out a yelp of pain. Good. Served it right.

As we all lay there, trying to catch our breath, I looked down the bluff towards the stadium. It was about three hundred yards behind us. We had travelled quite a way in the quig pen. It was hard to believe that a huge stadium was dug below the surface, and even more amazing was how, beneath the stadium, was an elaborate, multilevelled palace.

A moment later I realised that we weren't safe yet. The Bedoowan knights had finally figured out what we were doing. Several of them were now climbing up out of the stadium to come after us.

"We've got to move," I announced while pointing back to the palace.

Without another word we all jumped up and ran for the woods. Our best hope was to lose them in the dense forest that surrounded the Milago village. Compared to what we had just come through, this was going to be a piece of cake.

Loor led the way again. She took us on another romp through the forest, but this time I knew what to expect. I was in for another gruelling cross-country trek, but I didn't care. The further we got away from the palace, the more I realised that we had done exactly what we had set out to do. Uncle Press was running next to me because we had saved him. We went in, we found him, and we got him out. How cool was that? Better still, my adventure was almost over. As soon as we got him back to the Milago village, he could take charge of their rebellion and I could go home. So even though we were running like scared deer through the forest, I began to relax because my job was nearly complete. I already started plotting how I would go back down into the mines, make my way to the flume, and launch myself home, for good.

Loor ran us a long way around. We were on the far side of the farmland, maybe a half mile from the Milago village.

"Can we rest awhile?" asked Alder.

I was happy that it wasn't me who burned out first, for a change. So we stopped and the four of us stood together to catch our breath. After a few seconds I looked to Loor and smiled, but she didn't smile back. Neither did Alder. I looked to Uncle Press and he scowled back at me. What was going on? Was it because I had used the dog whistle from home? Okay, maybe it was against the rules, but if I hadn't done it, we'd all be on the inside of some quig by now. I think I deserved a little more credit than I was getting. Before I had the chance to say something about it, we heard a sound. It was a loud, sharp *pop,* like a firecracker. No, it was louder than that. It was more like a cherry bomb. Both Loor and Alder tensed. Uncle Press shot a glance in the direction of the sound too. From the look on his face I could tell that something was wrong. It didn't seem out of the ordinary to me, though. I hear sounds like that at home all the time. It could be a car backfiring, or fireworks, or even somebody's TV. But we weren't at home. Whatever made that sound was something out of the ordinary for Denduron.

There were two more pops. *Crack. Crack.* Uncle Press jogged towards the sound. The rest of us followed.

We travelled a short distance through the woods until we came upon the edge of a clearing. This was an area I hadn't seen before. It was past the Milago farmland and not exactly on the beaten track. Uncle Press hid behind a tree to watch what was going on. We all followed his lead. What we saw seemed to be some kind of target practice. On one side of the clearing was a line of scarecrow-type figures that were crudely made out of straw. Opposite them was a group of Milago miners, each holding one of the catapults I had found down in the mines. The miners were practising throwing stones at the scarecrows. They each had a pile of rocks at their feet that were about the size of walnuts. They would put one of the stones in the catapult, spin it overhead, and release it. They were pretty accurate, too. But still, a small stone being flung from a catapult wasn't going to do much to stop a knight in full armour.

I then found out how very wrong I was.

Someone stepped forward holding a small basket. It was Figgis, the crafty little salesman. He walked up to each of the throwers and held the basket out to them. The throwers reached inside and took out another kind of rock. These new stones looked very different. They were about the same size as the stones they had been flinging, but they looked soft and rusty red coloured. It seemed to me these new rocks would do even less damage than the rocks they had been flinging, yet the shooters held them gingerly as if they were precious. The first shooter loaded a new stone, spun the catapult over his head and let it fly. The rust-coloured stone shot across the clearing towards its target. When it hit the scarecrow, the scarecrow exploded in a ball of fire!

Whoa! The Milago had some kind of explosive that detonated on impact! Those were the loud pops we were hearing. I looked to Loor and Alder. They were just as shocked as I was. Uncle Press watched intently. Nothing surprised him.

The next miner flung his stone at a scarecrow and it too erupted in a ball of fire. Figgis jumped up like a child and clapped with delight.

"Where did they find such a thing?" asked Loor.

"They didn't find it," answered Uncle Press. "He did," he said, pointing to Figgis.

The odd little man held the basket of explosives over his head and danced a jig. He was having a great time.

"I knew that little guy was up to something," said Uncle Press. "But I didn't know what . . . until now. He must be selling the stuff to the Milago."

One word sprang to mind. Tak. That's what Figgis was trying to sell me. It was a weapon. An explosive. He said that "tak was the way" and maybe he was right. If there was enough of that stuff around, the Milago could use it against the Bedoowan and the odds of beating them would suddenly be very good. Maybe there was hope for them after all. Tak may indeed have been the way.

But Uncle Press looked worried. He didn't like what he saw.

"What's the matter?" I asked him.

"If the Milago use that, it will be the end of Denduron," he answered soberly.

We all looked to him in surprise.

"End of Denduron?" I said. "Am I missing something here? That stuff could help the Milago beat the Bedoowan. Isn't that the point?"

Before Uncle Press could respond, all hell broke loose. We were attacked. But it wasn't the Bedoowan knights who caught up to us, it was a group of Milago miners. They jumped us from behind and wrestled us to the ground. One put a knee to my back and jammed my face into the dirt.

"Hold them," someone commanded.

I struggled to look up and see who was giving the orders and saw Rellin stride up past the miners. What was happening? These were the good guys, right? Why were they attacking us? Did they think we were Bedoowan? Rellin surveyed the scene to make sure that none of us could escape, then his eyes fell on Uncle Press.

"Hello, Press," he said. "I wish I could say that I was happy to see you."

Two miners pulled Uncle Press to his feet and held him opposite Rellin.

"You can't do this, Rellin," said Uncle Press.

"I am glad that you are alive," said Rellin. "But do not try and stop us."

"Listen to me," said Uncle Press with passion. "I want you to defeat the Bedoowan. You know that. But using that weapon is wrong. It will change everything."

"Wrong?" spat Rellin. "How could it be wrong to end our misery? Without tak we have no hope of defeating the

Bedoowan. But with it, we can return centuries of pain and torture to them in a few short seconds."

"But at what cost?" asked Uncle Press.

Rellin smiled at him and then said, "Let me show you something." He walked towards the clearing and motioned to the miners to follow with us. The miners pulled us to our feet and we were dragged along after him. There was no use in fighting; there were too many of them. I wasn't really sure we should be fighting them anyway. Up until a few minutes ago they were on our side. Now, well, now I didn't know what was happening. Same old, same old.

Rellin entered the clearing and the Milago miners instantly stood to attention. That was a surprise. Maybe these guys were more organised than I knew. Could all of the cowering and silence have been an act to make the Bedoowan think they were pushovers? Rellin walked over to something that looked like a big box that was covered with a large, brown blanket. He stopped there and turned to us.

"Soon we will begin the battle of our lives," he said proudly. "But it will not last long thanks to you, Pendragon."

Me? What did I have to do with any of this? Uncle Press shot me a look. So did Loor and Alder. All I could do was shrug. I had no idea what he was talking about.

Rellin continued, "Tak is powerful, but it is delicate." Figgis appeared next to him and held up his basket. Rellin reached in and took out a piece of tak that was no bigger than a pea. "All it takes to release the power is a small impact."

Rellin threw the pea down on the ground and it exploded with a huge bang that echoed through the forest. There was a blast of flame and smoke that left a deep, jagged hole in the ground the size of a water barrel. Man, that stuff really *was* powerful. Figgis giggled. I wondered how much he charged for each piece of tak.

"It is dangerous to use any more than a small amount," said Rellin. "But we had to find a way to use more. We had to find a way to release the power of enough tak to deliver a single, crushing blow to the Bedoowan. We have not been able to find that way, until now."

He reached under the brown blanket and pulled something out that made my heart sink. It was a heavy-duty twelve-volt battery, the kind you use in big torches. At first it didn't make sense to me. Where did he get that? Then it hit me. I guess you guys sent me a torch after all. The reason I didn't find it was because Figgis must have stolen it from my pack when he took my Swiss Army knife.

Rellin held the battery up and said, "Such an interesting device you brought to us, Pendragon. I do not know why, but it too gives off power. And it is a power that can be controlled."

He then reached under the brown blanket and pulled out the torch. He looked at it admiringly and played with the on-off switch. I looked to Uncle Press. I wanted to apologize, but it was too late for that. Uncle Press didn't look at me. His jaw was set and he stared at Rellin.

Rellin then continued, "We can now use the power of this strange device to release the awesome power of tak." He said this while switching the flashlight on and off. "One little push will unleash as much tak as we desire. The Bedoowan will fall, and they will suffer greatly for how they have treated us."

I now realised where this was going. They were going to make a bomb. They weren't satisfied with throwing little bits of explosives in slingshots. No, they wanted a big bang, and I had delivered the means for them to do it. They were going to use the electricity in the battery to set off a huge bomb. Nice going, Bobby.

With a flourish Rellin pulled away the brown blanket that was covering the big box. What lay beneath wasn't a box at all. It was one of the ore cars from the mines. To my horror, I saw that it was filled with tak. There must have been a few hundred pounds of it. Judging from the big explosion that came from a very small bit of tak, if this load blew up it would be like a nuclear bomb going off.

"This is a mistake, Rellin," Uncle Press pleaded. "You think this will save the Milago? You're wrong. If you use this weapon, you may find yourselves free of the Bedoowan, and slaves to a new power. The power of tak."

I immediately realised what Uncle Press was worried about. The Milago were on the verge of creating a weapon of horrible power. If they used it, it would alter the course of Denduron forever. Not only would there be devastating destruction, but once these simple people used the power of this explosive, where would it end? Already they weren't satisfied with using small bits of tak. They wanted more power. It was like the Milago skipped over gunpowder and jumped right into the nuclear age . . . and Armageddon.

The crazy thing was, this all came about because of two people who never could have foreseen the outcome of their actions. There was me, who stupidly brought the last piece of the bomb puzzle from home. And there was Figgis, this strange little man who lived by scrounging things and selling them to whomever had the coin to pay. Figgis had struck the big time now. He wasn't selling jumpers and knives any more. No, Figgis was now a merchant of death, and the people he was selling to were eager to buy.

It was clear to me now. The turning point for Denduron

wasn't the battle between the Milago and the Bedoowan. It was the introduction of this strange and horrible new power into the territory. As I looked at that deadly load of explosive in the ore car, there was something else that became clear. I wasn't going home. Even if I could get to a flume, there was no way I could go back now. No way. Not after the damage I had caused. I had no idea what to do, or how to stop this horror from happening, but I resolved then and there to stay and see this through to the end . . . even if the end meant my own death.

This may be the last journal I write to you, Mark and Courtney. If it is, then please know that it wasn't your fault about the torch. All you did was help out a friend. The blame is all mine. If you don't hear from me again, then please know I did everything I could to undo the mess I created. I may not be successful, but at least I tried. Thank you for reading this, and for being my friends.

Hopefully this isn't a final good-bye.

END OF JOURNAL #3

◉ SECOND EARTH ◉

Mark threw the parchment pages down on to his bedroom floor angrily.

"We should have known!" he shouted. "It was as much our fault as it was Bobby's!"

Courtney and Mark had waited until they got back home to Stony Brook before reading Bobby's latest journal. After saying good-bye to Bobby in the abandoned subway station, their journey back home was uneventful. They travelled the same route as the one that brought them to the flume in the Bronx, taking the subway to 125th Street and catching the first commuter train back to Connecticut. Once back in their hometown, they went straight to Mark's house and locked themselves in his bedroom where they could read Bobby's journal in private.

"It's not our fault!" argued Courtney. "The Milago are like a step above primitive. How could we know they'd figure out how to make a bomb with that stuff?"

"Because we read the journal," countered Mark. "We knew the same things Bobby did. Press told him never to bring anything from one territory to the next. We read that, but we did it anyway!"

Mark paced the floor out of sheer nervous energy.

"We helped Bobby," argued Courtney. "And maybe we helped the Milago, too. To be honest, I hope they do make a bomb that'll blow those Bedoowan creeps away. They deserve it!"

"You don't get it," argued Mark. "The Milago aren't ready for this kind of power. They don't know how to control it."

Now Courtney was getting angry. She jumped up and said, "What are you saying? Only socially evolved, brilliant people are allowed to blow themselves up?"

"No," Mark shot back. "It takes socially evolved brilliant people to figure out how *not* to blow themselves up. Look at it this way. The Milago are pissed off and they should be. The Bedoowan have been torturing them for centuries. Now suddenly they're given a weapon that's so powerful they can wipe out their enemies with the push of a button. They don't really understand it. They really don't know how to control it, but they're angry enough to use it anyway. If that tak stuff is as powerful as Bobby wrote, then they could end up killing themselves as well."

This made Courtney stop. "Is it really possible to use a battery to set that stuff off?" she asked thoughtfully.

"I don't know," answered Mark. "I suppose so. If tak is that volatile then a small electric charge could set off a chain reaction and . . . boom."

The two fell silent for a moment, imagining the consequences.

"I guess the trick is to be somewhere else when the button gets pushed," said Courtney. "I don't think they're smart enough to figure out how to make a timer."

"It wouldn't matter," said Mark soberly. "Tak isn't like anything I've ever heard of. If a little bit can make an explosion that big, then the amount Bobby described in that ore car would not only destroy the Bedoowan palace, it would level the Milago village too. And if the explosion makes fire the way it did with those scarecrow targets, then it could create a firestorm. Every living thing for miles around would be torched . . . the Bedoowan, the Milago, the farm, the forest . . ."

"And Bobby, Alder, Loor, and Press, too," said Courtney slowly. "I guess this Figgis guy really is a merchant of death."

Mark picked up the latest journal and scanned it, looking for something. It didn't take him long to find it.

"Listen to this," he said. "This is what Loor said to Bobby." Mark read from the journal. *"My mother explained that there are many territories, and they are all about to reach an important time. A 'turning point' she called it. It is a time when the outcome will either send the territory towards peace and prosperity, or plunge its people into chaos and destruction."*

Courtney said, "Yeah, and if the Milago beat the Bedoowan then everything will be okay."

"I don't think that's it," said Mark. "I think it's all about tak. Think about it. The Milago have been slaves of the Bedoowan for centuries. If they fight them and lose, then it will be business as usual. But if the Milago tip the balance by using something as horrible as that explosive, then who knows what it could lead to?"

"Then we've got to try and undo it!" countered Courtney.

"How?" was Mark's obvious question. "It's not like we can go through the flumes. It doesn't work for us, remember?"

Courtney paced, her mind kicking into overdrive.

"Then maybe we can send something to Bobby," she said. "Like a . . . like a . . ."

"Like a what?" shouted Mark. "We can't send anything to him. It would only make things worse! The only thing we can do is – "

Ding dong. Mark was interrupted by the doorbell. The two instantly fell silent.

"You expecting somebody?" asked Courtney.

"We skipped school today," Mark said nervously. "Maybe they're coming to check up on me."

The doorbell rang again.

"L-Let's hide," said Mark.

Courtney gave him a sarcastic look and said, "Hide? Gimme a break, I think we have bigger things to worry about than getting caught for skipping school. Answer the dumb door."

Courtney was right, thought Mark. Who cared if they got busted for skipping school? Whoever was at the door he'd deal with them and get back to the bigger problem at hand. When he got downstairs, he hesitated a second and tried to look sick in case it really was somebody from school coming to check up on him. He gave a little sick cough and then called out with a weak voice, "I'm coming."

He got to the door, unlocked it, swung it open, and then shouted out, "Bobby!"

Indeed, Bobby Pendragon was standing at the front door wearing the same clothes he had worn the night he disappeared. The Milago leather clothes were history.

"Hey, Mark," he said casually. "Can I come in?"

Courtney came running down the stairs on a tear. "Bobby?" she shouted.

Bobby stepped into Mark's house and gave Courtney a little smile.

"Miss me?" he said.

Courtney grabbed him in a hug and Mark hugged the two of them together. Bobby was home. He was safe. Everything was going to be okay. When they finally pulled away from the group hug, Mark and Courtney looked at Bobby in disbelief. This was too good to be true. A few seconds ago they were worried about never seeing him again. Now here he was standing right in front of them. But Bobby looked different. Both Courtney and Mark noticed it. It was still Bobby, no doubt about that. But he looked tired, like he had gone through an ordeal that took a lot out of him.

"Are you okay, man?" asked Mark. "You look kind of . . . sick."

"I'm not sick; I'm totally beat," was Bobby's answer. "I gotta lie down."

Mark and Courtney quickly led Bobby up the stairs to Mark's bedroom. They watched him as he walked and saw that he was a little unsure on his feet. They also noticed streaks of blood on his cheeks that came from many tiny cuts all over his face. Obviously a lot had happened since they saw him leave through the flume on his way back to Denduron. To Mark and Courtney only a few hours had passed. But as they had already figured out, time here on Second Earth and time in the other territories weren't relative. Bobby could have been gone for much longer than a few days for all they knew. Bobby looked as if he'd been through a war, but neither Mark nor Courtney wanted to ask him about it. They both figured that he'd tell them when he was ready. So without another word, they followed Bobby into Mark's room and watched as he lay down on the bed.

"I've got to get home," said Bobby weakly. "But I want to rest up first. Is it okay?"

"Absolutely," answered Mark. "Whatever you want."

"Thanks, man," said Bobby and put his head down on the pillow. Mark cringed, wondering how he was going to explain the streaks of blood on the white pillowcase to his mother. But then he felt bad for even thinking so selfishly and put the thought out of his head.

"Will you guys come with me?" asked Bobby without opening his eyes.

"Sure, Bobby," answered Courtney. "Uh . . . where?"

Bobby spoke weakly, as if he were nearly asleep. "To my house. Everybody must be going nuts looking for me. I'm going to need you guys to help explain things."

Mark and Courtney exchanged looks. Both knew what the other was thinking. Bobby's house wasn't there any more. His family had disappeared and along with them so had any history of the Pendragon family ever having existed. His parents, his sister, even his dog were just . . . gone. The police had launched an investigation to try and figure out what had happened to them, but so far they had come up empty.

"Whatever it takes," said Courtney. "We'll be there for you."

Bobby smiled.

Mark, on the other hand, was dying with curiosity. He didn't want Bobby to nod off before finding out what happened on Denduron.

"So tell us what happened!"

Courtney gave Mark a punch in the arm.

"Ow!" yelped Mark and grabbed his stinging arm.

"Go to sleep, Bobby," said Courtney. "Tell us later."

Bobby didn't open his eyes, but he chuckled at his friend's curiosity. "Oh yeah, I almost forgot," he said while reaching up to his shirt. He unbuttoned a few buttons, reached his hand in and pulled out a roll of parchment paper.

"It's all there," he said fading fast. "Everything that happened since I wrote last. Wake me up when you're finished."

That was the last thing he said. Bobby was in dreamland, the roll of parchment paper still in his hand. Mark glanced to Courtney, hesitated a moment, then took the precious journal. Courtney took the folded-up duvet from the bottom of Mark's bed and laid it gently over Bobby, right up to his chin. This was probably the first time he had slept in a bed in a long time and she wanted to make sure he was as safe and comfortable as possible. Then the two of them walked quietly to the far side of the room.

"Should we go downstairs and leave him alone?" whispered Mark.

"No," was Courtney's reply. "Nothing we could do would wake him up now."

Mark nodded. He didn't want to leave either. He slipped the familiar leather twine off the rolled-up scroll and opened it enough to read the very first line.

"Journal Number Four?" asked Courtney.

"Journal Number Four," answered Mark.

The two sat down next to each other on the floor and began to read the final chapter in Bobby's adventure.

DENDURON

I can't believe I'm still alive. At least I think I'm still alive. Every muscle, every bone, every hair follicle I've got is sore as hell, which pretty much tells me I'm still among the living. As I write this final journal to you guys, I've still got one major task ahead of me before I can come home. But right now I don't even feel like moving. Even the effort of pushing this pen across the paper is painful. I'm going to try and rest up, write this journal, and then get myself psyched for the final push.

As hurting as my body is, it's just as painful to remember the events of the past few days. But I've got to do it and write it all down because once it's on the page, I'm going to do my level best to forget it all.

I should warn you that some of the things I'm going to write about I didn't see for myself. It has been an incredible few days and there was no way I could be everywhere at once to see it all. But I'll do my best to re-create those events in my journal as accurately as possible based on what others have told me. I don't have a problem doing this because I'm sure everything they described is true. So sit down, take a breath, and hold on. It's going to be a wild ride.

I finished my last journal right after we rescued Uncle Press, then got recaptured by the people whom we thought were our friends – the Milago. Their leader, Rellin, showed us the huge bomb of tak they planned on using to vaporise the Bedoowan. There is something you should understand here. The Milago are not our enemies, but they were afraid we would try to stop them from using that nasty weapon. And they were right. If they exploded that bad boy, the destruction would be horrible. If we could stop them, we would. So we were in the weird position of being friendly enemies.

They brought us back to the hospital hut I'd been to a few times and locked us up with guards at the door. They said that as soon as the battle was over, they'd let us go. Great. If they detonated that bomb, there wouldn't be any place *left* for us to go. So the four of us – me, Uncle Press, Loor, and Alder – were prisoners again.

As soon as we entered the hut, Uncle Press looked around quickly. "Osa isn't here," he said. "She must be in hiding."

Uh-oh. We hadn't gotten the chance to tell Uncle Press what had happened to her. I also realised that Osa's body wasn't there any longer.

"What happened?" he asked quickly.

Loor pointed to me and said, "She was killed while protecting him from the Bedoowan knights."

Perfect. As if I didn't have enough guilt going on at the moment, she had to remind me about my part in Osa's death. I guess I couldn't be angry with her. Osa was her mother. She deserved to be angry. But I wished she didn't have to lay all of the blame on me. Mallos and the Bedoowan knights had a little something to do with it too.

We all looked to Uncle Press for his reaction. It was a strange one. Rather than show any sign of grief, he simply nodded as if the news of Osa's death were nothing more than a simple fact to file away. I think he realised that the three of us were taking it harder than that, because he put his hand on Loor's shoulder and said, "Don't be sad. This is the way it was meant to be."

That was exactly what Osa said just before she died. Was that some sort of Traveller motto? If so, it was a lousy one. It didn't make me feel any better, and I doubted if it helped Loor at all.

"Everyone get some rest," Uncle Press ordered. "Tomorrow's going to be a tough day."

He was right; we all needed rest. So we took places apart from one another in different corners of the hut. This is when I wrote the last journal that I sent you. Loor wrote too, as did Alder. We were all documenting our experiences as Travellers, though I'm pretty sure we all had different opinions about how things were going. The only one who didn't write was Uncle Press. He lay down on one of the benches and closed his eyes. I wondered how much sleep he had got while a prisoner in the Bedoowan palace. Not much, probably.

As I wrote I sensed that there was tension in the room. Maybe it was just my own paranoia, but I had the feeling that the others were blaming me for the tough position we were in. Whenever I looked up, both Alder and Loor would quickly look away. The truth was, I didn't blame them. As I played out the events of the past few days in my mind, the sickening realisation came to me that the situation on Denduron was much worse because of me. If Uncle Press hadn't brought me here, then he probably wouldn't have been captured by the Bedoowan. And if he hadn't been captured then he wouldn't have needed to be rescued, and I wouldn't have written to you guys to send me the stuff from home. And if I hadn't got that stuff from home, then the Milago wouldn't have the ability to explode that huge bomb. And if I weren't here, Osa would still be alive because . . . if, if, if. Whenever you look back and say, "If", you know you're in trouble. There's no such thing as "if". The only thing that counts is what really happened, and the truth was that every chance I got, I screwed up. Even when I thought I had done something good, it always turned out bad.

Then, just to rub salt in everyone's wounds, my watch alarm started to beep. I had totally forgotten about my Casio. Alder and Loor shot a look at me. They had no idea what it was. Uncle Press just cracked an eye open and gave me a deadly look. Without saying a word I jumped up and ran to a corner of the hut where I pulled the watch off and threw it into the latrine. I think it was a safe bet that nobody would go down there after it. I even pulled my Swiss Army knife out of my pocket and dumped it in the ooze. I looked back at the others to see they were all staring at me. I couldn't take it any more.

"What?" I yelled. "So I messed up! Yeah, I got that stuff from home, but it was the only way I could think of to get Uncle Press out. And it worked, didn't it?"

Nobody said a word. They just stared back at me. It was making me crazy.

"It's not like you tried to stop me, Loor . . . Alder," I added. "You used the stuff too!"

"But we did not know it was wrong," said Loor quietly. "You did."

I couldn't argue with that, but I was still in an arguing mood so I yelled, "I didn't ask to come here, you know! It's not like I had a choice. I'm not a warrior like Loor or Osa. I'm not a knight like Alder. And I'm not a . . . not a . . . I don't know *what* you are any more, Uncle Press, but I'm sure as hell not like you! You never should have brought me here." I was ready for a fight. I wanted them to say what a loser I was because I had a great comeback. I'd agree with them. I never claimed to be anything more than a junior-high kid from the suburbs. That's it. I wasn't a revolutionary, or a fighter, or anything else they wanted me to be. It wasn't fair to blame me for not living up to their expectations. I was doing the best I could. If that wasn't good enough, well, too bad.

But that's not what happened. Instead Uncle Press sat up on the bench and softly said, "Come here, all of you. Sit down."

We all kind of awkwardly exchanged glances and walked over to him. I had no idea where this was going. Uncle Press then spoke to us in such a calm manner that it took all of the tension out of the room. It kind of reminded me of the way Osa always seemed to have the ability to chill everybody out.

"I understand how tough this is for all of you," he began. "You haven't known about being Travellers for very long, and it's gotta be confusing."

"I do not understand why this has happened to me," said Alder. "Why must we be Travellers?"

"I was not given a choice," added Loor. "It does not seem fair."

I then realised that I wasn't the only one who was freaking out. Loor and Alder hadn't known about being Travellers for very long either. The only difference was they were better equipped to handle the assignment than I was. The closest I ever came to that kind of training was in Saturday morning karate class when I was ten. I usually ended up getting a bloody nose and running home crying.

That's not exactly elite warrior training. I was definitely out of my league here.

Uncle Press smiled warmly and said, "If you want to know why you are Travellers, all you have to do is look back on what you've already done. The way the three of you rescued me from that palace was an amazing thing. You proved yourselves to be smart and brave and resourceful. But more important was the fact that you willingly put your lives at risk because it was the right thing to do. Ordinary people wouldn't do that. You want to know why you're Travellers? Look first to yourselves."

"But what are these powers?" asked Loor. "We understand words that we should not."

"There's a lot for you to learn," said Uncle Press. "But the best way for that to happen is for you to experience it. As time goes on everything will come clear, but you need to learn it on your own."

"Come on," I said impatiently. "You gotta give us more than that. Are there others? I mean, are there more Travellers?"

"Yes," said Uncle Press. "Every territory has a Traveller. When you arrive in a new territory, always find the Traveller. They know best about the customs and history of their home territory and can help you along."

"Like Alder," said Loor.

"Yes, like Alder," confirmed Uncle Press.

"And what about Mallos . . . Saint Dane?" I asked. "He's a Traveller too, right?"

Uncle Press's expression grew hard. "Yes," he said coldly. "This is something you should know about now," he said. "Every territory is in conflict. There are always wars and disputes and battles. That's the nature of things. Always was, always will be. But no matter what the conflict of a territory is, the true enemy is Saint Dane. Here on Denduron it's not the Bedoowan, or Queen Kagan, or even the quigs. The real threat is Saint Dane. He's the one who must be stopped."

"What's his deal?" I asked. "Why is he so dangerous?"

I could tell we were getting into hairy territory, because Uncle Press had his game face back on. "He's dangerous because you never see him coming," was Uncle Press's answer. "He changes himself. On Denduron he has become Mallos, advisor to the queen. Bobby, you saw him back on Second Earth. He took on the form of a policeman. I'm not sure if he physically changes, or if he uses some kind of mind control to make you think he looks different, but the bottom line is you don't always see him coming. And make no mistake about it, the guy is evil."

Uncle Press paced faster. We all listened closely because it was clear we needed to hear what he was now telling us. "But his evil isn't obvious," he continued. "He doesn't murder, or cause floods or fires. His methods are much more devious. He will go to a territory and move himself into a position where he can *influence* events. He's smart and convincing. He'll appear to be your friend while the whole time he's pushing you towards disaster."

"Like with the Bedoowan?" I asked.

"Exactly," shot back Uncle Press. "The Milago and the Bedoowan have been in conflict for centuries, but Saint Dane has pushed it to the edge. Before he got here things were rough for the Milago, but nowhere near as bad as they are now. He worked his way into the trust of Queen Kagan — "

"Who isn't exactly a rocket scientist," I added.

"No, she isn't," he agreed. "For a while it was looking as if the Bedoowan might cut the Milago some slack, but it was Saint Dane's influence that convinced the Bedoowan to push harder. He's the one who started the unreasonable demands for glaze and the Transfer ceremony and the horrible quig slaughters in the stadium. It looks to the Milago as if the Bedoowan wanted all this, but it was really Saint Dane, or Mallos as he calls himself here. He whispers suggestions to Kagan, and she makes them law."

"But . . . why does he do this?" asked Alder.

"To push the territory towards chaos," was Uncle Press's firm answer. "Saint Dane doesn't care about the Bedoowan or the Milago. He's using the Bedoowan to push the Milago into getting so desperate that they will fight back. He wants a war. But not just any war, he wants the Milago to use tak. I see that now."

"He wants them to blow everybody up?" I asked.

"Not exactly," he continued. "Yes, using that bomb will cause terrible damage, but the long-term effects are what Saint Dane is after. I should have seen it coming, but I didn't. I didn't know about tak."

"Could Saint Dane have brought it from another territory?" I asked.

"I doubt it. My guess is that it's natural to Denduron and somehow Figgis stumbled across it . . . and Saint Dane is taking advantage. Tak now represents power to the Milago. They've been held down for so long that they'll grab at anything to pull themselves up. But once they start using tak on the Bedoowan, where will it stop? They could create weapons that would make them the most powerful tribe on Denduron. There are thousands of tribes here. None of them have a weapon like this. Putting the power of tak into the hands of one tribe is like tipping the balance. The Milago may be a peaceful bunch now, but they've got years of pent-up anger. Put that kind of power in their hands and they could overrun Denduron. That's the kind of chaos Saint Dane is looking for."

There it was. Loor had told me about the mission of the Travellers, but Uncle Press had now spelled it out pretty clearly. If this war began and the Milago used tak, it would be disaster. It really was a bigger deal than just a battle between two warring tribes. But there was something else that was bugging me.

"What is Halla?" I asked Uncle Press.

Uncle Press shot me a surprised look. "Where did you hear that name?"

"From Saint Dane," I said. "Before he took us to the stadium he told me that Halla would fall and we would fall with it. What is Halla?"

"Halla is everything," he answered. "Every territory, every person, every living thing, every *time* there ever was. Halla is what separates order from chaos. If Halla crumbles, there will be nothing left but darkness. Everywhere. For everyone."

Whoa. Now there was a concept to try and get my mind around. None of us spoke for a long while. We had just shifted into a new gear here. Was it possible? Could it be that the battle between the Milago and the Bedoowan was not only about the future of Denduron, but about the future of *all* territories? If things turned sour here, could that somehow affect things back home? This was the most devastating thing I had heard so far. The stakes had become so huge that it was hard to comprehend. Before any of us had the chance to ask another question, the wooden door to the hut flew open and a Milago miner stormed in.

"Rellin wishes to see you," he announced.

Uncle Press stood, but the miner held his hand up to stop him.

"Not you," he said. "Pendragon."

"Rellin wants to see *me*? What for?"

"Go with him, Bobby," said Uncle Press. "Listen to what he has to say. You know how important it is."

Yeah, this was important all right. It was so important that I wished somebody *else* were going. But I got up to follow the miner out of the hut. Before I left, I looked at Uncle Press. "I messed up," I said. "I'm sorry."

Uncle Press smiled and said, "It's okay, Bobby. Mistakes will be made."

That actually made me feel better. We were still in deep trouble and it was still my fault, but at least I didn't feel like a total nimrod for what I had done. One thing I could say for sure though: I wouldn't do it again. I guess that's what Uncle Press meant by telling us we would have to learn about being Travellers by experiencing it ourselves. You don't truly learn something until it's real, and the bomb that was about to blow us all into dust was very real. It's a tough way to learn a lesson.

I followed the miner out of the hut. Night had fallen, though I had no idea what time it was. My watch was floating in the latrine, remember? The village was empty. I could see lights coming from the huts, but nobody was walking about. It felt like the calm before the storm. The miner walked quickly until we came to one of the larger huts. He motioned for me to enter. It wasn't like I had a whole lot of choices, so I went in.

Rellin was waiting for me. He sat near the fire and offered me a cup of some kind of liquid. I wasn't sure if I should take it or not. Maybe it was poison. Or maybe it was a peace offering and by not taking it I'd be insulting him. I decided to take the cup and only pretend to drink. Of course if it was poison and I didn't clutch my throat in agony he'd pretty much know I faked taking a drink. Maybe I was overthinking this.

Once I had taken the cup and faked the drink (with no reaction from Rellin) he stood up and walked to a wooden table. Lying there was the battery from my torch. But something was attached to it. I looked closer and my stomach twisted when I saw that it was a small piece of tak. The wires and the switch had been pulled out of the torch and were used to connect the tak to the battery. These guys learned fast. They had made a little bomb. If they flipped the switch from the battery, it would complete the circuit and send a jolt of electricity through the tak. It may be a small jolt, but probably enough to detonate the unstable explosive. Rellin picked it up and examined it. I wanted to shout for him to be careful, but I could see that he appreciated the power and was handling it with caution.

"We have been trying to find a way to control tak," he said. "But until now we have been unsuccessful."

My mind flashed back to the moment down in the mines when there was an explosion and Rellin had to be rescued. He was probably experimenting with tak and something had gone wrong. Slowly the pieces of the puzzle were coming together.

"This is how we will ignite the tak," he continued. "Tomorrow this small device will explode and that will set off the larger load. When my army hears the explosion it will be their signal to attack. They will then overrun what is left of the Bedoowan. It will all be so very simple, because of you."

Gee, thanks. I'm thrilled that I could help us all move closer to Armageddon. Rellin put the small bomb down and sat back by the fire. He motioned for me to sit across from him.

"You have seen our lives," he said sadly. "We are dying.

The Bedoowan will never allow us to be free. Tak is our salvation. With tak the Milago can pull themselves up from the dirt and become the proud people we were destined to be."

He was absolutely right. The Milago had it bad. They lived like tortured animals. Nobody deserved that. They had every right to fight back, but they didn't understand that they were going about it the wrong way.

"You and your people want to help us," he continued. "For that we are grateful. But there is one thing we need from you that will be more helpful than you can imagine."

"What's that?" I asked warily.

Rellin stood up and walked quickly back to his little homemade bomb. He picked it up and held it out as if it were the Holy Grail.

"Bring us more of these devices," he said with passion. "If we had more we could become the most powerful army on Denduron. Once the Bedoowan are defeated, the Milago would never have to live in fear again. We could turn our miserable lives around to become the leaders of Denduron!"

Oh, man. Uncle Press was absolutely right. Now that the Milago had a little taste of power, they weren't going to be satisfied with just beating up on the Bedoowan. They hadn't even won yet and they already had visions of taking over the rest of Denduron. The good guys were going to become the bad guys, and the result would be chaos.

"Will you help us, Pendragon?" asked Rellin sincerely.

This was my chance. Maybe my *only* chance to try and talk Rellin out of his plan. I couldn't argue against centuries of hatred, so the best thing I could do was try and make him see the downside to his plan. I had to choose my words carefully.

"I'm not an expert on these things," I said. "But if you blow up that big load of tak, there may not be much left of the Bedoowan to conquer. Heck, there may not be much left of the Milago, either. Where I come from, there are many weapons like this. But the biggest fear we have is that they will be used. You don't understand what you're doing, Rellin. Your lives may be horrible now, but you may be worse off after the explosion. There must be a better way."

"No!" he shouted angrily.

I hadn't chosen my words carefully enough.

"You do not understand!" he yelled at me. "You have not lived your life in fear, in pain, in hunger. This is the only way. This is how the Milago will defeat the Bedoowan. Now, will you help us?"

Key moment.

"I'll help you," I answered as firmly as I could. "We'll all help you. But not if it means using tak."

Rellin stiffened and said, "Then go back to your friends. You will not be harmed. When the battle is over you will be free to leave."

My mind was racing. I wanted to come up with something to change his mind, but I was drawing a blank. The truth was I didn't know how the Milago could possibly defeat the Bedoowan without the help of something like tak. I couldn't offer a better solution. I had one chance and I blew it. But then a thought hit me.

"How will you explode the bomb?" I asked. "If someone pushes that switch, then they'll go up with it."

Rellin straightened up proudly. "It will be an honour to die in the name of freedom for the Milago."

Oh, man. Rellin was going on a suicide mission. This wasn't about personal glory or power. This was a good man who cared about the future of his people more than he cared about his own life. There was nothing more for me to say, so I left the hut feeling sorry for him, but also feeling incredible respect . . . and fear. If someone was ready to die for his cause, a dweeb like me had no chance of talking him out of it. That bomb was going to explode tomorrow and there wasn't anything I could do about it.

The miner led me back to the hospital hut where I quickly told the others about my meeting.

"So then it is true," said Loor. "The Milago will become a powerful, warring tribe and destroy all of Denduron."

"That's if they don't blow themselves up with that humongous bomb first," I added.

There was still a big question to be answered. Where were the Milago going to explode the bomb? They couldn't very well do it around here or their own village would be vaporised. They may have been primitive but I'm sure they figured that little detail out. No, they must be planning on exploding it near the Bedoowan palace. But how could they pull that off? It's not like they could drop it off on the palace doorstep, ring the doorbell and run away. As soon as they got within a hundred yards of the place the Bedoowan knights would stop them. They must have a plan, but what?

The answer turned out to be so simple I probably should have figured it out myself.

The next morning we were all awakened by the same thing. It was a deep, constant booming sound. I was still asleep and at first it had worked itself into my dreams. I dreamed that I was in a battle. Explosions were going off all around me. No matter which way I turned, another explosion would go off in my face. It was like I was trapped in a minefield. As I began to wake up I realised that I wasn't in a minefield, I was in the hospital hut of the Milago village. But the deep booming sound continued. What was it? I lay there for a few seconds, trying to remember where I'd heard it before. Then suddenly, it hit me. I knew exactly where I had heard it before and the realisation shocked me wide awake. I sat up quickly to see that the others were already awake and looking out of the small windows of the hut. I didn't have to ask what they were looking at. I already knew.

The sound I heard was the sound of the drum calling the Milago to a Transfer ceremony. I could picture the single drummer standing on the wooden platform in the clearing of the Milago village, slowly but steadily hitting that drum. The memory wasn't exactly a pleasant one, because it ended in the horrible death of a Milago miner. I truly hoped that this Transfer wouldn't end the same way.

I jumped up and joined Uncle Press at one of the windows. Loor and Alder peered out of the other one. The hut wasn't far from the central clearing of the Milago village. We were going to see all that we needed to see.

The scene in the clearing was painfully familiar. The Milago villagers slowly gathered around the central platform; the seesaw device was in place, ready to weigh the next poor victim; the lone drummer stood on the platform, beating out the summons; and a handful of Bedoowan knights stood next to the platform with spears in hand. The drummer suddenly stopped pounding his kettle and an ominous silence fell over the village. Then, as if on cue, I heard the sound of a galloping horse. Mallos was on his way. The crowd parted and Mallos charged up to the platform and dismounted before his horse had come to a stop.

How could anyone be this evil? What was it that drove him to spread terror and chaos wherever he went? Was it because he enjoyed it? Did it give him some kind of thrill? Does evil exist just for evil's sake? There had to be answers to these questions, but they would have to wait for another time because the curtain was about to go up.

"Where is the glaze?" Mallos bellowed. "Why was I summoned before the glaze was ready to be transferred?"

He scanned the crowd waiting for an answer, but none was coming. Nobody could even look him in the eye. I was afraid he would blow a cork and send the knights on a rampage, but that didn't happen. Instead, Rellin stepped forward. The chief miner looked calm and in control.

"Mallos," he said. "I truly hope you will be happy with the news we bring you."

Mallos shot a suspicious look at Rellin, then stepped up to him and stuck his nose in the chief miner's face.

"Where are they, Rellin?" he seethed. "I know they are here. If you hide them from me, you cannot begin to imagine the punishment that will come down upon you."

Mallos was talking about us. He seemed incredibly ticked that we had got away and was accusing the Milago of hiding us. The four of us exchanged looks, but none of us were about to give ourselves up. Rellin was cool. He didn't back down.

"That is the news I bring you," he said. "We are sorry for all the trouble the outsiders have caused you. We thought they were our friends, but they are not. And knowing that they have caused distress to Queen Kagan, well, that now makes them our enemies as well."

Was he for real? Was he going to turn us over to Mallos and the knights after telling me he'd let us go? I didn't think Rellin was a liar, but this sounded bad. I could tell that Mallos wasn't sure where Rellin was going with this either. He looked at the miner suspiciously and asked through clenched teeth, "Where are they?"

"I do not know," answered Rellin. "But when we find them we will bring them to you immediately."

Okay, maybe he was a liar after all, but at least he hadn't lied to me. He wasn't going to turn us in. What was he up to?

"In the meantime," continued Rellin. "As an apology for the trouble we have caused you and Queen Kagan and all the Bedoowan, we would like to present you with a gift." He made a motion and the crowd parted. Three miners stepped forward carrying their load of glaze. But this was no ordinary load. They carried an entire ore car full of glaze! It was spectacular. The cart was piled high with the biggest, most brilliant glaze stones I had seen yet.

"Yesterday we struck a promising new vein of glaze," said Rellin proudly. "That is our good news. There is more glaze in this new vein than we could hope to bring up in a lifetime. It took us a full day and night to load this one car and I predict that there are hundreds of more cars to come that will be just as full."

Mallos seemed impressed. He should have been. It was a lot of glaze.

"This is our gift to you," said Rellin. "I ask only one thing in return."

"What is that?" barked Mallos.

"I wish to be able to present this to Queen Kagan myself," said Rellin. "I realise that a lowly Milago miner would never be allowed into the palace, but perhaps I could bring this car-ful of glaze to the Bedoowan stadium? I would be honoured to present this to Queen Kagan along with the promise of much more to come."

Rellin was brilliant. He was playing Mallos like a fish and the fish was about to bite the hook. Of course we all knew the truth. That ore car wasn't full of glaze at all. My guess is that if you dug about a quarter of the way down, the glaze would stop and the load of tak would begin. Yes, Rellin had figured out a way to smuggle his monstrous bomb right into the heart of the Bedoowan palace. It was like the story of the Trojan Horse where the Greeks were at war with the Trojans and gave them a gift of a giant wooden horse. Only the horse was loaded with Greek soldiers. As soon as the big horse was wheeled inside the city of Troy, the soldiers jumped out and gave a big helping of whup-butt to the surprised Trojans.

But this Trojan Horse wasn't full of soldiers. This was loaded with a deadly explosive that would level the Bedoowan palace and probably most of the Milago village. The plan was insane, and brilliant. The question was, would Mallos fall for it?

Mallos looked at the carful of glaze. He walked to it and dug his hand down into the precious stones. I could sense Rellin tensing, but he didn't make a move. Mallos pulled his hand out and clutched a load of brilliant blue stones. He then looked to Rellin and said, "Why make your promise to only Queen Kagan? I believe all of the Bedoowan people should be in the stadium to receive this gift and to hear your promise."

Rellin did his best not to smile and only said, "Yes, you are a wise man."

Unbelievable. Not only was Mallos going to let Rellin bring the bomb in, he was going to gather all of the Bedoowan around it.

Mallos then climbed back on his horse and bellowed, "Bring the glaze now. I will prepare the stadium!" With that he kicked his horse and charged towards the palace.

Rellin looked to the miners who had brought in the tak bomb. Without showing a hint of satisfaction, he walked to the ore car. No words were spoken. The men knew what they had to do. They all reached down, lifted the heavy car and began the long walk to the Bedoowan palace. Their death mission was under way.

Uncle Press backed away from the window and said, "Mallos knows."

"No way!" I said. "Why would he let them bring a bomb into the Bedoowan stadium?"

"Because he wants the Milago to use it," was his answer. "He doesn't care who wins, or who dies. He wants the Milago to use the tak. If that bomb goes off, he'll have succeeded."

Maybe Uncle Press was right. If Mallos wanted to start a war that would throw Denduron into chaos, what better way to kick it off than by letting the Milago have their big bang right in the Bedoowan backyard? For Mallos it was perfect. We all knew exactly where this was leading but there was nothing we could do to stop it because we were trapped in this stupid hut.

But not for long. Without stopping to tell us, Loor ran for the window and in one quick, acrobatic move pulled herself up and out. In seconds she was climbing up on to the roof. It happened so fast that none of us could react. We just sort of stared at each other, wondering what she was doing. We heard her quietly scamper across the roof until she was above the door to the hut. What followed was the sound of a brief scuffle outside, followed by a few quick grunts. Loor then poked her head back inside the door.

"We may leave now," she said with matter-of-fact calm.

None of us were exactly sure of what had happened, but we all ran for the door and followed Loor out. Outside we saw all three guards had been knocked unconscious and were leaning against the hut. Loor had struck before they knew what hit them and had managed to free us all in less than twenty seconds.

That was pretty cool, but there wasn't time for praise. We had to get out of the Milago village without being caught. As it turned out, it wasn't hard. Rellin's plan was being carried out, which meant the rest of the miners were preparing for their attack. As soon as they heard the explosion they would charge the Bedoowan palace. Those miners had more important things to worry about than guarding us. So getting out of the village and disappearing into the woods was easy.

The four of us ran until we felt we were a safe distance away. Uncle Press then raised his hand and we all stopped to catch our breath. Uncle Press looked at Loor and said what was on all of our minds.

"You are unbelievable!" he said with a laugh. "Why didn't you tell us you were going to do that? We could have helped."

Loor gave a very Loor-esque response. "I did not need your help. The best weapon in battle is surprise. The miners were watching Mallos and Rellin. They were not thinking about us. If I had waited, they may have turned their attention back to guarding us. I did not want to give them that chance."

"I'm proud of you, Loor," said Uncle Press. "Your mother would be too."

"She taught me well," said Loor.

My mother never taught me anything like that. She spent a lot of time drilling good table manners into me, but we never got to the lesson on how to disarm and crack heads with three guys twice my size. My education was definitely lacking in that area.

"What about the bomb?" said Alder. "We must do something!"

Uncle Press spun back to us and said, "Okay, first thing we have to do is get to the palace. We aren't doing any good here."

I wasn't so sure that going to the palace was on the top of my To Do list. The palace was the target and unless we had a real chance of stopping Rellin from setting off that bomb, the only thing getting closer would do is guarantee that we'd be killed the instant it went off. But I wasn't about to say that. The truth was if there was any hope of stopping Rellin, we had to get there.

"Alder, I want you to go back to the village," said Uncle Press.

"No!" he exclaimed. "I want to stay with you."

"Look," said Uncle Press firmly. "I have no idea if we're going to stop this thing. So get back to the village, talk to anyone who'll listen. Warn them that this bomb is going to be bigger than they could ever imagine. Try to get them to go down into the mines. Maybe if they get underground they'll be safe."

"But I – "

"No buts, Alder," said Uncle Press. "I know you want to be with us, but if we fail, you still might be able to save some of the Milago."

Uncle Press was right. If Alder could save even one person from being killed by the explosion, then his mission would be successful. He had to go back.

Alder nodded to Uncle Press, which told me he understood how important his job was. There wasn't time for long good-byes. I hadn't known Alder for very long, but I had grown fond of him. He was kind of a goof, but I didn't doubt for a second that he would have put his life on the line for any one of us. I'd like to say that I would do the same for him.

"Good luck, Travellers," he said, and smiled at each of us.

"You too, Alder," said Uncle Press. "Hurry."

Alder then spun around and ran back towards the Milago village. Now it was just the three of us. The warrior, the boss, and the kid who was so scared he had to pee. Guess which one I was?

"Come on," commanded Uncle Press and ran deeper into the forest. Our immediate goal was to get back to the Bedoowan palace. Beyond that, there was no plan. We would have to wing it once we got there, assuming we even got there. Since we were bushwhacking, it took us a long time. I could tell that Loor was getting impatient, but it was better to take a little longer to get there than to risk being captured again. We took a wide route and circled around towards the sea, then crawled along the bluffs until we were within eyesight of the outcropping that held the Bedoowan palace. Though we couldn't see it, we knew where it was because there was a long line of knights marching towards it. Behind them were the four miners carrying the ore car full of glaze and tak. They were almost at the palace. In a few minutes they would descend into the stadium.

We continued to move quickly along the bluffs, moving closer to the stadium. It was a smart thing to do because none of the knights expected anyone to be coming from the sea. They were ever vigilant, but always with their eyes towards the forest. We were able to quietly slip in from behind them and crawl the last several yards on our bellies until we reached the lip of the stadium. We had made it. Now the question was, what were we going to do?

The three of us peered down into the stadium to see that the line of knights was marching down the steep stairs towards the grass field below. Behind them came Rellin and the miners struggling with the heavy ore car. I glanced around the rest of the stadium and saw that two of the spectator sections were beginning to fill up. The Bedoowan people and the Novans were once again taking their seats in anticipation of a show. It was a horrible feeling. None of these people had any idea that the main event was going to be their own deaths. I looked to the section where the Milago were before to see that it was empty. Big surprise. These guys knew what was coming and didn't want to be any part of it. I then looked to Loor and to Uncle Press. Nobody said anything. That could mean only one thing. Nobody knew what to do. The thought ran through my head that we could run down the stairs screaming at everyone to run for their lives. But all Rellin would have to do is stop, press the button on his homemade bomb and it would be all over. That wouldn't work at all. But if we were going to come up with a better plan, we needed to do it fast, because Rellin and the miners had reached the grass field and were about to place the ore car dead centre in the ring.

"If I had an arrow I could kill Rellin from here," said Loor.

"Then one of the others would press the button," said Uncle Press.

I then heard the three chimes that signalled the arrival of Queen Kagan. Sure enough, when I looked at the royal box a few knights marched in, followed by the chubby queen. True to form, she was munching on something that looked like roast beef. What a piece of work.

"Mallos isn't there," said Uncle Press. "My guess is he's on a horse riding as fast as he can to get as far away from here as possible."

Indeed, Mallos was nowhere to be seen. That was further proof that everything was happening according to his plan.

And that's when it hit me.

"I . . . I've got an idea," I said without even thinking. Even as I said it I was still working it through my head, calculating the possibilities and the chances of it working.

Uncle Press and Loor looked at me, but I didn't respond to them at first. I still had to work things out.

"Don't take your time, Bobby," said Uncle Press. "We don't have much."

"Okay, okay," I said nervously. "There might be a way, but if it doesn't work, we're all dead."

"We are all dead anyway," said Loor.

Good point. I looked down to the stadium and realised that I was about to volunteer to do something crazy. If I did it, I'd probably die. If I didn't do it, we'd *definitely* die. Probably was better than definitely.

"I think I know how to stop this party," I said with as much confidence as I could muster, which wasn't much. Before I said another word, two more chimes sounded and the crowd fell silent. Rellin and the miners stood next to their wicked gift. Queen Kagan dropped her roast and leaned over the railing to look down on them.

"Tell me what it is you've brought me!" she shouted greedily.

If we were going to do something, now was the time.

DENDURON

"Good day, Queen Kagan!" shouted Rellin from the centre of the stadium field.

This was probably the first time a Milago miner had addressed a Bedoowan monarch. Ever. It was probably going to be the last. Rellin had everyone's attention in the stadium. I hoped that he had a lot to say, because if he decided to keep it short and reach for the bomb button, my plan had no chance of working. But if he took this opportunity to say what was on his mind and make some kind of grand political statement for the history books, then maybe we'd have a chance.

For my plan to work, we each had a different task. Unfortunately my job was probably the most dangerous. It's not that I wanted the most dangerous task, but it was the only job I was capable of pulling off. Lucky me.

I quickly told my idea to Uncle Press and Loor. They didn't even stop to discuss it. The time for debate was over and since nobody had any better ideas, my plan was a "go". The plan called for the three of us to split up. Before we had the chance to share a "good luck" or a "good-bye", Loor was off and running. Typical. Uncle Press didn't run off as quickly. He stayed long enough to give me this look of unclelike concern. I felt like I needed to say something important, but the only thing that came to mind was, "I really wish you had let me go to that basketball game." Okay, maybe not the most eloquent last words, but it was how I felt.

Uncle Press smiled and said, "No, you don't." Then he took off running.

I hesitated a moment because, well, I was scared. But I also had to think about what Uncle Press just said. Sure, if I had gone to that basketball game I wouldn't be lying here facing certain death. But that's not where my head went. This is going to be hard to explain because I'm not really sure I understand it myself, but as dire as the situation was, it somehow felt right. Believe me, it's not like I was having fun or anything. Far from it. But when I took a few seconds to do a gut check, I got the strange feeling that this was the right place, no, the *only* place for me to be. What was that Traveller motto? "This is the way it was meant to be." Okay, stupid motto, but it really felt to me as if this is the way it was meant to be. I don't mean to make this sound any more dramatic than it was, but the word that came to my mind right then was "destiny". Maybe this was my destiny. Now I could only hope that I'd get the chance to play a basketball game again sometime. But that wouldn't happen if I didn't get moving. So I jumped up and ran to do my part of the plan.

As I ran along the top of the stadium, I wasn't worried about getting caught because all eyes were focused on Rellin. It must have been amazing for the Bedoowan people to see this Milago miner addressing their queen. It was a spectacle that never would have happened if Mallos hadn't orchestrated it. I guess that's the kind of thing Uncle Press was talking about when he said that Mallos never did any of his own dirty work. He said how Mallos would influence others to do it for him. Well, Rellin was definitely about to do some dirty work, courtesy of Mallos.

"People of Denduron," Rellin continued. "I come before you today with a gift that is more valuable than you can imagine."

It seemed as if Rellin was indeed about to give a speech. That was good. Hopefully he was long-winded because I had no idea how much time it would take to pull off my plan.

"My gift is more valuable than the glaze you see before you," he bellowed. "It is more valuable than all the glaze that has ever been taken from the mines. It is the gift of a wonderful future, and it is for *all* the good people of Denduron to share."

Was this guy dramatic or what? Well, why not? He wasn't planning on being around long enough to hear any bad reviews. This was his moment in the spotlight. Keep going Rellin, I thought, make it good and long.

As I ran I saw that Loor and Uncle Press had already managed to pull off the first part of their jobs. They had each sneaked up on a Bedoowan knight from behind, whacked them and taken their armour. They needed to wear the armour so they could make their way down to the stadium field without being noticed. That's why I gave them the jobs I did. There was no way I was going to knock out a knight and steal his armour. And even if by some miracle I was able to do that, I was too small. If I put on the armour I'd look like a little kid wearing his daddy's clothes.

No, I had another job and I knew exactly where I had to go. It was only yesterday that I had been there. At the time I swore never to go near the place again but here I was, heading right back. It only took me a few minutes to get there. I was pretty fast, so running three hundred yards was nothing. But as I approached my destination I had a moment's hesitation. I thought that maybe if I ran fast enough and far enough, I could survive the blast from the tak bomb. But that thought lasted only about a nanosecond. There was no way I was going to bail on the plan.

At this point it wasn't even the bomb I was afraid of. That's because I had arrived at my destination: the horrible hole that looked down into the dark depths of the quig pens.

Yup, if my plan was going to work, I was going to have to climb down there and make my way to the stadium through a minefield of hungry quigs. And I didn't have my trusty whistle to protect me either. This could hurt. I stood on the edge of the hole trying to get the nerve to climb down. The rope ladder was in a heap at the bottom of the hole, right where it had fallen yesterday. But the thick rope that Loor had climbed to make her escape was still hanging there. That was my ticket down. I had to stop worrying and kick myself into gear because Rellin could hit that button at any second. So I grabbed the rope, swung my legs over, and slid down the rope into the pit of hell.

When I got to the bottom the first thing that hit me was the smell. It was as nasty as I had remembered it. Then I realised I had landed in a puddle of some kind of thick brown goo. I realised what it was and I nearly barfed. It was a congealed pool of blood from the quig that Uncle Press had skewered. I fought back the rising puke and quickly looked around. The injured quig wasn't there. Maybe it was dead. Better still, maybe it had been eaten by the other quigs. Can you believe this was the way my mind was working now?

My next goal was to get to the door that led to the stadium as fast as possible. I couldn't sneak quietly through the quig pen. No, I had to beat feet and get there fast, so I took off running in the direction I remembered travelling the day before. The run through the quig pen was terrifying. As I rounded each turn in the labyrinth, I kept expecting to see a monster quig waiting there with its mouth open, ready for dinner. My adrenalin was pumping so hard I don't think I could have walked slowly and cautiously if I'd wanted to. I should have been exhausted by now, but I wasn't. Fear will do that. If a quig didn't get me, then the bomb would. I wasn't sure which would be more painful. My guess is that the bomb would be quicker. But I forced those morbid thoughts away because the goal was to stay alive, not choose the least painful way to die.

After a few more turns I saw the door to the stadium. I had made it! Believe me, I never thought I'd get this far. I ran to the huge door and put my ear to it. I could hear Rellin still giving his speech. That was good. But there was another sound I wanted to hear as well. The job I had given to Loor was to get down to the stadium floor and unlock the door. That wouldn't be easy because as soon as she started to lift the heavy latch, somebody would certainly see her and try to stop her. Timing was everything. If she opened the door too soon, my plan would fail. If she opened it too late, my plan would fail. There was a small window of opportunity and it was getting close.

I listened again, and that's when I heard it. Two quick raps on the door. That was the signal. Loor had made it and was standing outside. Excellent! Now she had to wait for my signal before opening the door. Of course she had no way of knowing if I was on the other side or not. For all she knew I was being munched on by a quig who'd had a surprise treat fall into its lap. Still, I knew it didn't matter. She would stand there until I signalled for her to open the door, or the bomb blew up. Whichever came first.

Now came the hardest part of all. Talk about gut-check time. Everything that I had done up to this point was easy compared to what I had to do next. I looked around for something to help me and found a metal shield that one of the Bedoowan knights had dropped yesterday before he became quig food. I needed something else, too. I hoped to find one of the knight's spears, but for some reason they were gone. Time was running out, I had to move faster. I looked around again and saw the perfect thing. It turned my stomach to use it, but I couldn't let my squeamish belly stop me from doing what I had to do. So I picked it up. It was a leg bone. A human leg bone. As disgusting as it was, it was exactly what I needed. At least this one didn't still have the foot attached. I fought back my disgust, took a few steps back into the cavern, and rang the dinner bell.

Yes, I was using myself as bait. I used the leg bone to bang on the metal shield and hopefully wake up any napping quig that had missed my crazed run a few seconds before. "Come on!" I shouted. "Come and get it! Tasty meat, right this way!"

This was insane. Think about it. I was putting myself out there to be eaten by a beast that had already devoured three people. My hands were shaking with fear. Whose idea was this, anyway? Oh, right. Mine.

I banged on the shield a few more times and the annoying sound echoed throughout the cavern. Another horrible thought went through my head. What if they could hear this from the stadium? If there was even a hint of a problem, Rellin would hit the button and the game would be over. "Let's go!" I shouted. "C'mon, you losers! I'm the guy who killed your buddy up on the mountain! Come and get me!"

It came without so much as a warning. Yesterday when the quig attacked Uncle Press, it stalked him cautiously and slowly until it was close enough to pounce. That's not what was happening now. From far back in the depths of the rocky labyrinth I heard the bellow of a quig that was already charging! Maybe it was because of the annoying sound of the shield. Maybe it was my yelling. Maybe it was ravenously hungry. I'll never know, but whatever I had done, it worked. A quig was now charging towards me at a dead run. I could hear its giant paws pounding on the rocky surface as it rumbled closer, ready for the kill.

Now was the time. Now was the window of opportunity. Loor had to open that door fast or I'd be lunch. I dropped the shield, ran to the door and gave the secret, prearranged signal for Loor to do her thing.

"Open the damn door!" I yelled as loud as I could. How's that for a secret signal? Loor got the message. With my ear to the door I heard her fumbling with the heavy lock. This was the same lock that it took two knights to lift. I hoped that Loor had the strength to do it herself. Uncle Press could have helped, but he had his own job to take care of and was probably nowhere near the door. It was all up to Loor.

"Hurry!" I shouted. This was one time I didn't care about sounding cool or confident. I wanted her to know how close I was to being eaten. I heard a roar, turned back to look into the quig pens, and saw it. The quig. Its yellow eyes blazed as it charged through the pools of light, picking up speed, lusting for the kill. It was getting close enough that I could see bits of saliva flying from its open mouth. This thing was hungry and I was dinner. I threw my back against the door, hoping it would open. It didn't. I could hear Loor struggling with the lock. If she took any longer, someone would surely see her and stop her. Or Rellin would push the button. One way or another, this would all be over in a few seconds.

The quig crouched lower to the ground. It was getting ready to pounce.

"If you don't open the door," I shouted, "this quig is going to – " With a loud creak, the door swung open and I fell back. At that exact moment the quig sprang, but because I had fallen down it sailed over me and through the open door into the stadium. I swear I felt the breeze from its paws as they sailed over my head, inches from slicing me to pieces. I quickly jumped to my feet and ran into the stadium to see what was happening. The next few seconds were critical. It all came down to what the quig did . . . and Uncle Press.

The stadium was in total chaos. The quig was out of control. Several Bedoowan knights ran on to the field to try and capture it, or kill it. I saw that Loor had been attacked by two knights. But Loor wasn't their problem any more. They let her go and went after the quig. I helped her to her feet and the two of us took cover next to the open door. The monster quig had taken a stand. It went from offence to defence as the knights attacked it with their spears. I'm not sure who was doing more damage, the quig or the knights. For every spear they threw at the wild animal, the quig must have slashed two knights. It was in a total frenzy of anger, pain, and blood. But the main thing is that the battle to contain the quig had done exactly what I hoped it would. It disrupted the events that were taking place in the ring.

I looked to the centre of the ring to see what Rellin was doing. He must have been momentarily stunned by the sudden appearance of the quig, because he stood there with the other miners staring at the action. That didn't last long. He snapped out of it and went for the ore car full of tak. This was it. This was the moment. Rellin was going to push the button.

From the corner of my eye I saw a black streak headed towards Rellin. It was a flying spear. The missile flew at the chief miner and stabbed him right in the forearm, pinning him to the side of the wooden ore car. Rellin screamed out in pain, but I'm not sure if it was a scream of pain or of frustration because he couldn't get to the tak bomb. Then I saw a Bedoowan knight run up to the ore car. But I knew this wasn't a Bedoowan knight, it was Uncle Press. He was going for the detonator. Rellin couldn't move, but the other miners could. They realised what Uncle Press was doing and attacked him. These simple miners were no match for my uncle. Uncle Press was a blur of arms and legs as he took the miners on and knocked them down one by one. There was no way he was going to let any of them get to the detonator.

It was an amazing sight. The Bedoowan knights had all but killed the quig and Uncle Press was in full command of Rellin and the miners. I couldn't believe it. My plan had worked.

No sooner did I think that the worst was over than all hell broke loose again. I had forgotten there was another quig in the pen, and the door was still open. The second quig charged out on to the field with just as much fury as the first. But the knights were spent and they didn't have the strength or the will to kill another quig. This was going to be a slaughter. There was nothing to stop this murderous quig . . . except for Uncle Press.

Uncle Press had finished off the last miner, then quickly and carefully pulled the small homemade bomb out from under the ore car full of tak. Rellin tried to stop him, but he was literally pinned to the wooden car and could barely move. The quig crouched down on all fours and surveyed the scene.

It was looking for its first victim and it quickly made its decision. It wanted Uncle Press.

"Uncle Press!" I shouted. Uncle Press looked up to see the quig heading for him at a dead run. Without a second of hesitation he heaved the small bomb at the charging quig. I didn't know if he pushed the button as he threw or not, but whatever happened, the results were spectacular – and gruesome. The small bomb of tak hit the quig in midair and exploded. The force of the tak ripped into the beast and tore it apart, sending pieces of bloody quig raining down on the entire field. It was disgusting and beautiful at the same time. The quig was killed and the means to explode the bigger bomb was gone.

There was an odd calm in the stadium now. It was like no one understood what just happened, or what to do next. Many of the Bedoowan knights were injured or just plain exhausted from their battle with the quig. Kagan stood in her royal box looking down on the carnage. She must have been really confused because she wasn't even eating. The Bedoowan spectators watched in stunned silence. They had no idea if what had happened was planned, or some horrible mistake. Only the Novans reacted. They gave their typical polite applause. Gotta love those guys.

I looked to Loor and said, "What took you so long with the door?"

"I had two knights on my back," she answered. Not only had she lifted the heavy lock, she did it while fighting off two of the Bedoowan knights. Uncle Press walked over to Rellin and pulled the spear out of his arm, releasing him. He then gave him a rag to tie his wound. Loor and I joined them. Nobody knew what to say. I couldn't tell if Rellin was angry, disappointed, in pain, or all the above.

That's when Rellin started to laugh.

It was the last reaction I expected. It was the same kind of crazy laugh I heard from him down in the mines. It was like he knew something we didn't know. Again, it gave me the creeps.

Finally Rellin said, "You think this is over, but it is not."

"Yes, it is," said Uncle Press. "You have no way to explode this tak now."

Rellin laughed even harder. What was going through his mind?

"But this is not all the tak that was brought from the mines," he said. "This grand weapon may have failed, but the signal has been given just the same. It was you who gave that signal, Press, my friend."

The three of us looked at each other, befuddled. What was he talking about? Then it hit me. I remembered what Rellin had said to me the night before. He said that as soon as his miners heard the explosion, it would be their signal to attack. And there had certainly been an explosion. Granted it wasn't the big boom everybody was expecting, but it was pretty loud just the same. There were quig guts all over the place as proof. Could the Milago miners have heard it? The answer to that question came right away. A horn sounded from on top of the stadium. All eyes looked up to see a lone Bedoowan knight standing there.

"The Milago!" he shouted for all to hear. "They're attacking!" Instantly the Bedoowan knights scrambled. Even the knights who had bravely fought the quig and were wounded jumped to attention. They grabbed their spears, straightened their helmets and quickly climbed up the stairs of the stadium.

"Look!" said Loor and pointed towards Kagan's royal box. What we saw were more knights, hundreds of them, all piling out from inside the palace to join their comrades. Queen Kagan stood on her throne, laughing and clapping like a child, cheering them on. To her, this was a game. She had no idea that these men were heading into a very real battle. Or maybe she just didn't care.

The knights were now several hundred strong. They looked like a formidable fighting unit. They marched up the stairs of the stadium to join with their comrades and begin the defence of the palace. Then an odd thing happened. The Bedoowan spectators began climbing the stairs to the surface as well. They were excitedly laughing and chatting with anticipation. They were followed in turn by the Novans. This was unbelievable. It was like they wanted to watch the battle for themselves. Did they think this was going to be a show put on for their amusement, like the quig battles? Did they have any idea what was about to happen?

Rellin said, "We may not have made our grand statement, but we will still have our battle. We are armed with tak and we will triumph. Your efforts have been in vain. The battle is about to begin."

DENDURON

Much of what I am going to write about now was told to me after the battle. As I wrote before, I have no doubt that it is all true and I have no problem adding it to my journal. I'll try to recount it in the order that it happened.

When Alder left us to warn the Milago villagers about the bomb, nobody listened to him as he ran through the village shouting, "Everyone! Into the mines! You must protect yourselves!" But I guess none of the villagers even knew about tak, let alone about the huge bomb that was supposed to blow away the Bedoowan. So when Alder came running through like a nut job, they slammed their doors in his face and ignored him. I don't blame them. If a guy ran around all Chicken Little screaming that the sky was falling, I'd probably ignore him too. Alder quickly realised that trying to save them was futile. His last hope was to find the one group of people who might listen to him: the miners who were preparing for battle. They knew about tak and they knew about Rellin's mad plan. So Alder ran out to the training area where Rellin and his miners had captured us the day before.

What he found there was a frightening sight. All the

miners of the Milago had assembled. There were hundreds of them. It never seemed like there were all that many miners living in the village, but that was because most of them were usually in the mines. Not today. All the miners were now on the surface and they were ready to rumble. According to Alder they had emptied the secret stash of weapons from down in the mines and each of them was armed with either spears or bows and arrows. But more important, several of the miners carried a much more lethal weapon. Around their waists were leather pouches full of small tak bombs.

As Alder ran through the crowd looking for someone in charge, he looked into the eyes of these hardened miners. He told me that what he saw gave him a chill. Even though they were about to begin a battle that could cost them their lives, these guys showed no fear. I suppose a lifetime of slavery will do that to you. They wanted blood. Bedoowan blood. They may not have been trained warriors, but what they lacked in fighting skills was made up for with pure hatred for the Bedoowan. They were confident, too. Once Rellin exploded his bomb, they figured that most of the Bedoowan knights would die instantly. Any of the knights who survived would be easy to mow down with their precious tak. They thought the battle would be short and sweet.

They were absolutely, totally wrong.

Alder finally found the leader. It was a miner who stood towards the front of the group giving orders. Alder ran up to him and said breathlessly, "The bomb . . . the tak bomb. It is more deadly than you could imagine! If Rellin succeeds, it could kill us all! We must get everyone down into the mines to – "

That's when it happened. That's the moment when Uncle

Press threw the small bomb at the quig and made quigburger. The miners all looked in the direction of the Bedoowan castle as the explosion thundered through the hills. Then just as the last echo died away, the leader shouted, "Death to the Bedoowan!"

There was a huge cheer and the miners began running towards the castle. Alder had to dive out of the way for fear of being trampled by the stoked-up miners as they rushed to their destiny. They had no idea that they were headed right into the full force of the Bedoowan army.

The stadium was almost empty. Even Queen Kagan had left to watch the show. Four Novans had lifted up her throne and carried her up the stairs and out to the battlefield. Those pale little guys must be a lot stronger than they looked because that throne and that fatso must have weighed a ton. The three miners who brought the tak bomb with Rellin were gone too. They had run off to fight with their comrades. The only ones left in the huge stadium were me, Loor, Uncle Press, Rellin, and a dead quig. Actually two dead quigs, but the second one looked more like Hamburger Helper.

Rellin struggled to get to his feet. Uncle Press gave him a hand. These guys weren't enemies. They both wanted the same thing, sort of. Their only disagreement was how to go about getting it.

"Your miners aren't prepared to battle those knights," Uncle Press said to him. "The tak may prolong the fight, but the Bedoowan will crush them."

"Perhaps," said Rellin. "But better to die fighting, than as a slave."

Those were powerful words. I had seen the horrible lives the Milago lived. If they were going to die, at least now they would die with some dignity. It was a terrible choice, but maybe it was the right one. Rellin then said, "Permit me to join my men?"

Uncle Press picked up the spear he had used to stop Rellin from exploding the bomb. He looked at it, then handed it to the chief miner. "Good luck," he said.

Rellin took the spear, gave a small nod of thanks, then took off running to join his doomed men. We watched him run across the stadium grass and bound up the stairs towards the battle that was about to begin. I wondered if I would ever see the guy alive again. Uncle Press then picked up another spear.

"What are you doing?" I asked.

"I'm going back to the Milago village," he answered. "The Bedoowan are going to suffer casualties. That's never happened to them before. I'm afraid they'll get angry enough to continue on to the Milago village and take it out on some of the villagers."

"But how can you stop that?" asked Loor.

"I can't," was his answer. "But I can help Alder get them down into the mines. The knights won't go down there and it'll give them a chance to cool off."

"We're coming with you!" I said.

"No," ordered Uncle Press and pointed to the ore car full of tak. "See what you can do about that bomb."

"Like what?" I asked.

Uncle Press started to run off, but turned back to us and shouted, "I don't know. Get rid of it. Dump it in the ocean. Just don't let the Bedoowan have it."

I watched as Uncle Press ran up the stairs. After a quick wave back to us, he disappeared over the lip of the stadium and was gone. I looked to the ore car, then to Loor.

"Is he crazy?" I said. "This is too heavy to carry up those stairs!"

Loor started grabbing the glaze stones from off the top and throwing them aside like they were common rocks. "Not if we make the load lighter," she said.

"And what if we slip and drop it down those stairs?" I countered. "It'll make just as big a bang now as before."

"Then we must be careful not to drop it," she shot back.

Yeah, no kidding. I walked over to the cart and tested the weight. It was heavy! It had four wheels that rolled on the rails down in the mines, and handles both front and back that were used to push or pull it. I didn't care how strong Loor was, the two of us were not going to lug this thing up the stadium stairs. I reached in and dug down beneath the glaze until I found the tak. It was soft, like clay. I was thinking maybe we could pull it apart into smaller pieces and take it up that way, rather than transport the whole thing at once. I scraped it with my finger and pulled out a small piece. For something so deadly, it looked pretty innocent. Like I wrote before, it was rust-coloured and soft like Silly Putty. I easily rolled it into a marble-sized ball. The texture was kind of gritty and there was residue that stuck to my fingers as I rolled it.

"Are you going to help me?" asked Loor impatiently as she unloaded the glaze.

"I have an idea," I announced and ran towards the quig pen. Loor watched me as if I had lost my mind, but she needn't have worried. My plan didn't involve going back into quig world. No way. In fact, as an afterthought I stuck the little ball of tak into my pocket to free my hands and then closed the door to the pen just in case any more of those bad boys were wandering around inside. It was a smart thing to do, but it wasn't the main reason I went over there. I was looking for the water tap where the Bedoowan knight filled the water bucket that he used to wash away the blood of the Milago miner. When I found it, I turned the handle so that water poured out slowly. I then checked my fingers to find that they were still covered with the rusty-coloured tak residue. I stuck my fingers under the faucet, rubbed them together, and the tak dissolved! That was exactly what I hoped would happen. This stuff may be a powerful explosive, but it was still a natural mineral that would dissolve in water. Thank you, Mr Gill, and eighth-grade Earth science. He thought I was asleep in class most of the time. I wasn't.

"What are you doing?" shouted Loor.

I quickly grabbed one of the wooden buckets that was near the tap, filled one, and lugged it back to Loor and the ore car.

"We are wasting time, Pendragon," Loor said with growing impatience.

I ignored her and dumped the bucket of water into the ore car. Loor had this angry look on her face like I was being an idiot again. I stood back with the empty bucket and watched. In a few seconds my patience was rewarded. It was only a small drip, but the water had worked itself down through the tak and was running out between the wooden floorboards of the ore car. The water was rust-coloured, which could mean only one thing . . . the tak could be dissolved!

"We don't have to lug this thing out," I announced. "We can dissolve the tak like dirt."

Loor stuck her finger under the drip of water and saw that it was indeed full of dissolved tak. She thought a moment, then said, "More water!"

She jumped to her feet and ran back to the tap for another bucket. For the next ten minutes we ran back and forth between the tap and the ore car, dumping water inside. Little by little, the tak turned into liquid and ran out of the car. When enough of the tak dissolved so that we could move it, we began taking turns pushing it around. My idea was to spread the tak around enough so that its power would be diluted all over the field. The rusty liquid ran out of the car, poured on to the field and sank down below the grass like some deadly fertiliser. I had no idea what kind of problems this would cause later on. For all I knew, once the tak dried this could be like a minefield. But I didn't care. The main thing was that the power of the huge bomb was gone forever.

Finally I took a look inside the ore car to see that most of the tak was dissolved away. There were still some remnants clinging to the wooden car, but there wasn't enough left to do any big damage. I guess you could say that we had success-fully "liquidated" the bomb. I looked to Loor and smiled.

"Or we could have tried carrying it out," I said with a touch of sarcasm.

I didn't get many chances to dig Loor, so I took them where I could. She looked as if she wanted to say something in return, but was having trouble finding the words. I expected her to point out how I had done something stupid after all.

"I am a warrior," she finally said. "I was raised to fight my enemies with force. That is not what you were taught."

Uh-oh. Here we go. I was sure she was about to tell me what a weenie I was and that we should have muscled the ore car out of the stadium.

"But maybe that is good," she went on. "Maybe that is why we are together. You are not a warrior, yet you have shown more bravery than any warrior I have known."

Whoa. That was out of left field! After getting slammed by her at every turn, I wasn't expecting a compliment. I didn't know what to say.

I thought about what she said and realised that maybe she was right. I wasn't a fighter and wasn't planning on becoming one, so maybe our strengths complemented each other. I wrote to you before about the feeling I got that being here felt right. Well, as I stood there with Loor, I got the same feeling. The two of us being together felt right. We weren't exactly buddies, but maybe we were meant to be partners. It must have been hard for her to admit that I was her equal, at least when it came to the bravery department, and I wanted to say something back to her that let her know how great I thought she was. But I didn't get the chance. Before I could open my mouth, I saw something that I could barely believe.

"What is the trouble?" asked Loor.

All I could do was point. Standing in the royal box was Figgis, the little merchant of death who started this whole tak mess. What was he doing here? How did he get into the palace? Stranger still, he must have known what Rellin was trying to do with this bomb, so why did he hang around here knowing the whole place was going to blow up?

"This is strange," she said. "Why is he here?"

As if in answer, Figgis raised his hand to show us something he was holding. It was the yellow walkie-talkie that was taken from me in Queen Kagan's chambers. He held it up, and giggled.

"It is the talking toy," exclaimed Loor. "What is he doing with that?"

My heart sank. We had dodged a huge bullet, but here was another one aimed right at us. Loor looked at me and recognised how scared I was.

"Pendragon, what is the matter?" Loor shouted.

"The walkie-talkie works the same way the torch does," I answered. "It has a battery that gives off a charge of power."

"Could he use it to explode another bomb?" she asked nervously.

"Well, yeah," I answered soberly.

Now Loor looked sick as the reality of the situation hit her. "Do you think he has another bomb?" she asked soberly.

"I don't know," I answered. "But we better find out." I took a step towards the royal box and called out, "Figgis! We want to talk with you!"

In answer Figgis abruptly turned and ran back into the palace.

"C'mon!" I shouted and ran for the royal box.

Loor was right behind me. We both hit the stairs and ran up three at a time until we hit the royal box. Without hesitation we ran into the Bedoowan palace after the strange little man who was responsible for finding the power to destroy all of Denduron.

Outside the palace the two armies were drawing closer. The Milago miners were making their way through the dense forest, while the Bedoowan knights massed along the far side of a giant, open field. This grassy, sloping field was where the long-awaited battle would take place. Behind the Bedoowan was nothing but ocean. Behind the Milago would be forest. Between them was a huge expanse of empty field with nothing to use for protection but sea grass. The Bedoowan knights knew what they were doing. They had trained to protect their palace from marauders. They lined up in rows with shield carriers first, followed by archers, followed by spear carriers on horseback. They were ready.

Alder later told me how he ran through the forest with the miners, trying to get them to turn back. But no one listened. They were locked and loaded and primed for a fight. But when they got to the edge of the forest, the leader held up his hand and the miners stopped short of charging out into the open. It was a smart thing to do, for he saw something that the rest of the miners hadn't yet seen.

Standing across from them on the far side of this vast field were the Bedoowan knights. But they did not look like a straggle of injured survivors who were reeling from a devastating explosion. Just the opposite. There were more knights standing there than the Milago knew existed. They didn't look any worse for wear, either. They were strong and healthy and well armed. Obviously something had gone wrong. The explosion didn't do the damage they had hoped. This battle wasn't going to be the cakewalk they had anticipated. This was going to be a dogfight and they were going up against the best dogs in town.

The Milago leader held his army back, not entirely sure of what to do. The rest of the Milago miners had now seen the vast army of knights and it shook their confidence.

The only thing that Alder could do was watch, and pray.

When Loor and I ran into the palace, we found ourselves in Queen Kagan's empty chambers. We got our bearings, then dashed out into the corridor. I looked towards the stairs and caught a quick glimpse of Figgis scampering down.

"There!" I shouted and ran after him.

Loor was right behind me. We got to the stairs and started down. They were wide, spiralling stairs, and as we ran down we could see that Figgis was far below, heading for the lowest levels of the palace. We bounded down the stairs as fast as we could without taking a header and breaking our necks. When we hit the bottom, I saw that my boom box was there, only it was in pieces. That's how the knights finally got it to stop playing. They smashed it. I guess no one knew how to use the on-off switch. Idiots. I had the presence of mind to dig through the debris for the batteries. It may have been too little too late, but at least nobody could use these batteries to blow anything up.

We both took a quick look around for Figgis and heard a familiar giggle coming from down the corridor. The thought came to me that he was playing with us. But it didn't matter. We had to stop him. So we took off down the corridor.

"He is going for the mines," she said. "He must know the secret entrance."

She was right. That's probably how he got into the palace in the first place. Since we knew the way, we didn't bother looking down every corridor for the little guy. We headed right for the kitchen, which led to the pantry, which led to the trapdoor and the tunnels that would drop us down into the secret passage of the Milago mine that stretched beneath the palace.

In the forest, the Milago leader didn't know what to do. This wasn't the way it was supposed to happen. They weren't supposed to fight the Bedoowan army at its best. Should he attack or retreat? His decision would clearly decide the future of his tribe. Luckily for him, the responsibility for making a decision was soon taken away from him. With a roar of excitement from the miners, he looked to see a familiar face making his way towards him through the crowd. It was Rellin. He was here to take charge.

The sight of their trusted leader sent a rumble of relief

through the Milago miners . . . not to mention to the interim leader who no longer had to be in charge any more. It must have been a stirring sight, seeing their leader walking confidently to the front of his troops to take command. He jumped on to a rock so that all the Milago could see him and announced, "My brave Milago brothers! Today is the day. Now is the time. This is where our slavery ends!"

The miners all gave a cheer. Rellin was stirring them up again.

"Bring the tak to bear!" he commanded and all of the miners who had the tak and catapults came to the front of the group. "Are we prepared to take back our lives?"

Everyone let out a whooping cheer. They were no longer concerned about why he hadn't died. He was their inspirational leader, and they trusted him.

"Are we prepared to win our freedom?"

Another cheer.

"Are we prepared to make the Bedoowan pay for their crimes against us?"

That brought the biggest cheer of all. They were ready.

"Then do not stop until we have reached the throne room!"

That was it. The miners went nuts and the charge was on. With the tak throwers first, they charged out of the forest and on to the field to meet their enemy.

While this was going on, Loor and I dropped down the ladders into the Milago mine. No sooner did we hit the tunnel, than Loor stopped short, her ear to the air.

"Listen," she said.

I did, and after a second I heard what she was talking about. It was footsteps. Running footsteps. Figgis wasn't far away. But the strange thing was, they were coming from deeper in the tunnel. That didn't make sense because the tunnel didn't go on much farther. There was nothing beyond the end of this tunnel but a long drop to the sea. So where was that sound coming from?

Loor didn't stop to think, as usual. She headed deeper into the tunnel. Her senses told her that someone was back there running and she didn't bother to let logic stop her from following her instinct. All I could do was follow. We didn't go more than twenty yards before we came upon another offshoot from the main tunnel. It was a crudely dug side tunnel that was wide enough for one person to pass at a time. This is where Figgis went, so this is where we had to go too. As always, Loor went first. She ran into the tunnel, unafraid of what she might find. That was cool with me; she was the macho end of this duo, after all. Luckily the tunnel wasn't all that dark because there was enough light that seeped in from the main tunnel to let us see our way.

"I see the far end," Loor announced. "This tunnel connects with another tunnel."

I looked ahead and saw that she was right. This side tunnel connected with another large tunnel. But it soon proved to be more than just a shortcut. Before we reached the other end, the side tunnel grew wide and opened up into a large space. We stopped, trying to figure out why this cavern existed so deep inside the Milago mine. I took a step and felt something weird under my feet. It was a soft, springy sensation, like walking on tiny bits of rubber. I knelt down and scooped up a bit of the stuff to give it a close look. It had the feel of eraser dust. You know, the stuff you brush off your paper after erasing something. It didn't take me long to realise what it really was though, and my heart nearly stopped.

"What is it?" asked Loor.

"It . . . it's tak," I said with a dry mouth. "I think we just found out where Figgis got the tak. He mined it . . . from right here."

"That is right!" came a giggling voice from the tunnel ahead.

"Figgis!" shouted Loor and continued on to the end of the side tunnel.

I followed her out and into the wider tunnel on the far side. When I hit the intersection I saw that this next tunnel stretched out in two directions. Ore-car track was at our feet and an empty ore car sat on the tracks to our right. It was an ancient Milago mine tunnel. I looked at the floor and saw there was a lot more rusty tak dust coating everything. This must have been residue from when Figgis mined the stuff out of the rock. Like gold dust. A thin layer of the deadly stuff was everywhere. But there was something else strange about this place. It looked somehow familiar. The ore car, the opening to the side tunnel, the pile of rocks in front of the opening. I felt as if I'd been here before.

That's when my ring began to glow. I looked to Loor and she had already seen her own ring glowing. We had indeed been here before. This was the tunnel that held the gate to the flume. When we used the flume the other day, we had no idea that we were close to Figgis's source for tak. I looked to my left and sure enough, a few yards down the tunnel was the wooden door that led to the flume.

"Why does this whole setup give me the creeps?" I asked Loor.

She felt it too. Why would Figgis lead us down to the one place that he would want to keep secret? The answer came in the form of a rumble.

"What is that?" asked Loor nervously.

I listened. The rumble grew louder. It was either thunder, an earthquake, or . . .

"Cave-in!" I shouted.

I grabbed Loor's hand and ran along the track in the direction that would take us back to the main cavern of the mine. We passed the door to the flume and got only a few steps further when the ceiling in front of us collapsed! Tons of rock and gravel fell down, blocking our way out. My first thought was to go for the gate and jump into the flume, but we couldn't leave Denduron. Not now. So we ran back into the tunnel and dived into the side tunnel that led to Figgis's tak mine.

No sooner had we entered the tak mine than another cave-in sealed off the smaller tunnel ahead of us. Rocks tumbled down from the ceiling and poured into the small cavern. I took a few steps back and fell down on my butt. When I turned to get up, I came face to face with something that had tumbled down in front of me when the ceiling collapsed. It was a skeleton. I'm not ashamed to admit it; I screamed. Yes, I screamed like an idiot in a *Scooby Doo* cartoon. I quickly scrambled away and Loor helped me to my feet. The two of us stood there holding each other, not sure of what to do. It seemed as if the cave-in had stopped, at least for the time being.

Loor looked at the skeleton and said, "It must be a miner who was trapped here."

That made sense. But then I saw something that threw her theory out of the window. I took a closer look at the skeleton. He wore rotted-out leather clothing that marked him as Milago. But there was something else, something unique that made me want to scream all over again. The corpse wore an eye patch. The cloth was shredded and dangled down from the empty socket, but it had definitely once been a patch. And that's not all. On each of his bony fingers was a braided green ring. I had seen this only once before and remembered it all too well. This wasn't any miner.

"It's Figgis," I said, trying not to sound too freaked out.

"That cannot be!" exclaimed Loor. "Unless we have been chasing a ghost."

Then a voice came from behind us. "I am afraid it is indeed Figgis."

Both Loor and I spun to see someone standing in the opening to the tak mine. It was *Figgis*! Huh? The guy looked pretty healthy for a, okay I'll say it, for a ghost.

"The poor little man died a few years ago," he said. "Such a tragedy. He set traps to protect his little find here. That's why the ceiling collapsed. He didn't want anybody else to steal it from him. He died setting one of those traps. So sad. Such a visionary, and so . . . dead."

My mind was not getting around any of this. We stood there staring at Figgis, uncomprehending.

"I see you have not figured this out yet," he said with a smug smile. "Let me make things easier for you." And then, the little man began to transform. I had seen this happen once before, in a lonely subway station in the Bronx. His hair grew long and his body grew back to its normal height of seven feet. His leather Milago clothes changed into an all-black suit, and his eyes flashed with icy blue intensity. Yes, we were looking at Saint Dane, and he had us trapped under a ton of rock with no escape.

"I told you, Pendragon," he said with a smile. "You can't beat me."

DENDURON

The Milago miners charged out of the forest. The attack was on.

The Bedoowan knights didn't budge. They wanted to see what these bold peasants had planned. The first line of miners stopped and loaded their slingshots with tak. On command they flung their explosives at the waiting Bedoowan. The small tak bombs flew across the battlefield and exploded on impact. But they had fallen far short of the front line of the Bedoowan defence. If they were going to do any damage, they were going to have to get closer, which meant they had to put themselves within range of the Bedoowan archers.

The Bedoowan on the other hand, were surprised by the explosions that blasted down in front of them. Except for the quig that had been blown to bits in the stadium, they had never witnessed anything like this. There was a movement along the lines to retreat, but the Bedoowan commander wouldn't let them budge. They were going to hold their ground. The Bedoowan commander sent a line of shield carriers to the front. These brave men stood in line like a barrier of steel and flesh to protect their comrades from the incoming missiles. Behind them, the archers stood ready to release their arrows as soon as the Milago miners were in range. This was going to get real ugly, real quick.

But I didn't know any of this until afterwards. Right now I had my own problem to deal with, which was Saint Dane. There was no way out. We were trapped by two cave-ins that were caused by Figgis's booby traps. The only way out of this seemed to be through the flume. But it might as well have been a mile away because standing between us and the gate was Saint Dane.

"You brought the tak here, didn't you?" I spat at the guy.

"I did no such thing!" he said, acting all innocent. "Tak is natural to Denduron. Figgis discovered this vein several years ago."

He walked over to one of the walls and scraped off a layer of dirt with his hand. As the dirt fell away, I saw beneath it the familiar rusty red colour of tak. I looked to Loor and for the first time since we met, she looked scared. That's because she realised, as I did, that this entire cavern was made of tak. The bomb we had dissolved in the stadium was like a firecracker compared to this cavern . . . and we were standing in the middle of it.

"Figgis thought the miners could use the tak to help them tunnel through the rock," Saint Dane explained. "It was noble of him, but he was a merchant and he thought like one. He wanted to help the miners, but he also wanted to make a profit."

The evil Traveller walked over to the skeleton that used to be Figgis and nudged the bones with his foot. "I can't say that I blame him, but his greed proved to be his undoing. He set traps all over this cavern to protect his precious find. Unfortunately one of them backfired."

He kicked Figgis's skull and it rolled away from the body and landed at our feet. I wanted to kick it back just to keep it away from me, but that would have been gross.

"So you came to Denduron and took his place," I said. "And you showed the Milago miners how to use tak as a weapon."

"Of that, I am guilty," he said with a proud smile.

"But we stopped you," Loor shot back at him. "Rellin did not use the bomb."

Saint Dane answered this with a laugh. I didn't like that. When bad guys laugh it means they know something you don't.

"But it is better this way," he said with smug authority. "If that bomb had blown up it would have taken much longer for the Milago to regroup. Now, once they have won their little war they will still be strong enough to begin their march across Denduron. I suppose I should thank you, Pendragon."

Oh, man, was it possible? By preventing that bomb from going off, did I make things worse? "And what if they don't win the war?" I asked. "What if the Bedoowan win?"

Saint Dane brushed more dirt off the walls, revealing more tak. "No matter," he said with a shrug. "There is an endless supply of tak. It may take time, but the Milago will come back. They will find new ways to use this lovely weapon. It is inevitable, Pendragon. This will soon become a territory at war. Denduron will fall. And when it does, it will be the beginning of the end of Halla."

Halla. There was that word again. This was all about Halla.

On the battlefield above, the Milago miners had crept closer to the Bedoowan knights. They were now within range to catapult the tak into the front line of shield carriers. The frightened Bedoowans huddled beneath their shields as the tak bombs smashed into them. With small explosions the tak burst on impact against the shields and threw a blast of fire into the ranks. Several of the Bedoowan knights died right there. Others got smart and realised it wasn't a good thing to let the small rock bombs hit their shields. They began to dodge out of the way rather than shield themselves as the tak bombs rained down, setting off explosions that tore up the ground.

That's when the next line of Bedoowan knights began sending their arrows. They were too far away to take direct aim, so they arched their arrows high into the air towards the Milago. The black little streaks shot across the sky and rained down on the Milago silently. Some found their mark, others stuck harmlessly into the ground. But there were enough arrows in the air to prevent the Milago miners from flinging their tak uncontested.

Watching this all from a safe distance from the battlefield were the rest of the Bedoowans and the Novans. They had spread out along the grassy bluffs to witness the spectacle as if it were a show put on for their amusement. Children played, musicians performed, and food was passed around as though at some kind of summer festival. Queen Kagan was positioned in the centre of it all and stood on her throne to get the best view possible.

In the Milago village Uncle Press had found Alder, and the two of them tried again to warn the villagers to hide in the mines. The villagers knew Uncle Press, so at least they didn't slam doors in his face. But time after time they got the same response. To a person, the villagers were prepared to do battle with the Bedoowan. It didn't matter if they were women or children or the elderly or the sick. None of them feared death, nor did they fear the Bedoowan. Their only fear was having to continue to live the horrible lives they had been born into. No, these people were not about to run and hide. If the Bedoowan knights got past the miners, they would be ready, and they would fight.

Frustrated, Uncle Press and Alder ran quickly to the battlefield. Arrows rained down on the Milago while tak bombs scattered the front lines of the Bedoowan. Uncle Press and Alder were stymied. They wanted the Milago to defeat the Bedoowan, but not with tak. The true enemy here was tak. But if they somehow convinced the Milago to stop using it, the miners would be overrun by the Bedoowan. It was a no-win situation.

And speaking of no-win situations, Saint Dane had just said something that scared me to death. He said that the fall of Denduron was the beginning of the end for Halla. Uncle Press said Halla was everything that existed. Every place, every territory, every time that ever was. If Saint Dane succeeded in destroying Halla, did that mean that the entire universe would be destroyed? The thought was too huge to comprehend.

"Why do you want to destroy Halla?" I asked.

Saint Dane laughed. Great, more laughing. I hated that.

"You are young, Pendragon," he said. "There is much you do not know. But I will say this: When Halla crumbles, I will be there to pick up the pieces."

That sounded ominous. "I don't believe you," I said. "How can one man control the destiny of the entire universe?"

Saint Dane ran his hand over the wall of tak. "It is like lining up dominoes," he said. "Pushing over the first domino takes almost no effort, but when it falls it knocks down the next and the next and the next until before long there is nothing left but a pile of toys in complete disarray. The territory of Denduron is my first domino."

It was true. Denduron was only the beginning. Saint Dane would then turn to the next territory and the next. It would only be a matter of time before he worked his evil on Loor's home territory of Zadaa and set his sights on our home. On Second Earth.

"Your mother is dead," Saint Dane said to Loor. "But what of the rest of your family on Zadaa? And you, Pendragon, what of your family on Second Earth? And your friends, what are their names? Mark and Courtney? When the dominoes fall, they will all be caught in the crush."

I wanted to scream. It was like he had read my mind. This guy *was* evil.

"But this does not have to be a tragedy," he said with an oily smile. "Think of it as an opportunity. You two are strong. You have powers that you cannot imagine. If you joined me, I would teach you how to use them. Fighting against me is impossible, but fighting with me can bring you untold rewards. You could protect your loved ones, and live to rule Halla beside me. It is a wonderful thing I am offering you."

On the battlefield above, things were getting worse. The Milago had been able to keep the Bedoowan back while suffering only minor casualties. The Bedoowan side of the field was a mess. There were fires burning everywhere and the tak had chewed up the ground. However, the Bedoowan casualties were very few. They had mostly managed to avoid the incoming tak. Now the Bedoowan commander realised that the incoming bombs were slowing down. The Milago were running out of their strange and horrible weapon.

Rellin watched the action from behind the spear carriers. His worst fears were coming true. The Milago had used up most of their tak bombs, yet the Bedoowan were still a mighty force. Soon they would be out of tak altogether and the Bedoowan would overrun them. Their only hope of victory was to strike while the Bedoowan knights were still back on their heels. Rellin needed to summon every bit of courage he had in order to do what must be done. He stood up behind his miners, grabbed a spear, and shouted, "Freedom!"

The miners screamed in defiance and ran across the field towards their enemy. The Bedoowan commander seemed stunned that these peasant miners would have the audacity to challenge his vaunted knights. But if a fight was what they wanted, he was willing to oblige. He motioned for his spear carriers on horseback to come forward. With a sweep of his hand, he sent the knights charging towards the oncoming Milago.

Alder and Uncle Press watched in horror as these two tribes ran to meet each other in the centre of the field. Queen Kagan jumped up and down, giggling with delight. Only one thing was certain.

It was going to be bloody.

In the mine below, Saint Dane waited for our response to his offer. He had asked us to join him in his mad quest to control all that exists and threatened that our loved ones would die if we refused. It seemed as if we had run out of options. The guy scared the life out of me. I hated looking at him, so I looked down at the ground.

What I saw there started me thinking.

I saw rusty tak dust stuck to the Bedoowan shoes I had been wearing. I kept my head down and looked around the small cavern to see that tak dust was everywhere. It coated the floor and the walls and even seemed to hang in the air.

That's when I remembered something. It was something I had done a while ago without thinking. I didn't know it at the time, but it might turn out to be the key to saving Denduron. My mind raced. If I was going to make a move, it had to be now. I had no idea what was happening in the battlefield above, but after what Saint Dane had said, it really didn't matter. This wasn't about the Bedoowan or the Milago. This was about a horrible weapon that would change the course of a peaceful territory and send it to ruin. If anything must be stopped, it would have to be the supply of tak.

To be honest, it scared me to think about doing what I was about to do. But I didn't see any other choice. I wasn't even sure if it would work. I might end up looking like an idiot. No problem there, I was used to that. But if it did work, there was a good chance that Loor and I would die. Neither outcome was exactly a good one, but it was clear that I had to give it a try.

"Saint Dane," I said, trying to keep my voice from cracking with fear. "I believe you."

Loor shot me a surprised look. She didn't know where I was going with this . . . yet.

"I can't explain why we're Travellers, or how it's possible to travel through flumes, or how you can do the things you do, but I've seen enough to know that it's all real. I don't know if you have the power to bring down the universe, or Halla or whatever you call it, but I do believe that you can cause a hell of a lot of trouble. If toppling Denduron is the first part of your plan, then I can't let you do it."

I could feel Loor stiffen next to me. She knew I had something in mind and she wanted to be ready.

Saint Dane watched me with a smug smile and said, "And how do you plan to stop me?"

"I'm not," was my answer. "I'm going to stop the supply of tak."

That's when I reached into my pocket and pulled out the little ball of tak that I had taken out of the ore car in the stadium. I had put it into my pocket before closing the door to the quig pen. Now this little piece of explosive clay could be the only hope for Denduron. As I wrote before, I wasn't sure if this would work. But what I saw next made me think that it just might. For as soon as I pulled it out, I saw something that I didn't think was possible.

Saint Dane blinked.

The smug smile dropped off his face and I saw something in his eyes that made my heart leap. I saw fear. Up until then he had orchestrated everything that happened on Denduron. But things were about to change and he knew it. Seeing this in his eyes gave me a shot of confidence. I looked to Loor. She nodded. She knew what might happen to us, but she also knew that it was the only way. We were seconds away from salvation – or doomsday.

The battlefield above had erupted into a clash of bodies and clubs and horses and steel. The Milago were driven by their hatred and anger, the Bedoowan by their training and strength. It was going to be an even fight, which meant both sides were going to suffer huge casualties. The worst of the fighting was about to begin.

Saint Dane made a move to stop me. "No!" he shouted in panic.

But before he could take a second step, I threw my little

ball of tak down at the ground. There was an explosion. Not a big one, but big enough. The small ball of tak erupted and shot out a blast of flame. The explosion didn't do much damage, but that didn't matter. It was the flame I was counting on. That small, hot burst of fire ignited the tak dust on the floor. Instantly, the tiny little bits of tak began to burn. It looked like a Fourth of July sparkler on the floor of the cavern as the dust ignited and shot up into the air. But more important, the eruption began to spread. With each passing second the fizzing and popping circle of sparks grew larger. There was so much tak dust on the floor and in the air that this fire had plenty of fuel to burn.

Saint Dane jumped at the expanding ring of sparks and desperately tried to stamp it out with his feet.

"No! No!" he shouted at me in anger.

For all his ability to manipulate people and twist them into doing his dirty work, he was powerless against this simple, growing fire. There was an unlimited amount of fuel and as soon as it grew big enough, the sparkling ring of fire would ignite the large vein of tak that ran through the mine. Once that happened, well, we'd all find out soon enough.

Saint Dane gave up trying to stop it and shot me a look of hatred that froze the blood in my veins. "This isn't the end, Pendragon," he seethed.

"Don't be sad, Saint Dane," I said. "This is the way it was meant to be."

Saint Dane looked as if he were about to erupt with anger. His icy blue eyes flashed with hatred. I must have pushed a pretty raw button to get him that ticked off. Loor thought he was going to attack us because she took a threatening step towards him, daring him to charge. I think he might have done it too, but he took a quick look around at the rapidly growing fire and decided to back off.

"Until next time," he said, then turned and ran out into the Milago tunnel.

The sparkling ring of tak fire was growing larger by the second. It was like a fuse that couldn't be stopped as it got closer and closer to setting off the mother of all bombs. I had no idea how much time we had, but if we had any hope of surviving we had to get out of there.

"The flume!" I said and ran towards the tunnel. Loor was right after me. We hit the mine tunnel and ran straight for the gate that led to the flume. The wooden door was already open because Saint Dane had the same idea. As I was about to turn into the doorway I heard Saint Dane inside.

"Cloral!" he yelled into the flume.

We ran inside the gate in time to see the sparkling light that was Saint Dane disappear into the depths of the flume on his way to . . .

"What is Cloral?" I asked.

"It must be another territory," Loor answered.

"Let's not go there, okay?" I said. "We should go – " Before I had the chance to say another word, we both saw something in the flume. The sparkling lights and musical notes were heading our way. Was Saint Dane coming back? As the lights grew closer, I heard a sound that didn't make sense. It sounded like . . . water. We took a curious step closer to the flume and saw that it wasn't a Traveller heading our way at all. It was an actual rush of water coming through the flume. What was Saint Dane doing? Was he trying to put the fire out?

The answer was no. He was trying to prevent us from escaping through the flume. But it wasn't just water he was sending back. There was something *in* the water, and it had teeth. Swimming towards us through the flume was a giant shark! As impossible as it sounds, the thing must have been twenty feet long and was heading straight for us, jaws first. There was one other thing I remember: It had vicious, glowing yellow eyes.

We didn't have time to move and were both hit with the crushing wave of water. The force hit us so hard that it sent us both hurtling back out of the gate and slammed us against the far wall of the tunnel. That force of water was the only thing that saved us. If we had stayed at the mouth of the flume, we would have been rudely introduced to shark teeth. I got my head together, grabbed Loor and pulled her to the side just in time because the huge yellow-eyed shark was propelled out of the gate and it smashed, head first, into the far wall of the tunnel. It was now a fish out of water, literally. It squirmed and thrashed in the mine tunnel and its giant jaws bit at the air only a few feet from our heads. I tried to crawl away, but saw that Loor was unconscious. She must have smashed her head when she hit the wall. I grabbed hold of her and was able to drag her farther back into the tunnel and safety.

Did I say safety? We may have got out of range of the monster shark, but the fuse was still burning on the tak mine. We had nowhere to go. We couldn't get to the flume because there was three thousand pounds of thrashing shark in the way. We couldn't get back through the small tunnel to the Bedoowan castle because of the cave-in. The only place we could go was deeper into the mine. To make things worse, if that was possible, Loor was unconscious.

I tried to shake her awake, but it was no go. Her lights were out and I was looking down at a deadweight. It's amazing what adrenalin will do, because I stood up and was actually able to pick her up and get her on my back in a fireman's carry. I had no idea how much time we had left, but moving slowly was not an option. I tried to run with her, but it was hard. I couldn't get very far this way. We got past the entrance to the tak mine and I glanced in to see that the entire floor was ablaze. The place looked alive with mad fireflies as the tak dust sputtered and burned. I didn't take the time to stop and admire it though. I had to get us farther into the mine.

That's when I saw something that could help. It was the wooden ore car. If this thing still moved I could put Loor inside and push her the way Alder had pushed us before. With Loor still on my back I gave the car a kick. It moved! Yes! Without worrying about being gentle, I dumped Loor into the empty car. I didn't think she'd mind a few bruises under the circumstances. I quickly jumped to the back of the car and pushed. It moved slowly at first, but with each turn of the small wheels it picked up speed. I kept both hands on the car while pumping my legs like a football lineman hitting a blocking sled. I went from a crawl, to a walk, to a jog, and finally to a run. I had no idea where this tunnel would lead, but we were on our way.

The thought flashed through my head that we might hit a piece of damaged track that would send the car crashing into the wall. I also feared that the tunnel would reach a dead end that we'd hit at full speed. That would hurt. Or a wheel could fall off. Or . . . or . . . I thought of a million other things that could derail our escape, but none of them mattered. This trip wasn't about caution, it was about speed. If we had any hope of surviving, we had to get as far away from that burning vein of tak as possible.

And then I heard it. It started as a rumble and quickly grew like an earthquake. It felt like a freight train was barrelling up from behind, but I knew what it was. The burning dust had finally reached the large deposit of tak. The chain reaction had begun. The rumble was actually a series of small explosions, and those small explosions would set off bigger explosions. And bigger and bigger until . . . well, there would be a very big bang. I didn't stop to think about it. If anything it made me push harder. I could feel the ground shudder. The finale of this baby was going to be a thousand on the Richter scale.

On the battlefield the miners and the knights felt it too. Alder described it as the ground beginning to move under his feet. The fighting continued until they realised the shaking wasn't going to stop. One by one they dropped their weapons and backed away from each other. There was now a more frightening enemy.

Queen Kagan stood on her throne and threw a fit because the fighting had ended. Before she had the chance to order anyone to continue the battle, the ground shook and knocked her throne over. She tumbled down right along with it, and lay flat on the ground, scared to death. The rest of the Bedoowans and the Novans did the same thing. They all fell to the ground in fear. The fun and games were over.

Uncle Press and Alder didn't move. They knew it was futile to seek shelter, so they stood together and waited for the end. They weren't going to have to wait long.

The rumbling grew louder. It began to sound more like deep, booming explosions. As I pushed the cart with every bit of energy I had, I began to feel heat at my back. The tak mine was probably a blast furnace by now. I'm sure the shark was already roasted. It wouldn't be long before the whole mine blew.

Up ahead the tunnel was growing brighter. We were reaching the end, but I had no idea what that meant because I was crouched down behind the ore car pushing for all I was worth. Still, whatever was up there meant we had a shot at getting out, so I dug down even deeper and pumped my legs even harder. The faster we moved, the brighter the tunnel became. We were definitely nearing the end. Now the tunnel was shaking so violently that I was afraid it would throw the ore car off the track. If we didn't get to the end soon, it would definitely be the end for us.

I don't know why I realised what was about to happen when I did, but I did. It hit me about three seconds beforehand. Maybe it was some kind of survival instinct, but whatever it was, those few seconds prepared me. As we were hurtling down that tunnel with the force of the exploding tak at my back, I remembered about the layout of the mines. We were flying along a track that ran parallel to the tunnel under the Bedoowan palace. I knew where that tunnel ended, and that meant this tunnel would end the same way. This was a ventilation tunnel that led to the ocean bluffs. We were about to be launched out of the end where there was nothing waiting for us but a long drop to the sea.

And that's exactly what happened. Without breaking stride I pushed the ore cart off the end. One second I was running, the next second we were falling. I tumbled out of control, not knowing which way was up. I was desperate to see the water and get my body in a position to take the impact. If I hit head first, I'd break my neck. So I corkscrewed into a position to avoid that. Splashdown was a second away. Believe it or not, the last thought I had before hitting the water was, "Loor can't swim!"

There's only one word I can use to describe the feeling of hitting the water at that speed. Rude. It was just plain rude. I was able to twist myself around so I hit on my side rather than my head, but the impact still knocked the breath out of me. What a jolt! It was worse than when I beefed it off the sled into the snow after the crazy sleigh ride down the mountain. But I didn't lose consciousness this time. Good thing. I didn't want to drown. After all we'd been through, that wouldn't be fair. I came to the surface and looked back up at the opening to the mine. The fall was a big one, maybe thirty feet. But that's not what concerned me at the moment because I also saw that the entire wall of bluffs was shaking. Remember, these were cliffs. It was like looking up at a wall of skyscrapers. If this thing came down, we'd be buried.

I looked around quickly and was relieved to see that Loor was floating near me. She must've fallen out on the way down. I swam to her and listened to her breathing. She was alive, but I didn't know how badly she was hurt. All I wanted to do was swim as far away from the bluffs as possible. I also found the wooden ore car that had been our transportation out of there. It was floating right next to us. Luckily it hadn't hit either of us when we fell. So I got Loor on her back, brought her over to the floating ore car and grabbed on. We had a better chance of surviving with this lifeboat than by my swimming skills alone. I wasn't sure what direction to go in, but I soon realised I didn't have a choice. There was a swift current running parallel to the shore that swept us along. We weren't moving farther out into the ocean, but we were moving steadily away from the mines. It was a good thing too because that's when it happened.

Ignition.

The whole world exploded. The sound was like a deep, powerful growl from a giant demon trapped below ground and struggling to force its way to the surface. A second later, the ventilation shafts along the bluffs blew out, spewing huge blasts of flame that shot over our heads like rocket engines on full power. There must have been twenty openings, all breathing fire that streamed a hundred yards out over the ocean. The water began to churn and roil. It took everything I had to keep Loor and myself afloat. The bluffs themselves seemed to be out of focus. But that was because they were shuddering from an immense force that was tearing them apart from within. My thoughts went to Uncle Press and to Alder. They were up there somewhere. If the top blew off like a monster volcano, they'd be done.

Mark, Courtney, what I saw then will haunt me until the day I die. The eruption had begun a good thirty seconds before, but the powerful flames continued to jet from the holes in the bluff with incredible intensity. I allowed myself one small bit of hope that most of the force from the exploding tak would be funnelled out through these openings. Maybe these man-made openings would act like release valves to get rid of the force of the explosion before it destroyed the land above, and every living thing on it.

That's when I heard the sound.

It was different to the rumble from the explosions. It sounded more like something was cracking. If you've ever heard the sound that a big tree makes in its last moments as it falls to a lumberjack's axe, that was what it sounded like. It's a horrible, screeching sound as the tree tries to hold on to the last sinews of its trunk. That high-pitched tearing sound was what I now heard, only multiplied by about a million.

I looked up to my left to see where the sound was coming

from. Imagine a huge, five-storey castle carved into the bluffs. That was the Bedoowan palace, and it was about to fall down. The horrible creaking sounds were the palace's last desperate gasp at trying to hang on to its perch. But it was no use. The force of the exploding tak was tearing it apart. Cracks appeared like spiderwebs all over the stone castle. For a moment I thought it would dissolve into a billion pieces. But with one last groan the giant palace pulled free of the bluff and slowly began to lean over. In a final thunderous crack, the palace let go and toppled into the sea with a monstrous splash.

If the swift current had been running the other way, Loor and I would have been right under it. And though we were clear of the tumbling palace, we weren't safe yet. When the huge building hit, it created a monster surge of water that was heading right for us. If we didn't ride this thing, we'd drown for sure. So I faced the oncoming rush, prepared to ride it like a wave. We both rose with the huge swell and came down on the other side safely. Unlike regular wave sets, there was no second wave to worry about. This was a one-time phenomenon, and we had survived it.

Once the immediate danger had past, I looked at the castle. Or should I say, at what was left of it. The giant structure had hit the water and rolled over. One whole side was above water. I looked up to the bluffs to see a gaping scar that used to be the palace. The only thing left was the heavy columns it had been built upon.

I then realised that the flames had stopped shooting out of the mine airshafts. The rumbling had stopped too. The explosion was over – and we were still alive! Now all we had to do was get to shore. I tried to push the ore car along, but that was more trouble than it was worth. So I kicked the car away, but not without a nod of gratitude, for it had saved our lives.

It didn't take long for me to get Loor to shore. When I got us close enough for my feet to touch sand, I stood up and put her on my back with a fireman's carry again. It wasn't easy. My adrenalin surge was gone, and along with it, most of my strength. So after a difficult struggle I fell to my knees and slid Loor off of me on to the sand.

Then I collapsed. I figured that as soon as I got my breath and Loor woke up, we'd make our way up the bluffs to find Uncle Press and Alder. I feared for what we would find up there, but didn't have the energy left to worry. I wanted to enjoy being alive for a few moments, so I lay down on the sand, closed my eyes and crashed.

I think I had earned it.

DENDURON

I probably would have slept on that beach for weeks if I hadn't been gently nudged awake by something tapping at my foot. As I slowly pulled out of slumberland, I remembered that giant freakin' shark in the flume. I felt the tapping on my foot again and somehow made the connection between that feeling and the shark. Suddenly I was convinced that the shark had survived and was getting ready to bite off my feet. So I yelped and jumped up while pulling my legs closer for protection.

Of course it wasn't the shark. It was Loor. She was awake and trying to rouse me. She hadn't expected my dramatic reaction though, and when I jumped, she did too.

"I am sorry, Pendragon," she said sheepishly. "I did not know you were ticklish."

Ticklish? I was too embarrassed to tell her why I really jumped. "No problem," I said. "How do you feel?"

She rubbed the nasty black and blue mark on her forehead and grimaced.

"My head does not hurt as much as my pride," she said.

"What do you remember?" I asked.

"There was something coming at us from the flume, but what I remember does not make sense."

"Yeah, it does," I said. "It was a shark. Saint Dane didn't want us to follow him."

Loor thought about this for a moment. I think she was hoping that her memory was a bad dream. "After that I do not remember much," she continued. "But I do have memories of you carrying me. Was that a dream?"

"No, it wasn't," I said.

Loor frowned. At some point I would give her all the gory details of our escape, but now wasn't the time. Loor was a proud warrior. It hurt her ego that it took a weakling like me to save her. I didn't need to rub salt in the wound. Not yet anyway. Believe me, at some point I was going to get mileage out of this, but not now.

"You continue to surprise me, Pendragon," she said. "You have proven yourself to be brave and clever, and now it seems you react as a warrior would after all." She paused, and then said, "Thank you."

She had just given me the highest praise she was capable of. In her mind I was worthy of being elevated to the lofty status of warrior. I wasn't sure I agreed with her though. I was no warrior. Everything I did was out of total panic. I never felt as if I had a choice. In fact, I'd just as soon she didn't consider me a warrior because I didn't want her to expect any more heroics. As far as I was concerned, my Indiana Jones days were over. But I couldn't say that so I gave her the simplest, best response possible.

"You're welcome."

I wondered if she had also forgiven me for the death of her mother, but I wasn't about to go there. Loor looked out towards the water. The Bedoowan palace was a giant wreck that barely poked above the surface. Small waves lapped over it and a few seagulls explored its walls. In time the sea would eat away the stone and this mighty symbol of Bedoowan power would turn to sand. But right now it served as a reminder of the fall of the mighty Bedoowan. It was a perfect monument to their destruction.

"Do you think many Bedoowan died?" asked Loor.

"I don't know," was my answer. "I think most of them left to watch the battle. They're going to get a big surprise when they go back home though."

"It is sad," Loor said.

She was right. The Bedoowan were a pretty advanced culture for this place. They could have used their knowledge to improve all of Denduron, but instead they chose to use their power and knowledge to enslave others. The truth was, none of this would have happened if the Bedoowan hadn't abused the Milago. Saint Dane may have pushed it along, but the Bedoowan were already on the path. They had brought this on themselves.

"What of the tak mine?" Loor asked.

"It was a hell of a show," I said. "I'll bet that every ounce of tak was blown away. I don't think we have to worry about the Milago using it any more."

Loor then turned and looked me right in the eye. "If the explosion did this to the palace," she said soberly, "then what of the Milago village?"

That was a good question. My thoughts went immediately to Uncle Press and to Alder. Had they survived? I looked up towards the towering bluffs.

"We've got to climb up," I said, not really wanting to.

We walked to the bluffs and searched for the best way up. This was going to be tough. It was steep and treacherous.

"I can climb rock," suggested Loor. "I will braid a rope

with vines and we will tie ourselves together for safety. It will be dangerous, but we can make it."

"That sounds good," I said while slowly scanning the bluffs. "Or we could take that path over there."

Loor looked to the path I was pointing to. It was narrow and there were dozens of hairpin bends because it was so steep, but it was definitely a path.

"Oh," said Loor. "That could work too."

"C'mon," I said with a smile, and started for the path. Loor followed silently.

The hike up wasn't horrible. The hairpin bends kept the path from getting too steep, but made the trek very long. We didn't talk much as we climbed. I can't speak for Loor, but the closer we got to the top, the more I dreaded what we might find. The last we saw of the Bedoowan and the Milago they were heading for battle. Was the fight over? Did one tribe win? Or would we arrive at the summit to find the tak explosion had created a burned out hole that looked like the bottom of a volcano? I tried to put the worst of those thoughts out of my mind. We would learn the truth soon enough.

When we were nearly on the top, I stopped and looked at Loor. I felt that she was just as worried about what we would find as I was. Neither of us said it, but we both wanted to wait one more second before having to deal with whatever horror was waiting there. After a few moments Loor took a deep breath and nodded. I nodded in agreement and the two of us climbed the last few yards to the summit of the bluffs.

What we saw on top was nothing like I had imagined. First off, it looked as if the surface had remained relatively intact after the tak explosion. There was no gaping volcano-like hole. That was good. Maybe the mine vents channelled away most of the power of the tak explosion after all.

But still, things had changed. It looked as if all the violent action from the explosion took place underground, and the result on the surface was like a huge earthquake had hit. What had once been relatively flat land now looked like a roller coaster of mounds and depressions. The large, flat battlefield of sea grass where the Milago and the Bedoowan fought had been torn apart. Huge boulders had forced their way up from underground and gaping holes had opened up elsewhere. The tak explosion had dramatically torn the terrain apart, changing it forever.

"We should get to the Milago village," I said.

The two of us walked cautiously back the way we knew would bring us to the village as quickly as possible. Though the terrain had become a tumultuous mess, there was something else that stood out even more dramatically. It was the people. There were hundreds of people wandering around in a daze. As we walked towards the village we saw Bedoowans and Novans and knights and miners. They all seemed to drift about in the same stunned haze. No one cared that they were among the enemy, either. Knights and miners passed each other without so much as a second glance. No one spoke, no one fought, no one was afraid. Everyone was just . . . stunned.

There were bodies, too. I didn't know if they were the victims of the tak explosion or the battle. They were being carried off the battlefield and laid next to each other. It didn't matter if they were Bedoowan or Milago, they were laid side by side. As horrible as this was, I had feared there would be way more bodies than this. Between the battle and the tak explosion, I expected everyone to be wiped out. But it now seemed as though nearly everyone had survived. Only a few unlucky victims lay next to each other beside the battlefield.

Loor and I watched this strange scene silently as we made our way towards the village. We looked for the path that would lead us through the woods, but the path was gone. Most of the woods were gone too. Hundreds of trees had fallen and were piled up like pickup sticks. Finding our way through this maze of trees was tricky.

Then I saw something that made me stop and stare. An injured miner was sitting near the stump of a fallen tree. His head was bleeding and he had to lean against the stump for support. A woman knelt beside him, tending to his wounds. She had a bucket of water and some rags. She dipped the cloth into the water and gently dabbed at the miner's wound to clean it. She wasn't rough, she wasn't in a hurry. Her actions looked like a mother taking care of her child. Given all that had happened you wouldn't think this scene was out of the ordinary, but it was. That's because the woman taking care of the Milago miner was a Bedoowan.

"I do not understand," said Loor. "They are enemies."

"Maybe they found a common enemy," was my reply.

We picked our way through the toppled forest and found the Milago village. The place was a mess. Many huts were still standing, but most of them were badly damaged. Some were nothing more than a pile of rubble. The path that led through the village was now a mass of ruts, rocks, and rubble. I looked to the centre of the village and to the platform where the Transfer ceremonies took place. It was destroyed. The large stone foundation was still there, but it was now scorched black. The platform was gone. I was about to suggest we look for Alder and Uncle Press when we heard a familiar voice.

"Loor! Pendragon!"

It was Alder. He was alive! The big bumbling knight came bounding towards us like a happy puppy. In his excitement he tripped over a rock and stumbled, and we caught him before he did a complete face plant. The catch turned into a hug for all of us.

"I feared you were dead!" he exclaimed. "How did you escape from the palace?"

"Long story," I answered. "What happened up here?"

"It was unbelievable!" he shouted. The guy was totally charged. "There was a battle. The Milago tried to defeat the Bedoowan with tak, but the tak ran out so the Milago charged and the two sides clashed and . . . and . . . that's when it happened!"

"What?" asked Loor, though she had a good idea what the answer was.

"The ground came to life!" he shouted. "The earth began to move like the sea! The Milago and the Bedoowan stopped fighting and turned to run, but there was nowhere to go! Trees began to topple and huts fell and the sound . . . the sound was like thunder under the ground. And then came the fire — "

He pointed at the charred remains of the platform in the centre of the village. "Giant pillars of fire shot from the openings to the mines! The flames were like water geysers that shot high into the sky. And then . . . it was over."

Alder fell silent, letting us get our heads around all that he had said. After a moment he asked, "And where were you when this all happened?"

I looked to Loor and she gave me a shrug. That meant she wanted me to answer.

"Well," I said. "We blew up the tak mine. I think that might have had a little something to do with all the excitement."

Alder stared at us with his mouth open in disbelief. He was having trouble processing the information.

"Close your mouth," I said. "Where's Uncle Press?"

"Uhhh, Press," he said, snapping back to reality. "Right. Follow me."

Alder stumbled off and led us through the remains of the Milago village. As we approached a hut that was still fairly intact, Alder gave us the "shh" signal. Whatever we were going to see, he didn't want us to be disruptive. He stayed close to the wall and peered around the corner. Loor and I joined him and looked around the corner as well.

Several yards ahead was the hut that had once been Rellin's. I remembered it because I had been there when he asked me to go back home and get more batteries. But the walls of the hut were gone. It was bizarre. There were people inside who acted as if they were in the hut, but they were really outside and . . . well, you get the picture. There were three people who looked to be having a heart-to-heart meeting. I'm thrilled to say that one of them was Uncle Press. He was alive and looking fine. I wanted to shout to him, but I realised he was in the middle of something heavy, so I bit my tongue.

The second person I saw was Rellin. He looked like he had been through a war, which, in fact, he had. His leather clothes were in shreds and his bandaged arm was caked with dried blood, but he was alive. It was the third person in the hut that was the shocker.

It was Queen Kagan. The woman sat on the floor, hugging her knees to her chest, crying. I swear, she was crying like a two-year-old. I couldn't hear what they were saying, but it looked as if Rellin was speaking to her softly, like a father might speak to a sad child. Uncle Press wasn't saying anything. My guess was that he was there to act as a neutral peacemaker.

It was then that Uncle Press saw us and broke out in a big grin. He excused himself and ran to us. He threw his arms around me like a big old bear and laughed like it was

Christmas. I think he was even crying a little. To be honest, it made me laugh and cry a little bit too. How's that for a couple of tough-ass Travellers to behave? He pulled us back around to the other side of the hut so we wouldn't disturb Rellin and Queen Kagan, then threw his arm around Loor as well. I hadn't seen Uncle Press act like that in forever. For the first time since this adventure began, he was my old Uncle Press again. It was good to have him back. He then pulled away and gave us both a good hard look.

"What?" I finally said.

"Was it you?" he asked. "I mean, all this?" He motioned around to the destruction of the Milago village and I knew exactly what he meant. I looked to Loor. She shrugged, which was becoming our signal that she wanted me to do the talking.

"Well," I said. "Yeah."

Uncle Press burst out laughing. "I told you to get rid of the bomb, not set it off underground!"

"We didn't," I said, and gave him a quick rundown as to what happened from the time he left us in the Bedoowan stadium. Though everything I told him was the absolute truth, I have to admit that it sounded pretty fantastic. I think the most amazing fact of all was that all of this destruction started when I threw down a pea-sized marble of tak. Talk about knocking over the first domino. Wow.

Uncle Press listened closely. So did Alder. I didn't think it was possible, but I believe that the story of our adventure in the tak mine shocked my uncle. I knew it stunned Alder; he still couldn't close his mouth.

"What about Saint Dane?" Uncle Press asked.

"Gone," I answered. "He jumped into the flume. We would have followed him except he sent back this giant monster shark to stop us. It worked."

"Monster shark? That means he's on Cloral," said Uncle Press thoughtfully.

"Exactly!" I exclaimed. "How did you know?"

"Because the quigs on Cloral are giant monster sharks," was his simple answer.

Of course! I should have known! Quigs on Second Earth are monster dogs, quigs on Denduron are monster bears, and quigs on Cloral are monster sharks. It was so simple. Everybody knew that. Mental note to self: Stay away from Cloral.

"What's going on over there?" I asked, referring to the meeting with Queen Kagan and Rellin. I was tired of thinking about quigs, no matter what form they took.

We all looked back around the corner to see the two leaders were still in deep conversation.

"You're looking at two people who are very frightened," Uncle Press said. "They both got a glimpse of the apocalypse. Rellin came close to losing every last one of the Milago and Queen Kagan saw her palace fall into the sea. There's nothing left of their worlds, except for their people."

"What are they talking about?" asked Loor.

"A lot of things," answered Uncle Press. "But the bottom line is, they're talking about how to survive, together."

A few hours ago the idea of the Milago and the Bedoowan living together in cooperation was a joke. They had centuries of baggage to deal with. That kind of thing doesn't go away in an afternoon. But then I thought back to the Milago miner who was being cared for by the Bedoowan woman. They were still people, after all. And since the palace had been destroyed, they were pretty much in the same dire situation. Their best chance of survival was to help each other. It seemed like a lot to ask of mortal enemies, but I guess a cataclysmic event that nearly destroys every living thing in sight will make you rethink your priorities.

"They have a lot to offer each other," added Uncle Press. "The Bedoowan have an advanced knowledge of engineering and chemistry that can help bring the Milago out of the stone age. The Milago are farmers and builders. Now they can finally get something back for their hard work."

"What about the mines?" asked Alder.

"The mines are gone," answered Uncle Press. "When the tak blew, the mines collapsed. It would take decades to get back to where they were. It's not worth it. The Milago are out of the mining business . . . for good."

"That means no more glaze," I added.

"Yeah, no more glaze," said Uncle Press. "The Bedoowan used glaze to trade with other tribes. Now they'll have to be more self-sufficient."

"How do the Novans fit into all this?" I asked.

"They can go back to their own tribe," said Uncle Press. "Or they can stay and help rebuild. It's their choice, but I think they'll stay."

"What if the Milago try to use tak again?" asked Alder. "That is what Saint Dane wanted, is it not?"

"There *is* no more tak," I said with authority. "Rellin couldn't get his hands on any even if he wanted to."

"Rellin is a good man," Uncle Press said sharply. "But he was blinded by his concern for his people. Now he can channel that energy into something more constructive. He's going to be a great leader. But he's going to have his hands full with Queen Kagan. She's a piece of work."

As if he knew we were talking about him, Rellin looked up to us. We made eye contact and Rellin smiled. That one little smile spoke volumes. He had been humbled, and though he looked tired, he also seemed to be at peace. There was a huge task in front of him, but he was the right man for the job.

"There are no guarantees," said Uncle Press. "These people have to work through centuries of hatred and mistrust. But at least now they've got a shot at building a society that can benefit everyone. It's not often that you get a second chance."

As I looked around the ruined Milago village it was hard to comprehend that the best thing that could have happened to these people was the near-destruction of their world. But maybe Uncle Press was right. Maybe the only way they could change was to clean the slate and start over. They were certainly going to get that chance. I truly hoped that they'd make the most of it.

"I'm hungry!" announced Uncle Press. "Loor, could you and Alder head over to the hospital hut? They've set up an emergency supply station there."

Alder and Loor quickly left us to search for some food. But I don't think Uncle Press was really interested in eating. I think he wanted to talk to me alone.

"Let's walk," he said. The two of us left Queen Kagan and Rellin to their discussion and walked through the Milago village.

"How do you feel, Bobby?" he asked me.

Now there was a simple question that didn't have a simple answer. How did I feel? I felt a million different ways. I felt tired. I felt sore from my escape with Loor and our plummet into the sea. I felt proud of myself for having kept my head on straight when things were crashing down around me.

I felt as if I'd learned a few things. I'd learned that it's sometimes okay to think like a weenie, so long as you don't *act* like one — at least not all the time. I'd learned that it's okay to be wrong, as long as you can admit it and are willing to listen to those who may know better.

I also felt sad. Sad for Osa, Loor's wonderful mother. She was someone I wish I had got to know better. And I felt sad for Loor, who lost her. I also felt sad for the others who lost their lives here as well. There was so much I had seen over these few days and not all of it was good. I saw the horrible way that people could treat each other. That may be the saddest thing of all. I saw greed and anger and murder and a total lack of concern for human life. It was the wicked side of the human soul that I saw here on Denduron and it saddened me to know that such a dark place existed.

How did I feel? I was frightened of Saint Dane. Not because I thought he would come after me or anything, but scared of what one man was capable of. He used his evil influence to manipulate people into doing horrible deeds. His power nearly brought about the destruction of an entire world. I feared that he might try again elsewhere and hoped that by stopping him here, his plan would go no further. But what I was mostly scared of, was being a Traveller. I didn't want the responsibility. I mean, I'm just a kid. If there is something that truly scares me, it's my own future.

How did I feel? I also felt a little glad. I was glad that the people of Denduron were going to get a second chance. I was proud of Uncle Press. I wasn't entirely sure of what his deal was, but he cared enough to help bring about the resurrection of a society headed for ruin. I was also glad that I met the people I did. Alder had a good heart and I'll always remember him as a friend. Rellin may have been misguided, but what he did he did for the good of his people and I respected that. Now he has the chance to help them in a more positive way. I'm glad that I met Osa. I don't think I will ever forget her calm wisdom and I hope that some of it rubbed off on me. I was glad that I had good friends like you two, Mark and

Courtney. You helped me when I needed it most and I will forever be in your debt.

But I think I was mostly glad that I met Loor. She was fiercely loyal and willing to put her life on the line for what she believed. She was brave and caring and smart and beautiful as all hell. But beyond that, there was something about Loor for which I couldn't even begin to thank her. When this adventure fades in my memory, and it will, I will still be grateful to her for having pushed me to think outside my own little world, and recognise my own strength.

So how did I feel? It was a complex question, but I had a simple answer.

"Uncle Press," I said, "I feel like I want to go home."

He was about to argue with me, but I cut him off.

"No," I said. "When you asked me to come with you, you said there were people who needed our help. I did everything you asked me to do. Now I want to go home."

He didn't even try to argue. How could he? "Okay, Bobby," he said warmly. "You're right. I am more proud of you than I can begin to say. Tomorrow, I'll take you home."

Now, *that's* what I wanted to hear! And that's what brought me to the place where I am right now, writing my final journal. We're spending the night in the hospital hut. Tomorrow we're going to make the long trek back up the mountain to the flume. Unfortunately the gate that was in the mines is now buried under a million tons of rock. Uncle Press assures me that the climb won't be hard. We will borrow some horses from the Bedoowan and take along a few whistles in case we run into any rogue quigs.

Alder and Loor are with me and they, too, are writing their journals. Alder filled me in on all that had happened during the battle, so that is how I know. I'm not going to send this journal to you through the ring. My plan is to hand it to you guys myself. I'm looking forward to seeing the expressions on your faces when I show up.

I'm also looking forward to seeing my family again. I'm not sure what to tell them, but I'll figure something out. I wonder if Marley misses me as much as I miss her?

Well guys, this is the last time I'm going to be writing to you. Thank you for reading. Thank you for being my friends. Tomorrow I'm going to leave Denduron for the final time. I can't wait to get home.

END OF JOURNAL #4

◉ SECOND EARTH ◉

Mark finished reading the pages before Courtney did, but didn't move until she looked up. They both looked at Bobby, who was lying on Mark's bed. They wanted to talk to him, but they didn't dare wake him up because he needed the rest. It was a strange feeling. This was their friend. They had known each other since they were little. Things were different now. Yes, this was still Bobby, but he wasn't the same Bobby who had kissed Courtney only a few days before. Could things go back to the way they were?

"I'm awake," Bobby said softly.

Mark and Courtney jumped up and went to him. Courtney sat on the edge of the bed. Mark paced.

"So I guess you got back to the flume on the mountain okay," said Courtney.

Bobby sat up, but it was a struggle. Obviously he was sore. Not hurt, just sore.

"Yeah, we got some Bedoowan horses and they took us most of the way."

"What about the quigs?" asked Mark.

"They didn't show, but I think that was because of the nasty ice storm." He pointed to the small cuts on his face. "The wind was blowing hard. It was like being cut by flying needles. Basically, it sucked. Sorry if I messed up your pillows."

"It's cool," said Mark. He meant it too.

"Who came back with you?" asked Courtney. "Uncle Press?"

"Yeah," answered Bobby. "But you know something weird? When we got to that subway station, his motorcycle was waiting for us right where he left it. The helmets, too. How strange is that?"

It was strange indeed, because when Mark and Courtney went to that station the motorcycle wasn't there. Someone must have been keeping it, waiting for Press's return.

Mark said, "Yeah, that's strange." He held up Bobby's last journal and added, "But you want to talk about strange?"

They all stared at the parchment pages, then burst out laughing. Mark was right. Compared to what Bobby had done on Denduron, a motorcycle mysteriously disappearing and reappearing was pretty low on the "strange" scale.

It felt good for Bobby to laugh and to be with his friends, yet he had the same awkward feeling that bothered both Courtney and Mark. A lot had happened. He was a different guy. Could he go back and pick up his life where he left off?

"What about Loor?" asked Courtney. "Did she stay on Denduron?"

Mark thought he caught a touch of jealousy in her voice, but he decided not to point it out.

Bobby stopped laughing. Courtney had touched a raw nerve. "She climbed with us to the top of the mountain," he said softly. "But when we got into the cave where the gate was, she just kept walking and jumped into the flume. No good-byes. No see ya around. No gee it's been swell. Nothing. I mean, it's not like we'd become best friends or anything, but we'd been through a lot. There were some things I wanted to say."

Obviously this hurt Bobby. He had grown to like Loor, but it didn't seem as if Loor cared about or liked him the same way. There was a long moment of awkward silence. Then Mark raised the key issue that was on everyone's mind.

"Bobby," he said tentatively. "There's some crazy stuff in your journals. The deal with the Milago and the Bedoowan is only part of it. What about this Traveller stuff; and flumes that shoot you between times and places; and people who live on territories all over the universe; and Halla? What is Halla? How can every *place* and every *thing* and every *time* still exist? And who is this Saint Dane dude? Is he gonna show up here someday and do what he did on Denduron? The stuff you wrote tears apart everything we know about how things work and I gotta tell you, it's freaking me out."

"I wish I could make you feel better," Bobby began. "But it's freaking me out too. I don't know anything more about it than what I wrote in those journals. I wish I could turn back the clock to the other night and tell Uncle Press to find somebody else to help him, but I can't. Part of me is okay with that. I learned some things about myself that are pretty cool. I also found out some things that I gotta change. That's all good. But as for the whole Traveller deal . . . I haven't got a clue."

"So, what are you going to do?" asked Courtney.

Bobby pulled himself across the bed and stood up. His legs were a little shaky, but otherwise he was okay. "I'm going to try to get back to normal," he announced with certainty. "If Uncle Press needs help again, he can find somebody else. Would you guys come home with me? It might make things easier."

This was the moment Mark and Courtney were dreading. How could they possibly tell Bobby that his family had disappeared? After what he had been through, he didn't deserve this. But still, he had to know.

"B-Bobby," said Mark nervously. "There's s-something you should – "

Courtney cut him off. "We'll go with you, Bobby," she said. "We want to be there for you."

Mark shot Courtney a look, but Courtney didn't back down. She felt there was only one way that Bobby should learn about what had happened and that was to see it for himself. If they told him, he'd want to see for himself anyway, so Courtney felt it would be better to get the news all at once.

It was a short walk to Bobby's house on Linden Place. As they walked along the familiar paths of Stony Brook, Bobby looked around with a smile. He had walked these streets a thousand times before, but he now had a whole new appreciation for them. He took in every sight, every smell, every sensation that he could. He wrapped himself in the feelings like a comfortable blanket and it made him feel whole again. He felt so good that he even allowed himself to think that it was possible to pick up his life where he had left off.

Mark and Courtney sensed this. It broke their hearts to know that soon his happy homecoming was going to crash and burn. Then just before they rounded the final bend that would bring them to 2 Linden Place and the empty lot where Bobby's house used to be, Courtney grabbed Bobby and stopped him. She held him by the shoulders and stared him right in the eye.

"You've got to know something, Bobby," she said sincerely. "We're here for you."

"I know that, Courtney," replied Bobby.

Courtney didn't let go of him. She knew that as soon as she did, he'd turn that corner to see that the life he so desperately wanted back, wasn't there any more.

"Hey, you okay?" Bobby asked her curiously.

Courtney nodded and let him go. Bobby glanced at Mark to

try and get a clue as to why Courtney was acting all strange, but Mark looked just as bad as Courtney did. Bobby knew right then that something was wrong. He spun and ran around the corner to get to his house. Mark and Courtney gave each other a nervous glance and followed.

When Mark and Courtney rounded the corner, they saw Bobby standing alone on the sidewalk, staring at the empty lot where his house used to be. He didn't move, he didn't shout, it didn't even look like he was breathing. He just stood there and stared. They didn't say anything. They had to let Bobby take the time to get his mind around what he was seeing. Or *not* seeing. Bobby walked forward and stepped on to the spot where his yard used to be. It was the yard he had played in since he was a toddler. It was the yard where he wrestled with Marley. It was the yard that led to the house he had called home for fourteen years. It was all gone.

"Hey there," came a familiar voice from behind them.

Everyone spun to see Uncle Press standing on the pavement. He was once again dressed in his jeans and long leather coat. Behind him was a small, black sports car he had just arrived in. A Porsche. Uncle Press always travelled in style.

"It's okay, Bobby," said Uncle Press softly. "Try to breathe."

Mark and Courtney took a few steps out of the way. Whatever was about to happen, it was between Press and Bobby. They saw that Bobby's eyes were red. He had started to cry. But the sad look turned to one of fury when he saw his uncle.

"Where are they?" Bobby said through clenched teeth. "And don't tell me this is the way it was meant to be. I don't want to hear that."

"They're fine, "Press said soothingly. "They're all fine."

Bobby took a few steps towards Press. He was angry, sad,

confused, and scared. But most of all, he wanted answers. "Then why aren't they here?" he demanded.

"This is the toughest part," said Press. "It was tough for me, it was tough for Alder and for Loor, too, but we all had to go through it. I would have told you on Denduron, but you had to see for yourself."

"See what? What is happening?" Bobby demanded.

Courtney reached out and grabbed Mark's hand for support. Mark didn't resist.

"Bobby, your family is gone because it was time for you to leave," said Uncle Press. "They raised you to be the person you are today, but it's time to move on."

Bobby took a few steps back as if Press's words had physically hit him. What was he saying? Was it planned for him to go to Denduron from the day he was born? Did his family know about this all along? How could that be? His life had been so . . . normal. Then a realisation came to Bobby.

"You're not my uncle, are you?" he asked.

"No, not in the traditional sense," answered Press. "But I've always looked out for you and I always will."

Bobby turned back to the empty lot and ran to the centre. He wanted to find a splinter of wood, a piece of glass, maybe even a piece of an old Wiffle ball. There had to be something that said he had passed through here. But there was nothing. Then Bobby heard something that came as another surprise.

"It will be all right, Pendragon," said another familiar voice.

Bobby spun back towards the road to see that standing next to the car was Loor. She was dressed in denim overalls and a tight pink sleeveless shirt that showed off her powerful shoulders and arms. She even had on Doc Marten black boots. Her long black hair was braided down her back and she wore a necklace made of small shells. She could have easily passed for a student at

Stony Brook High. No one would ever guess that she was actually a warrior from a far-off territory.

Courtney looked at Loor and sized her up, head to toe. Mark saw this and made a mental note to give Courtney a hard time later for being jealous. But who could blame her? Mark thought that Loor was even more strikingly beautiful than Bobby had described. She may have been dressed like a suburban girl, but she had the powerful presence of a warrior. Courtney Chetwynde had finally met her match.

Bobby walked to Loor. If anyone could tell him the truth, it would be her.

"Does this make sense to you?" he asked.

"It is starting to," was her answer.

"What about your mother?" he asked. "Was Osa your real mother?"

"No. I was told the truth before I first went to Denduron," answered Loor. "Osa raised me, she taught me all that I know. She was my mother in every sense, except that she had not given birth to me. But that did not stop me from loving her."

Bobby looked down, letting this sink in.

"On the mountain," continued Loor, "I did not say good-bye to you because my mind was elsewhere. Osa's body was already back on Zadaa. I had to return for the burial ceremony. It was difficult for me. I hope you were not offended."

Bobby shook his head. He understood all too well because he now knew what it was like to lose your mother. He looked to Press and asked, "So that's it? Travellers don't have families? They don't have lives? They only bounce around the universe looking for trouble?"

Press smiled and said, "You trust me, Bobby, don't you?"

"I think so," said Bobby sceptically. "But I'm losing faith fast."

"Don't," said Press quickly. "Believe me when I tell you that as time goes on, this will make sense to you. And I'll make you a promise. You will see your family again. You'll see your mum and your dad and your sister, Shannon, too."

"What about Marley?" Bobby asked.

"You'll run with your dog again too," said Press. "But not today."

"When?" asked Bobby.

Press gave this thought. He may have had all the answers, but this one eluded him. "That's one I can't answer," he said.

Bobby looked to Loor who gave him a slight nod of encouragement, then back to the empty lot. He took a long time to collect his thoughts. Finally he said, "You asked me how I felt before. You want to know how I feel right now?"

"How?" asked Press.

"I feel like I just found out there's no Santa Claus," he answered. "It's not a good feeling."

"It'll get better," said Press.

"So what happens now?" asked Bobby.

"Now you come with us," answered Press.

Bobby walked over to Mark and Courtney. He looked at his two friends and the memories of his life in Stony Brook came flooding back. He wanted nothing more than to turn around and see his house standing there so he could go back to the way things were before. But that was not meant to be.

"I . . . guess I've got to go," said Bobby.

"We'll always be here for you," said Courtney as tears began to well in her eyes.

Bobby leaned forward and grabbed the two of them in a hug. He tried hard not to break out in tears. He didn't want to do that. Not in front of Loor. But he didn't want to let go of his friends, either, because as soon as he did it would be the final act of letting go of his life here on Earth. Second Earth.

"Time to go, Bobby," prodded Press gently.

Bobby pulled back from his two best friends and looked them in the eye. Mark wiped away a tear, smiled and said, "Hey, don't forget to write!"

The three of them laughed at this. That went without saying.

"Are you sure?" asked Bobby. "Will you keep my journals?"

"I'd be pissed if you sent them to anyone else," Mark replied as he held up his hand to show Bobby the ring that Osa had given him.

Bobby gave a smile of thanks and fought back tears to say, "See you guys soon."

"Good-bye, Bobby," said Courtney. "Good luck."

Bobby nodded, then turned and headed towards the car. He stopped in front of Loor and looked at the warrior girl who was destined to be his partner.

"I know you do not want to hear this, Pendragon," she said. "But this is the way it was meant to be."

"Yeah, we'll see," said Bobby with scepticism. He gave one last look to the empty lot where his house used to be, then slid into the back of the Porsche. Loor looked at Mark and Courtney. Courtney stood up a little straighter. Loor chuckled, then she too got into the car.

"Keep his journals safe," Press said to Mark and Courtney. "He may need them again someday."

Mark and Courtney nodded a promise. Press then jogged around the car and hopped behind the wheel. With a roar of the engine, the little sports car blasted away from the kerb and flew down the street, heading for . . . somewhere.

Mark and Courtney watched it until it was out of sight and the sound died away. They stood there for a long time after, not sure of what to do next.

Finally Mark said, "There's no Santa Claus?"

Both of them laughed. It felt good, but it hid their true feelings.

Courtney said, "You'll call me if – "

"Soon as the next one comes in," promised Mark.

Then the two of them walked away from the empty lot, split up, and headed to their homes. Mark went right to his bedroom and waited for another journal from Bobby. The others had come pretty regularly and he expected his ring to start moving with the telltale quiver any second. But it didn't. He stayed awake most of the night, staring at the ring, willing it to move.

But it didn't.

Courtney called him twice a day to see if Bobby had written but kept getting the same answer, "Nothing yet." Whenever she saw Mark in school she would make eye contact as if to ask: "Anything?" But Mark would always answer with a shrug and a shake of his head.

Days passed. The days turned into weeks, the weeks into months, with nothing from Bobby. Mark and Courtney realised that they couldn't live their lives around waiting for his next message, so they drifted apart. Besides their friendship with Bobby, they really had nothing in common. Courtney went back to playing volleyball and led the Stony Brook team to the county finals. The men's team, of course.

Mark went back to being Mark. He still ate too many carrots and spent most of his time huddled over books in the library. There was one big change in his life though. Andy Mitchell didn't bother him any more. Courtney didn't know it, but she became Mark's guardian angel . . . at least when it came to Andy Mitchell.

The investigation to find the Pendragons continued, but they found nothing. Sergeant D'Angelo and Captain Hirsch would sometimes call Mark or Courtney to ask if they had heard anything, but the answer was always the same. No. Even if they wanted to tell the truth, neither of them could begin to figure out what to say.

Mark and Courtney never forgot about Bobby. He popped into their thoughts at least once a day. But the more time that passed without a word, the less he stayed on their minds. It made sense. They had to get on with their own lives.

The times when they thought of Bobby were usually triggered by seeing things that reminded them of their friend. Mark would play Nintendo football and remember the times that Bobby kicked his butt at the very same game. Courtney would hear a comedian say something goofy on TV and she'd laugh because she knew it would have made Bobby laugh. One time Mark sat in the stands during gym watching the guys play basketball and it made him think of how great Bobby was at the game.

And that's when it happened. The ring twitched.

At first Mark didn't know what it was. But when he looked down, he saw the familiar glow coming from the stone. Mark nearly wet his pants with excitement. He ran out of the stands and right through the game. It didn't matter to him that he totally disrupted play and was getting yelled at by every guy on the court. He had to get out of there fast and he had to find Courtney. He found her in the girls' gym next door. She was taking a class on combatives and was in the middle of a judo match. With very little effort she picked up her opponent and threw her on her back with a loud, sickening *thud*. Then just as she was helping her victim to her feet, Mark ran into the gym and yelled.

"Courtney!"

Everyone turned to look at the mad dweeb. Courtney locked eyes with him and instantly knew the deal. She quickly bowed to her opponent and ran to Mark. They didn't have to say a word.

They knew what to do. The two of them headed right for Mark's fortress of solitude: the boys' bathroom on the third floor. Courtney wasn't shy, she barged in ahead of Mark. No sooner did they get inside than Mark took off the ring and put it on the ground. The ring twitched, the crystal lights flashed and the familiar process began. The little ring grew larger and with a final blinding flash, it was over.

On the floor was a roll of paper, but this one looked different to the others. It was a light green colour, rather than the yellowed pages they were used to. There was a tie around the roll, but rather than a piece of brown leather, this looked like some kind of dark green plantlike material. Mark pulled it off and carefully unrolled the pages. They were roughly the same size as the others, but these were oddly shaped. There were no squared edges. Mark felt the texture – they didn't appear to be paper at all. These pages were some sort of large, dried leaves that were sort of rubbery . . . and waterproof.

"You ready?" asked Courtney.

"My hands are shaking," replied Mark.

Then the two of them looked at Bobby's newest journal.

CLORAL

Hi, guys. I've got to apologise for taking so long to write. So much has happened since I left you two, I'm not really sure where to begin. First off, one mystery is solved. Remember the giant shark that nearly ate me down in that mine shaft on Denduron? Well, now I know where it came from. The territory I'm in now is called Cloral, and it's entirely underwater. No kidding. Underwater. The quigs on Cloral are giant, flesh-eating sharks. Nice, huh?

Now let me tell you about some of the new trouble I've been getting into . . .

To Be Continued.

D. J. MacHale is a writer, director, executive producer, and creator of several popular television series and movies which include: *Are You Afraid of the Dark?; Chris Cross; Encyclopedia Brown, Boy Detective; Tower of Terror; Ghostwriter;* multiple Afterschool Specials; and the new series *The Strange Legacy of Cameron Cruz*. In print D. J. has co-written the book *The Tale of the Nightly Neighbours*, based on his own teleplay, and written a poetic adaptation of the classic folk tale *East of the Sun and West of the Moon*.

The adventure continues in

PENDRAGON

THE LOST CITY OF FAAR

CLORAL

Hi, guys. I've got to apologise for taking so long to write. So much has happened since I left you two, I'm not really sure where to begin. First off, one mystery is solved. Remember the giant shark that nearly ate me down in that mine shaft on Denduron? Well, now I know where it came from. The territory I'm in now is called Cloral, and it's entirely underwater. No kidding. Underwater. The quigs on Cloral are giant, flesh-eating sharks. Nice, huh?

Now let me tell you about some of the new trouble I've been getting into.

I was almost eaten, again; I came dangerously close to drowning; my arms were nearly yanked out of their sockets;

and I think I cracked a couple of ribs – all in the first hour after I got here. Sounds like a fun place, no?

I'm writing this journal now because things have finally calmed down and I need the rest. I think it's best to start my story at the point when I last saw you two. Man, that already seems like years ago. Time sure flies when you're out of your mind.

I still have tons of questions about what's happened to my life, but two jump to the top of the list. Why is it that I, Bobby Pendragon, have been chosen to become a Traveller? I don't think that's a lot to ask since I've had to risk my butt about a thousand times over while performing my Traveller duties. The second is that I want to know what happened to my family. I keep asking Uncle Press these questions, but getting info out of him is like squeezing blood from a turnip. (Not that I've ever tried squeezing a turnip, but it seems like a tough thing to do.) He keeps saying, "It will all come clear with time." Great. Meanwhile, we keep jumping from one disaster to the next, and the best I can hope for is that I'll stay alive long enough to figure out why the heck I'm in the middle of all this when all I really want to do is go home and hide under my bed with the dog. C'mon! I'm only fourteen! Is that too much to ask?

I guess it is, seeing as my home isn't there any more. The last time I saw you two, you were standing in front of the empty lot where my house used to be. It's hard to describe the emotions that were banging around inside me back then. I was nervous about going on another adventure with Uncle Press and bummed to be leaving you two guys, again. But the worst part was the fear of the unknown.

Uncle Press promised me I would see my family again Mum, Dad, Shannon, and even my golden retriever, Marley.

But he stopped short of telling me where they had gone. He told me that they had raised me and prepared me for the moment when I would leave home to become a Traveller, but he didn't tell me why. Was it planned from the moment I was born? Was my family part of some secret plot? He also told me that he wasn't my real uncle. Meaning, a blood relative. But he hadn't yet answered the single most important question: *Why?* Why are there Travellers who blast through time and space, helping the territories through dangerous times? Who chooses them? Most importantly, why me?

To be honest, I've stopped asking these questions because his answers are always so freaking elliptical. It's like he's some kind of Jedi master who only drips out information on a need-to-know basis. Well, I need to know badly. But I guess I'll have to be patient and learn as I go along. I think Uncle Press is afraid if he lays it all out for me in one shot, the truth will make my head explode and I'll end up lying in a corner somewhere, drooling. He's probably right.

When I said goodbye to you two, I got into the car with Uncle Press and Loor, my partner from the adventure on Denduron. I was leaving my two best friends to take off with my new friend and partner. At least I considered Loor a friend. We had been through hell together on Denduron and even though I wasn't the warrior she was, I think I had earned her respect. At least I'd hoped I had.

I squeezed into the back compartment behind the two seats of the Porsche without being asked. Obviously Uncle Press was going to drive, and since Loor was bigger than me, there was no way she could fit in the back. She may have been dressed like she belonged on Second Earth, but she looked like no classmate I'd ever seen. I'm guessing she was around sixteen, but with her zero-body-fat, muscular bod, she looked ready for the Olympic decathlon. Her cocoa-dark skin made her look as if she were African, but I knew the truth. She was a warrior from the territory of Zadaa, which exists in an entirely different time and place from here. I think one of the first requirements for the Olympics is that you have to be from Earth. She didn't qualify.

"Comfy?" asked Uncle Press.

"Not even close," I answered.

With a laugh, Uncle Press hit the accelerator and once again we screamed away from my home town of Stony Brook, Connecticut. I didn't even ask him where we were heading, because I knew. We were going back to the abandoned subway station in the Bronx to find the gate that led to the flume that would take us . . . somewhere.

The last time we travelled this route I was on the back of Press's motorcycle, with no clue of what lay ahead. This time I had a clue, but not much more.

We blasted along the turnpike, out of Connecticut, heading for New York City. Within half an hour we had gone from the leafy-green suburbs of Stony Brook, to the concrete pavement of the borough of New York called the Bronx. It's the home of Yankee Stadium, the Bronx Zoo, the New York Botanical Garden, and a secret Traveller flume into the unknown.

As Uncle Press manoeuvred the quick little sports car through the city streets, people turned to stare. This was a rough neighbourhood. They weren't used to seeing a sleek sports car screaming through their 'hood. Or maybe they were staring in wonder at the guy riding in the back who was turning blue because his knees were jammed into his throat. That would be me.

With a final spin of the wheel, Uncle Press brought us

right up to the kerb next to the small green kiosk that was our destination. As I looked at that little building and the peeled paint on the sign above it that said SUBWAY, only one thought came to mind.

Here we go again.

I hadn't expected to see this place again so soon. No, I had expected to *never* see this place again. Uncle Press and I had come through this way only a few hours before, having returned from Denduron. My plan was to get back home, and do my level best to forget about this whole Traveller business. But things changed. I discovered that my family was gone, along with the life I knew. I think Uncle Press brought me back to Stony Brook to see for myself. It was a smart move, because if he hadn't, I never would have believed it. I would always be thinking about how to get home. But there was no home to get back to any more. The cold, hard reality hit me that my destiny was to go with Uncle Press and learn more about being a Traveller. What a difference a few hours can make.

So there we were again, back in the Bronx, on the verge of starting my new life. I wanted to cry. Yes, I admit it. I wanted to cry. If Loor wasn't there, I probably would have.

Uncle Press hopped out of the car first, leaving the keys in the ignition. Loor and I crawled out after him. Actually, I did most of the crawling. I was so mashed up in the backseat that my legs were now totally asleep, and when I tried to stand, I fell over. Loor caught me and held me up until I got the feeling back. How embarrassing is that?

Uncle Press didn't stop to see if I was okay. He headed right for the stairs that led down into the subway.

"Uh, Uncle Press?" I called. "You sure you want to leave the car here?" I remembered back to our first trip here. We had left the motorcycle and the helmets right where the Porsche was now. I thought for sure that somebody would pinch them, but when we returned that morning, the bike was right where we had left it. The helmets were there too. Unbelievable. Pure luck. But this was really pushing it. A hot sports car sitting alone with the keys in the ignition was too tempting a prize. Worse, it was in a no-parking zone. If thieves didn't get the car, the cops would tow it for sure.

Uncle Press said, "It's okay. The acolytes will take care of it."

Huh? Acolytes? That was a new wrinkle. I looked at Loor to see if she knew what he was talking about. She shrugged. Before I could ask any more, Uncle Press disappeared down into the subway.

I said to Loor, "Yeah, I know – we'll learn more as we go along."

"Don't ask so many questions, Pendragon," she said. "Save them for when it is truly important." She then followed Uncle Press.

Truly important? Wasn't all this bizarro stuff truly important? I wanted to know! But since I was now standing alone and feeling dumb out here all by myself, the only thing I could do was follow. I was getting good at that.

I hurried down the dirty stairs and squeezed through the opening in the wooden boards that were nailed across the entrance. To the rest of the world this was a closed and abandoned subway station that had outlived its usefulness. To us Travellers, it was the crossroads of Second Earth, my home territory, and our jumping-off point to all the other distant territories. Sounds romantic, doesn't it? Well, it isn't. It's scary.

The filthy subway station was all too familiar to me. Subway trains still flew by, but it had been a long time since any had stopped at this forlorn spot. When I hit the platform, I saw something that brought back a chilling memory. It was the pillar that Uncle Press had hidden behind during his gun battle with Saint Dane. It was a battle that had given me the time to escape and find the gate and the flume that sent me to Denduron.

Saint Dane. There's a guy I'd like to forget. Uncle Press says he's a Traveller, like us. But he isn't exactly like us because the guy is wicked. On Denduron he pushed two rival tribes to the brink of annihilation. But we stepped in and messed things up for him.

Unfortunately Denduron was only the beginning. Saint Dane promised to wreak havoc with all the territories in his quest to rule Halla. That's key. He wants to rule Halla. Now, I'm no genius, but since Uncle Press described Halla as "every territory, every person, every living thing, every *time* there ever was", then having a guy like Saint Dane be the ruler is not a very good idea.

What made it all so incredibly creepy was that Saint Dane enjoyed seeing people suffer. I saw that firsthand, too many times. This abandoned subway platform was the first. This was where he hypnotised a homeless guy into jumping to a gruesome death in front of a speeding subway train. It was a cold-blooded trick that Saint Dane said was "to give the boy a taste of what was in store for him".

The boy he referred to was me. Nice guy, huh? I told you before that the worst part about my new life as a Traveller was the fear of the unknown. Well, that's not entirely true. Right up there on my list of fears is knowing that somewhere, sometime, we will cross paths with Saint Dane again. The guy is worse than dangerous, and it is our job to stop him. Standing there on that platform, I was really wanting a different job.

"Pendragon!" called Loor.

I followed her voice to the end of the platform. I knew this route. We had to climb down on to the subway tracks, carefully avoid getting fried by the third rail, and make our way along the grimy, oil-stained wall until we came upon a wooden door. On this door would be a symbol that looked like a carved star identifying it as a gate. That was our destination.

With Uncle Press in the lead, we moved quickly along the tracks. We had to hurry because a subway train could come charging along at any moment. There wasn't much room between the tracks and the wall and a train speeding past our noses would hurt.

As we got closer to the door, I noticed that the ring on my finger began to grow warm. I looked at it and saw that the slate grey stone was beginning to transform. The dark grey colour began to melt away and the stone now sparkled. This was the sign that we were getting near a gate. It was amazing how many things I was taking for granted. Once upon a time, the idea of following a possessed, glowing ring to a mysterious door in an abandoned subway station would seem like an off-the-wall dream. Not any more. Now it felt natural. Sort of.

Uncle Press found the door, opened it, and hurried us all inside.

The cave inside hadn't changed. I immediately glanced into the dark tunnel that led off into the unknown. This was the flume that would sparkle to life and take us . . . somewhere. Right now it was quiet, waiting for us to tell it where we were going. I'd only travelled through the flume between Second Earth and Denduron. I had to believe that this time we were going somewhere else, and now was the time for Uncle Press to tell us where. Loor and I stood together, waiting for him to show us the way.

"We're going to split up," he said.

Whoa. Not a good start. Was he crazy? We shouldn't be broken apart! Uncle Press knew his way around the cosmos and Loor was a fierce warrior. The idea of fluming off to face Saint Dane by myself without any back-up was not something I could get psyched up about. A million thoughts and possibilities flashed through my brain — all of them bad. But just as I was about to break into full panic mode, Loor spoke.

"Why?" she asked flatly.

Nothing like keeping it simple. She was good to have around.

"Since your mother died, you are the Traveller from Zadaa," he answered. "They'll need you there soon. I want you to go home and be ready."

"What about me?" I asked, immediately flying into protest mode.

"You and I are going to Cloral," was his answer. "Saint Dane went there for a reason and I want to know what it is."

Good news, bad news. Good news was Uncle Press and I were staying together. Bad news was we were going after Saint Dane. Really bad news.

"But if I'm the Traveller from Second Earth, shouldn't I stay here?" I asked hopefully. "You know, to take care of stuff?"

Uncle Press gave me a smile. He knew I was trying to weasel out.

"No, it's best you come with me," was his simple answer.

Oh well. I wasn't surprised that my lame attempt at getting out of this trip had failed miserably. But hey, it was worth a shot, right?

Loor then stepped up to me and said, "If you need me, I will be there for you, Pendragon."

Wow, that blew me away. I guess I had earned her respect after all. I nodded and said, "I'll be there for you, too."

We held eye contact for a moment. The bond the two of us had created during the war on Denduron was stronger than I had realised. I felt safer with her around, but it was more than that. I liked Loor. In spite of her inability to give an inch on anything, Loor's heart was always in the right place. I didn't want to go on without her. And I really believe that if she'd had the choice, she'd have stayed with me. But before I could say another word, she turned and strode into the mouth of the flume. She stared into the dark abyss, took a deep breath, and called out, "*Zadaa!*"

Instantly the tunnel started to breathe. The rocky walls began to writhe like a giant snake slowly coming to life. Then there was the familiar sound – the jumble of sweet musical notes that came from somewhere deep in the tunnel and grew louder as they rushed toward us. The walls transformed from grey stone into brilliant crystalline gems, just as my ring had as we approached the gate. The light that shone from the tunnel was so bright that I needed to shield my eyes. Loor became nothing more than a dark silhouette standing before the brilliant display. She gave one last look back to us and waved good-bye. Then, in a flash of light, she was swept into the tunnel. The retreating light and music carried her away and back to her home, the territory of Zadaa.

In an instant the show was over and the tunnel returned to darkness.

"Your turn," said Uncle Press.

"Tell me about Cloral," I asked, stalling for time. As much as I knew a trip through the flume was kind of fun, I was nervous about what I'd find on the other end. I needed a few seconds to get my act together.

"You'll find out all you need to know once you get there," he answered as he nudged me closer to the mouth of the flume. "Don't worry, I'll be right behind you."

"Why don't you ever give me a straight answer?" I asked.

"I thought you liked surprises," he answered with a laugh.

"Not any more I don't!" I shouted back. Uncle Press used to surprise me all the time with great birthday gifts and helicopter rides and camping trips and – basically all the coolio things a kid could ever want from an amazing uncle. But lately Uncle Press's surprises weren't as fun as they used to be. Especially since they mostly involved me being chased by hungry beasts or shot at or blown up or buried alive or . . . you get the idea.

"C'mon, you're no fun any more," he teased as he pushed me into the flume. "*Cloral!*" he shouted, and stepped out as the tunnel sprang back to life. I didn't even look into the depths because I knew what was coming.

"Fun?" I shouted. "If you think this is fun, you're crazy!"

"Oh, one thing, Bobby," he said.

"What?"

"Remember the Cannonball."

"What 'cannonball'?" I asked. "What's that supposed to mean?"

The light grew brighter and the musical notes grew louder. I was seconds away from launch.

"Just before you drop into Cloral, hold your breath."

"What! "

The last thing I saw was Uncle Press laughing. Then the light grabbed me and sucked me into the tunnel. I was on my way.

☾ SECOND EARTH ☽

"What are you two doing in here?" shouted Mr Dorrico, the chief caretaker of Stony Brook Junior High. "This ain't a library. You can't sit here reading your – hey, you're a girl! Girls aren't allowed in the boys' bathroom!"

Mr Dorrico had been a caretaker at Stony Brook for most of his illustrious fifty-year caretaking career. There wasn't much you could put past him and this time was no different. There was indeed a girl in the boys' lavatory. Mr Dorrico may have been ancient and terminally cranky, but he could still tell girls from boys. Most of the time.

Courtney Chetwynde and Mark Dimond had been sitting on the floor, reading Bobby's first journal from Cloral. The bathroom on the third floor was near the art department. It was rarely used by anyone, boy or girl. It had become Mark's fortress of solitude. When the world got too busy, Mark would come here to escape and think and eat carrots and be alone. If he received one of Bobby's journals at school, this is the place he would come to read it. And since Courtney was now part of the picture, she would join him. The fact that she was a girl never seemed to matter, considering how important the journals were. But now they were faced with an angry chief caretaker who looked as if he were going to have a heart attack at the very thought of a girl being in the boys' bathroom.

Mark jumped to his feet and quickly grabbed up the pages of Bobby's journal. "It's c-cool. W-We were just leaving," he stammered nervously.

Whenever he got stressed, Mark stuttered. Courtney, on the other hand, was at her best under pressure. She stood slowly, walked up to Mr Dorrico, and stared him right in the eye.

"The only reason I came in here," she said confidently, "was because there were so many boys in the girls' bathroom. It was getting way too crowded in there – and they never lift the toilet seats."

"What!" shouted Mr Dorrico, his face turning three shades of red.

To him this was clearly an offence that threatened to crack the very foundation of etiquette that our society was founded on. He grabbed the mop that he was going to use to swab up the boys' bathroom and charged back out, ready to do battle with the rogue delinquents who mocked the sanctity of the girls' lavatory.

Mark stepped up to Courtney and said, "You are bad."

"Time to go," she replied with a mischievous smile.

They ran from the bathroom and down the hall, careful to avoid the girls' room.

Mark knew that he and Courtney Chetwynde made an odd pair. Mark was an introvert. He lived in a world of books and graphic novels. He didn't have many friends. His hair was always a little too long and a little too unwashed. Sports were a four-letter word to him and his mother still picked out his clothes, which meant he wore a lot of non-name-brand geek outfits that were always about two years out of date. But the thing was, he didn't care. Mark never wanted to be cool. In fact, being comfortable with his noncoolness made Mark feel pretty good about himself. Where everyone else was busy trying to impress their friends with the way they looked or who they hung out with or what parties they went to. Mark couldn't be bothered. So Mark considered himself cooler than cool – in a nerdy kind of way.

Courtney, on the other hand, had it all going on. She was tall and beautiful, with long brown hair that fell to her waist and piercing grey eyes. She got decent grades. Not world-class, but good enough. She also had a ton of friends. But the thing that defined Courtney was sport. Volleyball in particular. Courtney was so tall and strong that it was unfair for her to play against most girls, so she played on the guys' teams at Stony Brook. As it turned out, it was unfair for her to play against most boys, too. She absolutely crushed them. Guys feared her because they didn't want to be embarrassed by a girl, but more because they were afraid when they faced Courtney, they'd lose teeth. At fourteen she was already a legend.

So the differences between Mark Dimond and Courtney Chetwynde were so huge that a friendship wasn't something you'd expect. That is, except for one thing.

Bobby Pendragon.

The adventure continues in

PENDRAGON

THE NEVER WAR

Bobby has been busy leaping from territory to territory, following his mysterious uncle Press on his mission to save the world – all worlds – from the ultimate evil, a renegade called Saint Dane.

Now Bobby has returned to Earth – but something isn't quite right – it's only 1937 and our 21st century hero finds himself a little out of his depth. Why is this territory called 'First Earth' when Bobby is from 'Second Earth'? Can Bobby work out how and where Earth is being threatened in the year 1937 before it's too late . . . ?